...be scared off **by a big, gorgeous sheriff with eyes as cold as a winter wind.**

"If you think you're worrying me, you're wrong," she said.

Nathan stared at her. "I don't want you worried. I don't want you at all."

Direct hit, she thought as an icy fist slammed into her chest and squeezed her heart. But she wouldn't let him see it. "I don't want you, either, Nathan. I'm not that young girl anymore, dazzled because Nathan Battle noticed her—"

He grabbed her, yanked her close and kissed her with a fierce desperation that was fueled by desire and anger, all twisted up together. She could feel it in him as she felt it in herself. Past and present tangled together and memories as thick as honey on a winter morning.

But those memories were swamped by all of the new sensations cours...

Amanda would not be scared off by a big, dangerous-sized ... with eyes as old as a winter wind

RUMOUR
HAS IT

BY
MAUREEN CHILD

Published in Great Britain 2013
by Mills & Boon, an imprint of Harlequin (UK) Limited,
Eton House, 18-24 Paradise Road, Richmond, Surrey TW9 1SR

© Harlequin Books S.A. 2013

Special thanks and acknowledgement to Maureen Child for her contribution to TEXAS CATTLEMAN'S CLUB: THE MISSING MOGUL miniseries.

ISBN: 978 0 263 90478 9
ebook ISBN: 978 1 472 00616 5

51-0713

Harlequin (UK) policy is to use papers that are natural, renewable and recyclable products and made from wood grown in sustainable forests. The logging and manufacturing processes conform to the legal environmental regulations of the country of origin.

Printed and bound in Spain
by Blackprint CPI, Barcelona

Maureen Child writes for Mills & Boon® Desire™ and can't imagine a better job. Being able to indulge your love for romance as well as being able to spin stories just the way you want them told is, in a word, *perfect*.

A seven-time finalist for the prestigious Romance Writers of America RITA® Award, Maureen is the author of more than one hundred romance novels. Her books regularly appear on the bestseller lists and have won several awards, including the Prism, The National Readers' Choice Award, The Colorado Award of Excellence and the Golden Quill.

One of her books, *The Soul Collector,* was made into a CBS-TV movie starring Melissa Gilbert, Bruce Greenwood and Ossie Davis. If you look closely, in the last five minutes of the movie you'll spot Maureen, who was an extra in the last scene.

Maureen believes that laughter goes hand in hand with love, so her stories are always filled with humor. The many letters she receives assures her that her readers love to laugh as much as she does.

Maureen Child is a native Californian, but has recently moved to the mountains of Utah. She loves a new adventure, though the thought of having to deal with snow for the first time is a little intimidating.

To Rosemary Rangel Estrada
We really miss you, neighbor!

One

Amanda Altman's back in town.

It was all anyone could talk about and Nathan Battle was getting pretty damn sick of it. Nothing he hated more than being at the center of a gossip tornado. He'd already lived through it once, years ago. Of course, he'd escaped the worst of it by moving to Houston and burying himself in the police academy and then his job.

Wouldn't work this time. He'd built his place here. He wasn't going anywhere. Mostly because Nathan Battle didn't run. So he'd just have to ride this mess out until the town found something new to chew on.

But that was life in Royal, Texas. A town too small to mind its own business and too big to have to repeat the same gossip over and over again.

Even here, he thought, in the hallowed halls of the Texas Cattleman's Club, Nathan couldn't escape the talk—or the speculation. Not even from his best friend.

"So, Nathan," Chance asked with a knowing grin, "you see Amanda yet?"

Nathan looked at the man sitting opposite him. Chance McDaniel owned McDaniel's Acres, a working dude ranch and hotel just south of town. The man had built the place from the ground up on property he'd inherited from his family, and he'd done a hell of a job.

Chance's blond hair was cropped short, but he still couldn't get the wave out of it no matter how he tried. His green eyes were amused and Nathan shook his head, knowing that *he* was the source of his friend's amusement.

"No." One word. Should be concise enough to get his message across. And maybe it would have worked with anyone else. Of course, Nathan told himself wryly, it wouldn't be nearly enough to get Chance to back off. They'd been friends for too long. And nobody knew how to get to you better than a best friend.

"You can't ignore her forever," Chance mused, taking a sip of his scotch.

"It's worked so far," Nathan told him and lifted his own glass for a drink.

"Sure it has," Chance said, muffling a laugh. "That's why you've been such a cool, calm guy the last couple of weeks."

Nathan narrowed his eyes on his friend. "Funny."

"You have no idea," Chance agreed, lips twitching. "So, Sheriff, if you're avoiding the Royal Diner these days, where are you getting your coffee?"

His fingers tightened on the heavy, old crystal. "The gas station."

Now Chance didn't bother to hide his laughter. "You must be desperate if you're drinking the swill Charlie brews down there. You know, maybe it's time you learned how to make decent coffee yourself."

"And maybe it's time you let this go," Nathan told him. Irritating is what it was, he thought. His whole damn routine had been splintered when Amanda moved back home to Royal. Used to be he started off his day with a large coffee and maybe some eggs at the diner. Amanda's sister, Pam, always had his coffee ready for him when he walked in. That was a routine a man could count on. But since Amanda blew back into his world, he'd had to make do with Charlie's disgusting coffee and a packaged sweet roll.

Even when she wasn't trying, Amanda found a way to screw with him.

"Seriously, Nate," Chance said, lowering his voice a little so the other members of the TCC couldn't overhear, "from all reports, Amanda's here to stay. Seems she's been making some changes to the diner, settling in. Even talking about looking for a house of her own, according to Margie Santos."

Nathan had heard all the same talk, of course. Hard not to, when everyone in a ten-mile radius was more than eager to talk to him about Amanda. Margie Rice was the top real estate agent in Royal and one of the biggest gossips as well. If she was spreading the word that Amanda was looking for her own place, then Nathan had to admit that she was here for the long term.

Which meant he couldn't ignore her for much longer.

Too bad, because he'd finally gotten good at not thinking about Amanda. Wasn't always the case. Several years ago, Amanda was *all* Nathan thought about. The passion between them had burned hotter than anything he'd ever known. She'd filled his mind, waking and sleeping.

Of course back then, they'd been engaged.

He scowled into his glass of scotch. *Times change.*

"New subject, Chance," he muttered and let his gaze slide around the main room of the TCC.

While his friend talked about what was happening at the ranch, Nathan's mind wandered. Over the years, it seemed like inside the TCC, time stood still. Even the fact that women were now officially members of the long-standing, males-only club hadn't affected the decor. Paneled walls, dark brown leather furniture—sofas and club chairs—hunting prints on the walls and a big-screen TV so you didn't miss a bit of any Texas sporting event.

The air smelled of lemon polish and the wood floors and tables gleamed in the lamplight. The TV was on now, but muted so that members could sit and brood behind newspapers or chat without having to shout to be heard. The soft clinking of crystal against gleaming wood tables underlined the hushed conversations surrounding them.

A woman's laugh pealed out just then, shattering the quiet and Nathan grinned as he noted that Beau Hacket actually cringed at the sound. At nearly sixty, Beau was short, thick around the middle and with a lot more gray in what was left of his dark red hair. He had a big laugh and a narrow mind—he believed women belonged in the kitchen and didn't care who knew it.

Now, Beau fired a hard look around the room as if to silently say, *Did you all hear that? That's just wrong. Women don't belong here.*

No one said anything, but Nathan read the tension in the room and noted more gritted jaws than usual. Women were members, but they still weren't really welcome. Everyone was gathered for the weekly TCC meeting and none of the old guard were happy about having women included.

"Sounds like Abigail's enjoying herself," Chance muttered into the stillness.

"Abby always enjoys herself," Nathan mused.

Abigail Langley Price, married to Brad Price, had been the first female member of the club. And, of course, she was having a good time now, since she had women to talk to in here. But it hadn't been easy on her, gaining acceptance at the TCC. Even with the support of Nathan, Chance and several of the other members, she'd had to fight her way in—and Nathan admired that about her.

"Does it feel weird to you," Chance asked, "to have women in the club now?"

"Nope." Nathan finished off his scotch and set the empty glass down on the table in front of him. "Felt weirder when they weren't allowed in here."

"Yeah," his friend said. "I know what you mean." Leaning forward, he braced his elbows on his knees. "But men like Beau over there aren't happy about it."

Nathan shrugged. "Men like Beau are always complaining about something. Besides, he and the others are just gonna have to get used to it." Then he added what he'd been thinking a few minutes ago. "Times change."

"They really do," Chance agreed. "Like, for example, the vote we're taking tonight."

Relieved to be off the subject of Amanda, Nathan turned his thoughts to the upcoming vote. It had been the talk of the town for days. Once Abigail and the other women became members of the TCC they'd had some ideas of their own to put forth and tonight marked the vote for one of the biggest items.

"The child-care center?" Nathan asked and Chance nodded.

"It's a big deal and only going to make the hard-line members more irritated than ever."

"True," Nathan agreed, imagining the fireworks that would soon take place over the vote. "Only makes sense if you think about it, though. A safe place for the kids while their parents are here. Probably should have done it years ago."

"Right there with ya," Chance told him with a shake of his head. "But I'm not sure Beau's going to agree with that."

"Beau doesn't agree with anything," Nathan said with a chuckle. As town sheriff, Nathan had to deal with Beau Hacket on a regular basis. The man had a complaint about everything and everyone, and didn't mind taking up the sheriff's time with them. "A more contrary man has never lived."

"True."

The clock over the river-stone fireplace began to chime the hour and both of them stood up.

"Guess it's time to get the meeting started."

"This should be good," Chance told Nathan and followed him down the hallway to the official meeting room.

An hour later, the arguments were still being shouted out. Beau Hacket had some support for his Neanderthal opinions. Sam and Josh Gordon, the twins who owned and operated Gordon Construction, were getting to be just as hardheaded as Beau.

"Is it just me," Nate whispered to his friend Alex Santiago, "or is Sam Gordon starting to become more and more like Beau Hacket?"

Alex shifted a look at the twin who was spouting all the reasons why children didn't belong in the TCC.

"It's not just you," he answered quietly. "Even his twin looks surprised at Sam's arguments."

Alex hadn't lived in Royal very long, but he'd made lots of friends in town and seemed to already have a handle on the town and its citizens. A venture capitalist and investor, Alex was wealthy and had become, in his short time in Royal, very influential. Sometimes Nate wondered why a man as rich as Alex would choose to settle down in Royal. But at the same time, he told himself with a smile, people probably wondered why Nathan Battle chose to be the town sheriff. Since he owned half of the Battlelands Ranch, Nate was rich enough to not have to work at all.

But then what the hell would he do?

Shaking his head, Nate gave a quick look around the long table at the members gathered. Not all of them were present, of course, but there were more than enough for the voting. Ryan Grant, former rodeo star, was attending his first official meeting and Nate saw the bemusement in the other man's eyes. Dave Firestone, whose ranch ran alongside Nathan's family spread, was lounging in a chair, watching the goings-on as if he were at a tennis match. Beau was nearly purple in the face, shouting down anyone who argued with him. Chance was sitting beside Shannon Morrison, who looked as if she wanted to stand up and tell Beau Hacket exactly what he could do with his outdated opinions.

And then there was Gil Addison, the TCC president, standing at the head of the table. His dark eyes flashed and Nate knew that his friend had about reached the limits of his patience.

Almost at once, Gil slammed his gavel onto its pedestal until he had quiet. The echoes of arguments and recriminations were hanging in the still air like battle flags when Gil said, "Enough talking. Time for a vote.

All in favor of the child-care center being added to the TCC, say 'aye.'"

All of the women, including Missy Reynolds and Vanessa Woodrow, spoke up, but Nathan, Alex, Chance and several of the others were quick to contribute their votes.

"All opposed," Gil added, "say 'no.'"

A few loud voices were heard.

The gavel slammed down again sharply. Gil nodded at the group and smiled. "Motion's passed. A child-care center will be added to the Texas Cattlemen's Club."

Beau and a few of the other members, still bristling over the fact that women were now included in their group, were practically apoplectic. But, there was nothing they could do about it.

As Beau stormed out of the meeting, Nathan watched him go and almost felt a flicker of sympathy. He could see the other side of the situation, but you couldn't stay locked in the past. The world moved every damn day and you moved with it or you got steamrolled. Tradition was one thing, being stuck in the mud was another.

Change happened whether you liked it or not, so the best way to handle it was to hop on board the train as opposed to stretching your body across the tracks and being run over. Which was, he told himself, a good way to think about how to deal with Amanda.

"This is great," Abigail Price said with a wide smile for her friends and those who had supported them. "And our Julia will be the first child enrolled as soon as we're up and running."

"You bet she will, honey." Brad Price gave his wife's hand a squeeze. "Shame Beau and the rest are upset, but they'll get over it."

"You did," Abigail reminded him with a smile.

True enough, Nate mused thoughtfully. Not too long

ago, Brad and Abby were butting heads every chance they got. He'd done his best to keep Abby out of the TCC and now just look at them—in love, married, and with a great little girl.

While everyone around them talked, Alex suggested, "Why don't we head over to the diner and get some coffee and pie?"

"Good idea," Chance agreed and flicked a glance at Nathan.

Friends could be a real pain in the ass sometimes, Nathan told himself. These two were trying to maneuver him into a meeting with Amanda and it just wasn't going to work. He'd see her. In his own time. In his own way. And damned if he was going to put on a show for the folks in Royal.

"No thanks," he said, pushing up from the table. He didn't even look at the other members in the room. "I'm headed back to the office to finish up some paperwork, then I'm going home."

"Still in hiding?" Alex murmured.

Nathan bristled. "Pretty hard to hide in a town the size of Royal."

"You should keep that in mind," Chance told him.

Irritated, Nathan just gritted his teeth and left. *No point in arguing with a jackass,* he thought.

Amanda was so busy she almost didn't have time to worry about Nathan.

Almost.

Turns out, even running the family diner, looking for a new house and arranging to have the transmission in her car replaced *still* left her brain enough room to plague her with thoughts of Nathan Battle.

"Bound to happen," she reassured herself for the fortieth time that morning. Just being in Royal had brought the memories rushing back and, there were a *lot* of memories.

She'd known Nathan most of her life and had been nuts about him since she was thirteen. She could still remember the sharp, bright thrill of having Nathan, then an all-powerful senior, taking a lowly freshman to the senior prom.

"And, if we'd just stopped it right there, it would be all sunshine and roses," she murmured as she refilled the coffee urn with water, then measured in fresh coffee grounds.

She pushed the button to start the brewing process, then turned to look out at the diner. Even with the changes she'd made in the last couple of weeks, being in this place was as good as being home.

She'd grown up in her parents' diner, working as a busgirl, and then a waitress when she was old enough. The Royal Diner was an institution in town and she was determined that it stay that way. Which was why she'd come home after her father's death to help her older sister, Pam, run the place.

As that reminder rolled through her mind, Amanda squared her shoulders and nodded briefly to herself. She hadn't come home because of Nathan Battle. Even though a shiver swept through her at just the thought of his name, she discounted it as sense memory. Didn't mean a thing. Her life was different now.

She was different now.

"Amanda, my love, when're you going to marry me and run off to Jamaica?"

Startled out of her thoughts, Amanda smiled at the familiar voice and turned to look at Hank Bristow. At eighty, Hank was tall and thin and his skin was craggy from a lifetime spent in the sun. Now that his sons ran the family ranch, Hank spent most of his time in the diner, talking with his friends. His blue eyes twinkled as he held out his cup for a refill.

"Hank, you just love me for my coffee," she told him, pouring a stream of the hot, fresh brew into his cup.

"A woman who can make good coffee?" Hank shook his head and said solemnly, "Worth her weight in gold."

She smiled, patted his hand, then carried the carafe along the length of the counter, chatting with her customers, freshening coffee as she went. It was all so familiar. So…easy. She'd slid into life in Royal as smoothly as if she'd never left.

"Why did you order new menus?"

Okay, not completely smoothly. Amanda turned to face Pam. As usual, the shorter woman didn't look happy with her. But then, the two of them had never been close. Not growing up. Not now. Even though Amanda had primarily come back to Royal because Pam had needed help running the diner. But, she supposed, *needing* help and *wanting* it were two different things.

Amanda walked the length of the counter again, and set the coffeepot down on the warmer before she answered.

"Because the old ones needed to be replaced," she said. "The laminate was cracked and old and the menus themselves were outdated." Catching the look of interest on Hank's face, Amanda lowered her voice. "We don't even serve half the things listed anymore, Pam."

Her sister's chin-length brown hair was tucked behind her ears. She wore a red T-shirt and jeans and a pair of scarlet sandals wrapped around her feet. She was tapping the toe of one sandal against the shining linoleum floor. "But our regular customers know that. They don't need fancy new menus, Amanda."

She sighed, but stood her ground. "They're not fancy, Pam. They're just not ratty."

Pam hissed in a breath.

"Okay, sorry." Amanda dug deep for patience and said, "We're in this together, right? You said you needed help and I came home. The Altman sisters running the diner. Together."

Pam thought about that for a long second before finally shrugging. "As long as you remember I didn't ask you to come in and take over."

"I'm not taking over, Pam. I'm trying to help."

"By changing everything?" Pam's voice spiked, then she seemed to realize that everyone in the place was no doubt listening because she spoke more softly when she continued. "There's such a thing as tradition around here, you know. Or did you forget, living off in Dallas for so long?"

A small twinge of guilt nibbled at her insides. Amanda hadn't been around much the last few years, it was true. And she should have been. She knew that, too. It had been just Amanda, Pam and their father, since her mother had died years before and the three of them had sort of drifted apart. For the rest of her life, she knew she'd regret not spending more time with her dad when she had the chance.

But she had grown up in the diner just as Pam had. Changing things wasn't easy for her, either. A part of her hated getting rid of things that her father had put in place. But times changed whether you wanted them to or not.

"Dad told us himself that when he took over the diner from *his* father, he made lots of changes," she argued, defending the new, still red—but unscarred red—counter and tables.

Pam scowled at her. "That's not the point."

Amanda took a deep breath and inhaled the aroma of fresh coffee, eggs and bacon. "Then what is the point, Pam? You asked me to come home and help, remember?"

"Help, not take over."

Okay, maybe she had been a little quick with changes. Maybe she hadn't taken the time to include her sister in decisions being made. That was her fault and she was willing to take the blame for it. In her defense, Pam had made herself scarce since Amanda got back to town. But, if she mentioned that, it would only start a new argument, so she let it go.

"You're right," Amanda said and watched surprise flicker in her sister's eyes. "I should have talked to you about the menus. About the countertops and tables and I didn't. I just…" She paused to look around the diner before adding, "I guess I didn't realize how much I'd missed this place. And when I got home, I just dove right in."

"I can't believe you missed the diner," Pam muttered.

Amanda laughed. "I know. Me, neither. You and I spent so much time working here as kids, who knew that I'd look forward to working here again?"

Pam sighed and leaned against the counter. She shot a frown at Hank, who was still listening in. The old man rolled his eyes and looked away.

"It's good you're here," Pam finally said. "And between the two of us, we should be able to both run the diner *and* have lives."

"We will," Amanda said, smiling a little at the tiny bridge suddenly springing up between the sisters.

"But it *is* the two of us, Amanda," Pam told her firmly.

"You don't get to make all the decisions and then let me find out later when the new menus arrive."

"Absolutely," she said. "You're right. I should have talked to you and I will from now on."

"Good." Pam nodded. "That's good. Now, I'm heading out. I've got a line on a new supplier of organic vegetables and—"

Amanda smiled and let her mind wander while her sister rattled off information on local farmers. Her gaze slid across the familiar faces filling the diner, then drifted out to the street beyond the wide glass windows. Main Street in Royal. Sidewalks crowded with early shoppers. Cars parked haphazardly along the curb. The sheriff stepping off the sidewalk, headed for the diner.

Sheriff. Headed for the diner.

Amanda's heart jumped in her chest. Her mouth went dry and her gaze locked on the one man in the world she couldn't seem to forget.

Nathan knew it was past time to face Amanda.

He left the sheriff's office with his deputy, Red Hawkins, in charge and stepped out onto Main Street. The morning was clear and promised another red-hot day. Summer in Texas was already off to a blistering start. The sun was a ball of fire looking to combust.

God, he loved it.

Walking down the sidewalk, his boots clattering out a sharp rhythm, Nathan nodded at those he passed and paused to hold a door for Macy Harris as she struggled to carry a baby and cling to her toddler's hand.

This was his place. Where he belonged. He'd actually had to leave and spend a few years in Houston as a city cop to figure that out. But now that he was back, Nathan knew he'd never leave Royal again. He'd found his place and damned if he was going to let Amanda Altman make him uncomfortable in it.

He loped across the street, dodging the occasional car, and headed straight for the Royal Diner.

The place was a landmark in town. He could remember going there as a kid with his folks and then later, as a teenager, he'd gathered there with his friends after football games and on long, boring summer afternoons.

It was the unofficial heart of town, which meant that at any time during the day, there would be a crowd inside. A crowd that would watch his and Amanda's first meeting with interest.

"Well, hell," he muttered as he marched up to the glass door. "Might as well get it done and let the gossips loose."

He pulled the door open, stepped inside and stopped, letting his gaze slide over the familiar surroundings. *Mostly* familiar, he corrected silently.

The walls had been painted. No longer a bright white that seemed to sear your eyes on a hot summer day, the walls were now a soft green, dotted with framed photos of Royal through the years. The counter had been changed, too—the old chipped and scarred red was now a shining sweep of a deeper, richer red. The black-and-white checked floors had been polished and the red vinyl booth seats had all been revamped. There were new chairs pulled up to the scatter of tables and sunshine streamed through the windows lining Main Street.

But none of it really mattered to him.

How could it?

He was too focused on the woman standing behind that new counter, staring at him.

Amanda Altman.

Damn. She looked way too good.

Nathan took a breath, forcing air into lungs suddenly

starving for sustenance. He hadn't really expected to feel the rush of heat swamping him. He'd convinced himself he was over her. Had forgotten what it had been like to be with her.

Big mistake.

"Hello, Nathan."

"Amanda," he said and ignored the swell of whispers sliding around the room as if carried along by a west Texas wind.

She moved toward the end of the counter, positioning herself behind the cash register. Defensive move?

Oddly enough, that eased him some. Knowing she was no happier about this public meeting than he was took some of the pressure off. In fact, he thought, it sort of tossed the power back into his lap.

She was new here. Okay, yeah, she'd grown up in Royal, just as he had. But Nathan had been here for the last three years and she'd been back in town only a couple of weeks. He'd made his place here and she was still treading water.

With that thought firmly in mind, he walked toward her and noted her chin came up defiantly. Damned if he hadn't missed that stubborn move of hers.

"Morning, Nathan," Pam chirped loudly. "We've missed you in here lately."

"Been busy," he said and ignored Hank Bristow's snort of derision.

"You want your usual?"

"That'd be good, Pam, thanks," he said, his gaze never leaving Amanda's.

She looked the same and yet…different. Maybe it was just that she was older now. Maybe it was the fact that her eyes weren't shining with adoration when she looked up at him. Didn't matter, he assured himself. Amanda was his past, in spite of his body's reaction to her.

"So," he said, knowing everyone in the diner was holding their breath, waiting to hear what might happen next, "you back to stay or this just a visit?"

Pam walked up to him then and handed him a to-go cup filled with black coffee. He didn't even glance at her as he took it and reached into his pocket for cash.

"On the house," Amanda told him.

"Not necessary," Nathan said and laid a couple of dollars on the counter. "You didn't answer the question, Amanda. You here to stay or just blowin' through?"

"I'm home to stay, Nathan," Amanda said. "I hope that won't be a problem for you."

He laughed shortly, and took a sip of coffee. Deliberately then, he said loudly enough for everyone to hear, "Why would that be a problem for me, Amanda? You and I are long since done."

He could almost *see* every customer in the place perking up their ears and leaning in closer so as not to miss a single word.

"You're right," Amanda said, lifting her chin even higher. "We're not kids anymore. There's no reason why we can't be friendly."

Friendly? His entire body was jittering with heat and she thought they could be friends? Not a chance. But he wasn't going to give her the satisfaction of knowing that.

"None at all," Nathan agreed tightly.

"Good. I'm glad that's settled," she said.

"Me, too."

"Oh, yeah," Hank muttered with a snort. "We can all see that this has worked out fine."

"Butt out, Hank," Nathan told him and turned for the door.

"Walk me to my car, Nathan?" Pam blurted and had him stopping for one last look behind him. But instead of seeing the woman headed toward him, his gaze darted straight to Amanda and he felt a surge of heat zap him.

The past might be dead and gone, but whatever hummed between them had just enough life left in it to be annoying.

When Pam threaded her arm through his, Nathan led her out and didn't bother looking back again.

Two

"That went well," Amanda told herself as she entered the tiny apartment over the diner that was now home.

All day, she'd been thinking about that brief, all-too-public meeting with Nathan. Which was, she thought grimly, probably exactly what he'd been hoping for. Nathan had always been the kind of man to assume command of any given situation. He was the take-charge type and so it was like him to make sure their first meeting was just the way *he* wanted it. That's why he'd come into the diner during the morning bustle—so that there would be so many witnesses to their conversation, neither one of them could really *talk*.

Honestly, the man hadn't changed a bit. Still stiff-necked and hardheaded. She'd seen that familiar, stony glint in his eye that morning and known the minute he opened his mouth that nothing between them would be settled. But then, she thought, why would it be?

She dropped onto an overstuffed, floral sofa that was older than she was, and propped her feet on the narrow coffee table in front of her. The romance novel she was currently reading lay beside an old ceramic pitcher filled with daisies and bluebells. Their scent was a soft sigh of summer in the too-warm room and, not for the first time, Amanda wished the apartment boasted more than a thirty-year-old air conditioner with a habit of shutting down every now and then for no particular reason.

The sofa held bright, boldly colored accent pillows and the two chairs in the room were more comfortable to look at than they were for sitting. There were pictures on the walls, a few throw rugs across the scarred wooden floor and the walls were still the dusty sand color Amanda's mother had preferred.

Folding her arms over her chest, Amanda stared up at the lazily spinning ceiling fan. A tired breeze of air sulkily drifted over her. This little apartment above the diner was like a security blanket. Her parents had lived here when they first married and opened the diner. Then later, they'd rented it out, furnished, to different people over the years. Pam had lived here for a while, then it had been Amanda's turn while she was in college. Having her own place had given her the chance to find her independence while staying close enough to home to feel safe.

Plus, she and Nathan had met here a lot back in those days. Those memories were imprinted on the tiny apartment, with its outdated, yet cozy furniture. If she tried, Amanda thought she'd be able to hear his voice, whispering to her in the dark.

She didn't try.

Instead, she concentrated on what he'd had to say that morning. Or rather what he *hadn't* said.

"He didn't want to talk anything through," she said to

the empty room and paused, as if waiting for the shadows to agree with her. "He only wanted to let me know that seeing me again meant nothing. He was trying to lay down the rules. Just like before. He tells you what things will be like, lays out his orders, then steps back, giving you room to follow them."

Well, he was in for a shock. She didn't *take* orders anymore. In fact, looking back at the girl she had once been made her nearly cringe. Back then, she'd been young enough and in love enough, that she had never once argued with Nathan—at least until that last night. When he announced his choice of a movie, she hadn't said she hated action movies. She'd never told him that she didn't like going to car shows or that she found fishing to be the most boring activity in the world.

Nope. Instead, Amanda had sat through countless movies where the only storyline revolved around demolition. She'd spent interminably long days watching Nathan fish in local streams and rivers and she didn't want to think about the hours lost staring at car engines.

Looking back now, Amanda couldn't believe how completely she'd given herself up to Nathan. Then, he was all she had cared about. All she thought about. And when everything fell apart between them…she'd had no idea what to do with herself.

It had taken a while to find her feet. To find *Amanda*. But she'd done it and there was no going back now— even if she wanted to, which she *so* did not.

Lifting her chin, she narrowed her eyes on the fan blades as if facing down Nathan himself. "I'm all grown up now, Nathan. I'm not going to roll over and speak on command. I don't *need* you anymore."

As her own words rang out in the room, Amanda

gave a tight smile. Good words. Now if she could just *believe* them.

Oh, she didn't need Nathan like she had then. Like she had needed air. Water. No, now what she needed was to get rid of the memories. To clear Nathan Battle out of her mind and heart once and for all, so she could move on. So she could stop remembering that when things were good between them, they were *very* good.

What she had to concentrate on, she told herself firmly as she leaped off the couch to pace the confines of the small living area, was the bad parts. The times Nathan had made her crazy. The dictatorial Nathan who had tried to make every decision for her. The man who had insisted they marry because she was pregnant, then the minute that pregnancy was over, had walked away from her so fast, she'd seen nothing but a blur.

That was what she had to remember. The pain of not only losing the baby she'd had such dreams for, but also realizing that the man she loved wasn't the man she'd thought he was.

If she could just do that, she'd be fine.

She walked to the galley-style kitchen and rummaged in the fridge for some of yesterday's leftovers. Working with food all day pretty much ensured that she wasn't hungry enough to cook for herself in the evening. But tonight, pickings were slim. A bowl of the diner's five-star chili, a few sandwiches and a plate of double-stuffed baked potatoes that hadn't sold the day before.

None of it looked tempting, but she knew she had to eat. So she grabbed the potatoes—and a bottle of chardonnay—then closed the fridge. She pulled out a cookie sheet, lined the potatoes up on it and put it in the oven. Once the temperature was set, she poured herself a glass of wine and carried it with her to the doll-sized bathroom.

It only took her a few minutes to shower and change into a pair of cutoff jean shorts and a tank top. Then she took her wine and walked barefoot back to the living room to wait for dinner.

The crisp, cold wine made the waiting easier to take. Heck, it even made thoughts of Nathan less…disturbing. What did it say about her, she wondered, that even when she was furious with the man, she still felt that buzz of something amazing?

Sad, sad Amanda.

In the years since she and Nathan had broken up, she hadn't exactly lived like a nun. She'd had dates. Just not many. But how could she think about a future when the past kept rising up in her mind? It always came back to Nathan. When she met a man, she waited, hoping to feel that special *zing* she had only found with Nathan. And it was never there.

How could she possibly agree to marry someone else if Nathan was the one who made her body burn? Was she supposed to settle? Impossible. She wanted what she'd once had. She just wanted it with someone else.

Heck, she had known Nathan was there the minute he'd walked into the diner. She hadn't had to see him. She'd *felt* his presence—like the electricity in the air just before a thunderstorm. And that first look into his eyes had jolted her so badly, it had been all she could do to lock her knees into place so she wouldn't melt into an embarrassing puddle of goo.

No one else had ever done that to her.

Only him.

She took a sip of her wine and shook her head. "This is not a good sign, Amanda."

It had been *years* since she'd seen him, touched him, and it might as well have been yesterday from the way her own body was reacting. Every cell inside her was jumping up and down, rolling out the red carpet and putting on a party hat.

But there weren't going to be any parties. Not with Nathan, at any rate. She'd never get him out of her system if she let him back in.

Trying to distract herself from the hormonal rodeo going on inside her, she walked to one of the windows overlooking Main Street and looked out at Royal. Only a few cars on the road and almost no pedestrians. The silence was staggering. Streetlights dropped puddles of yellow light on the empty sidewalks and, above the town, a clear night sky displayed thousands of stars.

Life in a small town was vastly different than what she'd known the last few years living in Dallas. There, the city bustled with life all night. Shops and clubs and bars glittered with neon lights so bright, they blotted out the stars overhead. Tourists flocked to the city to spend their money, and the nightlife was as busy as the daytime crowds.

It had been so different from the way she'd grown up, such a distraction from the pain she was in—Amanda had really enjoyed city life. At first. But over time, she had become just another nameless person rushing through the crowds, going from work to an apartment and back again the next day. Nights were crowded with noise and people and the gradual realization that she wasn't happy.

Her life had become centered around a job she didn't really like and a nightlife she didn't actually enjoy. She had a few friends and a few dates that always seemed to end badly—probably her own fault since she never had been able to meet a man without comparing him to Nathan. Pitiful, really, but there it was.

Then her father passed away and, a few months later, she got the call for help from Pam. Even knowing that she would have to eventually deal with Nathan again, Amanda had left the big city behind and rushed back home to Royal.

And she had slid back into life here as easily as if she'd never left. The truth was, she was really a small-town girl at heart.

She liked a town where nighttime brought quiet and families gathered together. She liked knowing that she was safe—without having to have two or three locks on her apartment door. And, right now, she liked knowing that she wouldn't have to talk to anyone until at least tomorrow morning.

She could have stayed at her family home, where Pam was living. But Amanda had become accustomed to having her own space. Besides, as evidenced by her sister's behavior today, just because Pam had needed her help didn't mean that she wanted Amanda around. She'd never been close with her sister and, so far, that situation looked as though it wasn't going to change any.

She took another sip of her wine and let that thought, along with all the thoughts of Nathan, slide from her mind. She wasn't going to solve everything in one night, so why drive herself nuts?

Her gaze slid to the darkened sheriff's office. No one was there, of course. In a town the size of Royal, you didn't need an on-duty police presence twenty-four hours a day. Besides, Nathan and his deputy were only a phone call away.

She wondered if Nathan still lived out on his family's ranch, the Battlelands. Then she reminded herself firmly it was none of her business where Nathan lived.

"Thinking about him is *not* the way to stop thinking about him," she told herself aloud.

The scent of melting cheese and roasting potatoes was beginning to fill the air and her stomach rumbled. Apparently she was hungrier than she had thought.

When the knock sounded on her door, she was more surprised than anything else. She took a step forward, then stopped, staring at the door leading to the outside staircase at the side of the diner. A ripple of something familiar sneaked across her skin and she took a gulp of her wine to ease the sensation. Didn't really help. But then, nothing could. Because she *knew* who was knocking on her door.

When she was steady enough, she walked to the door and asked unnecessarily, "Who is it?"

"It's me, Amanda." It was Nathan's voice, low and commanding. "Open up."

Wow. Skitters of expectation jolted through her. Amazing that just his voice could do that to her. After all these years, he could still stir her up without even trying.

She put one hand flat against the door and she could have sworn that she actually felt heat sliding through the wood. She took a breath, smoothed out her voice and tried to do the same for her racing heart. It didn't work.

"What do you want, Nathan?" she asked, leaning her forehead against the door panel.

"What I want is to not be standing out here talking through a door where anyone in Royal can see me."

Not that there were a lot of people out there at night. But all it would take was one busybody happening to glance up and word would fly all over town. *Nathan was at Amanda's doorstep last night!*

Okay, she thought, straightening, *good motivation for opening the door.* So she did.

Under the porch light, his brown hair looked lighter, his shoulders looked broader and his eyes…too shadowed to read. But then, she thought, it wasn't difficult to guess what he was thinking, feeling. His stance was stiff, his jaw tight. He looked as though he'd rather be anywhere but there.

Well, fine. She hadn't invited him, had she? "What is it, Nathan?"

He scowled at her and stepped inside.

"Please," she said, sarcasm dripping as she closed the door against the hot, humid air, "come in."

"We have to talk," he said, striding across the room before turning to face her. "And damned if I'm going to do it in the diner with everyone in town listening in."

Her fingers tightened on her wineglass. "Then maybe you shouldn't have come into the diner this morning."

"Maybe," he muttered and stuffed both hands into the pockets of his jeans. "But I needed some decent coffee."

She hadn't expected that. But he looked so disgusted, so…frustrated, Amanda laughed. His head snapped up, his gaze boring into hers.

"I'm sorry," she said, shaking her head as another laugh bubbled out. "But really? Coffee is what finally brought you in?"

"I've been getting mine at the gas station."

"Poor guy," she said, and he frowned at the humor in her voice.

"You can laugh. But I don't think Charlie's so much as rinsed out that coffeepot of his in twenty years." He grimaced at the thought and made Amanda smile again.

Shaking his head, he nodded at the wine in her hand. "You have any more of that?"

"I do. Also have beer, if you'd rather."

"Yeah, that'd be good." Some of the tension left his shoulders and one corner of his mouth tilted up into what might have been a half smile if it hadn't disappeared so fast.

She walked to the kitchen, opened the fridge and pulled out a beer. Amanda paused for a second to get her bearings. The moment she'd been dreading for years was finally here. Nathan and her were together again. Alone. And there was just no telling what might happen next. But whatever it was, she thought, at least it would be *something*. Better than the vacuum they'd been in for the last few years. Better than the rigid silence that had stretched between them since she came back to Royal.

With that thought in mind, she walked to the living room, handed him the cold bottle, then took a seat on the couch. Mainly because her knees felt a little wobbly.

Looking up at him, she watched as he opened the beer and took a drink. He looked so good it was irritating. His skin was tanned and there was a slightly paler line across the top of his forehead where his hat usually rested. His brown eyes were watchful as he glanced around the apartment, no doubt taking in everything in that all-encompassing sweep. She wondered if he was remembering all the nights they'd been together, here in this room. Could he still hear the whispered words between them? Probably not, she thought. Nathan wouldn't want to be reminded of a past that had no bearing on his life anymore.

She studied him as he studied the apartment. He wore scuffed brown boots, blue jeans and a short-sleeved, dark green T-shirt with Battlelands Ranch emblazoned on the shirt pocket. He stood stiff and straight as if awaiting a military inspection.

He was off-duty and yet everything about him screamed *police*. Nathan was just that kind of man. Devoted to duty, he preferred order to chaos, rules to confusion. He would take a road trip and stay on the highway, where Amanda would prefer the back roads, stopping at everything interesting along the way. No wonder they had clashed.

And even knowing all of that, she still felt the rush of attraction that she couldn't deny. She *wanted* to be immune to him and, clearly, she wasn't.

But this was exactly why she needed to be here. Because until she *was* immune to Nathan Battle, she'd never be able to move on. Instead, she'd go on being haunted by memories, by thoughts of what might have been.

He took another drink of his beer and looked down at the bottle in his hand. "I was sorry about your dad."

She blinked against the sudden sting of tears. The one thing she hadn't expected from Nathan was kindness. It was…disarming. "Thanks. I miss him."

"Yeah, he was a good man."

"He was." Safe ground. Talk about their families. Don't mention the tension coiled so tightly between them.

"Why did you come back?"

And *there* was the Nathan she knew best. So much for the pleasantries—it was on to Round One. "Excuse me?"

"Well, hell, Amanda." He frowned down at her and looked a little surprised that she didn't seem affected by his displeasure. "You were gone for years. Why come back at all?"

"Are you in charge of Royal's borders now, *Sheriff?*" she asked. "Do people have to check in with you before they move in?"

"I didn't say that."

She pushed to her feet. Even though she stood five foot ten, she was forced to tip her head back to meet his gaze, but she did it. "Royal's my home as much as it is yours, Nathan Battle."

"Couldn't tell from how you acted," he said, completely ignoring the hard glare she fired at him.

"I seem to recall you living in Houston for quite a while. Were you interrogated when you moved back home?"

"I'm not interrogating you, Amanda," he countered. "I'm just asking a damn question."

"That you already know the answer to," she shot back. "Pam needed help with the diner. I came home. That's the story. None of this concerns you, Nathan. This is my business."

"Damn straight it is, but now that you're back, it's *my* business, too." He stood as still and cold as a statue.

"How do you figure?"

"I'm the sheriff here. This is where I live. For you to come back now and start stirring things—"

"What am I stirring, Nathan?" she interrupted, and saw with a jolt of glee that he still hated being cut off. It infuriated her to remember that in the old days. She'd have shut her mouth so he could keep talking. Well, that time was gone. "I'm working at my family's diner."

"And getting tongues wagging again," he pointed out.

"Please. People in Royal gossip about everything. I didn't have to *be* here to have them talk about me."

"They're not talking about you," he elaborated grimly. "They're talking about *us*."

"There is no us," she said flatly, and was surprised by the twinge of pain that clutched at her heart.

"I know that and you know that, but the folks in town—"

"Forget about them," she interrupted again.

He took a long deep breath from between clenched teeth. "Easy for you to say. But as sheriff, I need to have the respect of the people I'm protecting. I don't like being the subject of gossip."

"Then tell them that. Why tell me?"

"Because if you leave, it'll stop."

She set her wineglass down before she was tempted to throw it at his rock-hard head. "I'm not leaving. And, it'll never stop, Nathan."

That statement hit him hard. She saw the proof of it flicker in his eyes. But she wasn't finished.

"Until we're ninety, people around here will be speculating and remembering...."

"Damn it, Amanda, I want you out of town."

"And I want you to stop caring what other people think," she snapped. "I guess we're both doomed to disappointment."

He set his beer bottle on the table beside her glass and moved in on her. He was so tall, he didn't have to put much effort into looming. She supposed it just came naturally to a man used to having his own way. A man accustomed to telling people what to do and having them do it.

It might have worked on her years ago, Amanda told herself, but no more. She was her own woman now. She made her own choices and decisions and lived with the consequences. She wouldn't be ordered out of town and she wouldn't be scared off by a big, gorgeous sheriff with eyes as cold as a winter wind.

"If you think you're worrying me, you're wrong."

"I don't want you worried."

"Good, because—"

"I don't want you at all."

Direct hit, she thought, as an icy fist slammed into her chest and squeezed her heart. But she wouldn't let him see it. "I don't want you, either, Nathan. I'm not that young girl anymore, dazzled because Nathan Battle noticed her. I'm not going to follow you around all doe-eyed, hoping for a smile from you. I'm—"

He grabbed her, yanked her close and kissed her with a fierce desperation that was fueled by desire and anger, all twisted up together. She could feel it in him as she felt it in herself. Past and present tangled together and memories were as thick as honey on a winter morning.

But those memories were swamped by all of the new sensations coursing through her. Amanda didn't try to pull free. Didn't pretend that she wasn't as hungry for him as he was for her. Instead, she moved into him, wrapped her arms around his neck and held on.

This is what she'd missed for so long. This man's touch. His kiss. The feel of his hard, strong body pushed up close against hers. She parted her lips for him and took him inside her. When he groaned and held her even tighter, Amanda felt bolts of heat shoot through her system like a summer lightning storm. So much electricity between them. So much heat.

Was it any wonder they had flashed and burned out too quickly?

His hands slid up and down her back, holding her, pressing her as close as he could. His mouth took hers again and again, and she met every stroke of his tongue with eager abandon. God, she'd missed him. Missed *them.* She had found nothing that could compare to what happened when they came together. No other man she'd ever met could compare to Nathan. Which meant that she was in very deep trouble.

Her mind raced even as her body lit up like a sparkler

factory. This was a huge mistake. Falling into Nathan's arms was *not* the way to get over him. But right now, all she was interested in was feeling her body come back to life as if waking up after a seven-year nap. Her skin tingled, her heartbeat crashing in her chest, and in the pit of her belly, heat settled and began to spread.

What was wrong with her, anyway?

Three

When Nathan suddenly released her and took one long step back and away, Amanda swayed unsteadily and gasped for air like a drowning woman. Her mouth burned from his kiss and her body was trembling.

"See?" he practically growled at her. "*This* is why you shouldn't have come back home."

"What?" She blinked up at him and saw that, once again, Nathan's expression seemed to be etched into stone. He looked hard, untouchable and about as passionate as a slab of granite. How did he turn it on and off like that? And could he teach her how to do it?

"I kissed you and you were all over me."

A sudden spurt of ice water flowed through her veins and put out all the lingering fires inside. Maybe he wouldn't have to teach her after all.

"Excuse me? I was all over you?" She took a step closer and stabbed her index finger at him. "Just who grabbed who, here? Who came to whose house? Who started kissing?"

His mouth worked and his lips thinned into a tight line. "Not the point."

"It's exactly the point, Nathan." Furious now, more at herself for falling so easily into old habits than at him, Amanda said, "Just like before, *you* came after *me*. You started all of this, then and now."

"And I'm going to end it."

Hurt raged inside, but was soon swallowed by a wave of fury. He decided when to start things. When to end things. And she was supposed to go quietly along. Nathan Battle, Master of the Universe.

"Big surprise. You like ending things, don't you?"

His eyes narrowed on her and his jaw muscle twitched so violently she was pretty sure he was grinding his teeth into powder. *Well, good.* She'd hate to think she was the only furious one in the room.

"I'm not the one who ended it seven years ago," he finally said, his voice a low throb of barely leashed anger.

"Not how I remember it," Amanda countered, the sting of that long-ago night still as fresh as if it had happened just yesterday. "You're the one who walked out."

"It's what you wanted." His gaze drilled into hers.

She met him glare for glare. "How would you know, Nathan? You never *asked* me what I wanted."

"This is pointless."

A long minute or two of tense silence stretched out between them. The only sound—the oven timer going off—rang out like a bell at a boxing match signaling the end of a round.

It worked to jolt both of them out of their defensive stances and a second later, Nathan was heading for her door. When he got there, he paused and turned back to look at her.

"This town chews on gossip every day, but I'm not going to be gnawed on."

"Good for you!" She picked up her wine and took a swallow she didn't really want before setting the glass down again. If he thought she was looking forward to being the topic of whispered conversations, he was nuts.

"The Battle family has a reputation in this town—"

"And the Altmans aren't in your circle, are we?" she interrupted again and felt a small swift tug of pleasure, knowing it irritated him.

"I didn't say that."

"You didn't have to." Walking toward him, Amanda glared up into his dark brown eyes. "I'm amazed you ever deigned to propose to me in the first place."

If possible, she thought his eyes actually went black for a second or two. How twisted was she that she *still* thought him the most gorgeous man on the planet?

"You were carrying my child," he told her flatly.

That statement, said with such frigid control, sliced at her like a blade and Amanda fought against the pain.

They hadn't spoken about their lost baby since the night he'd walked out on her. For him to bring it up now… "That was low."

He paused for a long minute or so, just studying her through narrowed eyes. "Yeah, it was." He scrubbed one hand across his face. "Damn it, Amanda, we've got to find a way to live in this town together."

She slid her hands up and down her arms. Funny—even with the hot, humid air of summer, she felt a chill. Maybe it was him being here, so close. Maybe it had been the loss of heat when their kiss ended. And maybe, she thought, it was because of the memories he'd brought up and waved in her face.

The memory of the child she'd carried and lost. The baby she had wanted so badly. Whatever it was, she wanted to be alone until that icy sensation was gone. She needed time to herself. To think. To regroup. And she couldn't do that until she convinced Nathan to leave.

"I'm guessing you have a plan," she said with a sigh.

"Damn straight, I do," he told her. "We go about our business. We live our lives. If we see each other, it's friendly, but distant. No more private chats. No—"

"Kissing?" she finished for him.

"Yeah. No more of that."

"Fine. Agreed." She threw both hands high. "Nathan's rules of behavior. Will you print me out a copy? I'll sign it. You want it notarized, too?"

"Funny."

"Well, blast it, Nathan, you haven't changed a bit. Still issuing orders and expecting them to be followed. Who made you the grand pooh-bah of the Western world?"

"Pooh-bah?"

She ignored that. "You come to my house. You kiss me. Then you lay down rules for me to live my life by and what? You expected me to just salute and say, 'Yes, sir'?"

"Would've been nice," he muttered.

She laughed. In spite of everything. "Yeah, well, not going to happen."

"You make me crazy," he admitted, shaking his head slowly. "You always did."

His voice was softer, deeper, and his eyes held a heat she remembered too well. So she stiffened her spine, refusing to be swayed by the urges she felt deep within her.

"Good to know," Amanda said, tipping her head back to look into his eyes. "That's some consolation, anyway."

He blew out a breath and muttered something she didn't quite catch before saying, "Fine. No rules. We go along. Stay out of each other's way."

"Fine."

"Eventually, people will stop talking or waiting for something to happen between us and—"

"You're still doing it," Amanda interrupted.

"Doing what?"

"Making rules. Setting down how things will be," she said. Tipping her head to one side, she stared up at him in complete frustration. "You can't regulate life, Nathan. It just...happens."

Like losing a baby you had loved from the moment of conception. That familiar twinge of pain, muted slightly because of time and her deliberate attempts to bury it, twisted inside her briefly.

"Unacceptable."

"You don't get to make that call, Nathan," she said softly.

"You're wrong." His eyes were hard, flinty chips of frozen chocolate. Whatever softness had been there before had completely dissipated. "My life moves just as I want it to. No exceptions." He paused. "Not anymore."

There it was, she thought. Once upon a time, *she* had been the exception to Nathan's carefully laid-out life. She'd thrown a wrench into his plans, made him scramble for a new strategy and then it had all fallen apart again. This time, though, she was older—and wiser, she hoped—and she wouldn't be sucked into Nathan's tidily arranged world. She preferred her life messy. She liked the adventure of not really knowing what to expect.

Of course, then scenes like tonight would probably rise up again to torture her, but that was a risk she'd rather take. Better than having your life plotted out on a ledger sheet, with no surprises, no jolts of pleasure or pain.

"Royal's a small town," he was saying and Amanda pushed her thoughts aside to pay attention. "But not so small that we can't comfortably ignore each other."

"That's how you want this to play out?" she asked. "We each pretend the other doesn't exist?"

"Better that way," he said.

"For who?"

He didn't answer. He just opened the door and said, "Goodbye, Amanda."

The sound of his boots on the stairs rang out like a too-fast heartbeat. A few seconds later, she heard a car engine fire up and then he was driving away.

Amanda closed her door on the world, wandered to the kitchen and retrieved the stuffed potatoes that were just a little too well-done. She idly stood there and watched steam lift off her dinner and twist in the barely moving air.

"Damn it," she whispered and stared through the window to the night beyond the glass. Her dinner was burned, her stomach was spinning and her temper was at war with her hormones.

Nathan was a force of nature. One that apparently was destined to crash in and out of her life whether she wanted him to or not. And the worst part?

"He walked away. Again."

She poured a fresh glass of wine, forced herself to eat the overdone potatoes and promised herself the next time she and Nathan were in the same room, *she* would be the one doing the walking.

* * *

The Battlelands Ranch glowed in the darkness. It stood like a proud dowager, waiting to welcome home its prodigal children. Practically every window shone with lamplight. Even the outbuildings—the barn, the foreman's house and Nathan's own place—boasted porch lights that formed brightly lit pathways.

Just like always, Nathan felt tension slide away as he drove down the oak-lined drive and steered his 4Runner toward the house he'd had built for himself when he moved back to Royal. He might not be a rancher these days, but the land was in his blood as much as it was in his younger brother Jacob's. The Battles had been on this land for more than a hundred and fifty years. They'd carved out every acre. Bled for it. Wept for it, and managed to hold on to it through all the bad times that had come their way.

The heart of the main ranch house was the original structure, a stately Victorian that the first Battle in Texas had built more than a hundred and fifty years ago to please his new bride. Over the years, that turreted, gingerbread-adorned structure had been added to, with wings spreading from each side and spilling into the back. Most of the ranch houses in the area were more modern, of course. Some mansions, some simple houses, they were all interchangeable in Nathan's eyes.

This place was unique because the Battles didn't tear something down just because it was old. They fixed it, improved on it and kept it, always to remind them of where they'd come from. Now that stately old Victorian was the centerpiece of a ranch bigger and more prosperous than that first Battle could ever have dreamed.

Gnarled, twisted live oaks stood like ancient soldiers on either side of the drive and gathered in clumps along the front and rear of the house. As Nathan parked his car and climbed out, he heard the swish of leaves in the grudgingly moving hot air.

From the main house came the sharp, clear sound of children's laughter, and Nathan smiled to himself. Lots of changes here at the Battlelands—mostly thanks to Jacob and his wife, Terri. They and their three kids were making this place come alive again as it hadn't since Nathan and Jake were kids themselves.

He glanced quickly at the wading pool and the nearby wooden swing set and climbing gym he'd helped Jacob put together for the kids. That laughter spilled from the house again and Nathan instinctively quelled the small twist of envy he felt for what his brother had. He knew Jake was happy. He had a family and the ranch he loved and Nathan didn't begrudge him any of it.

Still, it was a stunner that his younger brother had a wife and kids, but Jake had taken to life as a family man as easily as he had assumed control of the ranch years ago.

Nathan loved the place and it would always be *home* to him, but the ranch had never been at the heart of him as it had for Jake. As long as Nathan could remember, he had wanted to be a cop, while Jake wanted nothing more than to ride the range, and deal with the cattle grazing on the thousands of acres the family claimed. It had worked out well, Nathan told himself. Didn't matter that he was the eldest. It was enough for Nathan that the Battlelands was in good hands—even if those hands weren't *his*.

And, since Terri was pregnant again, Nathan knew that the family ranch was going to be in Battle hands for many more years to come. He couldn't help wondering what Jake thought of that, if his brother ever sat down and realized that his sons and daughters would be working the same land that had been handed down to him.

That twist of envy grabbed at him again and Nathan couldn't help wondering how his life might be right now if Amanda had carried their child to term. Would they still be together? Would there be more children? He tried to imagine it, but couldn't quite pull it off.

The ranch house door opened just then and a spill of light from inside poured onto the wide front porch. Grateful for the distraction, Nathan watched as his brother stepped out of the house. Talking to Jake would help him get his mind off of Amanda. Hopefully. His thoughts were crowded with her....

God, the taste of her. The scent of her. The feel of her body aligning with his and the hush of her breath on his skin—*damn it*.

Jake leaned against one of the porch posts and asked, "Late night?"

"A few things to see to," he answered vaguely and headed toward the main house.

Jake came down the steps, holding a beer in each hand. He was as tall as Nathan, but where Nathan was broad and muscled, Jake was wiry. His dark brown hair was a little too long, his jeans were worn and faded and his boots were as scarred and scuffed as Nathan's own. He was slow and steady and more at ease with himself and his world than Nathan had ever been.

Jake went his own way and managed to have a good time while he was doing it. Nathan had always admired that trait in his younger brother.

With a wide grin, Jake handed over one of the frosty bottles. Grateful, Nathan accepted it and took a long drink. When Jake wandered off, Nathan followed his brother across the yard toward the swing set. Apparently,

Jake wanted to talk—away from the house. But nothing would get Jake talking before he was good and ready, so Nathan just enjoyed the night and the returning sanity now that he was a safe distance from Amanda.

He'd thought he was well and truly over her. Nathan had deliberately put her out of his mind years ago. He'd lost himself in work and in the arms of the willing women who'd come and gone from his life without leaving so much as a trace of themselves behind. So yeah, he'd figured with Amanda back in town, he'd face her down and keep moving on.

But the hard ache in his body let him know that though his mind had let her go, the rest of him hadn't. And there she was again, he thought in disgust. Right back in his thoughts, front and center. He closed his mind to the memories and focused on the now.

There were a few dawn-to-dusk lights around the play area and he took a second or two to look it over. He and Jake had dug out the wide area beneath the playground equipment and then poured enough fine sand to sink an aircraft carrier. It had taken the two of them nearly two weeks to get everything set up and finished off for safety, but knowing his niece and nephews loved it made all the work worth the effort.

Made of sanded, polished wood—to prevent splinters in tiny hands—the climbing gym sprawled across the pristine lawn as if it had grown in that spot. Jake's five-year-old twin sons and their two-year-old sister loved climbing on it and especially enjoyed the castle-like room at the top. Gave him a good feeling, seeing the next generation of Battles clambering all over the structure, hooting and hollering at each other, just like he and Jake had done when they were kids. It also made him remember that if things had turned out differently, his own child might have been playing here as well.

He shook off that disquieting thought and buried it under another long drink of his beer.

Jake slapped one hand against the swing set and blurted, "So, how's Amanda?"

Nathan almost choked on his swallow of beer. When the coughing ended and he could breathe again, he looked at his younger brother. "How the hell did you know I went to see her?"

Jake shrugged. "Mona Greer was walking that tiny excuse for a dog of hers and saw you going into the diner apartment. She called Sarah Danvers, Sarah talked to her daughter and Amelia called Terri a while ago."

The Royal hotline was already buzzing.

"Well, hell," he muttered. So much for keeping his private life private. He hadn't seen a damn soul around the diner. Mona Greer should look into a career with the CIA or something. Even at eighty, her eyesight was damn good and she clearly had a sneaky streak.

Jake laughed. "Seriously? You thought you could slide in and out of Amanda's apartment and nobody would catch on?"

"A man can dream," Nathan mumbled.

Jake laughed even louder and Nathan told himself there was nothing more irritating sometimes than a younger brother. "Did you come out here just to bushwhack me with gossip then laugh at me?"

"Of course," his brother said with a good-natured shrug. "Not every day I get to give you grief over something."

"Glad you're enjoying yourself."

"Yeah? Well, *I'm* glad to see Amanda back. Glad to see it bugs you."

"Thanks for the support," Nathan told him and took a drink of his beer. His gaze moved over the play equipment. In the moonlight, the slide gleamed like a river of silver and the pennant flag on the castle top fluttered in the hot Texas wind.

Irritation swelled inside him. Three years he'd been sheriff. He had respect. He had the admiration of the townspeople. Now, he was just grist for the mill.

"You want support? Go back to the TCC and talk to Chance. Or Alex." Jake toasted him with his beer. "From family, you get the truth, whether you want it or not."

"I don't." Nathan leaned against one of the posts as visions of Amanda roared into his brain again. He shouldn't have gone to her. But how could he not have? They'd had to talk. But then, there hadn't only been *talking,* had there?

"I know you don't want to hear it but you're going to anyway." Jake paused, ran one hand over the heavy chain from which one of the swings hung. "So here it is. You missed your chance with Amanda back in the day."

Nathan snorted. "I didn't miss a thing. Trust me."

Shaking his head, Jake said, "You know what I mean. You let her get away."

"I didn't *let* her do a damn thing, Jake," Nathan said tightly as he pushed away from the heavy wooden post. "Her decision to walk."

Jake was unaffected by the anger in Nathan's voice. "Right. And you didn't try to talk her out of it."

"Why the hell should I have?" Stalking off a few paces, Nathan's boots slid in the sand he and his brother had laid beneath the swing set. This was his place. The home he'd grown up in. The town where he'd carved out a spot for himself. Damned if he'd let the past jump up and ruin what he'd built.

At the far end of the play equipment, Nathan turned to look at his brother. Jake looked relaxed…amused, damn him.

Well, why wouldn't he be? Jake had everything he'd ever wanted. He ran the ranch. He was married to his high school sweetheart and they had three great kids plus another on the way. Everything was riding smooth in Jake's world—not that Nathan begrudged his brother's happiness. But at the same time, you'd think Jake could manage a little sympathy.

"I'm not going to *beg* a woman to stay with me."

"Who said anything about *begging?*" Jake shot back. "You could have asked."

"No," Nathan said, shaking his head and looking away from his brother's too-sharp eyes to stare out over the moonlit lawn. "I couldn't. There were…reasons."

Reasons he'd never talked about. Never even mentioned to Jake, and Nathan was closer to his brother than to anyone else on the planet. Those reasons tried to push into his mind now and Nathan resolutely pushed them out again. He'd dealt with them all years ago. He wouldn't go back, damn it.

"You listened to the gossip. You believed the rumors instead of talking to Amanda about them."

His head snapped up and his gaze locked on his brother like a twin pair of dark brown lasers. "What do you know about the rumors?"

Jake took a sip of his beer. "Chance told me what was going on—" He held up one hand to keep his brother quiet. "And don't blame him for it. You sure as hell didn't bother to tell me. You're my brother, Nate. You could have said something."

He shook his head and squelched the burst of anger struggling to come alive inside him. "I didn't want to talk about it then—" He paused and added for emphasis, "I still don't."

He didn't like remembering those days. Remembering how he'd felt when Chance told him what people were saying. Nathan had been in the police academy in Houston, unable to get to Amanda. Hell, he hadn't even had time for a damn phone call. And when he had finally been able to go to her...

Shaking his head, Nathan mentally closed the door on the past. It was done and he wouldn't be revisiting it anytime soon.

"You always were the hardhead in the family," Jake said on a sigh.

Nathan managed a short laugh at that. "Seems to me your Terri might argue with you there."

"Probably," Jake admitted with a wince. "Nate, I don't know what happened between you two seven years ago—" he held up a hand again "—and I'm not asking. I'm just saying, she's home to stay now and you're going to have to find a way to get past whatever happened so long ago. You're going to have to deal with her. Maybe the two of you should actually try talking about what happened to break you guys up."

Nathan grimaced, took a pull at his beer and let the icy froth cool down the temper that was still simmering inside him. "Where is all this talking, share-your-feelings stuff coming from? Is Terri making you watch Dr. Phil again?"

"No." Jake looked embarrassed. "But I'm not an idiot any more than you are and I *know* you know you have to make your peace with Amanda."

Another sip of ice-cold beer slid down Nathan's throat as he thought about what his brother said. And then a fresh memory of Amanda, molding her body to his. The heat of her kiss. The scent of her filled his mind. The feel of her beneath his hands again. His body stirred and he winced at the ache that he had a feeling was going to become all too familiar.

"Jake," Nathan said softly, "you don't get it. I learned a long time ago, where Amanda's concerned, there *is* no peace."

Four

One thing Amanda had always loved about living in Royal was the big farmers' market held every weekend in the park.

Ranchers and farmers from all over the county showed up to sell fresh vegetables, fruit and preserves. There were always craft booths as well, with local artisans selling everything from jewelry to ceramics and handmade toys.

At barely 9:00 a.m., the sun was already a hot ball of misery glowering down on the town. By afternoon, the only people not huddled in an air-conditioned room would be the kids. But for right now, the park was buzzing with activity. The busiest vendors in the park were those who had claimed a spot beneath the shade of a live oak.

Amanda had the day off and she was determined to enjoy it. But, as she wandered through the market, it was clear that the Royal rumor mill was in high gear.

She felt the speculative glances thrown her way as she passed and she lifted her chin defiantly in response. No point in hiding, she told herself. Instead, she would just ignore the fact that whispered conversations would stop when she got close and pick up again as she moved off. Clearly, *someone* had seen Nathan at her place the other night and it hadn't taken long for tongues to start wagging.

Amanda stopped at a booth displaying hand-thrown pottery and idly picked up a kiln-fired, sky-blue pitcher.

The artist, a young woman with waist-length blond hair and bright green eyes, smiled at her. "I'm running a special today on the cornflower-blue pottery."

And if she'd picked up one of the earthenware jugs, Amanda thought, *that* would have been the special of the day. But she couldn't blame the woman for doing her best to make a sale. Besides, she was going to be looking for a house in town soon and she'd need to furnish it, wouldn't she? Smiling, she said, "It's lovely work. How much?"

"Only thirty-five."

"Sold," Amanda told her and set the pitcher down to reach for her wallet. She probably could have haggled, but it was beautiful and she really did want it.

Purchase made, Amanda left a satisfied artist behind her, tucked her new pitcher into the cloth shopping bag slung over her shoulder and wandered off toward the next booth.

"Amanda, hi!" Piper Kindred waved her over with a wide grin. Piper's curly red hair was drawn back into a ponytail and her green eyes were shining. "Haven't had a chance to talk to you since you moved back home."

"I know. Things have been so busy, but we have got to get together soon." Amanda had known Piper most of her life and seeing her friend now made Amanda realize again how much she'd missed being a part of Royal.

"I hear you and Nathan are getting cozy again…"

"Of course you did," Amanda said. A few days ago, Nathan had shown up at her apartment and kissed her senseless. Ever since then, she'd had dozens of customers who spent most of their time at the diner watching *her*. Including Nathan, she reminded herself. He made time to come in at least once a day. He'd order coffee, sit at the counter and watch her as she moved around the room.

Nerve-racking on all fronts.

"Anything you care to share?" Piper teased.

"Not a thing," Amanda assured her old friend, then abruptly changed the subject. "So," she asked, stepping back to read the sign strung across the front of the booth Piper was manning, "what're you selling?"

"Raffle tickets," Piper told her and used her thumb to fan a stack of them. "We're raising money to help pay for the new child-care center at the TCC."

Grinning, Amanda said, "I heard the motion passed. Beau Hacket must have been purple with fury."

"By all reports," Piper assured her. Then she sighed. "I only wish I'd seen it myself. You remember Shannon Morrison? She tells me she came within a breath of hog-tieing the old coot just for the hell of it."

Beau was possibly the last living true chauvinist in the world. He liked women fine, as long as they stayed in their "place." Amanda had never been able to figure out why a woman as nice as his wife, Barbara, had married the man in the first place. "Sorry I missed it."

"More and more women are becoming members of the TCC now that Abby Price paved the way." Piper paused. "I'm not a member or anything, but I wanted to help with this raffle. How many tickets are you going to buy?"

Shaking her head, Amanda reached for her wallet and laughed. "Give me five."

"Atta girl." Piper peeled off the tickets and waited while Amanda wrote her name and phone number on the stubs. When she was finished, Piper dropped the stubs into a steel box and said, "The draw's in a week. Who knows? You might win the grand prize."

"What is it?"

"A weekend getaway in Dallas." Piper shrugged. "Personally, I'd rather win the free dinner at Claire's."

"Hey," Amanda countered, in a mocking insulted tone, "how about you come eat at the diner instead? We've got lemon meringue pie tomorrow."

"Now you're talking," Piper said. "I'll come in around lunch. Maybe we can sit and talk over pie. You can give me the real story behind the gossip."

"You'll be disappointed. There is no story." Except for that kiss, Amanda thought. She waved a goodbye, then moved on. She was still smiling when she caught the scent of fresh-brewed coffee along with a delectable aroma of cinnamon coming from nearby. Marge Fontenot had probably brought in her homemade cinnamon rolls to sell in the coffee booth her husband ran. Amanda's stomach growled in anticipation as she headed for the vendor cart with the long line snaking in front of it.

"Doing some shopping?"

She stopped and looked at Alex Santiago as he approached her.

"I am." As the sun shone down on her, she was grateful she'd tucked her hair into a ponytail that morning. But Alex looked cool and comfortable in khaki slacks and a short-sleeved white shirt. "Living in the city, I really missed farmers' market days."

His gaze swept across the crowded park. "I admit, I

enjoy them as well. Last week I bought a new pair of boots...."

She glanced down and nodded in approval at the hand-tooled brown leather boots he wore. "Very nice."

"Thank you. And just now, I've purchased what I am told is the—" he paused to reach into a paper bag and draw out a jar long enough to read the label "—world's best huckleberry jam." He shrugged and gave her a smile that could probably melt ice at a hundred yards.

Amanda just chuckled. "If you bought that jam from Kaye Cannarozzi, I guarantee it *is* the world's best. She's won prizes for her jam every year at the state fair."

"Good to know," he said and folded up the bag again. "You can find just about anything here, I've discovered."

Amanda watched him as he looked around the park. He was dark and gorgeous and his accent made every word sound like seduction. Alex was also nice, funny and, except for his dubious taste in friends—Nathan for example—he was pretty much perfect. Too bad for Amanda that the only bell he rung for her was one of friendship.

"Hmm," Alex mused. "I'm curious as to what put a frown on your face just then. Dark thoughts?"

She forced a smile and shook her head. "Not at all. Um, I'm headed for the coffee wagon over there." She pointed and asked, "Would you like to join me?"

"I could use some coffee as well, so, yes." He fell into step beside her. "I'm looking forward to the Fourth of July celebration. I hear it's quite the event."

"Oh, it's great," Amanda told him. "Most of the town gathers right here for an all-day party. There are contests and games and the fireworks show is always amazing. If I do say so myself, we put on a terrific Fourth."

Funny how good it felt to say *we*.

"Sounds as though you've missed it."

"I really did," she admitted, glancing around the park at the people wandering from booth to booth. Kids raced away from their parents, laughing as they headed to the playground. Dogs on leashes strained against their owners' restraining hands and a hot summer wind kicked up out of nowhere.

Royal was home. There was no other place like it and she'd never really been happy anywhere else. "You know, I told myself while I was gone that I was fine. That life in the city was better, somehow. But now that I'm back, it's like I never left."

"Going home isn't always possible," he mused. "I'm glad you're finding it easier than you'd thought."

Amanda looked up at him and saw that while his stare was fixed on the distance, a slight frown was etched into his features. She didn't know Alex well, but she sensed something was bothering him. Before she could offer to help, though, he spoke again.

"I'm pleased to see that the gossip hasn't upset you."

She sighed. The downside to small-town life. She'd already had several people stop her in the park that morning, asking questions, giving her sly winks and knowing smiles. Nathan and she were the talk of the town and until something really juicy came up, that wasn't going to change.

"You've heard it, too?"

He gave her a rueful grin. "I think you would have to be on the moon to miss it."

"Know anyone who could give me a ride?"

"Sadly, no." He shrugged and added, "Though a beautiful woman shouldn't let loose talk from small minds worry her."

Amanda stopped, cocked her head and looked up at him. "You really *are* perfect, aren't you?"

His mouth quirked. "I like to think so, though I'm sure others would disagree."

"Not from where I'm standing."

"For that, I thank you. Besides, gossip isn't a static thing, Amanda," he said. "Very soon, they'll find something else to talk about."

"I suppose," she said, looking at the crowds in the park. Most of the people she'd known her whole life. Oh, there were plenty of outsiders who had come into town solely for market day. But the great majority were familiar to her. Which was probably why everyone felt free enough to talk about her.

She knew they were watching her now, too. Wondering why she was walking with Alex when it was clear she and Nathan were starting up again. A tiny twist of pain wrapped itself around her heart. "As much as I love Royal, it's not always an easy place to live."

"No place is easy," Alex said, his expression becoming thoughtful again, as if there were things chewing at him.

Somehow, she'd struck a nerve, Amanda thought. From what she knew, Alex Santiago hadn't been in town very long and she wondered if anyone really knew him well. Reaching out, she threaded her arm companionably through his. "Everything okay, Alex?"

Immediately, his handsome face brightened as he flashed her a smile. "You've a kind heart Amanda, but there's no need for concern. I'm fine."

"Am I interrupting?"

Amanda looked up when Nathan's deep voice demanded her attention. He was only a few feet away, headed right for her. The sunlight winked off the sheriff's badge pinned to his broad chest. He wore his favorite scuffed boots and a uniform shirt tucked into black jeans. The gun at his hip made him look even more formidable than usual. His gaze was fixed on hers, but still he managed to fire a brief glare at Alex.

A flash of heat shot through Amanda at Nathan's nearness and made the heat of the summer sun seem no hotter than a match-head in comparison. She wanted to fan herself, but she knew it wouldn't do any good, so she settled for sarcastic indifference instead.

"If I said 'yes you are,'" Amanda quipped, "would you go away?"

His eyes flashed. "Not until I know what you guys are talking about."

Alex grinned at his friend. "About small towns and smaller minds."

Nathan frowned and nodded. "You mean the gossip."

"Among other things," Amanda said, drawing Nathan's eyes back to her. She knew him so well she could see the tension in his face. The gossip was irritating to her. To Nathan, it had to be infuriating. "What do you want, Nathan?"

"Coffee, one of Margie's cinnamon rolls and to talk to you. Not necessarily in that order."

So, there wasn't even going to be a pretense of friendliness between them. He was acting as if the kiss they'd shared hadn't happened. As if putting it out of his mind made the whole scene disappear.

"I'm busy," she said. "Alex and I are shopping."

She should have known that men would stick together. Alex immediately said, "Actually, there are a few things I have to take care of. I've enjoyed myself, Amanda." Shifting his gaze to his friend, he nodded and said, "I'll see you later, Nathan."

"You don't have to go," Amanda told him quickly. Without Alex there, she and Nathan wouldn't have a buffer. And she suddenly wanted one really badly.

"Yeah, you do," Nathan said at the same time.

Alex only laughed. "You two are very entertaining. I'll be on my way."

Around them, conversations rose and fell. A sultry wind teased the hem of her shorts and in the distance, children played and laughed. Amanda knew that she and Nathan were now the center of attention, but she didn't care anymore. Alex had been right about one thing. Sooner or later, everyone would find a new topic of interest. Until then, her best choice was simply to ignore them all. People would talk and she couldn't stop them. So instead, she continued on toward Margie's coffee cart and wasn't surprised to have Nathan right at her side.

"Mona Greer saw me at your place when I was there a few nights ago," he told her, his voice low and deep.

"Well, that explains a few things," Amanda said wryly.

"That woman should have been a spy."

"Maybe she was. Now she's retired," Amanda mused, "and she's looking for new things to occupy her."

He snorted a short laugh. "That'd be something. Mona in the CIA."

Amanda laughed, too, then Nathan looked down at her and she caught the confusion in his eyes.

"This doesn't bother you? Being talked about?" Nathan asked.

"A little," she admitted. "Okay, a lot. But I can't stop it, so why make myself nuts?"

"Healthy attitude."

"I try," she said, and fell into line at the coffee cart. Nathan stayed beside her and, keeping his voice low, he said, "I still think we need to set some ground rules, Amanda."

"Like you coming around the diner to keep an eye on me?"

He frowned.

"Or are you talking about when you kissed me?"

She had the satisfaction of seeing a flash of temper spark in his eyes. Then he spoke as if she hadn't said a thing. "We agree that there's nothing between us anymore and—"

Amanda didn't have to speak. She only looked up at him, making no attempt at all to hide the smile curving her mouth. Nothing between them? Hadn't they proven just the other night that if nothing else, there was still plenty of heat between them?

He scowled, clearly understanding what she wasn't saying. Then he muttered, "That doesn't count."

"Felt like it counted to me." In fact, that one kiss had kept her awake most of the night feeling restless, edgy. Memories had crowded in on her until all she could think about was Nathan and how things used to be between them. That kiss had stirred up everything for her, making the last few days really uncomfortable. And now Nathan wanted to pretend it hadn't happened?

Nathan looked down at her and watched her meadow-green eyes narrow. She was mad. He liked that. Better than amused. Or accepting. Anger was safer. For both of them. Except for the fact that she looked so damn good when she was pissed off at him. Gave her a fire he'd never found in any other woman.

Her light brown hair was pulled into a high ponytail at the back of her head. She wore gold hoops in her ears that dangled long enough to skim her smooth shoulders, displayed nicely in a navy blue tank top. Her white shorts showed off her tan and made her legs look as if they were a mile long, and the sandals let him see she still wore the gold toe ring he'd given her on her left foot.

A breeze sent her ponytail dancing and it was all Nathan could do to keep from reaching up and twining that silky mass around his fingers. Damn it, she was in him again. As fiercely as she had been years ago. For days now, he'd been tormented by thoughts of her. By memories so thick they'd nearly choked him. He'd hardly slept for dreams of her and when he woke, it was to a body that was hard and aching for want of her.

His talk with Jake hadn't helped any. He'd meant it when he said there was no peace with Amanda. But back in the day he hadn't been looking for peace, had he? All he'd been able to think about was her. Her laugh. Her eyes. Her scent. Her taste. The feel of her hands on his body and the sweet brush of her breath when she kissed him.

Hell, no, that wasn't peaceful.

It was…consuming.

And it was happening again. Only this time, he'd come up with a plan to combat it. It had hit him in the shower just that morning—another damn cold one—that what he needed to do was get Amanda back in his bed.

Over the years, Nathan had convinced himself that he'd idealized what he and Amanda had shared. That was why he hadn't been able to find another woman to compare to her. His own mind had set him up for failure by making the memories of Amanda so amazing that what woman *could* hold a candle to her?

What was needed here was a little reality. And sex was the key. Get her in his bed, and get her out of his mind once and for all.

It was the only road to sanity.

Once he'd had her again, he could let her go. This tension between them would finally be over.

As his plan settled into his mind, he smiled to himself.

"What?" Amanda asked.

"What do you mean?"

"You're smiling," she pointed out.

"And that's bad?" He laughed a little and moved forward as the line continued to snake ahead.

"Not bad," Amanda said, still watching him warily. "Just…suspicious."

Behind them in line, someone chuckled.

Nathan frowned. Damned hard to work on seducing a woman when you had half the town watching your every move. "So when I'm angry, you're mad and when I'm not, you're worried."

She thought about it for a second, then nodded. "That's about right."

For just a moment, Nathan enjoyed the confusion in her eyes and found himself laughing briefly. "There really is no one else like you, is there?"

"Probably not," she admitted and moved a bit closer to the head of the line.

She could always drive him out of his mind, Nathan thought, letting his gaze move over her in appreciation. He'd always liked tall women—they were right in easy kissing range. Amanda, though, was like no one else. Or at least that's how he remembered it. Even in high school, when she was a freshman and he a senior, he'd been drawn to her. His friends had given him grief over it, of course—but he hadn't been able to stay away.

And then, years later, those same friends had told him about the rumors that had eventually torn him and Amanda apart.

"So tell me, Nathan," she said, shattering his thoughts and drawing him back to the moment, "are you interested in my sister?"

"What?" He goggled at her. "Where did that come from?"

She shrugged, glared at the man behind them, openly listening to their conversation, then leaned in closer to Nathan to say, "I've seen the way she watches you."

Nathan thought about that for a minute. He hadn't noticed Pam looking at him in any particular way. Okay, yes, he'd dated her a couple times a year or so ago, but it hadn't gone anywhere and they'd parted friends. Or he'd thought they had. Until now. Frowning slightly, he said, "We went out a few times a while back, but—"

Her eyes went wide. "I can't believe you dated my *sister*," she said, cutting him off sharply.

The man behind them in line let out a long, slow whistle, but when Nathan gave him a hard look, the guy got quiet fast.

"It was a couple of dates. Dinner." He thought back. "A movie."

"It was *my sister*." She fisted her hands at her hips. "How would you like it if I dated Jake?"

"I think his wife would mind it even more than I would."

"You know what I mean."

"Yeah, I do. But we were over, remember?" Nathan whispered and moved with the line. How long *was* this line, anyway? And were there even more people crowded around them than there had been a few minutes ago? "Besides, Pam was here and—"

"So she was *here*," Amanda said, interrupting him again and making Nathan grind his teeth together in frustration. "Well, then. Of course I can understand that. The whole proximity factor."

The whistler behind them chuckled now and only shrugged when Nathan gave him another hard stare. This conversation was going to be all over town by suppertime, he told himself, and still he couldn't keep from saying, "At least Pam never lied to me."

She sucked in a gulp of air and her eyes shone with fury. "*Lie* to you? I never lied to you. You were the one who—"

"That's it," he muttered and grabbed hold of her arm.

He wasn't going to do this with a couple dozen people watching them with all the avid interest of a crowd at a football game.

Dragging her out of the line, he headed toward the nearest deserted spot. A shade tree close to the now-empty baseball diamond. Naturally, nothing with Amanda came easy. She tugged and pulled, trying to get out of his grip, but no way was he letting her go until they had this settled. And for this talk, they needed some damn privacy.

"Let go of me!" She kicked at him, but missed.

"In a minute," he muttered.

"I want my coffee. I do *not* want to go anywhere with you."

"That's too damn bad," Nathan told her and never slowed down. When they finally reached the shade of the oak, he let her go and she stared up at him, furious.

"I don't know who you think you are, but—"

"You know exactly who I am," he told her, voice low and filled with the temper crouched inside him. "Just like you know that I hate putting on a show for the whole damn town."

"Fine." She lifted her chin, met him glare for glare

and then said, "You want to talk, here it is. I never lied to you, Nathan."

"And I'm supposed to take your word for that?"

"Damn right, you are," she shouted, obviously not caring who was listening. "When did I *ever* give you a reason to *not* trust me, Nathan?"

She had a point, but he didn't want to admit to it. All he remembered were the rumors she hadn't been able to disprove. The sympathetic glances from his friends. The gossip that insisted on a completely different story than the one she'd told him. And his doubts had chewed on him until, ragged with temper and tension, he'd faced her down and in one night, they had lost everything.

"What was I supposed to think?" he demanded. "My best friends told me that story. Why wouldn't I believe them?"

Shaking her head, she looked at him now with more hurt than fury and that tore at him.

"Because you were supposed to *love* me. You should have taken my word for it."

Shame rippled through him and was gone an instant later. He'd done what he thought was right. Hell, he'd been half-crazed back then anyway. When he heard she had lost the baby, he was enrolled in the police academy in Dallas and hadn't been able to get to her. Hadn't even been able to call her. To figure out truth from lies.

"It was a long time ago, Amanda."

"Was it?" she asked quietly. "Doesn't feel like it right now."

No, it didn't. The past was there, in the park with them. Shadows of memories crowded together, dimming the sunlight, making the other people in the park fade away until it was just he and Amanda. He looked into her eyes and said, "All right then. Tell me now. The truth."

She sighed. "I shouldn't have to tell you again, Nathan. You know me. You knew me then. You should have believed me. I *lost* our baby."

Pain slapped at him but he pushed it away. Now that the past was here, it was time to finally settle it. If he wanted to get her out of his mind, then he was going to have to make a start right here.

"Then who the hell was it who made sure I thought you had *ended* the pregnancy on purpose?"

Five

"I don't know," Amanda said, shaking her head. She still couldn't believe anyone had spread that rumor. Couldn't believe that Nathan had thought for even a minute that she would ever do such a thing.

In a flash, Amanda was back there, on the night when everything crashed down around her. They'd been engaged for two weeks—because Nathan had insisted on a wedding the moment he found out she was pregnant. But that night, she had been the one doing the insisting.

"The wedding's off, Nathan."

"Just like that?"

"The only reason you were marrying me was because of the baby, right?" Those words cost her. *She so wanted him to say that wasn't true. That he loved her. Always had. That they would be okay, they would get past this.*

But he didn't.

*And she couldn't marry a man who didn't love her—
no matter how much she loved him.*

"So that's it?" he demanded. "Now that you're not
pregnant, you don't need me anymore, that it? Find
someone richer?"

Stunned, she could only look at him. She had never
cared a damn about his money. She'd loved him for as
long as she could remember. And she'd convinced herself that he cared for her, too. Even though he'd never
actually said the words. Now she could see she'd been
living in a dream world. "How can you say that?"

"Oh, I'm not done," he told her flatly. "You said you
lost the baby, but that's not the whole story, is it?"

Amanda stared up at him. She had expected him to
be supportive. To share the pain that was still tearing
through her. The loss of the baby, her hopes, her dreams
for the future. They were all gone now.

She'd needed Nathan so badly. Now that he was here,
she only wanted him gone.

"I don't know what you mean," she said finally.

"Yeah, I think you do." He stalked around the perim-
eter of her tiny Midland apartment. "Hell, you hated
the thought of marrying me so much you got rid of my
baby?"

"What?" Shock held her in place. Outrage made her
want to scream. Pain held her in such a tight grip she
could hardly breathe. "You think—"

"Thought I wouldn't find out, didn't you?" he asked,
his voice dripping with ice.

"There was nothing to find out, Nathan." Through
her pain, anger began to blossom like a black rose. She
gave it free rein. "I lost the baby. I had a miscarriage.
I told you."

He scrubbed one hand across the top of his head.

"Yeah, that's what you told me. Others told me something different."

"And you'd believe them? Believe that I could do something like that to our child?"

His eyes were hard, his expression distant, remote. "Why would anyone say that if it wasn't true?"

Good question, but that was for later. Right now, the most important question on her mind was how could he think for even a second that it was true?

"How do I know?"

"Exactly," he said. "How do I know what to believe, either?"

"I guess you have to trust me," she said, knowing he didn't. Knowing he wouldn't.

"Yeah." His eyes were as cold as the moon. Suddenly he looked like a stranger to her and Amanda knew she wouldn't be able to reach him because he didn't want to be reached.

So much lost, all in a blink of time. She swayed with the impact of what was happening.

He turned and walked to the door. There, he stopped and looked back at her. "You're right about one thing, though. The wedding's off. I was only marrying you because of the baby. With the reason gone, there's no point, is there?"

The fact that his words echoed what she had thought herself only moments before just made the pain that much deeper. Sharper. When Nathan left, the quiet click of the door shutting behind him sounded like a gunshot. It seemed to echo in the empty room long after he'd left her. Long after Amanda had curled up on the couch to cry herself to sleep.

Shaking her head as if she could somehow dislodge the painful memories, Amanda looked up at him through eyes that were no longer starry with love for a man who refused to love her back. She wasn't young and foolish anymore. If she still loved Nathan, that was her problem and she'd find a way to get over it. But he would never know that he still had so much power over her heart.

"You walked out, Nathan," she reminded him in a voice that was low and throbbing with remembered hurt.

"Yeah," he admitted, "I did. But you were the one to end things between us. Hell, I walked in the door and you handed me the ring."

"You agreed with me about calling off the wedding," she reminded him.

"Damn straight, I did. You weren't pregnant. You'd already handed me the ring—"

"You wouldn't *talk* to me," she said.

"You didn't give me a chance to say anything and even if you had, what the hell could I say?" he countered. "It was done. The baby was gone and your ring was in my fist. What do you think I should have said, for God's sake?"

"That you believed me." That was the one thing that had always stung. He had known her better than anyone else—or so she had thought. And he'd taken the word of malicious gossips over her.

How was she supposed to forget that?

He scrubbed both hands across his face as memories crowded so close he could hardly draw a breath. The rumors had driven him crazy when he couldn't get to her. At first, she was in the hospital and then when she was out, he was confined to the academy. Couldn't even talk to her. Couldn't look into her eyes and see for himself truth from lies. But by the time he finally reached her side, the crazy had taken over. The doubts. The disappointment and fury had him so tangled into knots it was all he could do to hold it together.

Hell, he prided himself on control. On being in charge of every damn thing around him. He had his own personal rules of conduct. And he'd blown them all on that long-ago night. Duty. Honor. They'd both gone out the window when anger made him blind to common sense.

Blowing out a breath, he stared up at the sky for a long minute, then lowered his gaze to hers. Doubts still gnawed at the edges of his heart, but being with her, looking into her eyes, clouded with hurt, he could see the truth that had eluded him for so long. "I do believe you."

The moment he said it, he knew it was right. Back then, he'd been young and stupid. He'd wanted her to rush into his arms looking for comfort. He'd wanted her to cry and mourn their lost child so he would *know* that she hadn't ended her pregnancy. Instead, she'd handed him the ring he'd given her and told him, more or less, to move on.

So his own self-assurance took a hit and then delivered one right back. Hurt, he'd made sure that she hurt, too. He wasn't saying he was right. He was only saying—screw it.

A sheen of tears filmed the brilliant green of her eyes, but before he could panic or kick his own ass for making her cry, she blinked them back. She took a breath, steadied herself and said, "Thanks for that, anyway. Better late than never, huh?"

"I guess," he said, but this conversation still felt unfinished.

She hitched her bag higher on her shoulder. "Now, I've got to go."

"Damn it, Amanda—don't walk away."

"What else is there to talk about, Nathan? We're over

and done, and standing here in the park together is only
going to fire up the gossip train you hate."

True.

He did hate knowing that, but there didn't seem to
be much he could do about it. For days now, he'd lived
with everyone in town watching his every move. With
having people drop by the jailhouse for a "friendly chat"
when what they were really looking for was more grist
for the rumor mill. They wanted exclusive news about
Nathan and Amanda so *they* could be the ones to spill
the next part of the story.

Hell, he was actually getting used to it.

He'd come here today, knowing the gossips were
chewing on them, knowing that meeting her like this
would only make things worse. But this was his plan. Talk
with her, bed her, then move on and—damn it—he was
going to stick to it. It was a good plan, even if it had gotten more involved than he'd originally thought it would.

Nathan hadn't meant to dig into the past. Hadn't intended to throw up that night between them like a damn
battle flag. He didn't want her pissed—despite how good
she looked when fire was in her eyes. He didn't want her
sad. Or resigned.

He wanted her hot and ready and as eager to be with
him as he was to get his hands on her. But he couldn't
do that until he ended the war.

"You're off tonight, right?"

"What?" She looked as surprised as he was over his
blurted question.

Taking hold of her arm again, he drew her around to
the far side of the old oak, using the tree to block most
people's views of them.

"Let go, Nathan."

He did, though his fingers still felt the warmth of

her skin long after he drew his hand back. Through the years, through the old pain and shared memories, the heat between them lingered. He was more convinced than ever that he was doing the right thing. Get her back into bed, feel the burn again so that he could finally let it—and her—go.

"We need some time, Amanda," he said, keeping his gaze locked with hers. "Time to talk. To find a way to be in this town together."

She was shaking her head so he talked faster, refusing to give her enough room to back away. "Come out with me tonight. We'll have dinner—and time."

"I don't know...."

Confusion etched itself onto her features. He could see her weighing her decision, so he gave her a little push. "Not afraid to be alone with me, are you?"

It worked.

Her head snapped up and she snorted. "Afraid? Please."

He grinned. "Then it's settled."

"Fine." She nodded at him. "Where do you want to meet?"

"I'll pick you up at your place about seven."

She laughed a little uneasily. "This is Saturday. Everyone for miles around will be in town. You're not worried about how many people will see us together?"

He glanced up at the crowd milling around the park before looking back to her. What was the point of hiding now? They were already the center of every conversation in town. No sense trying to fight it. "They're already talking, remember? Besides, damned if I'm going to sneak around."

She nodded. "Good point."

"All right, then. See you at seven."

* * *

Over at the diner, Pam leaned on the counter and tapped her fingernails against it in a sharp staccato. "People have been talking about them all day."

"You shouldn't be listening."

"How can I not?" She shook her head and gave a quick look around at the people sitting at the booths and counters. Peggy, the other waitress on duty, was laughing with her customers and in the kitchen behind her, Pam could hear the cooks talking while they worked. The diner was busy and that was a good thing. The fact that it was all because of Amanda made it harder to appreciate.

"She's been back home for a couple of weeks and she's taking over again."

She looked at the man sitting in front of her. JT McKenna had been her friend since school. He ran his own ranch just outside of town where he raised a small herd of cattle and his pride and joy, quarter horses.

His dark brown hair curled over the collar of his shirt and his tanned face showed a line of white across the top of his forehead where his hat normally rested. He was tall and lean and according to Pam's friends, gorgeous. She'd never really noticed because JT had always been just her friend.

Now, he cupped his hands around a cup of coffee and shook his head. "Pam, you're the one who asked her to come home."

She sighed. Hard to admit, but he was right. Pam had tried to run the diner on her own, but it just hadn't worked. She'd been overwhelmed with trying to handle the whole place on her own. But she still hated to acknowledge that Amanda had made a difference. Her younger sister had always been the golden one. Her parents' favorite. Taller, smarter, prettier… Pam's finger-nails sounded out like a jackhammer.

It wasn't that she didn't like her sister. But did Amanda have to be so perfect?

"You're getting wound up over nothing, Pam," JT said.

His brown eyes were on her and she had to sigh. "You're probably right, but—"

"No buts," he teased and gave her a grin that lit up his eyes. "You're so focused on Amanda and Nathan you can't see anything else around you."

"Like what?"

JT blew out a breath and said, "Like I could use some more coffee."

"Oh, sure." She turned to reach for the pot and told herself she needed to calm down. But the last few days had made that nearly impossible. Everyone was talking about Nathan and Amanda again. Just as they had all those years ago.

Nathan.

Her heart ached at the thought of him. Without even trying, her little sister had even gotten the man Pam had always wanted. All those years when Amanda was living away from Royal, Pam had done everything she could to capture Nathan's attention. But it was as if he was com-pletely oblivious to her. Even the couple of times she'd managed to get him out to dinner and to a movie, noth-ing had come of it.

"Still," she said thoughtfully, "according to Dora Plant, Nathan and Amanda were arguing at the park today."

"You're doing it again," JT told her flatly. "I can see it in your eyes. You're thinking on how you can get around your sister to Nathan and it's not going to get you anywhere. You best watch your step, and move careful, Pam."

"What?"

"You and Amanda," he said gently, "you're *family*. Always will be."

"I know that—" she argued.

He cut her off. "Maybe you do, but I'm thinking you tend to forget what you don't want to think about. My point is, you should open your eyes, Pam. Nathan's not interested in you that way and probably never will be."

She flushed, but couldn't seem to stop it. Pam had hungered after Nathan for so long, it had become a way of life for her. All the time he was with her sister, that knowledge had eaten away at her like acid. But then the two of them broke up and Pam began to hope again. All right, nothing had come of their few dates, but that didn't mean she should give up.

"You don't know what it's like, JT."

He laughed shortly, shook his head and dug money out of his wallet. Laying the bills on the counter, he said, "You'd be surprised by what I know, Pam."

She watched him go, then turned back to her customers, still wondering what JT had meant.

A few hours later, Amanda was standing in front of her mirror, trying to figure out how Nathan had maneuvered her into this. She wasn't even sure why she was going along with…what was it? A date? Her stomach swirled at the thought.

"It's not a date," she said, just to hear it said out loud. She dragged a brush through her hair. "It *feels* like a date. It shouldn't, but it does. God, I haven't been on a date in—" She stopped because even if there was no one else there to hear her, admitting out loud that it had been *three years* since she'd been on a real, live, guy-picks-you-up-and-pays date was too humiliating.

No wonder she was nervous.

Music pumped from the radio in the living room and Amanda smiled at herself in the mirror. Looked more like a grimace, but she'd take it. She had no idea where Nathan was taking her, so she'd changed her outfit three times, finally settling on a pale blue skirt that hit just above her knees, a white, short-sleeved blouse that buttoned up the front and a pair of sandals with a heel that would bring her almost to eye level with Nathan.

And there was the swirl of nerves in the pit of her stomach again.

Notadate...notadate...notadate...

The chant went through her mind but couldn't seem to find anything to hold on to. Because she'd been off balance ever since she'd returned to Royal. Those first two weeks, waiting to see him again. Then that first meeting in the diner, when he'd been so cold, so remote. Only to have him show up later, right here and, after demanding she leave town, kiss her until her head was spinning.

No wonder she felt as if she were at the center of a madly spinning tornado. She had no sense of direction. Only the instinctive drive to keep her heart intact this time. To become so immune to Nathan and what he could do to her with a glance that she could finally move on. Find a nice man—one who didn't drive her to impossible highs and heartbreaking lows—and build a life. A life with the children she longed for. A life filled with the love she'd lost so long ago.

So *why* then was she putting herself through this not-a-date? Because she wasn't immune to Nathan yet and just maybe a night spent alone with him might start her on that path.

When a knock sounded at her door, she slapped one hand to her abdomen in a futile attempt to quell all the butterflies nestled in there, then told herself to get a grip. To get over Nathan, she was going to need to restrain her natural tendency to go up in flames around him. She walked across the room, deliberately casual, opened the door and nerves slid away to be replaced by something more elemental. More…hazardous, to her already iffy sense of control.

He wore black jeans, a red, button-down long-sleeve shirt open at the collar and the boots that seemed to be a part of him. He gave her a slow, thorough once-over, then an appreciative smile curved his mouth. "You look great."

Fire licked at her insides, but she squashed the flames flat before they could take hold. This wasn't a romantic thing, for heaven's sake. This was just…who knew what it was?

"Thanks." She grabbed her purse from the nearby table. God, he smelled good. "I'm ready to go."

That smile of his deepened as he turned her toward the stairs. "Always liked that about you, Amanda. None of this make-him-wait stuff." Taking her hand, he led her down the stairs and then to his car, a big, black SUV he'd left parked on the street.

Saturday night was date night in Royal for young and old alike. A lot of the local ranchers came in to treat the family to dinner out. There were shoppers hitting the stores on Main Street and pedestrians, just out watching other people. And she was sure that most of them were avidly watching her and Nathan.

Nothing could have proven to her more completely that he didn't give a damn about the gossips any more than picking her up on a Saturday night for the whole town to see.

To her left, the wide front windows of the diner shone with light and she knew that everyone in there, too, would have a perfect view of her leaving with Nathan.

As if he knew just what she was thinking, he squeezed her hand briefly and gave her a conspiratorial wink. Her heart clenched—it was almost as if the two of them were a team again. To underline that sensation, his hand around hers felt warm and strong and...right. She nearly stumbled when that thought zipped through her mind.

Thankfully, she recovered quickly, since an older woman with a crown of gray braids wrapped around her head stopped them on the sidewalk.

"Well, now, what might you two be up to on such a nice summer evening?" Hannah Poole was easily seventy-five. Her eyes—shining with glee—were razor-sharp and her nose was practically twitching with interest. If there was a gossip train in Royal, then Miss Hannah was the engineer. There wasn't a thing that went on in town that she didn't know about.

"Hello, Miss Hannah," Amanda said, tugging at Nathan's hand to stop him. "It's nice to see you."

"I'm sure it is, honey," she said as her gaze locked briefly on their joined hands. "Going somewhere, are you?"

"Yes, ma'am, we sure are," Nathan answered, then surprised Amanda by letting go of her hand only long enough to snake one arm around her waist, steering her toward the car. "And if we don't hurry we'll be late."

"Well, I wouldn't want to keep you," the woman said thoughtfully, eyes gleaming. "I've got to get on home, myself. You two young people have fun, now. Good to see the two of you back together again."

"Oh, we're not—" Amanda began.

"Thank you, Miss Hannah," Nathan said over her. "You have a good evening."

He got Amanda settled, stalked around to the driver's side and climbed in.

"Of course she had to get home," Amanda said, watching as Hannah Poole scurried down the sidewalk. Her feet, clad in sensible brown shoes, moved faster than Amanda had ever known them to go.

"What she meant was, she had to get on the phone and tell everyone who wasn't in town tonight that she saw the two of us together."

"Yep."

She turned her head to stare at him. "Doesn't that bother you?"

"Yep." He fired up the engine, checked traffic, then pulled out onto Main Street.

"That's it? Just 'yep'?" Amanda's gaze locked on him. In the old days, Nathan would have been rigidly furious to be the center of attention. This Nathan was a stranger. Mysterious. Intriguing. "Who are you and what have you done with Nathan?"

His lips quirked briefly. "What am I supposed to do? Shoot Miss Hannah? Throw her into a jail cell to keep her off the phone?" He shook his head and turned left. "Nope. No way to stop her or anyone else from talking."

"Did you have a temper transplant?"

Unexpectedly, he glanced at her and grinned. "No, but not a bad idea."

She was charmed. How could she not be? Not only was this Nathan—the man she'd been in love with since she was fourteen years old—but tonight he was…different. More relaxed. More…approachable.

Which could be risky, her mind warned. Logically,

she should pay attention to that warning. Unfortunately, her body was too busy celebrating Nathan's nearness to worry about possible future problems. And that was a whole different problem. She was supposed to be weaning herself from the allure of Nathan and now he'd made it that much more difficult.

Amanda settled back in the car seat, kept her gaze locked on the street in front of them and tried to stifle the sensations already building inside her.

It wasn't easy.

"So where are we going?"

"You still like surprises?" he asked.

"Yes…"

"Then sit back. Won't take but a minute to get there."

That narrowed down the choices. Even if he was taking her to Claire's restaurant, it was clear on the other side of town. But he wasn't headed in that direction, anyway. They'd only driven a mile or so, when Nathan pulled into a familiar parking lot.

"The TCC?" she asked.

"Problem with that?"

"No." She looked at the building that had been a part of town life since long before she was born. Built in the 1900s, it was a huge, rambling, one-story building constructed of dark stone and wood with a tall, slate roof.

She'd been inside a couple of times before—not as a guest, but as a server when her father had catered meetings. She knew the ceilings were high, the furniture and floors were dark and old-world style and the ambiance was loaded with testosterone. Sure, they were allowing female members now, but not many and not without a battle that had made the Alamo look like a playground tussle.

"I've just never—" She caught herself and shrugged. "I'm just...surprised, I guess."

"Why?" Nathan shut off the engine and looked at her. "The dining room's been open to women for years."

"True, but you never took me there before."

"Yeah," he said, "there's a lot of things I didn't do that maybe I should have."

She didn't even know what to say to that. Did he have the same kind of regrets she had for the way things had ended between them? Nathan was a master at hiding what he was feeling so unless he came right out and said so, she might never know for sure.

"Maybe that's true of both of us." She offered a truce and was pleased to see his smile in response.

"Could be you're right. But for now, let's just say I'm a changed man." He got out of the car and as he walked around the hood to come to her side, Amanda found herself hoping he hadn't changed *too* much.

Over dinner, she realized that she had forgotten just how charming Nathan could be. His gaze fixed on hers, he led their conversation to happier times. To the years before they'd split up in such a crash of emotions.

All around them, the clink of silver against china and the tinkle of crystal became no more than quiet background noise. The people, the servers, seemed to fade away. She had even stopped noticing the hunting trophies on the walls. With Nathan's full attention on her, it was impossible to be aware of anything else.

The dark paneled walls, the soft lighting and the flickering candles on the tables all made for a romantic setting that Amanda wasn't sure how to interpret. She hadn't expected romance, yet it seemed Nathan was determined to give it to her. Why?

And why couldn't she just enjoy it while it lasted?

They talked about old times, without touching on the painful parts. They talked about what each of them had been doing over the last seven years and slowly, began to work into…what? A friendship? No. That was too pale a word for the connection that hummed between them, whether they were acknowledging it or not.

Of course, because they were in a small town where they knew everyone, their dinner wasn't completely private. Several people paused at their table to say hello and Amanda watched as Nathan became what he was: the sheriff. A man respected and trusted by everyone in town, he answered questions patiently and promised a couple of people to look into their problems. He carried power easily and she realized that the last several years had made a difference. He wasn't the young, arrogant man she'd known back then. Oh, he was still cocky, that came across just fine, but there was an underlying thread of patience that the old Nathan had lacked.

It wasn't just him that had changed. The years had left their mark on both of them. They weren't the same people they had been seven years before. And maybe, if faced with the same situation today, they'd each react differently.

Not that it would change anything now, but she couldn't help wondering how things might have been if only they had trusted each other more. *Talked* to each other, rather than reacting to the pain of the moment.

When they finished their meal, Amanda took a moment to glance around at the elegant dining room, filled with TCC members and their guests. No doubt every one of them would be spreading the word about this dinner she and Nathan had shared—but at the moment, she just didn't care.

Seated across the linen-draped table from him drinking a cup of coffee, Amanda said, "Thank you. For... bringing me here. I had a great time."

"Good." He glanced at their bill, tucked money inside, then set the black leather folder at the edge of the table. Lifting his own coffee cup, he toasted her and said, "So did I, but the night's not over yet."

"Really? What could possibly top that fabulous dinner?"

"Dessert."

She had to laugh. "Nathan, we both passed on dessert, remember?"

"You won't pass on the one I've got in mind," he assured her.

Amanda looked into his eyes and in the dancing candlelight, she read *desire* in those depths. Tingles of something expectant, something amazing, went off like sparklers in the pit of her belly and even lower.

A deep, throbbing ache pounded out inside her to the rhythm of her own heartbeat and the longer she held his gaze, the faster that rhythm became. Here was the danger, she told herself sternly. And if she had a single ounce of common sense, she'd ask him to take her home. Now.

But she knew she wasn't going to do that.

It had been seven long years since she and Nathan had been alone together. Seven years since she'd felt this sizzle of bone-deep attraction. Years since she'd been able to look into those chocolate-brown eyes and see the need she saw now.

No. No matter what happened next, she wouldn't be leaving him. Not yet.

"Well, now I'm intrigued," she managed to say.

"Then let's get going." He stood up and held one hand out to her.

She only hesitated a moment before laying her hand in his and allowing him to draw her to her feet. Their gazes met and in the quiet elegance of the room, it felt as if explosions were going off all around them but only *they* could feel them. If interested gazes followed them as they left, Amanda was oblivious to them.

Nathan led her out of the club, into the warm, moist air of a Texas summer's evening. Wherever they were headed next, she knew there was nowhere else she'd rather be.

Six

As they drove through town and took a turn in the direction of the Battlelands, Amanda looked at Nathan's profile. There was a slight smile on his face, but that told her nothing other than that he was pleased with himself. *Hmm.*

"Are we going to the ranch house?"

He glanced at her and smiled. "You'll see."

Why was he being so secretive? What was he up to?

She could play along, so she said, "It'd be nice to see Jake and Terri again. Been a long time since I've seen their kids."

"Uh-huh. You will eventually."

So, probably not going there right now. Okay, fine. She could be patient. To a point.

"How're you and Pam getting along these days?"

The question caught her off guard and made her a little uncomfortable at the same time.

"About the same," she said. "She's glad I'm there in the diner, but I think she'd rather if I could phone in the work from somewhere else."

He frowned. "She's got some issues with you."

"There's a news flash," she murmured. She had a couple of issues with Pam, too, now that she knew her sister had dated Nathan. Probably shouldn't matter since she and Nathan were *so* done when it had happened. But it *did* matter, darn it. She didn't like her big sister making a move on her ex. And one of these days, she and Pam were going to have to talk about that. But for now, she changed the subject. "Speaking of families, how're Jake and Terri doing?"

Now he gave her a *real* smile. "They're great. I know you've kept up with what's going on here in Royal, so I'm guessing you know they have twin boys and a little girl?"

"Yeah," she said, smiling wistfully. "Last time I came home to visit my dad before he—well, I made sure you were nowhere around and I met Terri and the kids in town."

Nodding, he said only, "The twins are in kindergarten now and Emily's talking all the time."

A small ache settled in her chest, thinking about Nathan's nephews and niece. Children always did that to her, though—made her remember that she'd been cheated out of her child. Amanda had been playing what-if for more than seven years—wondering how her life might be different if only she hadn't lost Nathan's child. They'd have married, of course—Nathan wouldn't have had it any other way. But would they be happy? Or would he have always felt trapped by circumstances? Would she always wonder if he really loved her or had married her solely out of duty? Questions she would never have the answers to.

She tried to shake them off. "Emily's almost two now, isn't she?"

"Yeah, and a beauty. Has Jake wrapped around her tiny fingers, too." He chuckled and shook his head. "Hard to believe sometimes that Jake's a father, but he's damn good at it."

So would you have been, she couldn't help thinking. And maybe his thoughts were mirroring hers because his features slid into more somber lines.

A few miles of silence filled the big black car before Nathan took a turn she recognized.

"So we're not going to the ranch house at all."

"Nope."

"We're going to the river."

"That's the plan."

Nerves jittered and Amanda told herself not to build anything out of this. After all, Nathan had grown up on this land. He and Jake had spent most of their childhoods at the river, fishing, swimming, avoiding chores. For him, this place was just a part of his life. There was no reason to believe that Nathan felt the same…affection for this spot that she did. For Amanda, this river was magical. This one slice of his family's ranch would always be special to her.

Cutting right through the heart of the Battlelands, the fast-moving river was shaded on either bank by ancient live oaks. It was cool and green and lush. As they approached, she couldn't help remembering—and didn't try too hard to stop—that she and Nathan had been in this private place when they made love for the first time so long ago.

Her heartbeat quickened as the memories inside her mind played out like a movie. She could see them both so easily. Young, eager, and for her at least, so much in love she was drowning in the overflow of emotions. Nerves had been thick, but desire was more prominent. It was as if in this one place, time had stopped. The world had dropped away and she became a part of the one man she had always wanted.

Was he remembering? Did he think about that night and all the nights that had followed? Did he have the same regrets she did? Or had he really moved on from their shared past—and if he had, why were they here together now?

The sun was so low now, that only the barest hint of color remained in the sky. Amanda turned her head to the side, looking away from Nathan. What was she supposed to think about this? What was he expecting? Was he deliberately trying to recreate that night? Did he really think that after all these years, all it would take is this one romantic setting and time would roll back?

Oh, God. What if he was right?

The Texas landscape stretched out for miles beneath a faintly rose-colored sky. Grasses waved in a sultry wind on either side of the lonely road and Amanda drew an uneasy breath. Years without Nathan and now, in a single day, he was wiping away the emptiness and drawing her back into a net designed to reawaken emotions she'd thought long buried. How could he take her from fury to desire so easily? And how could she defend her heart against him when all she really wanted was what they'd once had?

"Look familiar?" he asked, voice deep enough to rumble along her spine like tentative fingertips.

"Really does," she said, steeling herself before she turned to look at his profile in the growing darkness. She couldn't read on his face what he was thinking. As always, he had tucked his emotions away, offering the world no peek at what he was feeling. "Why are we here, Nathan?"

He glanced at her, then shifted his gaze back to the road. "We need to talk and I couldn't think of a more private place."

Oh, it was private all right, Amanda thought as another slow swirl of anticipation spread through her. This could be dangerous, she warned herself, but at the same time, she wasn't that young, desperately-in-love girl anymore. She'd grown and changed and lived through a heartbreak she had thought at the time would kill her. She was strong enough now to withstand the churning emotions inside. Strong enough to hold her own against a man who was an overwhelming presence in her life.

At least, she hoped she was.

Otherwise, history would repeat itself tonight—and she honestly couldn't have said which she was hoping for.

He pulled the car off the road and steered it toward a stand of oaks. She took a breath and let it out slowly, determined to keep what she was feeling to herself. Shouldn't be hard since her feelings right now were so jumbled even she was confused.

He parked the truck beside the trees, then gave her a look she couldn't interpret. "Everything should be ready. Let's go."

She had no idea what he was talking about but there was only one way to answer her questions. Besides, Amanda wasn't about to let him know that being here made her feel as if she were off balance on a high wire. She opened the door and stepped out into the warm embrace of the summer air. Tipping her head back, she glanced up at the sky. The first stars were just blinking in and out of existence as clouds scudded past. The wind was soft, like a warm caress, as she walked around the front of the car to join Nathan. "What're you up to?"

He smiled. "Come with me and see."

He held out one hand toward her and Amanda hesitated only a moment before laying her palm against his. She was in this far, she told herself, no point in trying to back out now. Besides, she was curious.

Why had he brought her here? What was *ready?* And who was this man, anyway? Less than a week ago, he'd told her flat out that he wanted her to leave town. Tonight, he was being Prince Charming. Tall, dark, gorgeous and using his smile like a well-honed weapon.

She was completely unsteady and she thought that was exactly the way he wanted her.

Nathan gave her hand a gentle squeeze, then led her through the trees to the river. The whisper of leaves sounded overly loud, like hushed conversations you couldn't quite make out, and the muted roar of the river grew louder as they walked closer. Wind plucked at her hair, her heels wobbled on the sunbaked ground. Nathan lifted branches out of their way as they passed and she felt herself slipping further and further into the past as memories became as thick as the shadows.

They stepped free of the trees and Amanda stopped dead, pulling her hand free of Nathan's to stare at what lay in front of her. A blue-and-white quilt was spread out on the grass. A hurricane lamp was lit, the flame flickering in the soft breeze. A cooler sat at one side of the blanket and two place settings of china and crystal were laid out, just waiting for them.

It had been different in the past, she thought, mind racing as the years rolled back and suddenly she was a shy, nervous high school senior again. Nathan was home from college and he'd brought her here, to "their spot."

He had talked about school, what he was doing, who he was meeting, and all she could do was look at him, storing up image after image in her mind so that when he left again, she wouldn't feel so alone.

They'd had a picnic, right here. Nathan had positioned his car so that the headlights shone down on them and the car radio had provided music. They'd talked and laughed and made plans for a misty future neither of them could fully imagine.

And then they'd made love, right here, beneath the stars, for the first time. Everything had changed for them that night. She could still remember his face, as he rose over her, as she took him inside her. The surge of love, of need, filled her now as it had then and had her turning to look at the man beside her.

"What are you doing, Nathan?"

"Remembering," he said, his gaze fixed on the scene laid out in front of them. Then he turned those eyes on her. "Since you've been back I've been doing a lot of that."

"Me, too."

"And you remember what happened here?"

"Not likely to forget," she said with a lightness she didn't feel.

"Good," he said and took her hand again, drawing her toward the scene so meticulously laid out.

It really didn't matter, but she heard herself ask, "Who did all of this?"

"Louisa," he told her just before he eased down to the quilt and drew her down beside him. "She probably had Henry drive her out here and help, but she packed the cooler and set everything up."

Louisa Diaz, the housekeeper at Battlelands. She'd been running that ranch house for twenty years. Of course Nathan would go to her for help. "Wasn't she curious about why you wanted this set up?"

"If she was, she'd never admit it," he said, opening the cooler to draw out a bottle of chilled white wine. He poured two glasses and handed her one. "We've got strawberries and whipped cream and some of Louisa's famous pecan cookies, too."

She stared at the golden liquid in her glass. She was still off-kilter. He'd gone to so much trouble, setting all of this up, it made her wonder what was behind it all. Just memories? Or was there something more? "It seems you've thought of everything."

"I think so."

"The question remains," she said. "Why?"

He sighed heavily, impatiently. And suddenly he seemed more like the Nathan she'd been dealing with since returning to Royal rather than the younger man she'd given her heart to.

"Does there have to be a reason? Can't we just enjoy it?"

Enjoy it. Reliving a memory that was so cherished it still haunted her dreams? Remember a time when she'd had the world at her fingertips—only to lose it a year later? Pain floated just beneath the surface and Amanda had to fight it back. If she knew what he wanted, expected, maybe this would be easier. But because she couldn't read him, she was left to stumble around in the dark. She took a sip of wine, letting the dry, icy flavor ease the tightness in her throat.

Silence blossomed between them and seemed to grow unchecked for what felt like an eternity before Nathan spoke, shattering the stillness.

"There's no great plan here, Amanda." His voice was deep, and each word seemed to rumble along her spine.

"I just wanted to bring you to a place where we could talk."

"And you chose *here*."

A flicker of a smile touched his mouth then faded almost instantly. "You're not the only one who remembers, you know. This was a good spot for us, once."

"Yes," she agreed, her own voice sounding strained and rough. "It was. But Nathan—"

He shook his head. "But nothing. We're here. We'll talk. Have dessert. Relax, Amanda."

Relax?

This from the most tightly wound man she'd ever known?

She looked into his brown eyes and tried to see beyond what he was showing her. But he'd clearly gotten more adept over the years at hiding what he was thinking, feeling, and Amanda was left to take him at his word. Dangerous? Maybe.

But she couldn't ask him to take her home now. She'd look as though she were afraid to be here alone with him and she wouldn't give him that much power. Besides, she could consider this a test of her own resolve. If she and Nathan were going to live here in Royal together, then she had to get past the desire that swept through her every time he was near. She could hardly live her life in a constant state of expectation.

"Okay," she said at last, taking another sip of her wine. "We'll talk."

He gave her a quick, disarming grin that jolted her heartbeat into a thundering gallop and she knew that for her, at least, there wouldn't be any *relaxing* happening tonight.

"I came better prepared this time, too," he said and reached behind the cooler for a small, battery-operated radio. He turned it on and a woman's voice soared into the shadows, singing of love. "Remember the battery on my old truck died that night? Left the radio playing too long and we had to use the ranch walkie-talkie to get Henry to come out and give us a jump?"

She remembered. She also remembered the knowing look Henry had given the two of them. But the ranch foreman hadn't said a word. He'd only gotten Nathan's truck running again and then left.

"That was embarrassing," she said with a sad smile.

"It was," he agreed, then gave her another quick grin. "But it was worth it."

Her hand tightened on the slender base of the crystal wineglass. Nathan was pushing past all of her defenses, one smile at a time.

She turned away from him and looked out over the river. At its widest point, it was no more than six feet across, but it was a wild river, fed from the distant mountains and left unchecked. The water frothed on the surface, slapping against the banks and over rocks worn smooth over time. While she watched, a trout jumped from the water only to splash back down. Wind sighed through the trees, rattling the leaves.

It was perfect.

A summer night, with the stars overhead. Soft music playing accompaniment to the roar of the river and the man who had been the great love of her life at her side. How many times had she wished for just this over the years?

She looked at Nathan as he reached into the cooler and pulled out two cookies. Handing one to her, he smiled and said, "You always did like Louisa's pecan cookies."

Her heart fisted in her chest. He looked so damn… harmless. And he so wasn't.

"You're evil," she said, nipping the cookie from his fingers and taking a bite.

He nodded. "You used to like that about me."

"There are a lot of things I used to like."

"But not anymore." The words were clipped. Cool.

"I didn't say that."

"Didn't have to," he told her and then shrugged as he took a bite of his cookie. "I feel the same way."

"Good to know," she muttered, as her foolishly hopeful heart sunk a little in her chest.

"Things've changed," he said.

"If that's what you brought me out here to tell me," Amanda said, "you wasted your time. I already knew that."

"But the thing is," he said, as if she hadn't spoken at all, "*some* things don't change."

He reached out and stroked the tip of his fingers down the back of her hand and along her arm. Amanda shivered.

"Not fair." She pulled her hand free of him and dropped the cookie to the quilt before she stood up and moved to the edge of the river.

Music continued to sail into the deepening night. The river rushed on and, above her, the stars were glittering against the dark sky.

She heard him stand, then walk up behind her. When his hands dropped onto her shoulders, she was already braced for the heat that poured from his body into hers.

"Why the hell should I play fair?" he demanded and turned her around to face him.

"Why are you playing at all?" she countered and waited, watching his features in the indistinct light.

"Because I can't get you out of my head," he admitted, his voice harsh and deep, as if it were crawling up from the center of him.

If he could admit at least that much, then she could, too. "I feel the same way."

He slid his hands up and down her upper arms as if chasing away a chill she didn't have. In fact, she was so hot at the moment, she couldn't imagine *ever* being cold again.

Amanda took a breath, tipped her head back to look up at him and said, "Wine. Cookies. Music." She waved one hand at the frothy river beside them. "This place. What is it you want, Nathan? Truth."

"Truth." He tasted the word as if trying to decide if he liked the idea of it or not. Finally, though, he nodded and said, "Truth is, Amanda, there's a lot of history between us and until we get it sorted out, life in Royal's going to be harder than it has to be for both of us."

Disappointment flashed through her before she could stop it. Of course that's why he'd done all this. To soften her up. To make her malleable enough to agree to however he wanted to handle things. So much for change, she thought glumly.

"We've already had our 'talk,' Nathan."

"Yeah, we did," he agreed. "But it wasn't enough."

She pulled away from him and walked even closer to the river's edge, where spray reached up from the water's surface to kiss her skin. She turned her face up to the sky and fixed her gaze on one star in particular. It was a focus point, to center her thoughts, to gather her frazzled nerves.

She didn't want to talk about the past anymore. It only brought pain. Still watching that star, she asked, "What more is there to say, Nathan?"

She heard him move to stand behind her again. She

felt the heat of his body reaching out for hers. Felt the frisson of something incredible that she *always* felt when close to Nathan.

Once again, his hands came down on her shoulders and a whip of electricity snaked through her in an instant. She closed her eyes and took a breath to steady herself—an idea that went to hell the moment he started speaking. "Can we leave the past where it is, Amanda? Live here in town without going back there?"

"I want to," she said and it was the truth. The past was pain and she'd had enough of that to last a lifetime.

"Then we make a pact. We deal with the present. Starting fresh."

"Just like that?" Was it even possible? she asked herself.

"Won't be easy," he admitted, "but it's easier than hauling the past around with us wherever we go."

It sounded good, but she wasn't as sure as he was that it could be done. But, talking with him, being with him, without the hurtful memories, was worth taking the chance.

"A pact," she agreed and held out one hand.

He looked at it, smiled, then took her hand in his, smoothing his fingers over her knuckles. His voice was soft, low and as mesmerizing as the rush of the river below.

"You're still in my blood, Amanda."

Her heart jumped into high gear and she swayed on her feet. But his hands only tightened on her shoulders. He bent his head until his mouth was beside her ear. His voice came again and his warm breath dusted her skin.

"I think about you. Dream about you. *Want* you."

"Nathan…" Her blood felt as if it were bubbling in her veins.

He spun her around, pulled her close and took her right hand in his left. Confused, Amanda only stared at him, until he said, "Dance with me."

He didn't give her a chance to answer. To decide yes or no. Instead, he began to sway to the music and she let herself move with him. He held her tightly, her body pressed along the length of his and she felt…everything, just as he'd wanted her to.

Her body lit up inside as desire pulsed like a beacon deep within her. He must have sensed it. Must have felt her body's surrender because he dipped his head to steal a hard, fast kiss that left her reeling.

"Tell me you don't the feel the same damn thing," he demanded.

Amanda knew that if she looked into his eyes again, the very foundation of what little self-control she'd managed to cling to would be shaken. But she couldn't resist. Couldn't deprive herself of the chance to see those dark brown eyes flashing with need again.

The moment she did, she felt herself falling into a whirlwind of emotion. Long-buried feelings resurfaced with a vengeance and were tangled up with something new. Something still fragile, but so much deeper than anything she'd known before.

Their dance ended abruptly. He shifted his grip on her, sliding his hands up to cup her face. His thumbs traced the edges of her cheekbones and his gaze moved over her features hungrily. She felt every nerve in her body leap to attention. Every square inch of her wanted him so desperately she trembled with the need.

It would be so easy to give in, she thought wildly as she lost herself in the dark chocolate of his eyes. To surrender to her body's demands. To push away the past and think only of the now. But where would that put them? Where would they go from here?

"Nathan, this is crazy...."

"Nothing wrong with crazy," he murmured and leaned in to leave a light-as-a-feather kiss on her forehead.

She swallowed hard. "But if we do this—it will only make living in this town together harder."

He snorted a laugh. "I can't get much harder."

"Oh, God." Her breath caught in her lungs as he pulled her in close to him. Close enough to discover that he was right. Much harder and he'd turn to stone.

A burn started low and deep within her, spreading with a swiftness that made her feel as if she had a sudden fever. A fever only Nathan could assuage.

Shaking her head both at her own thoughts and at him, she pulled free and took a staggering step backward just for an extra measure of safety. Not that she was afraid of Nathan. No, she was more afraid that her good intentions would be blown out of the water by her own need.

"Damn it, Amanda," he said roughly. "You want this, too. I can feel it."

"Yes," she admitted when she could talk around the knot lodged in her throat. "I do. But I'm not going to do it."

"Why the hell not?"

"Because it wouldn't solve anything, Nathan."

He threw both hands high and wide then let them fall to his sides again. "Why the hell does it have to *solve* anything? We're not kids anymore. Can't it just be what it is and leave it at that?"

"Not between us," she said, a little steadier now that he wasn't touching her. "It's never simple between us, Nathan, and you know it."

He shoved both hands into his jeans pockets and let

his head fall back briefly as if looking for patience in the wide Texas sky above them. When he looked at her again, he said, "You can't let go of the past, can you?"

Bristling a little, she countered, "Can you?"

Shaking his head, he pulled one hand free of his pocket and ran it over his face. "Not entirely, no."

"Then how can us sleeping together help?"

"How can it hurt?" he argued.

"Nathan, sex doesn't solve a problem, it only creates *new* problems."

"Maybe that's enough for now," he said tightly.

"Not for me," she answered.

"What the hell do you want, then?"

A thousand disjointed thoughts swept through her mind in one confusing instant. What did she want? *Him,* mostly. She'd tried to fool herself into believing that she just wanted to move on. To find a new man and build a life with him.

But there were no other men for Amanda. There was only Nathan, now and always. She wanted what they hadn't had before. Trust. Love. A future. And she knew Nathan wasn't interested in anything like that.

So that left her exactly where?

Alone, she thought. She'd be alone.

He closed the gap between them in one long stride and grabbed her up close again. Here was the danger, she thought. Feeling him pressed close to her, knowing that he wanted her as much as she wanted him. But want wasn't enough, as they'd already discovered.

"Don't make this harder," she whispered.

"Why should I make it easy?" he asked.

She looked up at him and when he kissed her, Amanda lost herself in him. His mouth covered hers with a fierce tenderness that quickly became a dance of desperation.

Their tongues met again and again, stroking, caressing, tasting. Hunger built and spread, wrapping them both in a wash of heat that was inescapable. His hands swept up and down her back and finally came to rest on her behind. He held her tightly to him and ground his hips into hers. She gasped and lifted one leg instinctively, wrapping it around his thigh, trying, but failing to bring him even closer.

His mouth continued to overwhelm her and all of Amanda's good intentions were swept away on a tide of passion too staggering to fight. Her mind splintered under the onslaught of too many sensations. It had been so long, was her only coherent thought. So long since she'd felt his hands on her body, his breath on her face. How could she not have him? What did it matter what happened tomorrow, if tonight, she could have *this?*

One of his strong hands held her thigh up along his hip, his fingers digging into her flesh. With his free hand, he lifted the hem of her skirt, then slipped his hand beneath the hem of her panties and down to the trembling, heated core of her.

At the first brush of his fingers, Amanda gasped, and tore her mouth from his. Reeling, she tipped her head back and stared into his eyes as he stroked her hot, damp center. His brown eyes were flashing with fire and need. His breath came as fast and sharp as hers. Her fingers clutched at his shoulders, as she fought for balance and for the orgasm that was rushing toward her.

He dipped one finger and then two into her depths, stroking both inside and out as he plunged and withdrew in a rapid rhythm that tortured as it pleasured. Amanda's hips rocked into his hand as she struggled to find the release that he was promising her. Her mind was shutting down. Who needed to think when he was offering her so much to *feel?*

Again and again, she whimpered and twisted against his touch. His thumb rolled over one sensitive spot and she cried out his name in a broken voice torn from a throat nearly too tight to allow breath.

"Come for me," he whispered, kissing her mouth, her eyes, her nose. "Come now, Amanda, and let me see you shatter."

Stars shone overhead. A Texas wind caressed her bare skin. Her lover's eyes held hers. And Amanda surrendered to the inevitable with a groan of release and a whispered sigh that was his name.

Seven

She was limp in his grasp and Nathan had never felt more alive. His body hard and aching, his pulse scrambling, he continued to stroke her intimately, loving the feel of her slick flesh beneath his fingers. Her breath hitched and she jerked in his arms as her still-sensitive body reacted to his touch.

No woman in the world affected him like this one did. With just a sigh, she could inflame him or bring him to his knees. Which is why he was here, he reminded himself. This was the plan. To have sex with her again so that he could walk away. He looked down into her face and saw a soft, satisfied smile. Saw her meadow-green eyes glazed with passion. Saw the rapid pulse beat at the base of her throat and he wasn't thinking about walking away. He was thinking only of burying himself inside her. Feeling her body close around his again.

"Nathan…that was…"

"Foreplay," he groaned past the hard knot of need lodged in his throat and waited for her reaction. He touched her again and she trembled. In his arms, she felt vulnerable, soft, and every protective instinct he had roared to life. In that moment, he wanted to stand between her and the rest of the world. He wanted to always see her like this, looking up at him with stars in her eyes and a breathless plea on her lips.

Seconds ticked past as she looked into his eyes. He held perfectly still. He wouldn't touch her again until she said yes. Until she admitted that sex was the *one* thing they both could agree on. That they both needed. He hoped to hell she'd say it. If she still said no, it just might kill him.

She lifted one hand to cup his cheek and stroked her thumb along his cheekbone. "I'm tired of being sensible," she said. "I don't want to think about tomorrow. I only want tonight. With you."

He waited a beat or two, letting her words sink in. Then, for his own sanity, he demanded, "You're sure?"

She smiled and linked her arms behind his neck. "About this, yes."

"Thank God," he muttered and spun her around in a quick circle before lowering her to the quilt spread beneath the gnarled, twisted arms of the oaks surrounding them.

Quickly, they worked to clear the quilt, setting the wine aside and shifting the cooler off into the thick grass. The radio played on, music shifting now to a low, throbbing beat that seemed to echo what each of them was feeling.

They turned to each other, tearing at clothing, needing to touch only skin. Needing to feel the heat that flesh against flesh created. The summer wind slid over them as hands and mouths rediscovered the magic that pulsed between them.

Nathan couldn't seem to touch her enough. The feel of her soft, smooth skin beneath his fingers fed the fire inside that was engulfing him. His brain hazed out, his vision narrowed until all he saw was *her*. The woman who had haunted him for years. The woman he'd lost and never forgotten.

He eased back, taking a moment to just look at her, enjoy this moment when she was his again. Her hair spilled across the quilt beneath her. Her long, tanned limbs were lean and smooth and her breasts were high and full. His hands itched to cup them, to tease those pebbled nipples until she was moaning and arching into his touch.

Shaking his head, he murmured, "Been thinking about this since that first day I saw you in the diner."

She laughed a little and the sound rose over the roar of the river to become part of the music of the night. "You mean when you walked in all fiery-eyed, wanting me to leave town?"

"Yeah, only I didn't want you out of town as much as I just *wanted* you," Nathan told her, dipping his head to taste first one dark nipple and then the other.

She gasped, then sighed, a slow exhalation of breath that seemed to slide right into the heart of him. When he lifted his head again, she looked up into his eyes and said, "You hid it really well, being all crabby."

He gave her a quick grin. "Couldn't let the town gossips know what I was thinking. Hell, I didn't want *you* to know what I was thinking."

"Oh, me neither," she admitted, holding his head to her breast. Her fingers threaded through his short hair, her nails dragging across his scalp.

He was on fire. His whole damn body felt as if it were lit up from the flames about to swallow him. "Shoulda done this days ago."

"Oh, yeah," she whispered and arched into him as he moved down her body, trailing damp kisses along her skin…down her chest, along the line of her stomach and across her abdomen. She tasted of summer and smelled like a spring meadow. He was surrounded by her taste, scent, touch. And still it wasn't enough. His body ached like a bad tooth. He needed her and damned if he wanted to *need*. Being sucked into a maelstrom of emotions hadn't been the plan. The plan was simply to bed her, so he could get her out of his system once and for all.

The plan. He fought to hold on to it. To remember why it was important. Nathan Battle didn't do anything without a damn plan and once it was made, it was golden.

And yet…his brain shied away from thinking at all. Nathan wanted to concentrate solely on this moment, not what had led to it or what might come after. All he wanted right now was to revel in finally having her here, beneath his hands again.

Her body was long and slim with just the right amount of curves to tempt a man. In the starlight, her skin seemed like warm honey. He dragged the tips of his fingers across her flat belly and smiled to himself when she sucked in a gulp of air. He traced the tan lines that striped over her breasts and then along the narrow strip of paler skin that lay across the triangle of light brown curls at the juncture of her thighs.

"You wear a tiny bikini," he murmured and wished he'd seen her in it.

She smiled. "No point in wearing a big one, is there?"

"Nope, guess not," he agreed, sliding one hand down to cup her heat. "What color is it?"

She gasped and rocked her hips into his hand. "What? Color? What?"

"Your bikini, Amanda," he whispered, "what color is it?"

He dipped a finger into her heat and she hissed a breath. "Is that really important right now?"

"Humor me," he told her and swirled the tip of his finger around an already sensitive spot.

"Okay, okay, just don't stop," she ordered, then swallowed hard. "It's white. With red…" She broke off and shuddered, as he continued to stroke her with slow deliberation.

"Red what?"

"Huh? Red? Right." She nodded, licked her lips and wiggled her hips into his touch. "Red, um, dots. Polka dots."

"Sounds nice."

"Uh-huh," she whispered. "I'll be sure to show you sometime. But for right now could we…"

"You want more?" he asked, knowing she did, drawing out the suspense, the waiting, the wanting, for both of them.

"I want it all." Her eyes snapped open and she met his gaze squarely. "Honestly, Nathan, if you don't get inside me within the next minute or so…"

"You'll what?" He grinned at her, enjoying the frustration in her eyes, in her voice. "Leave?"

She blew out a breath and scowled at him. "Funny. No, I'm not leaving, but Nathan—"

He rose up over her, looked down into her eyes and whispered, "You're still so beautiful."

"I'm glad you think so." She sighed and reached for him, but he pulled back, grabbed the jeans he'd tossed aside a few minutes before and rummaged in the pockets until he came up with a foil square.

"Pretty sure of yourself, weren't you?" she asked wryly.

"Pretty sure of *us*," he told her as he ripped the foil open, then took another moment to sheathe himself.

Her expression was carefully blank as his gaze met hers and she asked, "Is there an us, Nathan?"

That was a good question, he thought, his eyes locked on hers. And he didn't have an answer. Yesterday, he might have flatly said no. Tomorrow, he might do the same. But now... "There is tonight."

A flicker of sorrow danced across her eyes and was gone again so quickly he could almost convince himself he hadn't noticed it at all. He didn't want to hurt her, but damned if he'd pretend something that wasn't so. Besides, he didn't want to think beyond the moment. *Us?* No, there was no us. But there was *now*.

"No more thinking," he murmured and ended any further conversation by taking her mouth in a kiss that left them both breathless. His brain went blank and his body took over. Her hands slid up and down his back, her neat nails scraping across his skin, letting him know that the hunger that crouched inside him lived within her, too.

The past dropped away as they found each other again in the most elemental way. Every touch was a reaffirmation of what they'd once been. Every kiss and gasped breath was a celebration of what they were discovering now. In the warm summer air, they gave and took from each other until passion was a living, breathing entity, wrapping them so tightly together they might never completely be apart again.

They rolled across the quilt, arms and legs wrapped around each other as the river rushed on and the music continued to pump into the night air. Wind whispered through the trees and their strained breathing added to the symphony.

His hands moved over her body and every touch was achingly familiar while, at the same time, it all felt new, electrifying. As if this were their first time coming together.

He pushed her over onto her back and went up on one elbow to look down at her. She looked like a summer goddess, stretched out on that blue-and-white quilt, with starlight dancing on her skin. His breath caught when she licked her lips and smiled up at him. Her eyes were glazed with a burning desire that reached out to engulf him in the same flames. The fire felt good after so many years in the cold, he thought wildly. But he wasn't about to wait another damn minute before claiming her and all she was.

He shifted, kneeling between her legs and when she parted her thighs and lifted her arms to him in welcome, he groaned in satisfaction. He pushed himself home in one long, smooth stroke and hissed out a breath at the sensation of her hot, tight body gripping his.

She gasped, lifted her legs and locked them around his hips, pulling him deeper, tighter. She arched, her hips rising to meet his, drawing him as close as she could. Then she trembled as pleasure whipped through her—a bright, white-hot thing that glittered in her eyes. He felt her pleasure with her every sigh. Felt the tension coiling in her body just from the way she moved with him.

As if they were somehow connected on a deeper level than just physically, he felt what she did, knew when he looked into her eyes how close she was to climax. He knew her as he'd known no other woman. Her body was as familiar to him as his own. Her passion as important as his own.

Her hands clutched at his back, his shoulders, his arms. Every strangled breath and sigh fed the fires inside him. His hips pistoned into hers as he withdrew from her body only to plunge deep inside her heat again.

Her gasps and sighs filled him, pushing him harder, faster, as he quickened the rhythm between them and she rushed to meet him. He took her mouth, his kiss demanding, hungry. She had demands, too. Silent, desperate demands that he met eagerly.

"Nathan. Nathan." His name became a chant that was caught up by the wind and tossed into the night sky. She whispered and pleaded, moving her body into his, fighting for the release that waited for her.

And when the first tremor hit, she clung to him, riding out wave after wave of pleasure tearing through her. Nathan felt her body fist on his as her completion took her. Only then did he give himself up to the coiled tension inside, finally releasing his stranglehold on control, surrendering to what only Amanda could do to him.

His body exploded, his mind shattered and when he collapsed against her, Amanda's arms came around him in the darkness.

Amanda's heartbeat was racing. With Nathan's heavy weight covering her, she felt, for the first time in years, *complete*. Ridiculous to admit, even to herself, but without him in her life she'd always felt as though something was missing. Something vital.

Now, here it was.

But she didn't know how long this could last.

He'd already told her that as far as he was concerned they weren't together. This was just sex. *Stupendous* sex, but just sex. If she made more of it than that, she would be setting herself up for pain and disappointment.

He shifted and rolled to one side of her, drawing her with him until she was nestled against his chest. Amanda listened to the sound of his rapid heartbeat and knew that he was as affected as she was. Some consolation in that, she supposed.

The silence between them stretched on for what seemed forever until she simply couldn't stand it anymore. Best, she told herself, to be the one to speak first. To set a tone that would let him know that she wasn't going to swoon into his arms or cry and beg him to stay.

Not that she didn't want to, but he didn't have to know that, did he?

"Nathan, that was—"

"Yeah," he agreed. "It was."

"So," she said, lifting her head to look at him, "come here often?"

He grinned, fast and sharp and her breath caught.

"Haven't been here in years," he said. "Not since—"

He stopped, but now she knew that he hadn't brought another woman to what was most definitely "their" place. Funny how much comfort that brought her. Oh, he was no monk and during the time they were apart—there had no doubt been *dozens* of women in his life. She winced at that thought. But at least he hadn't brought them here.

"It's beautiful here," she told him, glancing at the moonlight on the water.

"Yeah, it is. Look, Amanda…"

Oh, that sounded like the beginnings of a we-have-to-talk speech. Which she really didn't want to hear at the moment. She preferred the teasing, tempting Nathan who had just shattered her so completely. She didn't want to talk to the dutiful and honorable Nathan. Not now.

So she just wouldn't give him the opportunity to turn this moment into a regret-filled this-will-never-happen-again speech. Abruptly, she sat up and reached for her shirt. Dragging it on over her head, she flipped her hair back over her shoulder and asked, "How about some of that wine?"

He studied her for a long minute, then sat up and reached for his own clothes. "Sure, that'd be good."

"And cookies," she reminded him, determined to keep a cheerful, nonchalant attitude. Standing up, she stepped into her panties and then her skirt, smoothing the material before sitting down on the quilt again. "I think we need more cookies."

Once he was dressed, he sat down opposite her on the quilt and watched her warily, as if she were a time bomb with a faulty fuse and could go off any second. "Cookies."

"Why not?" she asked. "Don't you remember? Sex always gives me an appetite."

Unexpectedly, he smiled as he poured them each a fresh glass of wine. "I do remember all of the picnics we had in bed."

Stillness washed over her as memories slammed into her mind. So many nights they'd spent in bed, laughing, loving and then feeding each other whatever they'd been able to find in the refrigerator. "We had a lot of good times, Nathan."

He handed her a full glass, then clinked his to hers. "Yeah, we did. But, Amanda…"

She cut him off and saw his jaw tighten at being interrupted. "Let's just leave it there, okay? We had good times back then and we had a good time tonight. Isn't that what you said earlier? We have tonight?"

"Yeah, I did."

"So, let's enjoy it."

"You are the most confusing woman I've ever known."

Amanda laughed. "I think I'm flattered."

"You would be," he said wryly. "You always knew how to twist me around until I didn't know which end was up."

He sounded almost wistful and Amanda's heart lurched in her chest. Memories were swimming in the air between them, rising and falling as swiftly as the frothy waves on the nearby river. Amanda took a sip of her wine to ease the knot in her throat before she trusted herself to speak. "You used to like that about me."

"Yeah," he admitted. "I did."

Her gaze caught with his. "I've missed you, Nathan."

"I've missed you, too."

And maybe, Amanda told herself, for tonight, that was enough.

"You had sex."

"Piper!" Amanda jolted and looked around the diner guiltily, making sure no one was within earshot. Thankfully, most of the lunch crowd was long gone and she and her friend had the back of the diner practically to themselves. Amanda grabbed her cup of coffee for a sip, then asked, "Could you say that any louder?"

"Probably," Piper said. "Want me to try?"

"No!" Amanda shook her head and tried for a little dignity. What? Was the truth stenciled on her forehead? *I had sex with Nathan last night.* Who else had noticed? Oh, God.

"I don't know what you're talking about," Amanda told her, deciding to plead ignorance and let it go at that.

"Sure," her old friend said with a smirk. "I'll buy that. And any bridges you might have lying around."

Amanda frowned and leaned back into the rush of cool air pouring down on her from the overhead air-conditioning vent. Irritating to be read so easily—and by someone she hadn't even seen in years. Well, clearly there was no point in pretending with Piper. "Fine. Yes. You're right, Ms. Mind Reader."

Piper laughed and took a bite of the lemon meringue pie Amanda had promised her the day before. "Honey, I don't need to read your mind. It's in your eyes—not to mention the whisker burn on your neck."

She slapped one hand to the right side of her throat. A quick tingle whipped through her as she recalled how it had felt, having Nathan's whiskery cheeks buried in the curve of her neck. Of course that didn't mean she wanted the world noticing what she'd been up to. Amanda had been so sure she'd managed a makeup miracle. Now she didn't know why she had bothered.

"Honestly, I don't know how they can call that foundation 'full coverage,'" she muttered. "I should send them an email, complaining."

"You do that," Piper said with a chuckle. "So, how is Nathan?"

"He's…*good*." Better than good. Fabulous, really. A smile curved her mouth as she remembered the night before.

By the time Amanda had gotten home, she was more tired and more energized than she'd been in years. Every cell in her body had felt as if it had just come to life after long years of sleep. She'd felt almost like Sleeping Beauty, except that Nathan wasn't exactly Prince Charming and she was no damsel in distress waiting to be rescued.

No, last night hadn't been the beginning of anything. She wouldn't fool herself into hoping for more when she was pretty sure that Nathan was considering what had happened at the river to be just a good time.

But it had been more. For her, at least. Despite what she had said to Nathan, Amanda wasn't a sex-is-just-sex kind of girl. If sex didn't mean anything, what was the point to it all? No. The only reason she had slept with Nathan was because she still had feelings for him.

"And so," Piper persisted, "this means you're back together?"

"No," Amanda said, shaking her head. "I'm not kidding myself about that. Last night was just…last night." She wasn't going to invent dreams and let them soar only to come crashing back to earth again. She'd already lived through that pain once and really had no desire to do it one more time. "Nathan and I didn't work out before, remember?"

Piper winced. "I know, but you're both different now."

"Are we?" she wondered aloud. Amanda had been doing a lot of thinking about this since the night before. Sure, they were older, hopefully wiser, but was it enough to make a new relationship possible? Did Nathan even want a new relationship with her?

She was getting a headache.

"I don't know," she said finally. "Nathan will always be important to me. But—"

"No buts," Piper insisted. "There don't have to be any buts."

Amanda chuckled. "In a perfect world…"

A loud noise from across the room caught her attention and Amanda glanced at her sister, who was slamming the coffeepot back onto the warming burner. It was a wonder the pot hadn't shattered. Amanda frowned when Pam turned her head long enough to fire a glare at her.

"Wow, Pam's in a good mood today."

"Yeah," Amanda said. "She's been like this all morning."

"Not surprising," Piper told her. "She's been after Nathan for years and she's probably guessed by now that she's never going to get him."

"What?"

"You probably know that she and Nathan went out a couple times while you were gone." When Amanda nodded, Piper continued. "Well, it didn't go anywhere. Nathan wasn't interested. And let's just say if I could notice the whisker burn on your neck, then Pam noticed, too."

"Perfect." So not only was her life in turmoil over Nathan, but she also had to worry about her sister's anger, too.

Piper shot a quick glance at Pam over her shoulder before turning back to Amanda. She leaned in closer to say, "Everybody knows Pam's been crazy about Nathan since school. Just like everyone knows that she's jealous of you."

"Everyone but me," Amanda said and picked up her coffee for a sip. Yes, she knew Pam had had a crush on Nathan when they were in school. What girl *hadn't* back then? But jealous? "Why should she be jealous of me?"

"Hmm…" Piper pretended to ponder the question. "Let's see. You're younger, prettier, you've got a college degree she never bothered to go after and most importantly—you have Nathan."

"Had."

Piper's eyebrows lifted. "You sure about the past tense, there?"

The old-fashioned jukebox was playing in the corner, some classic rock and roll song streaming through the one large speaker. A couple of people sat at the counter having a late lunch and two elderly women occupied a booth and shared tea and cake. Most people around here stayed home on Sunday and had family meals together so it was a slow day for the diner, which was both a burden and a blessing.

Since Amanda hadn't gotten much sleep the night before, she was grateful to not be so busy. But not being busy meant that Pam had the time to make Amanda's life miserable. Which, she had to say, her sister was getting really good at.

But the worst part about a slow day at the diner? It gave Amanda too much time to think. Too much time to wonder about what had happened the night before between her and Nathan. And no matter how much thought she put into the situation, she was no closer to understanding it.

She knew that the two of them together were magical. But she also knew that didn't guarantee a happy ending.

"Whatever you're thinking," Piper said quietly, "you should stop it. Doesn't look like it's making you happy."

"It's not." Amanda took a bite of her pie and let the dense lemon flavoring explode on her tongue. When she'd swallowed, she said, "I don't know that last night meant a darn thing, Piper."

"If you want it to mean something, it will."

She laughed shortly. "Not that simple. What if I want it and Nathan doesn't?"

"*Make* him want it," Piper suggested with a shrug.

"Oh, well, that should be easy," she mused.

"No, it won't," Piper told her. "Nothing worth having comes easy. The question is, do you want him?"

"Wish that was the only question," she murmured and finished off her pie.

Eight

A few days later, Amanda realized she had forgotten just how much she enjoyed small-town Fourth of July celebrations.

All of Royal seemed to be gathered at the park. The sun glared down from a brassy sky and promised to get even hotter as the day wore on. Nobody seemed to mind much. Texans were a tough bunch and no matter how miserable the heat and humidity, they didn't let it get in the way of a good time.

There was a community baseball game in full swing on the diamond. Picnic blankets dotted the grass and families settled in for a long day that wouldn't end until after the big fireworks show. Kids raced through the park, laughing and shouting, oblivious to the heat that was already beginning to wilt their parents.

Dozens of game booths were scattered around the park, each of them offering chances to win everything from goldfish to teddy bears. And at the far end of the parking lot, a small carnival had set up shop and the taped calliope music was fiercely cheerful.

Amanda grinned at the little boy in front of the booth she was manning. He was about six, with a missing front tooth, hair that was too long and a T-shirt already stained with what looked like mustard. At the moment, he was biting his lip and considering the last softball he held. He had already gone through most of his pocket money, buying chances to knock over bowling pins with the softball to win a prize.

"It sure is harder than it looks, ma'am," he said with a shake of his head.

"It is, isn't it?" Amanda was trying to figure out a way she could "help" the boy win, when Nathan walked up.

A now familiar flash of excitement zipped through her at just the sight of him. He wore a beige uniform shirt, with the sheriff star on his chest glittering in the sunlight. His jeans were faded, his boots were scuffed and his hat was pulled low enough on his forehead to throw his eyes into shadow.

It had been a few days since their night by the river and since then, things had been…different between them. Well, of course—they'd had sex. Things would be *different,* not that they'd slept together since. But there was less tension between them. And, she thought wistfully, more confusion.

"Afternoon, Amanda," he said, then shifted his gaze to the boy. "Carter, how you doing?"

"Not so good, Sheriff," the boy answered and scowled at the one softball he had left to throw. "I figured I'd win one of those teddy bears for my baby sister." He shrugged. "Girls like that sort of thing, but like I told Miss Amanda, it's a lot harder than it looks."

"What're you doin' running around on your own? Where're your folks?"

Carter pointed over one shoulder at a young family sitting on a blanket under a tree. "They're all right there."

"That's good." Nathan dropped one hand on the boy's narrow shoulder, then ruffled his hair. "Maybe we can try together, what do you think?"

The boy looked up at him as if Nathan were wearing a cape and had just swooped in to the rescue.

Amanda watched Nathan with the child and swallowed a sigh. If she hadn't lost their baby, it would now be about this boy's age. Boy? Or girl? It had been too early to know at the time, but that hadn't stopped her from wondering. From picturing what her child with Nathan might have been like. And in this boy, with the light brown hair and brown eyes, she saw…what might have been. And the tiny ache that settled in the corner of her heart felt like an old friend.

"How about I give you a hand?" Nathan asked, then flashed a smile at Amanda. "That is, if Miss Amanda doesn't mind."

"That'd be great, Sheriff," Carter answered, then turned to Amanda and asked, "Is it okay?"

"Well, you know, back when the sheriff was in high school, he was the star pitcher."

Nathan smiled at her as if pleased she remembered. How could she forget? She'd spent hours in the bleachers at Royal high school, watching Nathan play ball. And every time he went up to bat, he'd look at her first, as if he were checking she was still there, still watching.

"Really?" Carter brightened up even further.

"No pressure," Nathan muttered with a shake of his head.

"C'mon, Sheriff," she said and stood back as Nathan

took the ball from Carter and tossed it in the air a couple times to get its weight. "Show us what you've got."

He nodded at the boy then winked at Amanda. "Well, now, let's see what we can do."

He wound up, threw the ball and sent three bowling pins clattering to the floor. Carter whooped with delight and even Amanda had to applaud.

"You won, Sheriff!" Carter clapped, too. "Nice throw!"

Amanda picked up one of the teddy bears lining the prize shelf and handed it to Nathan, who gave it to Carter.

"My baby sister's gonna like this a lot. Thanks, Sheriff!" Clutching the bear, the boy took off and was swallowed by the crowd moments later.

Amanda looked up at Nathan and smiled in approval. "That was nice of you."

"Carter's a good kid." Nathan shrugged and leaned one hip against the edge of the booth. His gaze swept up and down her body thoroughly until she felt a heat that had nothing to do with a hot Texas day.

"So," he said, "how'd you come to be running the PTA booth?"

"Patti Delfino had to take care of the baby so I offered to help."

"Falling right back into life in Royal, huh?"

"It wasn't that hard," she said. Although being around him *was*. She didn't know where they stood. Didn't know what was going to happen next. They'd had that one incredible night together and since then…nothing. Well, except for him stopping in at the diner a few times a day. But they hadn't been alone again and she was hungering for him. Did he feel the same? Or had he considered that night a one-time thing? A sort of goodbye to the past?

The questions running through her mind were driving her crazy.

A little girl ran up and patted Nathan's thigh to get his attention. When he looked down at her, the girl's big blue eyes fixed on him. "I wanna teddy bear, too."

"You do, huh?" He grinned and looked at Amanda. "Apparently Carter's bragging how he got hold of his bear."

"And what are you going to do about it, Sheriff?" Amanda teased.

He dug in his wallet and slapped down a twenty-dollar bill. "Guess I'll be throwing softballs."

The little girl clapped and bounced up and down in excitement. Amanda handed him three softballs to get him started and then stood back and watched as he mowed through the prize shelf. Over and over again, he threw the balls at the bowling pins and soon he had a crowd of kids surrounding him, each of them waiting to be handed one of the stuffed bears.

Amanda watched him, saw his eyes shining with pleasure, heard him laughing with the children and a part of her wept for what they might have had together. He was so good with kids. He would have been a wonderful father if only…

By the time it was over, the bears were all gone and the last of the children had wandered off, clutching their prizes. When it was just Nathan and Amanda again, he said, "Looks like you're out of business. What do you say we find Patti and hand over the cash box, then you and I go join Jake and Terri for some lunch?"

"Aren't you on duty?"

"I can keep an eye on things—and you—at the same time."

Pleasure whipped through her as she grabbed up the metal cash box and swung her legs over the side of the booth. "I think I'll let you."

He took her hand in his and as they walked through the mob of people, Amanda felt that sense of rightness again. Did he feel it, too?

The rest of the day went by in a sort of blur. It had been so long since Amanda had really enjoyed a Fourth of July. When she was away, she would sit on the balcony of her apartment and watch distant fireworks alone. She could have gone out with friends, but her heart hadn't been in it. Instead, she had wished to be back here. At home in Royal.

And the town wasn't disappointing her.

After lunch with Jake and Terri and the kids, Nathan and Amanda spent the rest of the day with them. Nathan was called away a few times to settle disputes ranging from an argument over the umpire's call on the baseball field to a broken windshield in the parking lot. He always came back, though, and Amanda saw that with his family, Nathan was more relaxed. More ready to enjoy himself than she remembered him ever being before.

Back in the day, he'd been too driven, too determined to carve out the life he wanted to take the time to slow down with family. Maybe, she thought, they'd both changed enough over the years that they could find a way back to each other.

With the fireworks about to start, Jake and Nathan walked the kids over to get some Sno-Kones, while Amanda and Terri settled on the quilt and waited for the show.

"I'm so glad you're home," Terri said abruptly.

"Oh, me, too. Believe me." Amanda looked around the park at all the familiar faces and smiled to herself. Older couples sat in lawn chairs, holding hands, gazes locked on the sky. Young marrieds herded small children and the older kids raced through the park waving sparklers, flashes of light trailing behind them like high-tech bread crumbs.

Whatever happened between her and Nathan, Amanda was home to stay. "I really did miss this place."

"Hmm," Terri mused. "You missed Royal? Or Nathan?"

"Sadly, both." Terri knew her too well to believe a lie, so why not admit the truth? "But that doesn't mean anything, Terri."

"Sure it does," she said, biting into one of the last pecan cookies with relish. "It means you guys belong together. Everybody knows that."

"Everybody but Nathan," Amanda muttered, glancing at her friend. Terri was tiny, trim and summer cute in a hot pink sundress with spaghetti straps. Her long, dark brown hair was in a single braid that hung down the middle of her back.

As Amanda watched her, Terri licked a crumb from her bottom lip and popped the rest of the cookie into her mouth. As she chewed, she said, "Nathan's been on edge since you got back."

"Great. On edge."

Terri just stared at her for a second, then shook her head. "Seriously? Do you know nothing about men? On edge is just where you want them. That way they're never sure which way to turn."

"And that's a good thing?" Amanda asked with a laugh.

"Absolutely." Terri grabbed a bottle of water and took a long drink. "Why would you want Nathan all relaxed and complacent about you?"

She hadn't thought about it that way, but now she was. Maybe Terri had a point. Kicking off her sandals, Amanda folded her legs under her. Bracing her elbows on her knees, she cupped her chin in her hands and looked at her friend. "So, you keep Jake guessing, do you?"

"All the time, sweetie," Terri assured her with a laugh. "Why do you think he adores me so?"

"Because he's smart enough to know how good he's got it?"

"Well, that, too." Terri laughed. "But mostly because I keep him on his toes. He's never sure what I'll do next."

As she reached for another cookie, Amanda shook her head. "How do you stay so thin when you eat like this?"

"Won't be thin for long," Terri said with a smile and a gentle pat on her belly. "I'm pregnant again."

Instantly, Amanda felt a quick slice of envy poke at her. Terri had three wonderful kids and a husband who really did adore her. While Amanda was happy for her friend, it was hard not to wish that her own life was as full.

"I saw that," Terri said and reached out to pat Amanda's hand. "Sweetie, I'm sorry. I didn't mean to make you feel badly."

"Don't be silly." Amanda squeezed her hand and shook her head. "I'm happy for you. Really. I just…" She looked out over the park again, toward the booth where Jake and Nathan shepherded twin five-year-old boys and a darling two-year-old girl. As she watched, Nathan scooped up little Emily and cradled her in one arm. The girl laid her head on Nathan's chest and snuggled in. Smiling sadly, she looked at Terri and admitted, "Sometimes I just wish things were different."

Terri sighed. "Sweetie, maybe it's time to stop wishing and start *making* things different."

Amanda looked back at Nathan in time to see him laugh at something one of the twins said. A jolt of longing hit her hard. That smile of his would always turn her to butter.

Maybe Terri was right, she thought. Maybe it was time to take a stand. To fight for what she wanted. And what she wanted was Nathan.

When the fireworks started, Nathan settled down beside her and Amanda leaned her head back against his broad chest. They stared up at the sky, which was exploding with sound and color. He wrapped one arm around her and held her close and, despite the fact that they were surrounded by people, Amanda felt as if they were the only two people in the world.

The next morning, Amanda woke up to Nathan's kiss at the back of her neck. She smiled lazily, remembering the long night before. After the fireworks, they'd come back to her apartment over the diner and created a few fireworks of their own.

"Good morning."

"Mmm," he murmured, dragging one hand down her side, following the dip of her waist and the curve of her hip. "It's looking pretty good right now."

She smiled, then sighed as his hand moved to slide across her behind. Somehow, they'd crossed a bridge yesterday. Maybe it was the hours spent with his family. Maybe it was just that enough time had passed for them both to realize that they wanted to be together. Whatever the reason, Nathan had stayed here with her last night, not caring that the town gossips would surely notice his car parked in front of her place all night.

When he shifted his hand to cup her breast, Amanda hissed in a breath and rolled onto her back so she could look up at him. She didn't think she'd ever tire of that. His dark eyes could flash with temper, shine with kindness or, like right now, glitter with desire. She lifted one hand to his cheek and scrubbed at his whiskers with her thumb.

Smiling, she whispered, "I'm glad you stayed last night."

"Me, too," he told her and gave her a long, slow, deep kiss that quickened the still-burning embers inside her. "And I'd really like to stay now, but I've gotta get to work."

She glanced at the window, where the soft, early-morning light was sifting through the curtains. "Me, too."

He kissed her again and tenderness welled up between them, stinging Amanda's eyes and tearing at her heart. This is what she wanted. Nathan, all of Nathan. Not just the fire that quickened her blood and made her heart race—but the warmth that touched her soul and made her yearn.

When he lifted his head and looked down into her eyes, he whispered, "Maybe I don't have to leave right this minute."

She nodded and cupped his face in her hands. "I think I could spare some time, too."

And this time when he kissed her, she forgot about everything else and let herself slide into a sensual haze that only he could create.

"Did you hear that?" Pam stopped in front of JT and automatically refilled his coffee cup.

"Hear what?"

"Hannah Poole was telling Bebe Stryker about Nathan's car being out front of the diner all night."

JT sighed, shook his head and took a sip of coffee. "What do you care about that?"

She looked at him as if he'd just grown another head. "The whole town's talking about Nathan and Amanda. If it gets bad enough, he'll leave again."

"Not a chance," JT muttered but Pam hardly heard him.

"I can't believe Amanda's starting up with him again." Huffing out a breath, she added, "I can't believe Nathan would *want* her again. After what she did…"

JT's eyes narrowed. "Thought you didn't like gossip."

She flushed. "I don't."

"Then maybe you should give your sister the benefit of the doubt on all that old stuff." Frowning, he added, "I never believed it for a second."

"You, too?" she demanded in a harsh whisper. "You're going to be on Amanda's side?"

"Not taking sides," he said, pausing for a sip of coffee. "I'm just saying, you're her sister. You should know her better than anyone else and I'm thinking you didn't believe any of that nonsense people were talking about years ago, either."

She flushed again and wasn't happy about JT making her feel guilty. "It's always Amanda," she said bitterly. "Nathan's never looked at me the way he looks at her. How can *anyone* be so blind?"

"Was wondering the same thing myself," JT answered and stood up. He dropped money on the counter and said, "I'll see you tomorrow, Pam."

She watched him go and felt a twinge of regret for fighting with her best friend, but honestly. Since he *was* her best friend, shouldn't he understand how she felt about all of this? Shouldn't he be on *her* side?

The more she thought about it, the angrier she became, and watching Hannah Poole scurry to yet another

table to spread the word about Nathan and Amanda was
all the impetus she needed to go and face down her sister.

"What is wrong with you?"

Amanda's sister stormed into the office at the back
of the diner a couple of hours later. Morning sunshine
streamed through the window and the scent of coffee
and fresh cinnamon rolls flavored the air-conditioned
air. Amanda sighed and dropped her pen to the desk as
the last, lingering effects of early-morning lovemaking disappeared with one look at the woman facing her.
Pam's eyes were narrowed, a flush stained her cheeks
and her mouth was set in a tight, grim line.

Amanda set aside the paperwork she was laboring
over and thought she'd even take a fight with Pam over
filling out the supply list for the coming week. She *hated*
paperwork and Pam knew it. So, naturally, her sister
had completely abdicated that task the minute Amanda
came back to town.

She had really hoped that Pam calling and asking for
her help meant that her older sister was going to welcome
her home. But, if anything, Pam's antagonism seemed
fiercer than ever.

Her conversation with Piper ran through Amanda's
mind as she looked at Pam, quietly fuming. *Jealousy?*
Was it possible? If so, Amanda didn't know how she
would fix what was wrong between her and her sister.
Because she wasn't about to give up Nathan to make
Pam feel better.

"What're you talking about?"

Pam stepped into the office and closed the door quietly behind her with a soft click. Then she leaned against
that door, hands behind her back. "You know exactly

what I mean, Amanda. The whole town is talking about you. And Nathan."

Her stomach jittered a little, but she'd known going in that she was going to be the hot topic of conversation in Royal. Ever since their dinner out at the TCC, people had been whispering. And Nathan leaving his car parked outside her place all night had pretty much put the capper on the whole situation.

"I know," she said with a helpless shrug, "but there's nothing I can do about it."

"Well, you could stop chasing after him, that might be a start," Pam snapped, pushing away from the door to stalk to the window overlooking the parking lot behind the diner.

Okay, she was willing to talk. To try to smooth things over with Pam. But she wasn't going to sit there and be attacked without defending herself, either.

"Chasing him?" Amanda stood up. "I'm not chasing Nathan. I've *never* chased him."

Pam whirled around and glared at her, eyes flashing. "Oh, you *love* being able to say that, don't you?"

"What, the truth?"

Pam laughed harshly, walked toward the desk and leaned on the back of the visitor's chair, positioned directly opposite Amanda. Shaking her short hair back from her face, she stared at her sister and blew out a breath before saying, "That just makes it better for you, doesn't it? It's the truth. Nathan chased after you all those years ago and now he's doing it again."

Just for a second, Amanda saw a sheen of tears in her sister's eyes and she felt terrible. Then Pam spoke again and all sympathy went out the window.

"Hannah Poole is sitting out there right now," Pam said, stabbing one finger toward the diner, "telling *ev-*

eryone how she saw Nathan's car parked outside your place *all night*."

Amanda winced a little. Well, they'd both known it would happen. They'd just have to ride out the gossip and wait for the first wave to dissipate.

"And this is *my* fault?" Amanda demanded.

"Oh, please." Pam pushed off the chair, making the wooden legs clatter against the linoleum. "Like you don't do everything you can to make sure he notices you. Big eyes. Soft voice."

Amanda laughed shortly. This was getting weird. And how come she had never noticed before just how jealous of her Pam really was? "What are you talking about?"

"When you guys broke up before, it nearly ruined him," Pam told her flatly. She took a deep breath and blew it out again before adding, "He stayed away from Royal for three years. He only saw his brother when Jake went to Dallas to visit him."

They'd both lost a lot, Amanda thought. They had been so young that neither of them had reacted the way they should have to the tragedy that had torn them apart. They'd cut themselves off from not only each other, but also from their friends, their families. It was time they'd never get back, but hopefully, they'd learned something from all of that, too.

But even as she thought it, she wondered if she'd ever really be able to trust Nathan again. He hadn't believed her. Hadn't *loved* her when she had needed him most. Those dark days came back in a rush, swamping her mind with painful shadows until all she could do was whisper, "I stayed away, too, remember?"

Pam waved that off as if Amanda's pain meant nothing. "This was Nathan's home and he didn't come back because he didn't want to deal with having the town gossips tearing him apart. Over *you*."

And just like that, old pain gave way to fresh anger. Pam was her sister and she was taking Nathan's side in this? *"And?"*

"And now they're doing it again." Pam folded her arms over her chest and tapped the toe of one shoe against the floor. "And just like before, it's all because of you."

In a blink, Amanda's temper ratcheted up to match her sister's. Funny, when they were kids, Amanda had always looked up to Pam. And in an argument, Amanda had always backed down, both intimidated by her sister and unwilling to risk alienating Pam entirely. Well, she thought, those days were long gone. They were both adults now and Pam had been on her case for weeks already. Fine. They had problems—they'd either work them out or not. But damned if Pam was going to wedge herself between Amanda and Nathan.

"This isn't any of your business, Pam. So back off."

Pam drew her head back in surprise. But her stunned silence only lasted a second or two. "I'm not backing off. I'm the one who's been here, Amanda. I'm the one who saw what you did to Nathan before. And I'm the one telling you to stop ruining his life."

"Ruining his life? A little dramatic, don't you think?"

"Hah. If the gossips chew on him for too long he'll leave again."

"Has it occurred to you that they're gossiping about *me*, too?" She tipped her head to one side, mirrored Pam's stance and waited. She didn't have to wait long.

"That's your own fault," Pam scoffed. "For God's sake, you lured him up to your bed and then were too stupid to tell him to move his car. You *wanted* the whole damn town to see."

"I didn't *trick* him into bed, Pam."

"You didn't have to." Pam blinked frantically to clear away the fresh sheen of tears in her eyes. "All you have to do is be there and he can't see anything else."

Amanda steeled herself against feeling sympathy for her sister. Of course she was sorry to see Pam in pain, but not sorry enough to back away from Nathan so her sister could try to get him. Again. "I still don't see how that's my fault *or* your business."

"Of course you don't," Pam said with an exasperated huff. "It's my business because I care about Nathan. When he came home, I was the one who helped him settle in. He was unhappy for a long time. And, Amanda—" she paused and took a breath "—I just don't want to see him like that again."

That much, Amanda could understand. She didn't want that, either. Because it would mean that whatever was between them had shattered again. Just the thought of that had a cold ball of ice settling in the pit of her stomach. Oh, God, she was never going to get over Nathan. How could she, when she was still in love with him?

Staggered by the sudden acknowledgment of what she was really feeling and worried about what it meant to her present—let alone her future—Amanda plopped down into her desk chair. Love? She hadn't counted on that at all. She'd hoped to make her peace with her memories—not build new ones.

She was in deep trouble. Nausea rolled through her stomach in a thick wave that had her swallowing spasmodically.

"Hey…" Pam's tone changed from banked anger to concern. "Are you okay?"

"No," Amanda told her, and cupped her face in her

hands. Oh, God, she was still in love with Nathan. A man she wasn't sure she could trust. She didn't even know how he felt about her! Seven years ago, Nathan had never told her that he loved her. Had left her the moment the reason for marrying her was gone.

Okay, yes, she was the one who had called off the marriage. But he hadn't fought her. He'd simply walked away. As if losing her and their baby meant nothing to him.

Today, there was still no mention of the *L*-word and that hadn't stopped her from once more falling for the only man she would ever love. She'd just tossed her heart into the air not knowing if it was going to crash and burn or find a safe home. "I really don't think I'm okay at all."

"This isn't just a cheap ploy to end the argument, is it?"

On a sardonic laugh, Amanda looked up and met her sister's eyes. "Trust me when I say, I really wish this was a ploy."

Nine

Summer was rolling along like a runaway freight train. Temperatures were high, tempers were even hotter and Nathan spent most of his time stepping in between arguing parties. Nothing unusual about any of it but for the fact that his head just wasn't in the game.

Hadn't been since that night with Amanda by the river.

Scowling, Nathan was alone in his office, thinking about that morning with Amanda. Waking up in her bed, her body wrapped around his, had eased a sore spot inside him he hadn't even realized was there. Making slow, languid love to her had carried that feeling further, until he was so caught up in her, he'd had to force himself to crawl out of that bed and go to work.

"So much for the plan," he muttered, taking a sip of his coffee.

He guessed it was safe to say his plan was shot. Not

only had he not gotten her out of his system, but she was also all he could think about anymore.

It had all seemed so simple. Get Amanda back into his bed and finally get over her. Let go of the past and move the hell on. Instead, she was deeper into his gut than she had been before. Not quite sure how that had happened, Nathan was even less sure about how to reverse the damage already done. Especially when all he wanted to do was make love to her again.

Hell, he was walking around town with a body so hard and tight, it was all he could do to keep from groaning in public. He needed…hell. He just *needed*.

Worse, he didn't want to need Amanda. He wanted to be free of her. Didn't he? Nathan scrubbed one hand across his face and tried to wipe away all of the thoughts clashing together in his mind.

To distract himself, he stared around the inside of his office, letting his gaze sweep across the familiar symbols of the life he'd built for himself in Royal. But none of it brought him the pleasure he usually found in just being there. Until Amanda came back to town, he'd been content. Now, contentment just wasn't enough. He wanted more. Wanted *her*.

The problem was…how to get her.

Oh, sex was great, but that was easy. What he wanted would be more difficult. Hell, he could admit, at least to himself, that he wanted it all. Not just Amanda, but the life they could make together. House. Family. A damn white picket fence.

But he knew the past still loomed between them, a big ugly wall they'd both ignored rather than dealt with.

He leaned back in his chair, kicked his feet to the corner of his desk and crossed them at the ankle. Staring up at the ceiling, he told himself that maybe the past should stay right where it was. Maybe they didn't have to dissect it. Maybe all they had to do was learn from it and let it go.

Trust would be an issue between them for a while, of course, but he could *show* Amanda that he had her back now. Over time, she'd eventually come to believe it.

Nodding to himself, he could see the future play out in his mind. He and Amanda, living in his house on the ranch. Having kids that would play with Jake and Terri's bunch. Long nights and lazy mornings in his bed, wrapped in each other's arms. It was what they should have had years ago.

And what they would have now.

When the door opened, Nathan looked over at the doorway, a scowl on his face.

"Nice welcome," Chance said.

"Sorry. I was doing some thinking." Nathan's feet dropped to the floor, then he stood up and held out a hand to his friend. "What's going on?"

Chance's blond hair looked as though he'd been stabbing nervous fingers through it for hours. His green eyes were troubled and he didn't meet Nathan's gaze directly. Not a good sign.

"Everything okay, Chance?"

"Not really," his friend muttered and rubbed one hand across the back of his neck.

He was backlit by the bright afternoon sunlight and when he turned to close the door, Nathan noticed he locked it, too.

"Okay, what's this about?"

"Nathan, I wouldn't be here if I didn't think you should know about what people are saying."

Instantly, Nathan's back went up and he shook his head. Seven years ago, Chance had been the one to tell

Nathan about the rumors spreading. The rumor that Amanda had deliberately ended her pregnancy. Back then, Nathan had been young enough to listen and stupid enough not to question.

Today was different.

"Don't want to hear it," he said and turned his back on Chance to walk to a file cabinet on the far wall.

"Don't you think I know that?" Chance's voice was reluctant but firm. Clearly, he wouldn't be leaving until he'd had his say.

Nathan spun around and said, "I don't give a good damn what people are saying, Chance."

The moment the words left his mouth, he realized they were completely true. Somehow, he just didn't care about being the center of gossip. And damned if he was going to listen to anything people had to say against Amanda. He might make mistakes, but hell if he'd make the *same* ones.

"Well, you'd better listen." Chance glared back at him. "The word is you're not the only guy she's sleeping with. People are saying she's slipping out of town, meeting some other guy. So if she turns up pregnant this time, who's to say you're the father?"

He felt like he'd been punched dead-center in the chest. And for one miserable moment, he let those words slam into his head and heart, too. But they didn't stay because they weren't true and he knew it. Knew it down to his bones. Amanda wasn't a cheat and she wasn't a liar.

His hands curled into fists at his sides and he took one long step toward one of his best friends.

Chance held up both hands and took a step back. "Hey, I didn't say I believed any of the talk."

"Then why the hell are you telling me this?"

He pushed a hand through his hair. "I didn't want to,

but if you want a life with Amanda, then you'd better find out who's spreading the poison and get it stopped."

Chance was right. Years ago, someone had spread lies about Amanda aborting their baby. And yeah, now he could see the lies for what they were. Amanda never would have done that. Back then, he'd been too young and stupid to think past his own fury.

Now things were different.

"On that, we totally agree," Nathan muttered darkly. "I'll find whoever it is and when I do…"

A couple of days later, the diner was packed and Amanda was still reeling from the realization that she was in love. On top of that, her stress level was sky-high just from keeping what she was feeling from Nathan. Then there was the situation with Pam.

She shot a covert look at her sister, ringing up a customer at the cash register. Things were still strained there, but at least they hadn't argued again.

"Everything okay?"

Amanda turned and forced a smile for Alex Santiago. She refilled his coffee cup, then set the pot down onto the counter.

"Everything's fine," she lied.

He studied her for a moment or two then nodded. "Yeah, I can see that."

"What about you, Alex?" Now that she was looking at him, she noticed that he wasn't giving her one of his million-dollar smiles. His eyes looked shadowed, as if he hadn't been getting much sleep. "Are you all right?"

"I'm fine. Just…" He shrugged and tried, but didn't quite manage to smile at her. "You know how it is. Sometimes, you've got too much to think about."

"That, I understand completely." Whispered conversations from off to her left caught her eye, but Amanda ignored them. If people were going to talk about her, she couldn't stop them.

"I think you do," he said, then took a sip of coffee. "Don't worry about me, Amanda. Everything will be fine."

She might have said something else, tried to draw him out a little if only to erase some of the worry in his eyes, but a shout sounded out.

"Amanda, honey, how long till that burger of mine is ready?" John Davis slapped one meaty hand to his broad chest and gave a groan. "I'm a starvin' man, darlin'."

Alex laughed a little. "Go. Feed the man before he dies of hunger."

She rolled her eyes and patted Alex's hand. "I will. But if you need anything, all you have to do is ask."

He covered her hand with his briefly and said, "You've a kind heart."

Amanda went to pick up John's lunch, then delivered it, all the while wondering about Alex. But by the time she got back to the counter, he was gone. His coffee was still steaming and there was a five-dollar bill next to the saucer. She frowned and looked through the front window in time to see Alex hurry down the street.

A few days later, Nathan answered the phone at the sheriff's office and smiled. "Alex. What's up?"

"Nothing much," his friend said, then asked, "Are you going to be at the TCC meeting tonight?"

"I'll be there," Nathan said on a tired sigh. "With Beau Hacket still making waves over the child-care center, figured I should attend just to keep him in line."

"That's good," Alex said. "After the meeting, I'd like to talk to you. Privately."

Nathan frowned and straightened up in his desk chair. There was just something about the tone of his friend's voice that set off small alarm bells in Nathan's mind. "Everything all right?"

"Yes," Alex told him quickly. "Absolutely. I'd just like to talk to you."

"Okay, sure." Still frowning, Nathan suggested, "We could grab a late dinner."

"That would be good," Alex said and now relief colored his words. "I'll see you later, then."

"Right." Nathan hung up, but his mind raced with questions.

That night at the meeting, Nathan wished he could just leave. His heart just wasn't in being there. He'd have much rather been with Amanda.

What had he come to? He laughed at himself. Who would have guessed a few weeks ago that he'd be feeling downright…domesticated? He wasn't sure what it was they had going between them, but he was damn sure he didn't want it to end. Was this love? Hell if he knew. He'd imagined himself in love with her seven years ago, but what he felt now was different. Bigger.

He glanced around the meeting room, but didn't make eye contact with any of the people. They were all busy, talking, visiting, but Nathan wasn't in the mood. Hell, he wasn't in the mood for much here lately. Not until he found out who was behind the rumors designed to hurt Amanda.

And, now there was the question of what was bothering Alex, as well. He glanced at the empty chair behind him and wondered again where his friend was. Alex hadn't shown up for the meeting and though Nathan kept telling himself the man would appear at any moment, the meeting was almost over and there was still no sign of him. For the moment, though, he let thoughts of Alex slide away as Amanda's situation took precedence.

From the corners of his eyes, Nathan looked at the familiar faces around him and wondered if it could be one of them. One of his "friends" who had deliberately sabotaged his relationship with Amanda so long ago and was now trying to do the same. But what the hell did anyone have to gain by spreading lies? Not like anyone was going to stop eating at the diner. Or talking to Amanda, for that matter.

So what was the point?

Well now, he thought, he'd know that as soon as he found the bastard.

Raised voices caught his attention and Nathan dragged his thoughts back to the present. Just like every other weekly meeting, there were the same people gathered, having the same arguments. Beau and his bunch were still bitching about the new child-care center and Abby Price looked downright pleased to be able to tell them all to shove off. Couldn't blame her, Nathan thought. She'd fought hard to become a member here at the club. It had to be satisfying to now be able to ensure that not only more women were welcome here, but their kids as well.

Shaking his head, Nathan wondered why Beau couldn't let it go. It was a done deal. Move on.

He caught Chance's eye across the table and the two of them shared a smile.

"I tell you, it's disgraceful," Beau was sputtering. "Putting a babysitting club in the billiards room? Our founding fathers are probably spinning in their graves."

A few raised voices shouted in unison with Beau and the little man seemed to get bigger every time someone sided with him. So before he got out of line entirely, Nathan spoke up.

"No one even *plays* billiards anymore, Beau." The older man was nearly purple in frustrated rage, but Nathan wasn't impressed. He knew Beau was mostly talk. "Hell, when was the last time *you* played the game?"

"Not the point, Nathan Battle, and your own pa would be sore disappointed to hear you taking up on the side of these females." The man wagged a finger at Nathan as if he were a ten-year-old boy.

Chance smothered a laugh and Nathan felt all eyes on him as he said, "That's the thing, Beau. My dad would have been the first one to take a hammer to that moth-eaten old billiards table. And he'd have shamed *you* into giving us a hand remodeling that room for the kids, too."

Beau's color got even worse. His jaw worked and his lips pursed as if there were legions of words trapped inside trying to fight their way out. But he managed to hold on to them and Nathan thought that was probably for the best.

"Now, why don't we end this meeting so we can get on home?" Nathan looked over at Gil Addison, who gave him a wink and a nod before slamming his gavel down with a hard crash.

"Meeting is concluded," Gil announced a second later. "See y'all next week."

Chair legs scraped against the wood floor. Glasses were set onto the table with sharp clicks. Beau was the first one to storm out of the room and once he was gone, conversation picked up as people meandered toward the exit.

"Nice speech," Abby called out as she waved to Nathan.

He smiled and nodded and then turned to Chance when he walked up.

"You shut down Beau pretty well," Chance said.

"Not hard," Nathan answered. "The man's from the Stone Age. Don't know how his wife, Barbara, puts up with him."

"Must have his good points."

"I suppose," Nathan mused, his gaze scanning the TCC members as they filed out, still looking for Alex to come rushing in late. But he didn't show. A trickle of unease rolled along Nathan's spine. He was getting a bad feeling about this—and he'd learned to listen to those bad feelings.

Wasn't like Alex to miss an appointment. In the short time he'd been in Royal, the man had shown himself to be a fiend for schedules. So if he'd wanted to meet with Nathan, where the hell was he?

"Have you seen Alex?" Nathan asked suddenly.

"Not since a day or two ago. Saw him at the diner, talking to Amanda."

People got busy, Nate told himself. Maybe something had come up. But he'd made a point of setting up a private meeting with Nathan. So if he wasn't going to show, why wouldn't he have called to cancel? That bad feeling was getting stronger. He didn't have a concrete reason for it, he supposed, but he couldn't shake that niggling sensation chewing at the back of his mind. Nathan frowned to himself, because he knew a cop had to trust his instincts before anything else. "It's not like him to miss the meeting."

"You know," Chance said, as he also looked around the quickly emptying room, "now that you mention it, I had wondered where he was tonight."

"That's what I'm saying."

Chance shrugged. "Maybe he's on a date or something. Or maybe he just wasn't in the mood to deal with Beau tonight. God knows I wasn't."

"Yeah, but you came anyway," Nathan said firmly. "So would Alex." Especially since he'd wanted to speak privately with Nathan.

"Then where is he?"

"That's the question," Nathan said. "Isn't it? I'll go by his place see what I can find out."

"I've got another question for you." Chance shoved his hands into the pockets of his slacks and started for the door, Nathan walking alongside him. "Discover anything about our gossip starter?"

"No. Not yet." He'd been asking discreet questions all over town, too. Trying to wheedle information out of folks without letting them know that's what he was doing. Most he spoke to were embarrassed to talk to him about the rumors, but they all denied knowing who had started them. It was always, "I heard it from so and so who got it from what's her name." Didn't seem to be a starting point.

But there was one.

And Nathan was going to find it.

"A whole lot of weird going on all of a sudden," Nathan muttered the next morning. "Alex has dropped off the radar and now this at the diner. Doesn't feel like they're connected, but it's damn odd."

"Tell me about it." Amanda's stomach twisted with nerves and knots. "When I got home from your place I went up the back stairs to my apartment and took a shower. I came down after to open up the diner and found this. Then I went to your office to get you."

"Just the right thing," Nathan said as he eased past

her in the doorway. "You stay out here, I'll go in and check things out."

"I don't think so," she said and walked into the diner right behind him. "This is my place, Nathan. I'm not waiting outside."

Grimly, he looked at her, mumbled something she didn't quite catch, then said, "Fine. At least stay behind me and don't touch anything."

They walked through the back door directly into the diner kitchen. Amanda looked around the room and still couldn't believe what she was seeing.

The grill was smashed, as if it had been beaten with a hammer. Flour was strewn across everything, making it look like there'd been a snowstorm in the kitchen. Jars of spices lay shattered on the floor, their contents spilled across the flour in festive patterns. Plates were smashed, drawers yanked out and dumped. In essence, the kitchen was a disaster.

"Somebody did a number on this place," Nathan murmured more to himself than to her.

"If I'd been upstairs last night, I would have heard them, damn it." Anger was burning through her nerves.

"Yeah," he said thoughtfully, "you would have. Funny, isn't it, that whoever did this waited until you were spending the night with me on the ranch to do this damage?"

That clicked in immediately. Why hadn't she thought of that? "So who knew I went to the ranch yesterday?" As soon as she asked the question, she sighed in disgust. "Half the town, probably. Everyone saw me leave with you last night."

"Yeah," he said, tipping her chin up so he could look into her eyes. "But not many of them knew you'd be *staying.*"

She thought about that for a minute, realized he was right, then tried to make a mental list of who actually knew she'd be gone overnight. "There's Pam, of course. And Piper. I told her. And Terri." She shook her head, disgusted. "They could have told people, I suppose, but I just can't think of anyone who would do this."

"We'll figure it out." He glanced back at the mess. "I'll have the kitchen fingerprinted, but there are so many people in and out of this diner every day I don't know that we'll find anything."

"No," she grumbled, crossing her arms over her chest. "Probably not. When I first walked in and saw this, I was scared. Now, though, I'm just mad." She kicked at some flour and watched it puff into the air before settling. "This will shut us down for days."

"Might not be too bad," he said. "But you're gonna need a new grill."

She sighed, then tried to look on the bright side. "Well, that grill is older than I am, so maybe we needed a new one anyway. So, once you do your fingerprint thing, I'll call Pam and we'll get this mess cleaned up."

Nathan smiled, shook his head, then grabbed her and pulled her in close for a hug. "You're really something, Amanda Altman."

"Thanks, Sheriff," she said with a smile then sobered. "This is pretty ugly, but I know how concerned you are about Alex. Finding him is important, too."

"Not even really sure why I'm worried," he admitted. "The man could be off taking care of business none of us knew about."

"True," she said, staring up into his eyes. "But you said yourself that he wanted to talk to you about something. Wouldn't he have called to let you know he couldn't make it?"

"Yeah." Frowning, he said, "He would have. You haven't thought of anything else? What he talked about when he was at the diner the other day?"

"No," she said softly. "Ever since you asked me that last night, I've been thinking about it and there's just nothing." Shrugging, she added, "He seemed distracted. Worried about something maybe. But he didn't say anything specific."

He huffed out a breath and shook his head. "Damned strange. All of it."

"I know." She hugged him tightly then let him go. "I've got a lot of work to do here, Sheriff. So I'll get to it and you go find Alex and catch me a bad guy."

Ten

Nathan spent a couple of frustrating days trying to track down answers to his questions. He couldn't find Alex Santiago and he had no clue who had vandalized the diner kitchen. Frustration chewed at him. That bad feeling about Alex was intensifying, and as for Amanda…

This was damn personal. Someone was out there trying to hurt her and damned if he'd let them. Amanda was *his* and nobody was going to mess with her and get away with it.

Of course, he mused ruefully, he hadn't told Amanda yet how it was going to be between them. Now that he'd decided that they were going to be together, he wanted to take his time. Keep seducing her with sex, get her used to the idea of having him back in her life before he actually told her it was time to get married. He wasn't an idiot, after all. The last time he'd asked her to marry him it was because of the baby and none of it had ended well.

It shamed him to remember it now, but it was best to go into any tricky situation with your thoughts and goals straight. Looking back, Nathan was willing to admit he'd handled that situation badly long ago.

This time would be different.

Amanda was a hell of a woman, but she had a spine and was likely to fight him on this whole marriage thing if he didn't work it just right.

Not that it mattered if she fought him. He would have her, in the end. It would just be easier all the way around if he could just keep reminding himself to be patient.

But he wouldn't be patient in finding whoever was behind this mess at the diner. Because he knew, whoever it was, would also turn out to be the source of the rumors. Highly unlikely that two different people would both be harassing Amanda at the same time.

When the phone rang, he snatched it. "Sheriff's office."

"Hey."

"Chance." Nathan straightened, grabbed a pen and slid a pad of paper in front of him just in case he needed to take notes. "You hear anything?"

"Nada." Chance sounded disgusted. "I've talked to everybody I can think of and nobody's seen Alex."

"Damn." He sat back in his chair and tossed the pen to the desktop. "I talked to Mia Hughes yesterday—Alex's housekeeper. She hasn't seen him in days. Says he hasn't been home at all."

"Well, where the hell is he, then?"

"I don't know, Chance." Nathan shook his head and stared off into space. "It's like he dropped off the face of the earth."

"I don't mind admitting that I'm getting worried, Nate," Chance said. "This isn't like Alex."

Nathan was worried, too. It just didn't seem reasonable that *nobody* in Royal had heard from or seen Alex. And why the hell would he leave town without at least telling Mia? Something was definitely wrong here and Nathan didn't like it.

Usually, in a town like Royal, the "crimes" he dealt with were kids getting into trouble or the occasional battle between neighbors. Now he had a missing man and a break-in.

"Any news on what happened at the diner?" Chance asked.

"No." One word. Disgusted. Nathan had never felt helpless before and he didn't care for it. He couldn't find his friend and he hadn't been able to discover who was behind the vandalism to Amanda's place.

Though he did at least have a half-baked suspicion on that one. Didn't make much sense to him, but he'd check it out. And if he were right…it would help prove to Amanda that she could trust him—in spite of the mistakes in their past.

"What is *with* Royal this summer, man?"

"Wish to hell I knew," Nathan answered.

The upside of having her diner demolished, Amanda thought, was that she had more time with Nathan.

He hadn't wanted her staying alone in the apartment over the diner until he found whoever had done the damage. So, she'd been staying here, at the house he'd had built for himself on the Battlelands. Normally, she might have fought him over his bossy, take-charge attitude, but she hadn't wanted to stay there, either. As much as she liked the little apartment, it would never really feel safe to her again.

Nathan's place, as great as it was, was temporary

and she knew it. The only answer was to find a place of her own.

"Guess it's time to look for that house," she said aloud.

"You have a house," Terri told her firmly. "Right here."

"This is Nathan's," Amanda said, shaking her head as she took a sip of her tea. "Being here with him is wonderful, but it isn't permanent."

"Honestly, I don't know which of you has the harder head." As if accepting that she wouldn't change Amanda's mind, Terri sighed and went to a new subject. "How's the diner coming along, anyway?"

"We'll be able to open again on Monday. We've got a new grill and Pam's been helping me clean up and restock the kitchen."

"There's a miracle," Terri murmured. "Pam doesn't exactly strike me as the helpful type."

Amanda had to chuckle. She'd been surprised by her sister's assistance, too. "That's one good thing that came out of all of this. Pam did such a turnaround this last week—she's been so nice it's almost eerie."

"And all it took was the destruction of the diner."

"Whatever caused the change, I'm happy about it." Amanda had never wanted to be at war with her sister. Over the last week, they'd worked together in the kitchen, straightening up, restoring order. Not that she and Pam were joined at the hip or suddenly becoming best buddies…but it was a start. If this new relationship with her sister continued, then the vandalism would have been worth it.

Terri set a paper sack on the kitchen table and pushed it toward Amanda. "I got what you asked for at the store."

Amanda's stomach flip-flopped as she reached for the bag. She took a deep breath then blew it out again.

"Thanks, Terri. If I had gone into a store anywhere near here to buy it myself, everyone in town would have known by the end of the day."

"Amanda…"

She cut her friend off. "Remember, you promised. Not a word. Not even to Jake."

Terri made a quick cross over her heart and held her hand up. "I swear. But you're crazy, you know that, right? You should tell Nathan."

"I will," Amanda said. "If there's anything to tell."

"Stubborn," Terri said. "Okay, fine. Do it your way."

"Wow, thanks for that, too," Amanda said with a smile.

"Okay, I'm going. But if you need me, just call. It'll take me a whole ten seconds to walk over here from the main house."

"I'm fine, Terri. But thanks. I appreciate it."

"You're welcome. And I really hope you get this straightened out already. It'd be nice to have you here on the ranch permanently."

When the kitchen door closed behind her friend, Amanda picked up her tea and the small paper bag and wandered out of the room. Her gaze slipped over Nathan's place and in her mind, she instinctively added pillows, splashes of color, vases filled with summer flowers.

Terri was right about one thing. Amanda didn't want to buy another house. She wanted to live here. With Nathan. But she couldn't do that without love.

Nerves skittered through her already uneasy stomach and Amanda swallowed hard to settle everything down. She'd been here in this house with Nathan for nearly a week and it was becoming too comfortable. Being here with him, having breakfast and dinner together, waking up in his arms—it all felt just right. As it was supposed to have been seven years ago.

But no promises had been made. No talk of a future. No mention of love.

Amanda's heart twisted a little as she reminded herself of that. She couldn't let herself slide into a relationship with Nathan that had no chance of succeeding. And the longer she stayed here with him, the harder it was going to be to leave.

Especially now.

She stopped at a window overlooking the front yard of the main ranch house. Jake and Terri's kids were clambering over the jungle gym Nathan and Jake had built for them. Their shouts and laughter pealed through the morning air and Amanda smiled wistfully as she listened to them.

If things had been different, her child would have been out there with them. *Her child.*

Taking a breath, she turned around and headed for the stairs. She carried her tea up to the master bedroom, sliding her hand along the polished oak banister as she went. Nathan was in town at the sheriff's office. He'd be there for hours.

So, she told herself, there was no better time for her to find out the answer to a question that had been nagging at her for a week.

Pam looked horrible.

It was the first thing Nathan noticed when she opened the front door of her house to him. And that gave Nathan the answer he was looking for. In between his regular town duties and the unofficial search for Alex, Nathan had been working on the vandalism at the diner.

He'd spent hours thinking about this, looking for witnesses, anything to help him figure out who was behind Amanda's troubles. And the one name that kept coming back to him was Pam.

No one else in town had any real issues with Amanda. But her sister hadn't exactly made a secret of the fact that she resented Amanda's presence even though her return to Royal had been at Pam's request. So he was playing a hunch. Trusting his instincts. He'd come to Pam's house to talk to her about this, maybe get her to confess. Now, looking into her eyes, he knew he was right about it all.

"Nathan."

"We need to talk." Nathan walked past her into the darkened house. Drapes were drawn, shutting out the sunlight, as if she were in hiding.

He marched through the small, familiar house and stopped in the living room. Then he snatched off his hat and turned to face the woman following him.

Abruptly, tears filled her eyes and spilled over to run unchecked down her cheeks. "Nathan—"

"You're sitting here in the dark," he pointed out. "Looking mighty miserable and I think there's a reason for that. See, I came here on a hunch," he said, his voice clipped and hard. "The only person in town who has a problem with Amanda is *you,* Pam. No one else would have had access to the diner without breaking a window or something to get in." That fact had bothered him from the jump. The lock on the door hadn't been jimmied, so either he was looking for a skillful vandal with terrific lock-picking talents, or… "But you had a key. You went there in the middle of the night, let yourself in and tore that kitchen apart, didn't you?"

"I swear I didn't go there intending to wreck the place," she murmured, wrapping her arms around herself as if searching for comfort. "I went to get a bottle of wine from the fridge. Then I was there, alone and started thinking about you. And Amanda. And the more I thought, the angrier I got and before I knew it…"

His stance didn't soften, his voice didn't warm when he said, "Why? Why would you do that to your sister? To your own damn business?"

She unfolded her arms and wiped tears away with both hands before taking a long breath and saying, "I've been so angry for so long."

"Angry about what?" he demanded, his gaze locked on her as if seeing her clearly for the first time. She looked miserable, eyes gleaming with tears, her teeth biting into her lower lip and her shoulders hunched as if she were somehow trying to disappear inside herself.

"You," she admitted finally, staring up at him.

"What the hell are you talking about?"

She laughed harshly. "God, I'm an idiot. Look at you. You have no idea."

"Pam," Nathan growled, "my patience is stretched as thin as it can get. I've had a bad week and I'm not much in the mood for guessing games with you, so whatever's stuck in your craw, spit it out."

"Fine. Why not finish the humiliation?" She threw her hands high and let them slap down against her sides. Shaking her head, she blurted, "I was always crazy about you, Nathan, but you never looked at me. Never *saw* me."

"Pam—" Nathan said her name and watched her flinch.

She shook her head and held up one hand to keep him quiet. "Please don't say anything. Bad enough I have to say this. Bad enough that I wasted *years* pining after you when I never had a chance." She huffed out a strangled breath. "It was always Amanda for you, wasn't it?"

"Yeah, it was." He didn't feel sorry for her. She'd

caused a lot of trouble. He did feel badly that he'd never noticed that her fondness for him had become an obsession. That much was his fault. If he'd been paying attention, he could have spared everyone a lot of misery. As it was, he played another hunch. "What about the rumors attacking Amanda? The ones seven years ago and now? Was that you, too?"

She inhaled sharply and winced as if she were in pain. "Yeah. That was me." She turned away from him as if she couldn't bear to face him. "God, this is like a nightmare. Even I can't believe what I've done."

"Pam—" He broke off and shook his head. Hard to believe this one woman had caused so much damage. All of it stemming from jealousy. "You spread those lies about Amanda, suggesting she got rid of our baby. And you thought that would make me care for you?"

Her voice dropped to a whisper but in the stillness Nathan heard every word. "I never thought you'd find out."

"And the diner kitchen? What was that about?"

"God. I was in the diner alone." Her strained whisper sounded as if she were having to *push* every word through her throat. "Amanda was spending the night at the ranch. With you. I swear I didn't consciously mean to do all of that. But I picked up an iron skillet and just started beating the grill. I was so angry, so—it doesn't matter," she said brokenly. "It was like I lost my mind for a few minutes. I was so furious with her, for coming home." She looked around at him. "For taking you from me. I just lost it."

He wasn't moved by her confession. If anything, his jaw clenched tighter and his eyes narrowed more. All Nathan could think was that because of Pam, he and Amanda had lost seven years together. "She couldn't take me from you because I was never *with* you."

She dropped into a chair, wrapped her arms around her middle and rocked. "I know. And I'm sorry. I really am. For everything. I wasted so much time. But, Nathan—"

"No, there's no excuse for any of this, Pam," he told her flatly. "And if Amanda wants to press charges against you, I'll throw you into a cell so fast, the world will be a blur."

Her stomach sank. "You're going to tell her?"

"No," he said. "You are."

"Oh, God."

"Yeah," Nathan went on. "See, Amanda's going to marry me as soon as I get around to telling her how things are going to be. And I'm not going to be the one to break the news that her only family betrayed her."

Pam winced at that, but Nathan didn't give a good damn if her feelings were hurt. "Fine," she said. "I'll tell her."

"Do it fast." He stalked out of the house and slammed the door behind him.

Seven years wasted. But it wasn't all Pam's fault and he knew it. As much as he'd like to forget, Nathan had to acknowledge that if he'd had more faith in Amanda and more damn spine, he never would have believed a word of those rumors. Instead, he'd been young enough and stupid enough to let lies throw his life off track.

Well, no more.

Nathan was still fighting off the anger Pam had churned up in him when he parked outside his house. In no mood to talk to Jake, he was glad it was late enough that his brother and his family were already at dinner.

He got out of his car, slammed the door and took a minute to calm himself before going inside to see

Amanda. Like he told Pam, he didn't want to be the one to tell her that her own sister had been behind the harassment aimed at her. And if he went in there furious, she'd worm the information out of him whether he wanted to tell her or not.

Still, hard to believe that Pam was the vandal. And the one who'd started all the vicious rumors. But hell, at least he'd solved *one* mystery. Alex's disappearance was still chewing on Nathan. He was making calls, talking to people and, so far, he had nothing. As Alex's friend, Nathan was worried. As a cop, he was frustrated.

Shaking his head, he stared at his house and in spite of everything, the tension inside him easing. Lights were on, and it struck him suddenly that he really liked coming home to this. Always before, he'd leave work and drive up to an empty house, dark windows and a silence that grew thicker with every passing moment. But for the last week, Amanda had been here and she'd etched herself into every damn corner of that house—as well as his heart.

If she left him today—an option that would not be allowed to happen—he still would see her all over his house. He would hear her laugh, catch her scent on every stray breeze, reach for her across his bed.

Even after the rough day he'd had, Nathan smiled as he noted the pots of bright yellow and blue flowers Amanda had set on the porch yesterday. His chest tightened as he recalled her walking along the wraparound porch, muttering to herself about rockers and matching chairs and tables and how nice it would be to sit out on a summer night and watch the moon crawl across the sky.

He wanted that. With her. Wanted to come home to a well-lit house holding the woman he loved. All right, yes, he loved her. He hadn't told her, of course, because their past was still between them and he knew that though she might not admit it, she didn't completely trust him again yet. He couldn't blame her—hell, thinking back about what had happened between them years ago, how they'd ended, made him want to kick his own ass.

But he'd give her everything else. His name. His home. His children. And one day, he'd confess his love and she'd believe him. She'd trust him to not hurt her again as he had before.

He had to have her. Hell, he couldn't draw a breath inside that house without taking the essence of her into his soul. It had always been that way between them. Seven years ago, he'd just been too young to appreciate what he had when he had it. Now he was going to set things right.

Clutching his hat in one fist, he started for the porch. Time to get this done. He'd walk right in there and tell her they were getting married. Amanda was a logical sort of woman. She'd see it was the best plan right off. They'd have a small wedding, here on the ranch. Nathan took the front steps two at a time, a smile on his face.

The front door flew open just as he approached it and Amanda was standing there, staring at him through wide, wonder-filled eyes.

"Amanda?" He stopped dead. "Are you okay?"

"I'm pregnant."

Eleven

Okay, Amanda thought, she'd had that planned a lot better in her mind. She hadn't meant to just blurt it out like that, but on the other hand, even if she had taken ten or fifteen minutes to tell him, the result would've be the same.

She looked up at him and waited what felt like forever for his reaction. Would he be as happy as she was? Would he be upset? *Say something!*

He scrubbed one hand across his face. "You're what?"

"Pregnant." It felt so good to say. What felt like champagne bubbles were swimming through her system, making her nearly giddy.

"You're sure?"

"Positive." She laughed a little as she'd been doing all afternoon since taking that wonderful little test that Terri had picked up for her. "At least, that's what the test said. Positive."

He shook his head. "How?"

"Really?"

He laughed. "That's not what I meant. We used condoms."

"They don't always work, you know." She paused and added, "They didn't work seven years ago, either."

"I remember." He reached out and skimmed his fingers along her cheek.

Memories swirled around them, thickening the air with the haunting ghosts of shattered dreams and broken promises. They'd made an agreement to leave the past behind, but could it ever really be forgotten? Weren't you supposed to not dismiss your past, but learn from it?

Well, Amanda had. She'd lived through the pain, built a life, grown and changed. But the dreams of her heart were still there. Nathan. A family. She caught his hand in hers and held tight. Amanda had had a couple of hours to get used to this news and she figured it would take Nathan at least a few minutes to do the same. She wanted him to be happy about it, but the honest truth was, even if he didn't want the baby, *she* did.

Seven years ago, she'd been young and scared and too unsure about her own future to feel capable of raising a child on her own. But she was different now.

She had a home. A job. A place in this town. And if she had to, she would gladly raise this baby as a single mom. It was as if she'd been given a second chance to have all of the dreams she'd been denied so many years ago.

"This is..." He drew her into the house and closed the door. Tossing his hat onto the nearest chair, he laughed again. "This is *great*."

Relief and joy swept through Amanda on a tide so

high and wide, she could barely breathe through the richness of it. "You're happy about the baby?"

"Happy?" Nathan laughed, reached out, grabbed her and swung her in a circle before finally setting her on her feet and pulling her in close. "Amanda, it's like we've got a second chance, here."

"That's just what I was thinking," she agreed, wrapping her arms around his waist and holding on. She leaned her head on his chest and listened to his galloping heartbeat.

"We can get married here at the ranch," he said. "Actually, I was planning for us to be married, anyway."

She went still, then drew her head back and looked up at him. "I'm sorry. You were planning for us to be married?"

"Yeah. I was going to tell you about it tonight." He grinned at her. "But your news kind of threw my plan off."

"Your plan." A trickle of cold began to seep through the happy glow she'd been carrying inside.

He gave her a hard hug. "I figured we could get married here at the ranch."

"Did you?" The cold went a bit deeper now, but she steeled herself against it.

The past seemed suddenly so much closer. She was reliving it all. His announcement that they would be married. The baby she carried. Would she also relive the shattered dreams?

Nathan frowned a little. "We don't have to hold the ceremony at the ranch, but I thought it'd be easier. Terri will help you set everything up. I'll help when I can, but I'm still looking for Alex and—"

He had it all worked out. And with every word he spoke, her heart sank a little bit more. The buzz of excitement and joy she'd felt earlier was quickly being swamped by feelings of disappointment and, okay, yes, irritation. She couldn't believe this. Although, it was so typical of Nathan, she really should have expected it. Seven years ago, he'd done the same and she'd allowed it because she had wanted him badly enough to hope that one day he might tell her he loved her. Now, though, she wouldn't settle. Slipping out of his arms, she took a step away from him, folded her arms over her chest and stared at the man who had held her heart since she was a kid.

How could she be so dispirited and so in love with him at the same time? Had to be a sort of cosmic joke on her that the one man who could drive her to distraction was the only man she'd ever wanted.

"So you've got everything figured out, have you?" Amanda asked, her voice soft and cool.

"Not completely," he admitted. "But between the two of us it shouldn't take long."

"You're right about that," Amanda said, shaking her head as she looked up at him. "Won't take long at all, since I'm not going to marry you."

"Of course we're getting married."

"Nothing's changed, has it?" she asked, not really expecting a response. "Seven years ago, you decided we'd get married and I went along." He opened his mouth to speak, but she continued quickly. "But I'm not a kid anymore, Nathan. I make my own choices. My own decisions. I won't let you push me into a marriage you don't really want."

"What're you talking about?" He looked as astonished as he sounded.

"What I'm saying is, this is just like before. You're offering marriage because I'm pregnant. Because it's the *right* thing to do." She turned abruptly and walked away from him, into the living room. He was right behind her.

The huge room boasted views of the ranch from every window. Across the drive, the main ranch house was brilliantly lit and Amanda knew that inside, Terri and her family were cozy and happy. Envy curled inside her and twisted around her heart like tangled ribbons. She'd like that for herself. For her child. But she wasn't going to make the same mistakes she'd made seven years ago. She wouldn't be a duty. She wouldn't be a problem that Nathan felt honor bound to clean up.

"It's the right thing to do because we belong together," Nathan argued.

"Do we?" She didn't know anymore. She'd always believed it, but she'd been shot down before and now, if she went along with Nathan's plan she'd only be setting herself up for a possible repeat of history.

"I think we should talk this through," he said.

She shook her head, never taking her gaze from the scene sprawling outside the window. She would miss it here, but it was definitely time to leave. Glancing over her shoulder at him, she said, "I don't think so, Nathan."

He was looking at her as if she'd sprouted another head. She could almost smile about that. Nathan was so used to being obeyed, he didn't know what to do when someone simply said no.

So she took a breath and tried to explain. "Nathan, I know this is just instinct to you. To do the right thing. The honorable thing."

"And that's *bad*?"

"Of course it's not bad," she countered, and gave him a sad smile. "But it's no reason to get married. I went along with your demands last time because, frankly, I was too scared to have a baby on my own. But I've changed, Nathan. And I'm not going to be just another duty to a man with too much honor. I want to be loved Nathan, or I'm not going to get married at all."

He threw up his hands. "But I *do* love you."

Pain sliced at her. If he'd led with that, maybe things would be different right now. But he hadn't mentioned anything about love until he absolutely *had* to, so how could she trust it? How could she believe anything but that Nathan would use whatever he had to to win.

"I wish I could believe that," she said after a long moment. "I really do."

"Why the hell can't you?" he argued. "Is it so impossible to believe?"

"Yeah, it is," she said and moved farther away. God, she couldn't stay here. Couldn't be this close to him, knowing that she couldn't have him. She needed to be home. Back in the tiny, hot box of an apartment over the diner. She needed to think.

"Amanda," he said, stepping closer, keeping his gaze locked with hers. "You can believe me. I do love you."

"No, you don't," she said, shaking her head as she backed up toward the chair where she'd dropped her purse earlier. "You just want me to fall in line and you know this is the way to manage it. No. It's just a little too convenient, don't you think? I say I won't get married without love and boom. Suddenly you love me? I don't think so."

"It's not suddenly," he argued. "I've loved you most of my life."

That stopped her for a second as his words ricocheted around inside her, tearing at her heart. She wanted to believe, she really did, for both her own sake *and* the baby's. But how could she? And if she took a chance—

trusted him with her heart—and was wrong…then it wasn't only she who would pay the price. She had her child to think about now.

"Why is it, then, that you've never mentioned it before now, Nathan?" she asked quietly, sadly.

"I don't know," he muttered, shoving one hand through his hair.

She picked up her purse and rummaged one hand inside for her car keys. When she found them, she curled her fingers around them and said, "Until you know the answer to that, Nathan, there's nothing else to talk about. Now, I'm going home."

"You are home, Amanda."

That little arrow scored a direct hit on her heart. She had hoped this would be home. Had imagined it. But she couldn't have what she wanted—without first having what she needed. Amanda needed to be loved by the very man standing there giving her all the right words without the meaning.

"No, I'm really not." She shook her head and walked past him. He stopped her with a hand on her arm.

"Don't go."

She looked down at his hand then shifted her gaze to his eyes. "I have to."

He released her then and Amanda felt the loss of his touch all the way to her bones. It took everything she had to walk out the door and down the front steps. Before she reached her car, she looked back over her shoulder and Nathan was standing there, in the open doorway, watching her.

"This isn't over," he said, his deep voice carrying on the warm summer air.

Amanda knew that all too well. What she felt for Nathan would *never* be over.

* * *

"Anyway," Pam said later that evening. "What I'm trying to say is, I'm sorry."

What a day this had been, Amanda thought, staring at her sister in dumbfounded shock. A surprise pregnancy, a surprise proposal and now…a sister who had hated her enough to try and ruin her life. Her heart hurt at the realization that Pam had been behind the rumors that had torn Amanda and Nathan apart so long ago. But a voice in her mind whispered that Nathan shouldn't have believed those rumors. He should have loved her enough to know they weren't true.

And he hadn't.

"You're sorry." Amanda whispered the words and watched Pam flinch. "For all the rumors or for the diner?"

"Both." Pam dropped into a chair beside the sofa where Amanda was curled up.

The diner apartment was too warm, the air conditioner wasn't working again. Amanda reached for her glass of iced tea and took a long drink as she studied her sister. Pam looked awful. Her eyes were red and puffy from crying. Her hair was in a tangle as if she'd forgotten to brush it and misery pumped off of her in waves.

Right now, Amanda told herself, she should be furious. Should be raging at her sister for all the damage Pam had done over the years. But the bottom line was, Amanda's heart was already too broken to break again. And fury seemed to require more effort than she had the energy for at the moment.

"God," Pam said softly, "I was always so jealous of you."

"Why?" Amanda shook her head and stared at her. "You're my big sister, Pam. I always looked up to you."

Pam winced. "And I resented you. You were always the favorite. With Mom and Dad, with our teachers at school. With Nathan."

"I don't even know what I'm supposed to say to that," Amanda said quietly. "Mom and Dad loved us both and you know it."

"Of course they did, and I'm an idiot for clinging to all that junk from when we were kids and letting it chew on me until I lost it."

"Pam…"

"There's nothing you have to say. It was all me, Mandy," Pam whispered, unconsciously using the name Amanda hadn't heard since she was a little girl. "I got so twisted up inside, I couldn't see anything but my jealousy of you. And even if you don't believe me, I am really sorry."

"I do believe you." Funny. She could accept Pam's apology but she couldn't trust Nathan's proclamation of love. A very weird day.

Pam looked at her from where she was sprawled in the overstuffed, faded chair. "You do?"

"Yeah." She shook her head tiredly. "Not that it's okay with me, what you did. And we're going to have to talk about this more, figure out where we go from here, but you're still my sister…." Heck, Amanda understood better than anyone what it was to be so crazy about Nathan that you could lose yourself in the emotional pool. And, there was the fact that Amanda was going to need her sister in the coming months. She could raise a child alone, but she wanted her baby to have a family. An aunt to love him or her.

Pam drew a deep breath and let it out on a relieved sigh. Her lips curved in a tired smile that looked quivery at the edges. "I didn't expect you to forgive me so easily."

Amanda tried to find a return smile, but couldn't. "I didn't say it would be easy. You're paying for the damage to the diner."

"Agreed," Pam said.

"And," Amanda continued, since she had her sister at a disadvantage at the moment, "you're taking over the paperwork again."

Pam nodded. "I only dumped it on you because you hate it. I actually sort of like it. I was always good with numbers."

"I know, I used to envy that," Amanda mused, realizing that for the first time in years, she and her sister were having a real conversation. "Maybe you should think about going back to school. Getting an accounting degree."

Pam thought about that for a second and then smiled. "Maybe I will." She pushed her hair back behind her ears. "Gotta say, Amanda, you've been a lot nicer to me about this than I deserve."

"You know," Amanda said thoughtfully, "you're lucky you picked today to dump all of this on me."

"Why?"

Amanda frowned and tapped her fingernails against the glass she held. "Because I'm too tired from dealing with Nathan at the moment to work up any real rage for you."

"I'm so sorry, Amanda," Pam said again. "I know you and Nathan were having a hard time and I didn't make it any easier. But he made it clear today that you two were getting married and—"

Amanda went still as stone. "He what?"

Pam shrugged. "He said you would be marrying him as soon as he told you his plan and—"

"He told you he was going to marry me even before he bothered to mention it to *me?*"

"Yeah, apparently."

There was a part of Amanda that was excited to hear it. After all, he'd seen Pam *before* he knew about the baby. So he had planned to propose anyway—that was something. It didn't change the fact that he'd mentioned nothing about love, though, until he was forced to by the situation.

"Well," she murmured, "it doesn't change anything. I already told him I'm not going to marry him just because he decrees it to be so."

"You said no?" Incredulous, Pam's voice went high.

"Of course I said no. I'm not going to agree to marry him just because I'm pregnant again."

"You're pregnant?"

Amanda wrapped her arms around her middle as if giving her unborn child a comforting hug. "I am, and I can raise *my* baby all by myself. The baby will have a mom and an aunt, right?"

Smiling, Pam said, "Absolutely. Aunt Pam."

Amanda nodded. "I can do this and I can do it without Nathan Battle if I have to."

"If he lets you," Pam muttered.

"Lets me?" Amanda repeated, staring at her sister. "Did you just say if he *lets* me?"

Pam lifted both hands. "You know Nathan. He doesn't usually hear the word 'no.'"

"Well, he'll have to hear it this time. I'm going to live my life my way. I'm not going to be told what to do and where to go and who to love." She walked over to the window and stared down at Royal. It was dark and street-lights created puddles of gold up and down the street.

Overhead, the moon hung like a lopsided teeter-totter and the stars winked down on the world.

And over on the Battlelands, the man she loved was alone with his *plans*. She hoped he was as lonely as she was.

"Sure am glad the diner's back open."

It was a couple of days later when Hank Bristow lifted a cup of coffee and took a long, leisurely sip. He sighed in pure pleasure before picking up his coffee and heading for a group of his friends at a far table. "Didn't know what to do with myself when you girls were closed."

"We're glad to be open again, too, Hank," Amanda assured him as he walked away.

She glanced at her sister. Pam was like a different person. The old bitterness was gone and she and Amanda had spent the last couple of days building a shaky bridge between them. Someday, Amanda hoped the two of them would be close. It wouldn't happen overnight, of course, but at least now there was a chance that the Altman girls were finally going to have a good relationship.

"Earth to Amanda…"

She jolted a little and, laughing, turned to look at Piper, sitting on a stool at the counter. "Sorry. Mind wandering."

"It's okay, but since I'm starving, how about a doughnut to go with this excellent coffee?"

"You bet." It was good to have friends, Amanda thought as she opened the door to the glass display case and set a doughnut on a plate. Piper had been the one Amanda went to after Nathan's abrupt proposal. And Piper was the one who had insisted that Nathan *did* love Amanda, that he was just being male and sometimes that had to be overlooked.

Amanda wasn't so sure. She'd missed Nathan desperately the last couple of days. He hadn't called. Hadn't come to her. Was he waiting for *her* to go to *him?* How could she?

She set the doughnut in front of Piper and whispered, "Thanks again for everything."

"No problem," Piper told her and took a sip of coffee. "I'm guessing you still haven't heard from him."

"No." Amanda planted both hands on the counter. "I don't think I will, either. Nathan's a proud man—maybe *too* proud. And I turned him down and walked away."

"Then maybe you should go to him," Piper said matter-of-factly.

"How can I?" Amanda shook her head.

"Give him a chance, Amanda. Heck, everyone in town knows Nathan's crazy about you. Why can't *you* believe it?"

She wanted to. More than anything.

Walking along the length of the counter, Pam refilled coffee cups, chatted with customers and stopped when she reached JT in his usual spot. "More coffee?"

"Thanks." He watched her in silence for a second, then said, "Looks like you and Amanda got things sorted out."

She set the coffeepot down and glanced at her sister. "We're getting there. I guess you could say I finally grew up."

All around them, the diner was buzzing with morning conversations, so JT's words were almost lost in the sound when he said, "It's about time."

Pam smiled. "True enough. JT, why are you always so nice to me?"

In answer, he stood up and came around the end of the counter. When he was close enough, he grabbed hold of Pam, pulled her in tight, then bent her over in a dip as he kissed her, long and slow. Finally, he swung her back onto her feet and let her go.

"*That's* why," he said, grinning at her. "Any other questions?"

The whole diner was silent as everyone in the place focused on the drama playing out right in front of them. A second ticked past, then two. Pam lifted one hand and rubbed her fingertips across her lips, then grinned widely. "Only one question, JT McKenna. What in hell took you so long?"

Applause burst into the room as Pam leapt into JT's arms and kissed him back.

The rest of the day passed quickly as people came and went, and life in Royal marched on. Amanda did her work, smiled and talked with her customers all while trying to breathe past the knot in her throat. Thoughts of Nathan crowded her mind and the emptiness she felt without him left an ache in the center of her chest.

JT had taken up permanent roost at the end of the counter and Pam took every chance she could to stop for a kiss as she passed him. A patient man, JT had waited years for Pam to finally realize that *he* was the man for her.

Nathan wasn't patient, Amanda told herself. He didn't wait. He pushed. He nudged. He ordered and when that didn't work, just went ahead and did whatever he thought was the right thing to do.

As those thoughts wandered through her mind, Amanda realized that she'd always known that about Nathan. And she loved him for who he was, irritations and all. So how could she blame him for doing everything he could now to make sure she married him?

Sighing, she glanced out the front window toward Main Street and her breath caught when she saw Nathan headed for the diner. Just one look at him and her heartbeat jumped into a gallop. He had his hat pulled down low against the brilliant summer sunshine and his steps were long and determined. She could almost feel the intensity preceding him as he stalked ever closer, people instinctively moving out of his way.

Amanda fought for calm and didn't find it. Her heartbeat continued to race and her stomach swirled with expectation.

He stepped into the diner and his gaze swept the place in seconds, finally landing on her as if drawn to her by some immutable force. She felt the power of his stare from across the room and couldn't look away from those dark brown eyes that were filled with heat and charged with emotion.

The crowd in the diner took a collective breath and held it. Excitement fluttered through the room as people shifted positions to get a good view of whatever was coming next. Amanda didn't care. She wasn't thinking about anything but Nathan and why he'd come. If he was just here for more of the same, she'd have to tell him no and send him away again, though the thought of that tore at her.

Yes, he was arrogant and pushy and bossy and proud and she loved him desperately.

"Amanda," he announced, loud enough for everyone to hear, "I've got a few things to say to you."

"Here?" she asked. "In front of half the town?"

"Right here, right now," he told her, and his gaze bored into hers. "We've been trying to outrun or hide from gossip and rumor for so long... I think it's time we just took a stand." He moved a bit closer to her and his voice dropped a notch or two. "I don't care what they think. What they say. Let 'em look, Amanda. We're done hiding."

A flush of heat swamped her, but she found herself nodding in agreement. He was right. They had worried over rumors. They'd allowed vicious lies to split them up seven years ago. Maybe it was time to just be themselves without worrying over what the rest of the town had to say about it.

"You're right," she said. "No more hiding."

One corner of his mouth lifted into a brief half smile and she saw pride glittering in his eyes. For a second or two, the terrible tension in her chest eased and Amanda felt as if she and Nathan were a team. The two of them against the gossips.

Close enough to touch her now, he started talking. "I thought a lot about what we talked about the other night."

His voice was low and deep and seemed to reverberate up and down her spine. His eyes were locked on hers and she couldn't have looked away if she'd tried.

Reaching out, he stroked his fingertips along her cheek and Amanda shivered, closing her eyes briefly to revel in the sensation of his touch. When she opened her eyes again, he was still watching her.

"You were right, Amanda," he said. "The night you told me about the baby, I said the words you needed to hear to help convince you to marry me."

It felt as if all the air slid from her lungs at once. The tightness in her chest was painful and tears pooled at the backs of her eyes.

"But—" He cupped her face in his palms, and held her, forcing her to keep looking into his eyes. "That doesn't mean they weren't true."

"Nathan——" She shook her head and tried to look away. He wouldn't allow it.

"I do love you. I always have." He bent and kissed her gently on the lips and the taste of him lingered on her mouth. "Maybe telling you when I did was bad timing."

"Maybe?" she managed to ask.

He gave her a nod and a rueful smile. "You threw me that night, Amanda, but I *do* love you, with everything in me. If I hadn't been too young and too arrogant to say the words seven years ago…maybe things would have been different for us."

Amanda knew the whole diner was listening in and found she didn't care. The only person she was interested in now was Nathan. "I want to believe you," she said. "I really do."

"You *can,*" he told her, moving into her, until every breath she took drew the clean, fresh scent of him deep into her lungs. "We're meant to be together, and I think you know it."

He reached into his pocket and pulled out a small, red velvet jeweler's box. Her gaze landed on it even as her heart took another tumble in her chest. When she looked up at him again, he smiled.

"This is for you, Amanda."

She shook her head even as he opened the lid to display a brilliant topaz stone surrounded by diamonds and set in a wide, gold band.

"This stone is sort of the color of your eyes," he whispered, "at least, *I* think so. Every time I look in your eyes, I fall in love again. You're the woman for me, Amanda. The *only* woman. So I'm asking you now. The right way. Amanda Altman, will you marry me?"

She shook her head and blinked to clear away the tears blurring her vision. He was offering her everything she'd ever wanted. Love. The promise of a future together. All she had to do was trust her heart and take a leap of faith.

She looked away from the ring and into his eyes and nearly cried again when she read in his eyes the truth she'd needed so much to see. Warmth, passion, *love*.

Before she could say anything, Nathan continued. "When you left the other night, you took my heart with you," he said, gaze moving over her face like a caress. "I couldn't breathe. Couldn't sleep. Couldn't do anything but try to think of a way to bring you back home where you belong."

"Oh, Nathan." The diner, their audience, the whole world fell away and all that was left was the two of them. She and Nathan, together as she'd always dreamed they would be.

"I let you go once," he said tightly. "I don't know how I lived these years without you, but I *know* I can't live the rest of my life without you."

Her tears overflowed and tracked along her cheeks unheeded. Gently, he used his thumb to wipe the tears away and gave her a sad smile.

"I was young and stupid seven years ago," Nathan said, "but I've changed as much as you have. I know you could raise our child on your own—but I hope you won't." He took the ring from the box and slowly, carefully, slid it onto her ring finger, then kissed it as if to seal the ring in place. When he looked into her eyes again, he said, "I want to be with you, Amanda. Always. I need you. And our baby. And the family we'll build together. The family we should have started all those years ago."

She couldn't look away from his eyes and, in truth, she didn't want to. The ring felt warm on her hand and her heart felt even warmer. Amanda took a breath and slowly let it out, enjoying this moment, wanting to treasure the memory of this one small slice of time forever.

This was everything she'd ever wanted. He was saying the words that were so important to her. Offering her the life she craved. And she believed him. Nathan's eyes were filled with love as he looked at her and she knew that she would never doubt him again.

All around her, she sensed people's attention, knew they were all listening in and found she simply didn't care.

"I love you, too, Nathan," she said and smiled when he grinned down at her. "I just needed to believe."

"And now you do?" he asked, wrapping one arm around her waist to hold her to him.

"Now I do," she said and realized she'd never been more sure of anything than she was of what she and Nathan shared. For a while, she had allowed doubts and fears from the past to cast dark shadows over the present and the future. But she was through looking backward.

"I swear, you'll never be sorry." He swept her up tightly to him and kissed her so deeply, Amanda would never again have any doubts about his feelings.

And while the people in the diner broke into applause, Amanda knew that she finally had everything she had ever wanted.

The man she loved, loved her back, and there was nothing in the world more beautiful than that.

Epilogue

The wedding wasn't as small as Nathan wanted and not as large as Amanda had feared.

There was family—Jake, Terri and the kids. Pam and JT, practically joined at the hip. Amanda had the distinct feeling it wouldn't be too long before there was another wedding in Royal.

And there were friends. Piper and Chance and Abby and so many others gathered together to wish them well.

Nathan had surprised her by outfitting the wrap-around porch of their home with all of the rockers and gliders and chairs that she'd talked about once. She could see them in the years to come, sitting on that porch, surrounded by family, and it filled her heart to the point of bursting.

To avoid the steaming heat of a Texas summer, on the last day of July, the wedding was held in the evening. Lanterns were strewn across the yard, lending a soft glow that was matched only by the early starlight. Flowers in vases, wreaths and vines trailed from every available surface and sweetened the air with a perfume that flavored every breath.

Tables groaned with food and music played from the stereo situated on Jake's front porch. Children clambered all over the swing set Jake and Nathan had built while their parents chatted with friends. There was laughter and there was *love*.

Amazing how love, when it finally arrived, made the whole world shinier, brighter, more filled with promise.

"A bride as beautiful as you are shouldn't be standing here alone," Nathan said as he came up behind her and wrapped his arms around her waist.

She leaned back into him and smiled, loving the feel of him pressed close, knowing, *trusting* now, that he always would be. "I was just thinking how perfect today was."

"Agreed," he said and dipped his head to kiss her cheek. "The only way it could have been better was if Alex were here, too."

Amanda turned in his arms and looked up at him. She knew his friend's disappearance was haunting Nathan. It had been nearly a month now and there were just no clues to follow. "You'll find him, Nathan. And everything will be okay."

He nodded, glanced out over the crowd gathered at the Battlelands, then turned his gaze back to hers. "I'm going to have to officially declare him missing."

A twinge of worry caught her, but she let it go again because of her faith in Nathan. He would find a way to make this right. "You'll find him."

"I will," he said, then smiled. "But that's for tomorrow. Today is for dancing in the moonlight with the woman I love."

"I'm never going to get tired of hearing that, you know."

He led her onto the makeshift dance floor installed on the front yard specifically for the wedding. And as they moved to the music and their friends and family applauded, Nathan promised, "I'm never going to stop saying it."

Amanda gave herself up to the moment, to the magic, to the man who would always be the very beat of her heart.

* * * * *

"It takes everything I've got not to touch you when I see you sitting there like that."

There was a long silence, and then her voice again. "Why don't you?"

Liam's jaw was flexed tight, his whole body tense, as he tried to hold back the desire for her that was building inside. "I didn't think it was a good idea. I'm your boss. We have to work together. Things would get weird. Wouldn't they?"

Please let her say no.

"I don't think so," she said, slowly climbing to her knees. "We're both adults. We know what this is and what it means." She crawled leisurely across the elevator floor, stopping in front of him. Her hands went to his belt buckle as she looked up at him through her thick, coal-black lashes. "What happens in the elevator stays in the elevator, right?"

A *VERY* EXCLUSIVE ENGAGEMENT

BY
ANDREA LAURENCE

Published in Great Britain 2013
by Mills & Boon, an imprint of Harlequin (UK) Limited,
Eton House, 18-24 Paradise Road, Richmond, Surrey TW9 1SR

© Harlequin Books S.A. 2013

Special thanks and acknowledgement to Andrea Laurence for her contribution to the DAUGHTERS OF POWER: THE CAPITAL miniseries.

ISBN: 978 0 263 90478 9
ebook ISBN: 978 1 472 00617 2

51-0713

Harlequin (UK) policy is to use papers that are natural, renewable and recyclable products and made from wood grown in sustainable forests. The logging and manufacturing processes conform to the legal environmental regulations of the country of origin.

Printed and bound in Spain
by Blackprint CPI, Barcelona

Andrea Laurence has been a lover of reading and writing stories since she learned her ABCs. She always dreamed of seeing her work in print and is thrilled to finally be able to share her books with the world. A dedicated West Coast girl transplanted to the Deep South, she's working on her own "happily ever after" with her boyfriend and their collection of animals that shed like nobody's business. You can contact Andrea at her website, www.andrealaurence.com.

One

Figlio di un allevatore di maiali.

Liam Crowe didn't speak Italian. The new owner of the American News Service network could barely order Italian food, and he was pretty sure his Executive Vice President of Community Outreach knew it.

Francesca Orr had muttered the words under her breath during today's emergency board meeting. He'd written down what she'd said—or at least a close enough approximation–in his notebook so he could look it up later. The words had fallen from her dark red lips in such a seductive way. Italian was a powerful language. You could order cheese and it would sound like a sincere declaration of love. Especially when spoken by the dark, exotic beauty who'd sat across the table from him.

And yet, he had the distinct impression that he wasn't going to like what she'd said to him.

He hadn't expected taking over the company from

Graham Boyle to be a cakewalk. The former owner and several employees were in jail following a phone-hacking scandal that had targeted the president of the United States. The first item on the agenda for the board meeting had been to suspend ANS reporter Angelica Pierce for suspicion of misconduct. Hayden Black was continuing his congressional investigation into the role Angelica may have played in the affair. Right now, they had enough cause for the suspension. When Black completed his investigation—and hopefully uncovered some hard evidence—Liam and his Board of Directors would determine what additional action to take.

He was walking into a corporate and political maelstrom, but that was the only reason he had been able to afford to buy controlling stock in the company in the first place. ANS was the crown jewel of broadcast media. The prize he'd always had his eye on. The backlash of the hacking scandal had brought the network and its owner, Graham Boyle, to their knees. Even with Graham behind bars and the network coming in last in the ratings for most time slots, Liam knew he couldn't pass up the opportunity to buy ANS.

So, they had a major scandal to overcome. A reputation to rebuild. Nothing in life was easy, and Liam liked a challenge. But he'd certainly hoped that the employees of ANS, and especially his own Board of Directors, would be supportive. From the night janitor to the CFO, jobs were on the line. Most of the people he spoke to were excited about him coming aboard and hopeful they could put the hacking scandal behind them to rebuild the network.

But not Francesca. It didn't make any sense. Sure, she had a rich and famous movie producer father to support her if she lost her position with ANS, but charity was her *job*. Surely she cared about the employees of the company as much as she cared about starving orphans and cancer patients.

It didn't seem like it, though. Francesca had sat at the conference room table in her formfitting flame-red suit and lit into him like she was the devil incarnate. Liam had been warned that she was a passionate and stubborn woman—that it wouldn't be personal if they bumped heads—but he wasn't prepared for this. The mere mention of streamlining the corporate budget to help absorb the losses had sent her on a tirade. But they simply couldn't throw millions at charitable causes when they were in such a tight financial position.

Suffice it to say, she disagreed.

With a sigh, Liam closed the lid on his briefcase and headed out of the executive conference room to find some lunch on his own. He'd planned to take some of the board members out, but everyone had scattered after the awkward meeting came to an end. He didn't blame them. Liam had managed to keep control of it, making sure they covered everything on the agenda, but it was a painful process.

Oddly enough, the only thing that had made it remotely tolerable for him was watching Francesca herself. In a room filled with older businesswomen and men in gray, black and navy suits, Francesca was the pop of color and life. Even when she wasn't speaking, his gaze kept straying back to her.

Her hair was ebony, flowing over her shoulders and curling down her back. Her almond-shaped eyes were dark brown with thick, black lashes. They were intriguing, even when narrowed at him in irritation. When she argued with him, color rushed to her face, giving her flawless tan skin a rosy undertone that seemed all the brighter for her fire-engine red suit and lipstick.

Liam typically had a thing for fiery, exotic women. He'd had his share of blond-haired, blue-eyed debutantes in private school but when he'd gone off to college, he found he had a taste for women a little bit spicier. Francesca, if she hadn't been trying to ruin his day and potentially his year, would've been just the kind of woman he'd ask out. But complicating this scenario with a fling gone wrong was something he didn't need.

Right now, what he *did* need was a stiff drink and some red meat from his favorite restaurant. He was glad ANS's corporate headquarters were in New York. While he loved his place in D.C., he liked coming back to his hometown. The best restaurants in the world, luxury box seats for his favorite baseball team...the vibe of Manhattan was just so different.

He'd be up here from time to time on business. Really, he wished it was all the time, but if he wanted to be in the thick of politics, which was ANS's focus, Washington was where he had to be. So he'd set up his main office in the D.C. newsroom, as Boyle had, keeping both his apartment in New York and the town house in Georgetown that he'd bought while he went to college there. It was the best of both worlds as far as he was concerned.

Liam went to his office before he left for lunch. He put his suitcase on the table and copied Francesca's words from his notebook onto a sticky note. He carried it with him, stopping at his assistant's desk on his way out.

"Jessica, it's finally over. Mrs. Banks will be bringing

you the paperwork to process Ms. Pierce's suspension. Human Resources needs to get that handled right way. Now that that mess is behind me, I think I'm going to find some lunch." He handed her the note with the Italian phrase written on it. "Could you get this translated for me while I'm gone? It's Italian."

Jessica smiled and nodded as though it wasn't an unusual request. She'd apparently done this in the past as Graham Boyle's assistant. "I'll take care of it, sir. I have the website bookmarked." Glancing down at the yellow paper she shook her head. "I see Ms. Orr has given you a special welcome to the company. This is one I haven't seen before."

"Should I feel honored?"

"I don't know yet, sir. I'll tell you once I look it up."

Liam chuckled, turning to leave, then stopping. "Out of curiosity," he asked, "what did she call Graham?"

"Her favorite was *stronzo*."

"What's that mean?"

"It has several translations, none of which I'm really comfortable saying out loud." Instead, she wrote them on the back of the note he'd handed her.

"Wow," he said, reading as she wrote. "Certainly not a pet name, then. I'm going to have to deal with Ms. Orr before this gets out of control."

A blur of red blew past him and he looked up to see Francesca heading for the elevators in a rush. "Here's my chance."

"Good luck, sir," he heard Jessica call to him as he trotted to the bank of elevators.

One of the doors had just opened and he watched Francesca step inside and turn to face him. She could see him coming. Their eyes met for a moment and then she reached to the panel to hit the button. To close the doors faster.

Nice.

He thrust his arm between the silver sliding panels and they reopened to allow him to join her. Francesca seemed less than pleased with the invasion. She eyeballed him for a moment under her dark lashes and then wrinkled her delicate nose as though he smelled of rotten fish. As the doors began to close again, she scooted into the far corner of the elevator even though they were alone in the car.

"We need to talk," Liam said as the car started moving down.

Francesca's eyes widened and her red lips tightened into a straight, hard line. "About what?" she asked innocently.

"About your attitude. I understand you're passionate about your work. But whether you like it or not, I'm in control of this company and I'm going to do whatever I have to do to save it from the mess that's been made of it. I'll not have you making a fool out of me in front of—"

Liam's words were cut off as the elevator lurched to a stop and the lights went out, blanketing them in total darkness.

This couldn't really be happening. She was not trapped in a broken elevator with Liam Crowe. Stubborn and ridiculously handsome Liam Crowe. But she should've known something bad was going to happen. There had been thirteen people sitting at the table during the board meeting. That was an omen of bad luck.

Nervously, she clutched at the gold Italian horn pendant around her neck and muttered a silent plea for good fortune. "What just happened?" she asked, her voice sounding smaller than she'd like, considering the blackout had interrupted a tongue lashing from her new boss.

"I don't know." They stood in the dark for a moment before the emergency lighting system kicked on and bathed them in red light. Liam walked over to the control panel and pulled out the phone that connected to the engineering room. Without saying anything, he hung it back up. Next, he hit the emergency button, but nothing happened; the entire panel was dark and unresponsive.

"Well?" Francesca asked.

"I think the power has gone out. The emergency phone is dead." He pulled his cell phone out and eyed the screen. "Do you have service on your phone? I don't."

She fished in her purse and retrieved her phone, shaking her head as she looked at the screen. There were no bars or internet connectivity. She never got good service in elevators, anyway. "Nothing."

"Damn it," Liam swore, putting his phone away. "I can't believe this."

"So what do we do now?"

Liam flopped back against the wall with a dull thud. "We wait. If the power outage is widespread, there's nothing anyone can do."

"So we just sit here?"

"Do you have a better suggestion? You were full of them this morning."

Francesca ignored his pointed words, crossed her arms defensively and turned away from him. She eyed the escape hatch in the ceiling. They could try to crawl out through there, but how high were they? They had started on the fifty-second floor and hadn't gone very far when the elevator stopped. They might be in between floors. Or the power could come back on while they were in the elevator shaft and they might get hurt. It probably was a better idea to sit it out.

The power would come back on at any moment. Hopefully.

"It's better to wait," she agreed reluctantly.

"I didn't think it was possible for us to agree on anything after the board meeting and that fit you threw."

Francesca turned on her heel to face him. "I did not throw a fit. I just wasn't docile enough to sit back like the others and let you make bad choices for the company. They're too scared to rock the boat."

"They're scared that the company can't bounce back from the scandal. And they didn't say anything because they know I'm right. We have to be fiscally responsible if we're going to—"

"Fiscally responsible? What about socially responsible? ANS has sponsored the Youth in Crisis charity gala for the past seven years. We can't just decide not to do it this year. It's only two weeks away. They count on that money to provide programs for at-risk teens. Those activities keep kids off the streets and involved in sports and create educational opportunities they wouldn't get without our money."

Liam frowned at her. She could see the firm set of his jaw even bathed in the dim red light. "You think I don't care about disadvantaged children?"

Francesca shrugged. "I don't know you well enough to say."

"Well, I do care," he snapped. "I personally attended the ball for the past two years and wrote a big fat check at both of them. But that's not the point. The point is we need to cut back on expenses to keep the company afloat until we can rebuild our image."

"No. You've got it backward," she insisted. "You need the charity events to rebuild your image so the company can stay afloat. What looks better in the midst of scandal than a company doing good deeds? It says to the public that some bad people did some bad things here, but the rest of us are committed to making things right. The advertisers will come flocking back."

Liam watched her for a moment, and she imagined the wheels turning in his head as he thought through her logic. "Your argument would've been a lot more effective if you hadn't shrieked and called me names in Italian."

Francesca frowned. She hadn't meant to lose her cool, but she couldn't help it. She had her mother's quick Italian tongue and her father's short fuse. It made for an explosive combination. "I have a bit of a temper," she said. "I get it from my father."

Anyone who had worked on the set of a Victor Orr film knew what could happen when things weren't going right. The large Irishman had a head of thick, black hair and a temper just as dark. He'd blow at a moment's notice and nothing short of her mother's soothing hand could calm him down. Francesca was just the same.

"Does he curse in Italian, too?"

"No, he doesn't speak a word of it and my mother likes it that way. My mother grew up in Sicily and met my father there when he was shooting a film. My mother's Italian heritage was always very important to her, so when I got older I spent summers there with my *nonna*."

"Nonna?"

"My maternal grandmother. I picked up a lot of Italian while I was there, including some key phrases I probably shouldn't know. I realized as a teenager that I could curse in Italian and my father wouldn't know what I was saying because he's Irish. From there it became a bad habit of mine. I'm sorry I yelled," she added. "I just care too much. I always have."

Francesca might take after her mother in most things, but her father had made his mark, as well. Victor Orr had come from poor beginnings and raised his two daughters not only to be grateful for what they had, but also to give to the less fortunate. All through high school, Francesca had volunteered at a soup kitchen on Saturdays. She'd organized charity canned food collections and blood drives at school. After college, her father helped her get an entry level job at ANS, where he was the largest minority stockholder. It hadn't taken long for her to work her way up to the head of community outreach. And she'd been good at it. Graham had never had room to complain about her doing anything less than a stellar job.

But it always came down to money. When things got tight, her budget was always the first to get cut. Why not eliminate some of the cushy corporate perks? Maybe slash the travel budget and force people to hold more teleconferences? Or cut back on the half gallon of hair gel the head anchor used each night for the evening news broadcast?

"I don't want to hack up your department," Liam said. "What you do is important for ANS and for the community. But I need a little give and take here. Everyone needs to tighten their belts. Not just you. But I need you to play along, too. It's hard enough to come into the leadership position of a company that's doing well, much less one like ANS. I'm going to do everything I can to get this network back on top, but I need everyone's support."

Francesca could hear the sincerity in his words. He did care about the company and its employees. They just didn't see eye to eye quite yet on what to do about it. She could convince him to see things her way eventually. She just had to take a page from her mother's playbook. It would take time and perhaps a softer hand than she had used with Graham. At least Liam seemed reasonable about it. That won him some points in her book. "Okay."

Liam looked at her for a moment, surveying her face as though he almost didn't believe his ears. Then he nodded. They stood silently in the elevator for a moment before Liam started shrugging out of his black suit coat. He tossed the expensive jacket to the ground and followed it with his silk tie. He unbuttoned his collar and took a deep breath, as if he had been unable to do it until then. "I'm glad we've called a truce because it's gotten too warm in here for me to fight anymore. Of course this had to happen on one of the hottest days of the year."

He was right. The air conditioning was off and it was in the high nineties today, which was unheard of in early May. The longer they sat in the elevator without air, the higher the temperature climbed.

Following his example, Francesca slipped out of her blazer, leaving her in a black silk and lace camisole and pencil skirt. Thank goodness she'd opted out of stockings today.

Kicking off her heels, she spread out her coat on the floor and sat down on it. She couldn't stand there in those pointy-toed stilettos any longer, and she'd given up hope for any immediate rescue. If they were going to be trapped in here for a while, she was going to be comfortable.

"I wish this had happened after lunch. Those bagels in the conference room burned off a long time ago."

Francesca knew exactly what he meant. She hadn't eaten since this morning. She'd had a cappuccino and a sweet *cornetto* before she'd left her hotel room, neither of which lasted very long. She typically ate a late lunch, so luckily she carried a few snacks in her purse.

Using the light of her phone, she started digging around in her bag. She found a granola bar, a pack of *Gocciole* Italian breakfast cookies and a bottle of water. "I have a few snacks with me. The question is whether we eat them now and hope we get let out soon, or whether we save them. It could be hours if it's a major blackout."

Liam slipped down to the floor across from her. "Now. Definitely now."

"You wouldn't last ten minutes on one of those survival reality shows."

"That's why I produce them and don't star in them. My idea of roughing it is having to eat in Times Square with the tourists. What do you have?"

"A peanut butter granola bar and some little Italian cookies. We can share the water."

"Which is your favorite?"

"I like the cookies. They're the kind my grandmother would feed me for breakfast when I stayed with her. They don't eat eggs or meat for breakfast like Americans do. It was one of the best parts of visiting her— cake and cookies for breakfast."

Liam grinned, and Francesca realized it was the first time she'd seen him smile. It was a shame. He had a beautiful smile that lit up his whole face. It seemed more natural than the serious expression he'd worn all day, as though he were normally a more carefree and relaxed kind of guy. The pressure of buying ANS must have been getting to him. He'd been all business this morning and her behavior certainly didn't help.

Now he was stressed out, hungry and irritated about being trapped in the elevator. She was glad she could make him smile, even if just for a moment. It made up for her behavior this morning. Maybe. She made a mental note to try to be more cordial in the future. He was being reasonable and there was no point in making things harder than they had to be.

"Cake for breakfast sounds awesome. As do summers in Italy. After high school I got to spend a week in Rome, but that's it. I didn't get around to seeing much more than the big sites like the Colosseum and the Parthenon." He looked down at the two packages in her hand. "I'll take the granola bar since you prefer the cookies. Thank you for sharing."

Francesca shrugged. "It's better than listening to your stomach growl for an hour." She tossed him the granola bar and opened the bottle of water to take a conservative sip.

Liam ripped into the packaging. His snack was gone before Francesca had even gotten the first cookie in her mouth. She chuckled as she ate a few, noting him eyeing her like a hungry tiger. Popping another into her mouth, she gently slung the open bag to him. "Here," she said. "I can't take you watching me like that."

"Are you sure?" he said, eyeing the cookies that were now in his hand.

"Yes. But when we get out of this elevator, you owe me."

"Agreed," he said, shoveling the first of several cookies into his mouth.

Francesca imagined it took a lot of food to keep a man Liam's size satisfied. He was big like her *nonno* had been. Her grandfather had died when she was only a few years old, but her *nonna* had told her about how much she had to cook for him after he worked a long shift. Like *Nonno,* Liam was more than six feet tall, solidly built but on the leaner side, as though he were a runner. A lot of people jogged around the National Mall in D.C. Or so she'd heard. She could imagine him down there with the others. Jogging shorts. No shirt. Sweat running down the hard muscles of his chest. It made her think maybe she should go down there every now and then, if just for the view.

She, however, didn't like to sweat. Running during the humid summers in Virginia was out of the question. As was running during the frigid, icy winters. So she just didn't. She watched what she ate, indulged when she really wanted to and walked as much as her heels would allow. That kept her at a trim but curvy weight that pleased her.

Speaking of sweating…she could feel the beads of sweat in her hairline, ready and waiting to start racing down the back of her neck. She already felt sticky, but there wasn't much else to take off unless she planned to get far closer to Liam than she ever intended.

Although that wouldn't be all bad.

It had been a while since Francesca had dated anyone. Her career had kept her busy, but she always kept her eyes open to the possibilities. Nothing of substance had popped up in a long time. But recently all of her friends seemed to be settling down. One by one, and she worried she might be the last.

Not that Liam Crowe was settling-down material. He was just sexy, fling material. She typically didn't indulge in pleasure without potential. But seeing those broad shoulders pulling against the confines of his shirt, she realized that he might be just what she needed. Something to release the pressure and give her the strength to hold out for "the one."

Francesca reached into her bag and pulled out a hair clip. She gathered up the thick, dark strands of her hair and twisted them up, securing them with the claw. It helped but only for a moment. Her tight-fitting pencil skirt was like a heavy, wet blanket thrown over her legs. And her camisole, while seemingly flimsy, was starting to get damp and cling to her skin.

If they didn't get out of this elevator soon, something had to come off. Taking another sip of water, she leaned her head back against the wall and counted herself lucky that if nothing else, she'd worn pretty, matching underwear today. She had the feeling that Liam would appreciate that.

Two

"Sweet mercy, it's hot!" Liam exclaimed, standing up. He felt as if he was being smothered by his crisp, starched dress shirt. He unfastened the buttons down the front and whipped it off with a sigh of relief. "I'm sorry if this makes you uncomfortable, but I've got to do it."

Francesca was sitting quietly in the corner and barely acknowledged him, although he did catch her opening her eyes slightly to catch a glimpse of him without his shirt on. She looked away a moment later, but it was enough to let him know she was curious. That was interesting.

He'd gotten a different insight into his feisty executive vice president of Community Outreach in the past two hours. He had a better understanding of her and what was important to her. Hopefully once they got out of this elevator they could work together without the animosity. And maybe they could be a little more than friendly. Once she had stopped yelling, he liked her. More than he probably should, considering that she worked for him.

"Francesca, take off some of your clothes. I know you're dying over there."

She shook her head adamantly, although he could see the beads of sweat running down her chest and into the valley between her breasts. "No, I'm fine."

"The hell you are. You're just as miserable as I am. That tank you're wearing looks like it will cover up enough to protect your honor. The skirt looks terribly clingy. Take it off. Really. I'm about ten minutes from losing these pants, so you might as well give up on any modesty left between us."

Francesca looked up at him with wide eyes. "Your pants?" she said, swallowing hard. Her gaze drifted down his bare chest to his belt and then lower.

"Yes. It's gotta be ninety-five degrees and climbing in this oven they call an elevator. You don't have to look at me, but I've got to do it. You might as well do it, too."

With a sigh of resignation, Francesca got up from the floor and started fussing with the latch on the back of her skirt. "I can't get the clasp. It snags sometimes."

"Let me help," Liam offered. She turned her back to him and he crouched down behind her to get a better look at the clasp in the dim red light. This close to her, he could smell the scent of her warm skin mixed with the soft fragrance of roses. It wasn't overpowering— more like strolling through a rose garden on a summer day. He inhaled it into his lungs and held it there for a moment. It was intoxicating.

He grasped the two sides of the clasp, ignoring the buzz of awareness that shot through his fingertips as he brushed her bare skin beneath it. With a couple of firm twists and pulls, it came apart. He gripped the zipper tab and pulled it down a few inches, revealing the back of the red satin panties she wore.

"Got it," he said with clenched teeth, standing back up and moving away before he did something stupid like touch her any more than was necessary. It was one thing to sit in the elevator in his underwear. It was another thing entirely to do it when he had a raging erection. That would be a little hard to disguise.

"Thank you," she said softly, her eyes warily watching him as she returned to her corner of the elevator.

As she started to shimmy the skirt down her hips, Liam turned away, although it took every ounce of power he had to do so. She was everything he liked in a woman. Feisty. Exotic. Voluptuous. And underneath it all, a caring soul. She wasn't one of those rich women that got involved in charity work because they had nothing better to do with their time. She really cared. And he appreciated that, even if it would cost him a few headaches in the future.

"Grazie, signore," she said with a sigh. "That does feel better."

Out of the corner of his eye, he saw her settle back down on the floor. "Is it safe?" he asked.

"As safe as it's going to get. Thank you for asking."

Liam looked over at her. She had tugged down her camisole to cover most everything to the tops of her thighs, although now a hint of her red bra was peeking out from the top. There was only so much fabric to go around, and with her luscious curves, keeping them all covered would be a challenge.

"You might as well just take those pants off now."

Liam chuckled and shook his head. Not after thinking about her satin-covered breasts. He didn't even have to touch her to make that an impossibility. "That's probably not the best idea at the moment."

Her brow wrinkled in confusion. "Why—" she started, then stopped. "Oh."

Liam closed his eyes and tried to wish his arousal away, but all that did was bring images of those silky red panties to his mind. "That's the challenge of being trapped in a small space with a beautiful, half-naked woman."

"You think I'm beautiful?" her hesitant voice came after a long moment of silence between them.

He planted his hands on his hips. "I do."

"I didn't expect that."

Liam turned to look at her. "Why on earth not? I think a man would have to be without a pulse to not find you desirable."

"I grew up in Beverly Hills," she said with a dismissive shrug. "I'm not saying I never dated in school—I did—but there was certainly a higher premium placed on the Malibu Barbie dolls."

"The what?"

"You know, the blond, beach-tanned girls with belly button piercings and figures like twelve-year-old boys? At least until they turn eighteen and get enough money to buy a nice pair of breasts."

"People in Hollywood are nuts," he said. "There was nothing remotely erotic about me as a twelve-year-old. You, on the other hand…" Liam shook his head, the thoughts of her soft curves pressing against the palms of his hands making his skin tingle with anticipation. He forced them into tight fists and willed the feeling away.

"It takes everything I've got not to touch you when I see you sitting there like that."

There was a long silence, and then her voice again. "Why don't you?"

Liam's jaw was flexed tight, and his whole body tensed as he tried to hold back the desire that was building inside for her. "I didn't think it was a good idea. I'm your boss. We have to work together. Things would get weird. Wouldn't they?"

Please let her say no. Please let her say no.

"I don't think so," she said, slowly climbing to her knees. "We're both adults. We know what this is and what it means." She crawled leisurely across the elevator floor, stopping in front of him. Her hands went to his belt buckle as she looked up at him through her thick, coal-black lashes. "What happens in the elevator, stays in the elevator, right?"

Liam didn't know what to say. He could barely form words as her hands undid his belt buckle, then the fly of his pants. But he didn't stop her. Oh, no. He wanted her too badly to let good sense interfere. Besides, they had time to kill, right? Who knew how long they'd be trapped in here.

His suit pants slid to the floor and he quickly kicked out of them and his shoes. Crouching down until they were at the same level, he reached for the hem of her camisole and pulled it up over her head. Francesca undid the clip holding her hair and the heavy, ebony stands fell down around her shoulders like a sheet of black silk.

The sight of her body in nothing but her red undergarments was like a punch to his guts. She was one of the sexiest women he'd ever seen—and she was mostly naked, and on her knees, in front of him.

How the hell had he gotten this lucky today?

Unable to hold back any longer, he leaned in to kiss her. They collided, their lips and bare skin slamming into one another. Francesca wrapped her arms around his neck and pulled her body against him. Her breasts pressed urgently against the hard wall of his chest. Her belly arched into the aching heat of his desire for her.

The contact was electric, the powerful sensations running through his nervous system like rockets, exploding at the base of his spine. He wanted to devour her, his tongue invading her mouth and demanding everything she could give him. She met his every thrust, running her own silken tongue along his and digging her nails frantically into his back.

Liam slipped his arm behind her back and slowly eased her down onto the floor. He quickly found his place between her thighs and dipped down to give attention to the breasts nearly spilling from her bra. It didn't take much to slip the straps from her shoulders and tug the bra down to her waist. The palms of his hands quickly moved in to take its place. He teased her nipples into firm peaks before capturing one in his mouth.

Francesca groaned and arched into him, her fingertips weaving into his thick, wavy brown hair. She tugged him back up to her mouth and kissed him again. There were no more thoughts of heat or sweat or broken elevators as he lost himself in the pleasurable exploration of her body.

And when he felt her fingers slide down his stomach, slip beneath the waistband of his underwear and wrap around the pulsating length of his erection, for a moment he almost forgot where he was, entirely.

Thank heavens for power outages.

* * *

Francesca wasn't quite sure what had come over her, but she was enjoying every minute of this naughty indulgence. Perhaps being trapped in this hot jail cell was playing with her brain, but she didn't care. There was just something about Liam. Sure, he was handsome and rich, but she'd seen her share of that kind of man in Washington, D.C. There was something about his intensity, the way he was handling the company and even how he handled her. She'd been fighting the attraction to him since she first laid eyes on him, and then his shirt came off to reveal a wide chest, chiseled abs and a sprinkle of chest hair, and she lost all her reasons to resist.

When he told her that she was beautiful, a part of her deep inside urged her to jump on the unexpected opportunity. To give in to the attraction, however inappropriate, and make a sexy memory out of this crazy afternoon.

She still wanted a solid, lasting relationship like her parents had. They'd been happily married for thirty years in a town where the typical wedding reception lasted longer than the vows. But having a fun fling in an elevator was in a totally different category. Liam would never be the serious kind of relationship, and she knew it, so it didn't hurt. This was a release. An amusing way to pass the time until the power was restored.

Francesca tightened her grip on Liam until he groaned her name into her ear.

"I want you so badly," he whispered. He moved his hand along the curve of her waist, gliding down to her hip, where he grasped her wrist and pulled her hand away. "You keep doing that and I won't have the chance to do everything I want to do to you."

A wicked idea crossed her mind. Francesca reached out with her other hand for the half-empty bottle of water beside them. "Let me cool you off then," she said, dumping the remains over the top of his head. The cool water soaked his hair and rushed down his face and neck to rain onto her bare skin. It was refreshing and playful, the cool water drawing goose bumps along her bare flesh.

"Man, that felt good," Liam said, running one hand through his wet hair as he propped himself up with the other. "I don't want to waste it, though." He dipped down to lick the droplets of water off her chest, flicking his tongue over her nipples again. He traveled down her stomach to where some of the water had pooled in her navel. He lapped it up with enthusiasm, making her squirm beneath him as her core tightened and throbbed in anticipation.

His fingertips sought out the satin edge of her panties and slipped beneath them. Sliding over her neatly cropped curls, one finger parted her most sensitive spot and stroked her gently. She couldn't contain the moan of pleasure he coaxed out of her. When he dipped farther to slip the finger deep inside her body, she almost came undone right then. The muscles tightened around him, the sensations of each stroke building a tidal wave that she couldn't hold back for much longer.

"Liam," she whispered, but he didn't stop. His fingers moved more frantically over her, delving inside and pushing her over the edge.

Francesca cried out, her moans of pleasure bouncing off the walls of the small elevator and doubling in volume and intensity. Her hips bucked against his hand, her whole body shuddering with the feeling running through her.

She had barely caught her breath when suddenly there was a jarring rattle. The silence was broken by the roar of engines and air units firing up, and the lights came back on in the elevator.

"You have got to be kidding me," he groaned.

And then, with Liam still between her thighs and their clothes scattered around the elevator, the car started moving downward. Francesca threw a quick glance to the screen on the wall. They were on the thirty-third floor and falling. "Oh, no," she said, pushing frantically at his chest until he eased back.

She climbed to her feet, tugging on her skirt and yanking her bra back into place. She didn't bother tucking in her camisole, but shrugged into her jacket. Liam followed suit, pulling on his pants and shirt. He shoved his tie into his pants pocket and threw his coat over his arm.

"You have my lipstick all over you," she said, noting less than ten floors to go. Liam ran his hand through his still wet hair and casually rubbed at his face, seeming to be less concerned than she was with how he looked when they walked out.

By the time the elevator came to the first floor and the doors opened, Francesca and Liam were both fully dressed. A bit sloppy, with misaligned buttons and rumpled jackets, but dressed.

They stepped out into the grand foyer where the building engineers and security guards were waiting for them. "Are you two—" one of the men started to speak, pausing when he saw their tousled condition "—okay?"

Liam looked at Francesca, and she could feel her cheeks lighting up crimson with embarrassment. He still had some of her Sizzling Hot Red lipstick on his face, but he didn't seem to care. "We're fine," he said. "Just hot, hungry and glad to finally be out of there. What happened?"

"I'm not sure, sir. The whole island lost power. Wouldn't you know it would be on such a hot day. Might've been everyone turning on their air conditioners for the first time today. Are you guys sure we can't get you anything? Three hours in there had to be miserable."

"I'm fine," Francesca insisted. The engineer's expression had been a wake-up call from the passionate haze she'd lost herself in. She'd very nearly slept with her boss. Her new boss. On his first day after they'd spent the morning fighting like cats and dogs. The heat must've made her delirious to have thought that was a good idea.

At least they'd been interrupted before it went too far. Now she just wanted to get a cab back to her hotel. Then she could change out of these clothes, shower and wash the scent of Liam off her skin. "Just have someone hail me a taxi to my hotel, would you?"

The engineer waved to one of the doormen. "Sure thing. It might take a minute because the traffic lights have been out and there's been gridlock for hours."

Without looking at Liam, Francesca started for the door, stepping outside to wait on the sidewalk for her car.

"Talk about bad timing," Liam said over her shoulder after following her outside.

"Fate has a funny way of keeping you from doing things you shouldn't do."

Liam came up beside her, but she wouldn't turn to look at him. She couldn't. She'd just get weak in the knees and her resolve to leave would soften.

"I'd like to think of it more as a brief interruption. To build some anticipation for later. Where are you headed?"

"To where I was going before my whole day got sidetracked—back to my hotel. To shower and get some work done. Alone," she added if that wasn't clear enough.

"Do you have plans for dinner tonight?"

"Yes, I do." She didn't. But going out to dinner with Liam would put her right back in the same tempting situation, although hopefully without power outages. She'd given in to temptation once and she'd been rescued from her bad decision. She wasn't about to do it again.

Liam watched her for a minute. Francesca could feel his eyes scrutinizing her, but she kept her gaze focused on the passing cars. "You said things wouldn't get weird. That we both knew what this was and what happened in the elevator stayed in the elevator."

Francesca finally turned to him. She tried not to look into the sapphire-blue eyes that were watching her or the damp curls of his hair that would remind her of what they'd nearly done. "That's right. And that's where it will stay. That's why I don't want to go to dinner with you. Or to drinks. Or back to your place to pick up where we left off. We've left the elevator behind us and the opportunity has come and gone. Appreciate the moment for what it was."

"What it was is unfinished," he insisted. "I'd like to change that."

"Not every project gets completed." Francesca watched a taxi pull up to the curb. It was empty, thank goodness.

"Come on, Francesca. Let me take you to dinner tonight. Even if just to say thank-you for the granola bar. As friends. I owe you, remember?"

Francesca didn't believe a word of that friend nonsense. They'd have a nice dinner with expensive wine someplace fancy and she'd be naked again before she knew it. As much as she liked Liam, she needed to stay objective where he was concerned. He was the new owner of ANS and she couldn't let her head get clouded with unproductive thoughts about him. They'd come to a truce, but they hadn't fully resolved their issues regarding her budget and the way forward for the network. She wouldn't put it past an attractive, charming guy like Liam to use whatever tools he had in his arsenal to get his way.

She stepped to the curb as the doorman opened the back door of the taxi for her.

"Wait," Liam called out, coming to her side again. "If you're going to leave me high and dry, you can at least tell me what you called me today in the board meeting."

Francesca smiled. If that didn't send him packing, nothing else would. "Okay, fine," she relented. She got into the cab and rolled down the window before Liam shut it. "I called you *figlio di un allevatore di maiali.* That means 'the son of a pig farmer.' It doesn't quite pack the same punch in English."

Liam frowned and stepped back from the window. The distance bothered her even though it was her own words that had driven him away. "I'd say it packs enough of a punch."

She ignored the slightly offended tone of his voice. He wasn't about to make her feel guilty. He'd deserved the title at the time. "Have a good evening, Mr. Crowe," she said before the cab pulled away and she disappeared into traffic.

Three

Liam had just stepped from his shower when he heard his cell phone ringing. The tune, "God Save the Queen," made him cringe. Had he told his great aunt Beatrice he was in Manhattan? She must've found out somehow.

He wrapped his towel around his waist and dashed into his bedroom where the phone was lying on the comforter. The words "Queen Bee" flashed on the screen with the photo of a tiara. His aunt Beatrice would not be amused if she knew what the rest of the family called her.

With a sigh, he picked up the phone and hit the answer key. "Hello?"

"Liam," his aunt replied with her haughty Upper East Side accent. "Are you all right? I was told you were trapped in an elevator all afternoon."

"I'm fine. Just hungry, but I'm about to—"

"Excellent," she interrupted. "Then you'll join me

for dinner. There's an important matter I need to discuss with you."

Liam bit back a groan. He hated eating at Aunt Beatrice's house. Mostly because of having to listen to her go on and on about the family and how irresponsible they all were. But even then, she liked them all more than Liam because they kissed her derrière. And that was smart. She was worth two billion dollars with no children of her own to inherit. Everyone was jockeying for their cut.

Everyone but Liam. He was polite and distant. He didn't need her money. Or at least he hadn't until the ANS deal came up and he didn't have enough liquid assets to buy a majority stake quickly. Other people also were interested in the company, including leeches like Ron Wheeler, who specialized in hacking businesses to bits for profit. To move fast, Liam had had to swallow his pride and ask his aunt to invest in the remaining shares of ANS that he couldn't afford. Together, they had controlling interest of the company, and by designating her voting powers to him, Aunt Beatrice had put Liam in charge.

Liam had every intention of slowly buying her out over time, but he wouldn't be able to do so for quite a while. So now, at long last, Aunt Beatrice had something to hold over his head. And when she snapped, for the first time in his life, he had to jump.

"Dinner is at six," she said, either oblivious or unconcerned about his unhappy silence on the end of the line.

"Yes, Aunt Beatrice. I'll see you at six."

After he hung up the phone, he eyed the clock and realized he didn't have long to get over to her Upper

East Side mansion in rush hour traffic. He'd do better to walk, so he needed to get out the door soon.

It was just as well that Francesca had turned down his dinner date so he didn't have to cancel. That would've pained him terribly, even after knowing what she'd called him.

"Son of a pig farmer," he muttered to himself as he got dressed.

He opted for a gray suit with a pale purple dress shirt and no tie. He hated ties and only wore them when absolutely necessary. Today, he'd felt like he needed to look important and in control at the board meeting. He didn't want the ANS directors to think they were in the hands of a laid-back dreamer. But as soon as he had a strong foothold in the company, the ties would be gone.

Tonight, he left it off simply because he knew to do so would aggravate Aunt Beatrice. She liked formal dress for dinner but had given up long ago on the family going to that much trouble. She did, however, still expect a jacket and tie for the men and a dress and hosiery for the ladies. It was only proper. Leaving off the tie would be a small but noted rebellion on his part. He didn't want her to think she had him completely under her thumb.

It wasn't until he rang the doorbell that he remembered her mentioning something about an important issue she wanted to discuss. He couldn't imagine what it could be, but he sincerely hoped it didn't involve him dating someone's daughter. Aunt Beatrice was single-minded in her pursuit of marriage and family for Liam. He couldn't fathom why she cared.

"Good evening, Mr. Crowe," her ancient butler Henry said as he opened the door.

Henry had worked for his aunt Liam's entire life and a good number of years before that. The man was in his seventies now but as spry and chipper as ever.

"Good evening, Henry. How is she tonight?" he asked, leaning in to the elderly man and lowering his voice.

"She's had a bee in her bonnet about something all afternoon, sir. She made quite a few calls once the power was restored."

Liam frowned. "Any idea what it's about?"

"I don't. But I would assume it involves you because you were the only one invited to dinner this evening."

That was odd. Usually Aunt Beatrice invited at least two family members to dinner. She enjoyed watching them try to one-up each other all night and get in her good favor. It really was a ridiculous exercise, but it was amazing what the family would do just because she asked. His grandfather, Aunt Beatrice's brother, had never had much to do with her, so neither did that branch of the family. It was only after all the others of the generation had died that she took over as matriarch. Then, even Liam's part of the family was drawn back into the fold.

Liam held his tongue as Henry led him through the parlor and into the formal dining room. When a larger group was expected, Aunt Beatrice would greet her guests in the parlor and then adjourn to the dining room when everyone had arrived. Apparently because it was just him they bypassed the formalities and went straight to dinner.

Aunt Beatrice was there in her seat at the head of the long, oak table, looking regal as always. Her gray hair was curled perfectly, her rose chiffon dress nicely accented by the pink sapphire necklace and earrings she paired with it. She didn't smile as he entered. Instead, she evaluated him from top to bottom, her lips tightening into a frown when she noted his lack of tie.

"Good evening, Aunt Beatrice," he said with a wide smile to counter her grimace. He came around the table and placed a kiss on her cheek before sitting down at the place setting to her right.

"Liam," she said, acknowledging him without any real warmth. That's why he'd always thought of her as royalty. Stiff, formal, proper. He couldn't imagine what she would have been like if she had married and had children. Children would require laughter and dirt—two things unthinkable in this household.

Henry poured them each a glass of wine and disappeared into the kitchen to retrieve their first course. Liam hated to see the old man wait on him. He should be in a recliner, watching television and enjoying his retirement, not serving meals to privileged people capable of doing it themselves. The man had never even married. He had no life of his own outside of this mansion.

"When are you going to let Henry retire?" he asked. "The poor man deserves some time off before he drops dead in your foyer."

Aunt Beatrice bristled at the suggestion. "He loves it here. He wouldn't think of leaving me. And besides, Henry would never die in the foyer. He knows how expensive that Oriental rug is."

Liam sighed and let the subject drop. Henry placed bowls of soup in front of them both and disappeared again. "So, what have you summoned me here to discuss tonight?" He might as well just get it over with.

There was no sense waiting for the chocolate soufflé or the cheese course.

"I received a phone call today from a man named Ron Wheeler."

Liam stiffened in his seat and stopped his spoon of soup in midair. Ron Wheeler was in the business of buying struggling companies and "streamlining" them. That usually involved laying off at least half the employees and hacking up the benefits packages of the ones who were left. Then he'd break the company up into smaller pieces and sell them off for more than the price of the whole. No one liked to hear the mention of his name. "And what did he have to say?"

"He heard I'd bought a large portion of Graham Boyle's ANS stock. He's made me an extremely generous offer to buy it."

At that, Liam dropped his spoon, sending splatters of butternut squash all across the pristine white tablecloth. Henry arrived in an instant to clean up the mess and bring him a new spoon, but Liam didn't want it. He couldn't stomach the idea of food at this point.

"Aunt Beatrice, your holding is larger than mine. If you sell him your stock, he'll gain majority control of the company. The whole network will be at risk."

She nodded, setting down her own spoon. "I realize that. And I know how important the company is to you. But I also want you to know how important this family is to me. I won't be around forever, Liam. This family needs someone strong and smart to run it. You don't need me to tell you that most of our relatives are idiots. My two sisters never had any sense and neither did their children. My father knew it, too, which is why he left most of the family money to me and your grandfather. He knew they'd all be broke and homeless without someone sensible in charge."

Liam didn't want to know where this conversation was going. It couldn't be good. "Why are you telling me this? What does it have to do with Ron Wheeler?"

"Because I think you're the right person to lead the family after I'm gone."

"Don't talk like that," he insisted. They both knew she was too mean to die. "You have plenty of years ahead of you."

Her sharp blue gaze focused on him, an unexpected hint of emotion flashing in them for a fleeting second before she waved away his statement. "Everyone dies, Liam. It's better to be prepared for the eventuality. I want you to take my place and be family patriarch. As such, you would inherit everything of mine and serve as executor of the family trusts."

The blood drained from Liam's face. He didn't want that kind of responsibility. Two billion dollars and a family full of greedy suck-ups chasing him around? "I don't want your money, Aunt Beatrice. You know that."

"Exactly. But I know what you do want. You want ANS. And as long as I have my shares, you won't truly have it. I could sell at any time to Ron Wheeler or anyone else who gives me a good offer."

Liam took a big swallow of wine to calm his nerves. Aunt Beatrice had never held anything over him. She couldn't because until now he hadn't needed her or her money and she knew it. But he'd made a critical error. He never should've agreed to this stock arrangement with her. He'd given her the leverage to twist him any way she wanted to. "Why would you do that? I told you

I would buy that stock from you at what you paid or the going rate, if it goes higher."

"Because I want you to settle down. I can't have you leading this family while you play newsman and chase skirts around D.C. I want you married. Stable. Ready to lead the Crowe family."

"I'm only twenty-eight."

"The perfect age. Your father married when he was twenty-eight, as did your grandfather. You're out of school, well established. You'll be a prize to whatever lucky woman you choose."

"Aunt Beatrice, I'm not ready to——"

"You will marry within the year," she said, her serious tone like a royal decree he didn't dare contradict. "On your one-year wedding anniversary, as a gift I will give you my shares of ANS stock and name you my sole beneficiary. Then you can truly breathe easy knowing your network is secure, and I can know this family will be cared for when I'm gone."

She couldn't be serious. "You can't force me to marry."

"You're right. You're a grown man and you make your own decisions. So the choice is entirely yours. Either you marry and get the company you want and more money than most people dream of…or you don't and I sell my shares to Ron Wheeler. Tough choice, I understand." At that, she returned to her soup as though they'd been discussing the weather.

Liam didn't know what to say. He wasn't used to anyone else calling the shots in his life. But he'd given himself a vulnerability she had been waiting to exploit. She'd probably planned this from the very moment he'd come to her about buying ANS. Liam leaned his head into his hand and closed his eyes.

"If you don't know any suitable ladies, I can make a few recommendations."

He was sure she'd just love that, too. Thankfully she'd stopped short of deciding who he should marry. "I think I can handle that part, thank you. I've been seeing someone," he said quickly, hoping she didn't ask for more details about the fictional woman.

Aunt Beatrice shrugged off the bitter tone in his voice. "Then it's time the two of you got more serious. Just remember, you have a year from today to marry. But if I were you, I wouldn't dawdle. The sooner you get married, the sooner ANS will be yours."

Francesca had deliberately avoided Liam since they'd returned to D.C., but she couldn't put off speaking to him any longer. She needed to know if they were going to be sponsoring the Youth in Crisis gala or not. It was a week and a half away. It was already too late to pull out, really, but if he was going to insist they couldn't do it, she needed to know now.

She waved as she passed his assistant's desk. "Afternoon, Jessica."

The woman looked up at her with a wary expression. "You don't want to go in there."

Francesca frowned. Did she mean her specifically, or anyone? Liam couldn't still be mad about the whole elevator thing. Could he? "Why?"

"He's been in a foul mood since we left New York. I'm not sure what happened. Something with his family, I think."

"Is everyone okay?"

Jessica nodded her head. "He hasn't had me send flowers to anyone, so I would assume so. But he's not taking calls. He's been sitting at his desk all morning flipping through his address book and muttering to himself."

Interesting. "Well, I hate to do it, but I have to speak with him."

"As you wish." Jessica pressed the intercom button that linked to Liam's phone. "Mr. Crowe, Ms. Orr is here to see you."

"Not now," his voice barked over the line. Then, after a brief pause, he said, "Never mind. Send her in."

Jessica shrugged. "I don't know what that's all about, but go on in."

Francesca gripped the handle to his office door and took a deep breath before going inside. She'd dressed in her most impressive power suit today and felt confident she would leave his office with what she wanted. The emerald-green pantsuit was striking and well-tailored. Her black hair was twisted up into a bun, and she had a silk scarf tied around her neck. Not only did she feel good in the outfit, she felt well-covered. Liam had already seen too much of her body. She intended to keep every inch out of his sight from now on.

As she opened the door, she saw Liam sitting at his desk just as Jessica had described. He was flipping through an address book, making notes on his desk blotter. As she came in he looked up and then slammed the book shut.

"Good morning, Ms. Orr." His voice was a great deal more formal and polite than it was the last time they'd spoken. Of course, then they'd been recently naked together.

"Mr. Crowe. I wanted to speak to you about the Youth in Crisis gala. We don't have much time to—"

"Have a seat, Francesca."

She stopped short, surprised at his interruption. Unsure of what else to do, she moved to take a seat in the guest chair across from his desk. Before she could sit, he leaped up and pointed to the less formal sitting area on the other side of his office.

"Over here, please. I don't like talking to people across the desk. It feels weird."

Francesca corrected her course to sit in the plush gray leather chair he'd indicated. She watched him warily as he went to the small refrigerator built into the cabinets beside his desk.

"Would you like something to drink?"

"I don't drink at work."

Liam turned to her with a frown and a bottle of root beer in his hand. "At all? I have bottled water, root beer—my personal favorite—and some lemon-lime soda. I don't drink at work, either, despite the fact that if anyone wanted to be in a drunken stupor right now, it would be me." He pulled a bottle of water out of the fridge and handed it to her. "To replace the one we... *used up* in the elevator."

Francesca started to reach for the bottle, then froze at the memory of water pouring over his head and onto her own bare chest. Damn, he'd said that on purpose to throw her off her game. Pulling herself together, she took the bottle and set it on the coffee table unopened.

Liam joined her, sitting on the nearby sofa with his bottle of root beer. "I have a proposition for you."

She didn't like the sound of that. "I told you that I wasn't interested in dinner."

Liam watched her intently with his jewel-blue eyes as he sipped his drink. "I'm not asking you to dinner. I'm asking you to marry me."

Francesca was glad she hadn't opted to drink that water or she would've spit it across the room. She sat bolt upright in her seat and glared at him. "Marry you? Are you crazy?"

"Shhh…" he said, placing his drink on the table. "I don't want anyone to hear our discussion. This is very important. And I'm dead serious. I want you to be my fiancée. At least for a few months."

"Why me? What is going on?"

Liam sighed. "I've put myself in a vulnerable position with the company. I couldn't afford all of Graham Boyle's stock, so my aunt owns the largest share of ANS, not me. She's threatening to sell it to Ron Wheeler if I don't get married within a year."

Ron Wheeler. That was a name that could send chunks of ice running through her veins. Charity didn't help the bottom line in his eyes. Francesca, her staff and the entire department would be out the door before the ink was dry on the sale. And they would just be the first, not the last to go if he were in charge. "Why would she do that?"

"She wants me married and settled down. She wants me to be the strong family patriarch when she's gone and doesn't believe my playboy ways are appropriate. I think she's bluffing, really. I'm hoping that if I get engaged, that will be enough to soothe her. In the meantime, I'm going to work with my accountant and financial advisor to see if I can arrange for a line of credit large enough to buy her out. I have no expectation that we'll actually have to get married."

"I should hope not," she snapped. Francesca had some very strong ideas about what a good marriage was made of and blackmail was not the ideal start. "Don't you have anyone else you can ask? You've known me less than a week."

Liam looked over to the book on his desk and shook his head. "I've gone through every woman's name in my address book and there's not a single suitable candidate. All those women would look at this as a romantic opportunity, not a business arrangement. That's why you're my ideal choice."

A business arrangement? That's just what a girl wanted to hear. "So if this is just a business arrangement, that means you have no intention of trying to get me into bed, right?"

Liam leaned closer to her and a wicked grin spread across his face. "I didn't say *that,* but really, that's not my first priority here. I'm asking you for several reasons. First, I like you. Spending time with you shouldn't be a hardship. My aunt will expect the relationship to appear authentic and she'll sniff out the truth if she thinks we're faking it. After our time in the elevator, I think you and I have enough chemistry to make it realistic. And second, I know I can count on you because you want something from me."

Francesca opened her mouth to argue with him and then stopped. She knew exactly where this was going. Tit for tat. "The Youth in Crisis gala?"

He nodded. "If Ron Wheeler gets a hold of this company, everything you've worked for will be destroyed. The only thing I can do to protect this company and its employees is to get engaged as soon as I can. For your assistance, I'm offering the full financial support of ANS for the Youth in Crisis charity ball. I'll even pledge to top the highest private donation with my own money. I look at it as an investment in the future of the network. And all you have to do is wear a beautiful diamond ring and tolerate my company until my aunt backs down."

It felt like a deal with the devil and there had to be a catch. "You said it had to appear authentic. Define *authentic*."

Liam sat back in his seat and crossed his leg over his knee. "No one is going to follow us into the bedroom, Francesca, and I won't make you do anything that you don't want to do. But everything we can do to convince people we are a couple in love would be helpful."

She shook her head and looked down at her lap. This was all so sudden. The idea of being Liam's fiancée, even if just temporarily, wasn't so bad. She'd be lying to herself if she said she hadn't thought about their time in the elevator as she lay alone in bed each night. But his fiancée? Publicly? What would she tell her family? She couldn't tell them the truth. And her friends? She would have to lie to everyone she knew.

But the alternative was unthinkable. She cared too much about ANS and its employees to let the company fall into Ron Wheeler's hands. Going along with Liam's plan would protect the company and earn her the charity gala she wanted so badly. When the arrangement was no longer necessary, her friends and family would just have to believe that things had soured between them and they broke it off. She could live with that. It wasn't as though they were actually going to get married.

She looked up in time to see Liam slide off the couch to his knees and crawl across the floor until he was kneeling at her feet. He looked so handsome in his navy suit, his dark, beautiful blue eyes gazing into her own. He took her hands into his, his thumb gently stroking her skin. With him touching her like that, she'd probably agree to anything.

"Francesca Orr," he said with a bright, charming smile. "I know I'm just the humble son of a pig farmer, but would you do me the honor of being my temporary fiancée?"

Four

Liam watched Francesca's terrified expression, waiting for her answer. He could see the battle raging in her head. He understood. He was having to make sacrifices for the company and what he wanted, too. He felt guilty for dragging her into his mess, but she really was the perfect choice. If she could walk away from that elevator like nothing happened, she could do the same with this engagement. In the end, they could go their separate ways, both having gotten what they wanted.

Her dark brown eyes focused on him for a moment, then strayed off to his shoulder. Her expression of worry softened then, her jaw dropping with surprise.

Confused, Liam turned to look at his shoulder. Perched there on the navy fabric was a lone ladybug. He'd opened the window of his office this morning when he was suffocating from the pressure and needed some fresh air. The tiny insect must've been a stowaway.

Francesca untangled her hands from his and reached out to scoop the ladybug from his shoulder. She got up from her seat and walked over to the window. Opening it wide, she held her palm out to the sun and watched the bug fly out into the garden outside the network offices.

She stood looking out the window for several minutes. Liam was still on his knees, wondering what the hell had just happened, when he heard her speak.

"Yes, I will be your temporary fiancée."

He leaped to his feet and closed the gap between them in three long strides. "Really?"

She turned to him, her face calm and resolute. She looked really beautiful in that moment. Serene. The dark green of her suit looked almost jewel-like against the tan of her skin. It made him want to reach out and remove the pins from her hair until it fell loose around her shoulders. He liked it better that way.

"Yes," she said. "It's the right answer for everyone."

Liam was elated by her response yet confused about what had changed. There had been a moment when he had been absolutely certain she was going to tell him no. He'd already been mentally putting together a contingency plan. He was going to offer her obscene amounts of cash. And if that didn't work, he was going to find out if Jessica, his secretary, was married. "What helped you decide?"

"The ladybug. They're an omen of good luck. Having one land on you means you are a blessed soul. It was a sign that I should accept your proposal."

Liam knew better than to question her superstitions as long as they ruled in his favor. "Well, remind me to thank the next ladybug I come across."

Francesca chuckled. "I think you owe the entomology department at Georgetown a nice check."

"And I will get right on that. After I take my fiancée to lunch and let her pick out her engagement ring."

Her head snapped up to look at him. "So soon?"

"Yes," he insisted. "The sooner my aunt hears about this, the better. That means ring shopping, an announcement in the paper here and in New York and public sightings of the happy new couple. I intend to update my relationship status on Facebook before the day is out."

Her eyes widened with every item on his list. She wasn't sold on this arrangement, ladybug or no. "Before it hits the papers, I need to make a few calls. I don't want my family to find out from someone else. This is going to come out of the blue."

Liam nodded. That was understandable. He had a few calls of his own to make. First, to his mother and younger sister, both living in Manhattan.

His family was miserable at keeping in touch, but this was big enough news to reach out to them. They had always been like ships passing in the night, waving to one another as they went along their merry way. His parents were very outgoing and traveled quite a bit his whole life. But that changed after his father died three years ago when his car hit black ice on the highway coming home from a late business meeting. Since then, his mother had kept to her place in Manhattan, nearly becoming a recluse. He just assumed she was bad about calling until she stopped altogether—then he knew something was really wrong. His sister had moved in with her to keep an eye on the situation, but it hadn't helped much.

When he spoke with them, it was because he was

the one to reach out. Maybe the news of the engagement would be exciting for her. He felt bad lying to his mother about something like that, but if it got her up and out of the apartment, he didn't care.

Liam had often wondered, even more so in the past week, how things would be different if his father hadn't been in that accident. Where would everyone be now? Perhaps Aunt Beatrice would've wanted to hand the family to him instead, and Liam wouldn't be in this mess.

That was a pointless fantasy, but it reminded him of his next call. Once he was done with his mother, he had to inform Aunt Beatrice of the "happy" news. He didn't have many people to tell, but he could see by the expression on Francesca's face that she had the opposite problem. She must have a large, close family. An out-of-the-blue engagement would send up a hue and cry of mass proportions.

"I know this is a big deal. And not at all what you were expecting when you walked in here today. But it's all going to work out." He moved closer to her and put his arms gently around her waist. She reluctantly eased into his embrace, placing her hands on his lapels and looking up into his eyes. "I promise."

The dark eyes watching him were not so certain. He needed to reassure her. To make her feel more at ease with their new situation and prove they were compatible enough to pull this off. He only knew of one way to comfort a woman. He slowly lowered his lips to hers, giving her time to pull away if she needed to. She didn't. She met his lips with her own, her body leaning into his.

The kiss wasn't like the one in the elevator. They had come together then in a passionate and desperate rush. Two people in a stressful situation looking for any way to deal with their nervous tension. This kiss was soft, gentle and reassuring. They were feeling their way around each other. Her lips were silky against his, the taste of her like cinnamon and coffee. She made a soft sound of pleasure that sent a warm heat running through his veins. It reminded him of the cries she'd made beneath him that first day. It beckoned him to explore further, but he didn't dare push this moment too far. At this point, she could change her mind and no one would know the difference.

He couldn't risk running her off. They both needed this fake engagement to work. And if it did, he would eventually have his chance to touch her again. The thought gave him the strength to pull away.

Francesca rocked back onto her heels, her cheeks flushed and her eyes a little misty. She took a deep breath to collect herself and took a full step back from him. "Well," she said with a nervous laugh, "that authenticity thing shouldn't be an issue."

Liam smiled. "Not at all. Are you hungry?"

She straightened her suit coat and shrugged. "A little."

"Okay. You're not starving, so let's go ring shopping first. Then if we run into anyone at lunch, we'll have it and can share the news like a happy couple would."

"I need to get my purse from my office before we leave. I'll meet you at…" Her voice trailed off.

"The elevator?" he said with a grin.

She blushed. "Yes, I'll meet you at the elevator."

They strolled out of Pampillonia Fine Jewelry two hours later and, frankly, Francesca was exhausted. Who knew jewelry shopping could be so tiring? She almost wished that Liam had just popped the question with ring in hand like most men would and saved her the trouble of choosing.

Instead, they had spent the past couple of hours quibbling. She was worried that Liam was spending too much, especially considering it was a fake engagement. Liam insisted that Francesca needed to choose a ring large enough for people to see from a distance. Fake or not, the engagement needed to be splashy so people like his aunt would take notice.

They finally came to a compromise when she got tired of arguing and just let herself choose the ring she'd want if this were a real relationship and she had to wear the ring every day for the rest of her life. By the time they left, she was certain there was no doubt in the jeweler's mind that they were a real couple getting a head start on a lifetime of fussing at one another.

When it was all over, Francesca was the proud owner of a two-carat emerald-cut diamond solitaire framed with micro-pavé set diamonds in a platinum split band with diamond scrollwork. It was a stunning ring, and as they walked to the restaurant where they had lunch reservations, she almost couldn't believe it was on her hand. The weight of it pulling on her finger kept prompting her to lift her hand to look at it.

Francesca had dreamed her whole life of the day a man would give her a ring like this. The ring was right. But everything else was so wrong. Her life had taken a truly surreal turn since she had woken up this morning.

"Are you hungry now?" he asked as they approached the bistro with outdoor seating. It was perfect for an early May lunch; luckily, the Manhattan heat wave had not affected the D.C. area. It was pleasant and sunny in the high seventies with a breeze.

She still wasn't really hungry. Her stomach hadn't come to terms with the day's events. But she needed to eat or her blood sugar would get low and she'd spend the afternoon eating cookies out of the network vending machines. "I could eat. I think."

They followed the hostess, who took them to a shaded table for two on the patio. As nice as it was outside, she'd secretly hoped to get a table indoors. The street was so busy with foot traffic that she was certain to see someone she knew. Of course, she could just as easily run into someone inside. Between her and Liam, they knew a lot of people in this town. Francesca wasn't sure she was ready to play the gushing new fiancée for them yet.

Liam pulled her chair out for her and saw that she was comfortably seated before taking his own seat.

"I'm starving," he said, picking up the menu.

Francesca had to admit she wasn't surprised. Liam seemed to be constantly hungry when she was around him. "No breakfast?"

He shook his head. "I really haven't eaten much since I had dinner at my aunt's house. Killed my appetite, you know?"

"I do," she agreed. Nothing on the menu looked appealing, so she settled on a spinach salad with chicken. At the very least she was eating something figure-friendly.

She had a wedding dress to fit into, after all.

The thought crept into her brain, startling her upright in her seat. Where had that come from?

"Are you okay?" Liam asked.

"Yes," she said dismissively. "I just remembered something I need to do when we get back to the office."

Liam nodded and looked back at the menu. Francesca shook her head and closed her eyes. There would be no wedding and no wedding dress. It didn't matter how real their kisses seemed or how quickly her whole body responded to Liam's touch. It didn't matter that she had a luxury condo's worth of diamonds on her hand. Because she wasn't really engaged. She was Liam's fake fiancée. It was a business arrangement, nothing more, despite what she had to tell her friends and family.

The waiter took their orders and left with their menus. Feeling awkward, Francesca sipped her water and eyeballed her ring. She didn't know what to say to her new fiancé.

"Now that all the engagement stuff is arranged, I wanted to talk to you about something else, too."

She looked up at him with a sense of dread pooling in her stomach. She couldn't take any more surprises today. "No, Liam, I will not have your baby to make your aunt happy."

He laughed, shaking his head. "No babies, I promise. This is strictly work-related. I've been kicking around this idea for a few days, but the nonsense with my aunt sidetracked me. I wanted to ask…you're friends with Ariella Winthrop, aren't you?"

Francesca sighed. Her friend Ariella had been the media equivalent of the Holy Grail since the inaugural ball in January where it was revealed that the successful events planner was the newly elected president's long-lost daughter. How many journalists and garden-variety busybodies had asked Francesca about her friend since the scandal hit? More than she could count. Yes, they were friends. They had been for several years. That didn't mean she had anything useful to share with the press, even if she would tell—and she wouldn't. Ariella was adopted. She hadn't even known who her birth father was for sure until the DNA test results came back a little more than a month ago.

"I am," she said, her tone cautious.

"I was wondering if you could talk to her for me. I've got an idea that I think she might be interested in, but I wanted to run it by you first. I know ANS reporters and old management were responsible for the whole mess with President Morrow and her. I was hoping we could make a sort of goodwill gesture to them both."

"A fruit basket?" she suggested.

"A televised reunion show with Ariella and the president."

Francesca groaned aloud. That was a horrible idea. "Go with the fruit basket. Really."

Liam held up his hand. "Hear me out. I know lots of rumors and misinformation are swirling around on the other networks, especially because everyone involved isn't talking to the press. ANS obviously has stayed out of the story after everything that happened. I want to offer them the opportunity to publically set the record straight. Give them a chance to meet and clear the air without any spin or dramatic angles."

"That has 'exploitive' written all over it."

"And that is why I would give you total control over the show. You're her friend and she trusts you. You could work directly with the White House press secretary and see to it that no one is even remotely uncomfortable. No other network will offer them an opportunity like this, I guarantee it."

Francesca couldn't hold back her frown. She didn't like the sound of this at all. If it went badly and ANS ended up with mud on its face, there would be no coming back from it and Ariella might never forgive her. "I don't know, Liam."

"This is a win-win for everyone involved. Ariella and the president get to tell their story, their way. ANS will get the exclusive on their interview and it will help us make amends for the hacking scandal. It can't go wrong. You'll see to it that it doesn't turn into a circus. It's perfect."

Perfect for ratings. But Francesca wasn't so sure television was the right environment for her friend to be reunited with her famous birth father. That was an important moment for them both. A private moment. Ariella hadn't spoken much to her about the situation, but Francesca knew it was hard for her friend.

"Just promise me you'll ask her. If she doesn't want to do it, I'll let the whole idea drop."

The waiter came with their lunches, placing them on the table and briefly interrupting their conversation.

"I'll talk to her," Francesca agreed after he left. "But I can't promise anything. She made one short statement to the press, but aside from that, she's turned down every interview request she's received."

"That's all I ask. Thank you."

Francesca speared a piece of chicken and spinach with her fork. "At last, the dirty truth comes out. You're just marrying me for my political connections."

"A completely unfounded accusation," he said with a wicked grin. "I'm marrying you for that slammin' body."

Francesca met his gaze, expecting to see the light of humor there, but instead she found a heat of appreciation for what he saw. It was the same way he'd looked at her in that elevator when she'd had only a camisole to cover her. Today, she was deliberately covered head to toe, but it didn't matter. Liam apparently had an excellent memory.

A warmth washed over her, making her squirm uncomfortably in her seat with her own memories of that day. She had wanted him so badly in that moment, and if she was honest with herself, she still did. Things were just so complicated. Would giving into her desire for him be better or worse now that they were "engaged"?

She wished she hadn't opted for the silk scarf around her neck. It was strangling her now. Her left hand flew to her throat and started nervously tugging at the fabric. "I...well, I uh..."

A voice called to them from the sidewalk, interrupting her incoherent response. "Francesca, what is that I see on your hand?"

So much for not running into anyone she knew. On the other side of the wrought-iron railing that separated the bistro seating from the sidewalk was her friend Scarlet Anders. The willowy redhead owned a party planning company with Ariella that specialized in weddings and receptions. She could smell a new diamond from a mile away.

"Scarlet!" she said, pasting a smile on her face and hoping Scarlet didn't see through it. "How are you feeling?" she asked to distract her from the ring. Her friend had suffered a head injury earlier in the year and had temporarily lost her memory. It was a reasonable question that might buy Francesca a few minutes to get their engagement story straight.

Scarlet wrinkled her nose. "I'm fine, really. The doctors say there's not a single, lingering side effect from my accident. Now stop fussing over me, you staller, and let me see that hand."

Reluctantly, Francesca held out her left hand, letting the flawless diamond sparkle in the sunlight. Scarlet looked at the ring, then at Liam and back at her. "You are engaged to Liam Crowe. *Liam Crowe.* You know, when Daniel proposed to me, I told you and Ariella almost the moment it happened."

That was true, Francesca thought guiltily. And under any other circumstances, she would've done the same thing. This just didn't feel like a real engagement. Because it wasn't. "It just happened," she insisted, grinning widely with feigned excitement at her groom to be. "We just picked out the ring before lunch."

Scarlet smiled. "It's beautiful. You two are so sneaky. I didn't even know you guys were dating. How did this happen?"

"We, uh…" Francesca realized she had no clue what to say. They hadn't really gotten around to deciding what they're relationship history was. Certainly the truth wouldn't do, or people would think they were crazy. "Actually, um…"

"We started seeing each other a while back when I first started looking to buy ANS," Liam interjected. "With everything going on, we wanted to keep it quiet for a while. But after being trapped in that elevator with Francesca, I knew I had to spend the rest of my life with her."

Francesca swallowed her snort of contempt as Scarlet sighed with romantic glee. "That is so sweet. I can't believe you didn't tell *me,* of all people, but you two are just adorable together. So when is your engagement party? You have to let Ariella and I do it for you."

"No," Francesca insisted. "You've been so busy with Cara and Max's wedding and now, planning your own big day." The former newscaster and the public relations specialist for the White House press secretary had married at the end of March. Scarlet's beau, Daniel, had proposed to her at the wedding reception. "Don't worry about us. We're probably not going to—"

"Nonsense," Scarlet said. "I insist. I'm on my way back to the office right now. I'll tell Ariella the good news and we'll get right to work on it. When would you like to have it?"

"Soon," Liam interjected, cutting off another of Francesca's protests. "This weekend, if at all possible. We can't wait to share our excitement with all our friends and family."

Scarlet's eyes widened, but she quickly recovered with a pert nod. She was used to dealing with the unreasonable demands of powerful D.C. couples. "I'm sure we can make that happen. Short notice makes it harder to find a venue, but I've got a couple of people who owe me some favors. For you, I'm thinking an afternoon garden party. Something outdoors. Light nibbles, champagne punch. Maybe a gelato bar. How does that sound?"

Francesca choked down a sip of her water. "That sounds beautiful." And it did. It was just what she would've chosen for her engagement party. Her friend knew her well. She just wished they weren't wasting their efforts on an engagement that wouldn't lead to a loving marriage.

Scarlet was bursting with excitement. Francesca could see the lists being made in her head. Flowers, caterers, maybe even a string quartet to serenade the guests. Scarlet did everything with a stylish flair that was famous in elite D.C. society. "I will give you a call tomorrow and work out some details."

"Just tell me where to send the check." Liam smiled.

"Absolutely," Scarlet said. "Talk to you soon." She swung her bag over her shoulder and disappeared down the sidewalk with an excited pep in her step. She really did live for this stuff.

Francesca wished she could work up as much enthusiasm. And she needed to if they were going to pull this off. Because this was really happening. Really, *really* happening.

What on earth had she done?

Five

Liam hadn't planned on their having dinner that night, but seeing Francesca with Scarlet had made it absolutely necessary. They really knew nothing about each other. They had no relationship backstory. Once the news of their engagement got out, people would start asking questions and they needed to get their stories straight.

Usually this kind of discussion happened before the engagement, but they were working on a steep learning curve, here. After the waiter took their orders, Liam settled back into his seat and looked at his fiancée. He knew she was beautiful, feisty, caring and exciting. He knew that he desired her more than any other woman he'd ever known. And yet, he knew almost nothing about who she was and where she'd come from. That was a problem.

"So, Francesca, tell me all about yourself. I need to know everything to play this part properly and convince everyone we're really together."

"I feel like I'm trying to get a green card or something." She took a sip of wine as she tried to determine where best to start. "I grew up in Beverly Hills. My father is a Hollywood movie producer, as you know. He met my mother on a film set in Sicily and they eloped within a month of meeting."

"So they have no room to complain about our quick engagement?"

"Not at all." She smiled. "Although that didn't stop my father from giving me an earful on the phone this afternoon. I had to assure him that we would have an extended engagement to keep him from hopping a jet over here and having a chat with you."

"The longest engagement in history," Liam quipped.

"My parents are my model for what a marriage should be. It's what I've always hoped to have one day when I get married."

Liam took note. Francesca wanted the real deal for herself, just like her parents. This was probably not what she thought her engagement would be like. He felt bad about that. But she still had her chance to have the fairy tale with the next guy. This was just a temporary arrangement.

"I have a younger sister, Therése," she continued, "who lives in San Francisco. She's a fashion photographer. I moved to D.C. after graduation to go to Georgetown."

"I went to Georgetown, too. Maybe we were there at the same time." Francesca recited the years and, thankfully, they partially overlapped with his own. He'd graduated two years before she had. "That's excellent," he said. "I think if we tell people that we dated back in college and then met up again this year, it will make the speed of this relationship more palatable. What did you study?"

"I got a degree in communications with a minor in political science. I'd originally intended to become a political news commentator."

"It's a shame you didn't. I would've loved to have you on my big screen every night. It's funny we didn't meet until now. I had a minor in communications. I'm surprised we didn't have a class together."

Francesca shrugged. "Maybe we did. A lot of those classes were pretty large."

Liam shook his head. There was no way he could've been in the same room with Francesca and not have seen her. Even in one of those freshman courses they held in the huge auditoriums. His cocky, frat boy self would've picked up on those curves and asked her out in a heartbeat. "I would've noticed you. I'm certain of that."

Francesca blushed and started fidgeting with the gold pendant around her neck that looked like some kind of horn. For dinner, she'd changed into a burgundy wrap dress with a low V-cut neckline and an abundance of cleavage. He'd noticed the necklace earlier, but every time he thought to ask about it, he'd been mentally side-tracked by the sight of her breasts.

"So what's that necklace about? You seem to have it on whenever I've seen you."

She looked down at it before holding it out a little for him to see it better. "It's a *corno portafortuna*. My *nonna* gave it to me. It's Italian tradition to wear one to ward off the evil eye. You never know when someone might curse you, especially in this town. I wear it for good luck."

The way the horn rested right in the valley of her

breasts was certainly lucky for him. It gave him an excuse to look at the firm globes of flesh he could still feel in his hands and pretend he was admiring her jewelry. "In the elevator you mentioned spending summers in Italy with your grandmother."

"Yes, I spent every summer in Sicily from when I was about five until I graduated from high school. My mother would travel with me when I was younger, but once I reached junior high, I got to fly alone. My mother said it was important for me to keep in touch with my culture. My *nonna* would teach me authentic Italian recipes and tell me stories about our family. My sister and I both learned a good bit of Italian over the years. I don't remember as much as I should now."

"You know all the dirty words," Liam noted.

"Of course." She laughed. "You always remember the words and phrases that you shouldn't know."

"You picked up all your superstitions there too?"

"Yes. Italians are a very superstitious people. My *nonna* told me she only taught me a few of them. It's amazing. My mother never really cared for all that, but it was something special I shared with *Nonna*. She died last year, but the superstitions keep her alive in my mind."

"Thank goodness she told you the one about ladybugs or I might be in big trouble right now. Any bad luck omens I should keep an eye out for?"

"Hmm…" Francesca said thoughtfully. "There are the ones most people know about—broken mirrors and such. Never leave your hat on the bed. Never set a loaf of bread upside down on the table. Birds or feathers in the home are bad luck. If you spill salt, you have to toss some over your shoulder. The most unlucky number is seventeen. Never marry on a Friday. There are a million of these."

"Wow," Liam said. "I'm probably doomed. I've been running around for years, cursed, and never knew it."

Francesca smiled, easing back in her seat to let the waiter place their food on the table. "I think you've done pretty well for yourself without it."

That was true. He'd taken the seed money from his father and built quite a name for himself in broadcast media. He was only twenty-eight. Who knew what else he could accomplish with most of his career still ahead of him? Closing the deal with his aunt and taking full control of ANS could be the launching pad to bigger, better things. Especially if the two-billion-dollar inheritance came through.

His brain couldn't even comprehend having that much money. He tried not to even think about it. He could only focus on one thing at a time and right now, it was pulling off this engagement and buying ANS outright. He'd put his financial manager on the task before he even sat down to look for a bride. Hopefully, it would all work out. But even his worries were hard to concentrate on with such a beautiful woman sitting across the table from him.

"How about some more random trivia about you? Likes and dislikes," Liam said.

"My favorite color is red. I adore dark chocolate. I'm allergic to cats. I can cook, but I don't. I hate carrots and yellow squash. My middle name is Irish and impossible to spell or pronounce properly."

Liam had to ask. "Wait, what is it?"

"My middle name? It's pronounced *kwee-vuh*, which is Gaelic for *beautiful*. Unfortunately, in En-

glish it's pronounced absolutely nothing like it's written. *C-A-O-I-M-H-E*." She spelled out the name for him
and then said it again. "Try explaining that to the woman
at the DMV."

Liam laughed, not trusting himself to repeat the name
without slaughtering it. "My middle name is Douglas.
Not very exciting or hard to spell."

"I envy you."

"What about your dad's side of the family? You
haven't mentioned much about them."

"My dad isn't that close with his family, which is
silly considering they live in Malibu, only about thirty
miles from Beverly Hills. I only ever saw my grandpar-
ents on holidays and birthdays. I'm much closer with
my mother's side of the family."

"Sounds more like my family. I almost never see
them. Tell me something else about you."

"What else? I never exercise—I hate to sweat. And
I enjoy luxurious bubble baths and long walks on the
beach." She finished with a laugh. "This is turning into
a lame personal ad."

"It's not lame. If I ran across it, I'd be messaging your
in-box in an instant."

"Thanks. But enough about me. What about you?"
Francesca asked. "Your turn to tell me all about Liam
Crowe."

Dinner had been very nice. The conversation flowed
easily and Francesca had to admit she had a good time.
She enjoyed spending time with Liam. Honestly, she
liked him. He was handsome, smart, funny and easy
to talk to. It was nice to hear him talk about his family
and his work. He was so passionate about his career; it

made her understand just how important the success of ANS was to him. A part of her wished she had met him in college. Who knows what would've happened then?

Well, that wasn't true. She knew what would've happened. They would've dated, she would've fallen for him and he would've broken it off at some point, breaking her heart. Liam wasn't much of a long-term guy. They were only engaged now because his aunt had recognized that in him and twisted his arm.

Despite that, he seemed to be taking the whole thing pretty well. She wasn't exactly sure how Liam felt about their forced proximity, but he didn't let it show if he wanted to be someplace else. Actually, he'd been quite complimentary of her, listening to her when she spoke and watching her over his wineglass with appreciative eyes.

Liam pulled up his gray Lexus convertible outside her town house and killed the engine. He turned in his seat to face her, a shy smile curling his lips. He watched her collect her purse and sweater, not speaking but also not making a move to let her out of the car, either.

Their plotting dinner suddenly felt like a date and it made her a little nervous. It was silly considering he'd not only seen her naked, but they were engaged. Technically.

"I had a good time tonight," she said, feeling stupid the moment the words left her lips.

"Me, too. I, uh, wanted to say thank-you again for doing this for me. And, you know, for the company. I feel like I've hijacked your entire life today."

Francesca tried to think about what she was supposed to have done today. She certainly had plans of some kind, but Liam had wiped her memory clean along with her calendar. "I'm sure I didn't have anything important planned and if I did, it will still be around for me to do tomorrow."

"Do you have time on your schedule to have some engagement portraits taken? I wanted a picture to put with the newspaper announcement."

"I think so. Just have Jessica look at my calendar in the morning. Do I need to wear anything in particular or do something special with my hair or makeup?"

Liam watched her, shaking his head. "You're perfect just as you are. I couldn't ask for a more beautiful fiancée."

Francesca blushed. She couldn't help it. To hear him talk, she was the most beautiful woman in the world. It was ridiculous. She was a pretty enough woman but nothing special. He had a knack for making her feel special, though. "You're just sucking up so I don't change my mind."

"Absolutely," he admitted. "But it's easy when it's true. You don't know how much I've thought about you since that afternoon we spent together. And now, spending all day with you, I've been struggling with myself. I've spent the past three hours trying not to kiss you. I'm not sure I can hold out much longer."

Francesca couldn't help the soft gasp of surprise when he spoke so honestly about his desire for her. Before she could think of something intelligent to say, he leaned across her seat and brought his lips to hers.

It wasn't their first kiss. Or even their second, but somehow it felt like it. It lacked the raw heat of their time in the elevator and the reassuring comfort of this morning's kiss. This one felt like the kiss of a blossoming romance. His hand went to the nape of her neck, pulling her closer to him and gently massaging her with his fingertips.

His mouth was demanding but not greedy, coaxing her to open to him and give in to the pleasure he promised. She felt herself being swept up in his touch. It was so easy, just like letting herself flow with the current of a river. It felt natural to let her tongue glide along his, to let her fingers roam through the thick strands of his wavy hair.

His lips left hers, traveling along the line of her jaw to nibble the side of her neck. The sensation of it sent a wave of desire through her whole body. When his hand cupped her breast through the thin microfiber of her dress, she leaned into his touch, moaning softly in his ear.

It wasn't until her eyes peeked open and she saw the giant diamond on her hand that she came to her senses. This relationship was supposed to be for show. One that appeared authentic to friends and family. But as Liam had said, no one would follow them into the bedroom. Somehow, Francesca knew that if she crossed that line, it would be hard for her to keep this relationship in perspective.

Liam was her fiancé, but he would never be her husband. He wasn't in love with her, nor was she in love with him. Sex would just blur the lines.

Francesca gently pushed at Liam's shoulders. He pulled away, watching her with eyes hooded with desire. His breath was ragged. That was one hell of a kiss. And it was begging for one hell of a night together. She could tell that he intended to come inside. A nice dinner, a bottle of wine, good conversation, a dynamic kiss... now she was supposed to invite him in for coffee and take off her dress. That was all too much too soon, no matter how badly she might want him.

Francesca reached for the door handle. "Good night, Liam."

"Wait," he said with a frown as he reached out to her. "Good night?"

She nodded, clutching her purse to her chest as a subpar barrier between them. "It's been a long day filled with a lot of excitement. You went from my boss to my fiancé just a few short hours ago. I think adding 'lover' to the list tonight is a bad idea."

Liam sighed but didn't try to argue with her. Instead, he opened his car door and came around to help her out. He escorted her to her doorstep.

Francesca paused, clutching her keys in her hand. Right or wrong, she couldn't help leaning into him and placing a quick but firm kiss on his lips.

"I'll see you tomorrow at the office."

"Yes, I'm engaged." Liam sat back in his office chair and looked at the newly framed photograph of Francesca and himself that sat on the corner of his desk. They'd had it taken for the newspaper announcement, and Liam couldn't help sending a copy to the Queen Bee herself. When the phone rang the next afternoon, he wasn't surprised.

"Congratulations to you both. I didn't expect you to move so quickly on my offer," she noted, her tone pointed. She obviously thought that Liam was trying to pull one over on her somehow. She missed nothing. "I did give you a year, not a week, to get engaged."

"Well," Liam began, "I told you I had been seeing someone. You helped me realize that I needed to move forward in my relationship. Francesca and I are perfect for each other—I was just hesitant to take that last step. Thank you for the encouragement." He hoped he'd managed to work out the bitterness from his voice after practicing this speech several times before her call.

"That is wonderful, Liam. The picture of the two of you is lovely. I've sent Henry to have it framed for the mantle. She's quite the striking young lady. Where did you meet her?"

She was fishing for details. Thank goodness they'd worked all this out at dinner. "We met the first time in college through mutual friends and dated for a while." He recalled their fabricated past, linking it together with what he'd told Scarlet at lunch. "When I started looking into buying ANS, we ran into each other at a media event. She works there doing community outreach programs and we started seeing each other again."

Liam had no doubt that his aunt was taking notes and would have someone look into the fact that they had both attended Georgetown at the same time. "What a lovely coincidence that you two would find each other again. It must be meant to be."

"I think so."

"I hope both of you will be very happy together. I can't wait to meet her. In fact, I'm coming to D.C. later this month to speak to Congress. I'd love for the three of us to have dinner and celebrate while I'm there."

Liam frowned at the phone, glad for the miles between them and the lagging technology of camera phones that prevented her from seeing his pinched expression. He'd never known his aunt to have any political involvement before beyond writing checks. If she was coming to D.C., it was to check on him. She didn't trust

Liam a bit and rightfully so. They would have to perfect their lovey-dovey act before she arrived. Frankly, Francesca had been miserable at it when they ran into Scarlet.

It wasn't just the details of their relationship that had tripped her up. Her smile of engaged bliss had looked a little pained. She'd lacked the excited glow. She had had to be asked to show the engagement ring, whereas any other woman would thrust it out at anyone that would look.

Despite her hesitation to embark on a physical relationship the other night after dinner, something had to be done. She needed some real romantic inspiration to draw on because she couldn't fake it. Liam was all too happy to provide it.

He may have told Francesca that he didn't choose her with the intention of seducing her, and that was true. If they did become lovers, it would simply be a pleasant bonus to a potentially unpleasant scenario.

Heaven knew, he wanted Francesca. Every time he closed his eyes he saw her in the elevator. Red panties. Flushed cheeks. Soft, passionate cries of pleasure echoing in the small space. Yes, he didn't need a romantic entanglement complicating this arrangement, but he'd be lying if he said he didn't want to pick up where they'd left off.

Sex wouldn't be a problem as long as they both knew that's all it was. Given the way Francesca had writhed beneath him and walked away like nothing happened, she knew how to play that game. He just had to coax her into taking another spin at the wheel.

Gripping the phone, Liam struggled to remember what his aunt had just said. The mere thought of Francesca's red panties had completely derailed his train of thought. *Dinner.* Aunt Beatrice was coming to town and wanted to have dinner. "Absolutely," he said. "Francesca is very excited to meet you."

"I'm sure she is. I hope you two have a lovely engagement party tonight. I'm going to let you go. I need to call Ron Wheeler and let him know I'm turning down his proposal. For now," she added, making it clear they weren't out of the woods quite yet.

"It was good to speak with you," he said between gritted teeth. "I'll see you soon."

Hanging up the phone, he spun in his chair to look back at the photo of Francesca and him. His aunt made him absolutely crazy, but if this scheme landed that voluptuous, feminine form back in his arms, he just might have to send the Queen Bee a thank-you card.

Six

Francesca was fastening on her last earring when the doorbell rang. Giving herself one final look in the mirror, she was pretty pleased with how her outfit turned out. She'd purchased something new for the engagement party—a pale turquoise dress that was strapless and hit just below the knee. Around the waist was a cream-colored sash with a fuchsia flower for a pop of color. It came with a crocheted cream shrug to keep her shoulders warm when the sun went down.

She'd opted to wear her hair half up, with the front pulled back into a stylish bump and the rest loose in long waves down her back. Wearing her hair back highlighted her face and the sparkling aquamarine jewelry she was wearing at her ears and throat. And, of course, she was wearing the most important piece of her ensemble—her engagement ring.

Satisfied, she went down the stairs to the front door.

She watched Liam waiting patiently through the peephole. He was looking very handsome in a light gray suit, ivory dress shirt and turquoise tie to coordinate with her outfit.

Even though he'd dropped her off the other night after dinner, he hadn't been inside her town house yet. They'd decided he should pick her up and get familiar with her home just in case someone asked questions.

So far, no one had, and it was likely no one would. None of their friends in D.C. were remotely suspicious about their quick engagement. Romance seemed to be in the air this spring. So many of her friends had gotten married or engaged, so they were on trend. It was only Liam's crafty aunt they had to please.

"Hello," she said as she opened the door and gestured for him to come inside. "Come on in. This is my place."

"Very nice," he said, strolling into the living room and admiring his surroundings.

Francesca had always liked her home. She'd bought the small, red-brick town house near the university while she was a student. It was only two bedrooms, but the floor plan was open and the walled courtyard off the living room was the perfect oasis from the world. When she'd first bought it, nearly every room in it was white. She'd painted each room a warm, inviting color and filled them with lush fabrics and comfortable fixtures. That was her biggest update over the years. She loved her place.

She led him into the two-story living room so he could see out into her little garden and to the nicely remodeled kitchen she rarely used. "It's not very big, but it suits me. I love the location—right across from the park."

"You've done a lot with the place," he said. "It looks comfortably lived in. Very much what I'd expect for you. My town house still looks like a showroom model. I never got around to hiring a decorator. Who did yours?"

"I did," Francesca said, her nose wrinkling. "I couldn't let someone else decorate my house. That's too personal."

Liam shrugged. "You've got the eye for it. Maybe while we're engaged, I'll let you decorate mine."

She turned away from him without answering and went in search of her clutch instead. She didn't like the sound of that at all. It wasn't as though she would be moving into his house one day. She didn't need to put her own personal stamp on his space or leave anything behind of her once all this was over. That made things seem more permanent than they were. But she wasn't going to make much of it. They had a long night to get through without her adding more worries to the pile.

"Are you ready?" she asked.

"Absolutely."

Liam followed her out and then escorted her to the curb, where his convertible was waiting for them. Once he merged into traffic, they didn't have far to go. Scarlet and Ariella had secured a location at one of the large historical mansions in Georgetown. The two-hundred-year-old estate had acres of gardens with fountains and an overabundance of spring flowers this time of year. It was the perfect location for a sunny, happy engagement party.

As they pulled onto the property, the valet opened the doors, pointed them to the garden entrance and took the car around back to park it with the others.

Standing on the lawn, facing her engagement celebration, Francesca was more nervous than she cared to admit. Her knees were nearly shaking. She'd done okay enduring the excited hugs and fielding questions from her friends and coworkers, one by one. But this was almost everyone she knew at one time. It made her wonder if she could pull this off. An engagement party. *Her* engagement party.

Liam sensed her hesitation and approached her. Putting his hands on the back of her upper arms, he stroked her gently, reassuringly. "Everything will be fine. You look beautiful. I'm sure Scarlet and Ariella did a great job with all the arrangements. There's no need to be nervous."

"I know," she said with a shake of her head. She looked down toward the grass, but Liam's finger caught her chin and turned her face up to him.

"You can do this. I know it. But I have to say you are missing something."

Her eyes widened in panic. What had she forgotten? Ring? Check. Lipstick? Check. Overwhelming sense of paranoia? Check. "What did I forget?"

"You don't have the rosy blush of a young woman in love. But I do believe I can fix that." Liam leaned in and pressed his lips to hers.

As much as she had tried to deny her attraction to Liam, her body always gave her away. The heat of his touch immediately moved through her veins and she could feel the tingling of the kiss from the top of her head to the tips of her toes. She suddenly felt flush under her dainty sweater. Her knees were still shaking, although for different reasons than before. She gripped at his lapels to keep steady and pull him closer to her.

Liam's kisses were dangerous. She should've learned

that the very first day. A girl could get lost in one if she wasn't careful. And right now, it seemed like the perfect escape from everything else. Couldn't they just stay in each other's arms here on the front lawn? That seemed like the kind of thing a new couple might do, right?

When Liam finally pulled away, he held her close to keep her from swaying. She felt a definite heat in her cheeks as she looked up at him. "No lipstick on you this time," she noted.

"I was being more cautious today. But it worked— you officially have the bridal glow. Let's get in there before it wears off."

He looped her arm through his and escorted her down the stone pathway that led into the garden reception.

At first the party was a blur. There were easily a hundred and fifty people there, which was impressive on such short notice. Someone announced their arrival, and a rush of people came over to hug and congratulate them. There were pictures and toasts to the happy new couple. Francesca worried it would be hard to keep up the act, but after a little practice and a little champagne, showing people her ring and gushing about how beautiful the party was became easier and easier.

It wasn't long before Francesca was able to slip away from Liam and the crowds to get herself a drink and admire her friends' party-planning handiwork. Scarlet and Ariella really did an excellent job. The garden itself was beautiful, but she could spot the touches they'd added, like white paper lanterns in the trees and a gauzy fabric and flower arch behind the string quartet. The layout of the food and seating areas generated the perfect traffic pattern through the space. It was those details that made what her friends did special. Hassle-free events were their forte.

She picked up a glass and filled it at the four-foot-high silver punch fountain. Just as the lifted the frothy pink drink to her lips, she heard a woman's voice from behind her.

"That's got champagne in it, you know."

Francesca turned to find Ariella with a silver tray of pastel petit fours in her hands. "Am I not allowed to have champagne at my own engagement party?"

Her friend smiled and passed the tray off to one of the catering staff. "That depends on why you and Liam Crowe are in such a rush to get married."

"I am not pregnant," Francesca said with a pout. She should've known that rumor would be one of the first to start circulating. They liked nothing better than juicy gossip in these circles and they weren't above making some up if it was in short supply. She swallowed the whole glass of punch just to prove the rumor wrong.

"Good." Ariella refilled Francesca's glass and filled one of her own, then gestured over to a few chairs under a wisteria tree dripping with purple flowers. "So, just between you and me, what's going on?" she asked once they were seated.

Francesca knew her friend would grill her, although not in the same way that Aunt Beatrice probably would. She just wanted the details so she could understand and be happy for her. Or concerned, depending on if she thought she was being stupid or hasty. That's what good girlfriends did. They kept your head on straight. "It all happened so quickly, I can hardly tell you. The moment I saw him, it was like the last few years we've been apart never happened. There were fireworks." That wasn't exactly a lie. It was more like armed missiles, but there were explosions nonetheless.

Ariella looked into her eyes, searching her face for a moment. Then, satisfied, she smiled and patted Francesca on the knee. "Then I'm happy for you. I just wish you had told us what was going on."

Francesca wished she could really tell her what was going on. She could use a sounding board, but Liam had been adamant that no one know about their arrangement. No one. That was tough for her, considering how close she was with her friends and family.

"Everyone has been so busy with their own lives. I just decided to keep things quiet until there was something to tell."

"How'd your dad take the news?" Ariella asked.

"Ah." She sighed, "you know Dad. He'll adjust eventually. He's concerned that we're rushing things, and that he had no idea who my groom even was. I had to remind him that he and my mother met and eloped within a month. He didn't want to hear that."

Ariella smiled. "I imagine not."

Hoping to shift the subject, Francesca decided to use the topic of fathers to fulfill her first obligation to Liam. "Can I talk to you about something?"

"Sure," Ariella said. "Anything."

Francesca nodded. "Okay. Now I want you to tell me 'no' the moment you're uncomfortable with the idea, but I told Liam I would ask. Now is as good a time as any."

"He wants an interview?" she said wearily. Francesca could tell the last few months were really wearing on her friend.

"Not exactly. He wants to offer you and President Morrow the opportunity to meet and get your story out there. A televised reunion show. No spin, no intruding interview questions. Just you and your father, however you want to do it. Liam has even said he'd put me in charge of the show to make sure you'd be comfortable with it. I told him that I thought it was—"

"Okay."

Francesca's head shot up and she stared at Ariella. Surely she'd heard that wrong. "What?"

She shrugged. "I said okay. If the president is okay with doing the show, I think it's a great idea. We've gone too long without saying anything publicly, and I think it's starting to hurt both of us in the court of public opinion. Neither of us has done anything wrong, but the silence makes us look like we have something to hide."

"But do you think television is the right place for you to be reunited with your birth father? Won't that be hard for you?"

"Not any harder than anything else that's happened this year. Frankly, I'd be relieved to clear the air so the news networks can find some other story to sniff out. Tell Liam I'm in."

Francesca took another large sip of her champagne punch and sighed. Everyone had lost their minds—she was certain of it. "Okay, great," she said, feigning enthusiasm. "I'll let Liam know."

Liam had to admit that it was an excellent engagement party. One of the better ones he'd been forced to attend over the years. He was exhausted and well-fed, as he should be. If and when he did get married, he intended to keep D.C. Affairs Event Planners in his address book.

It was dusk now. The party was winding down, with

guests making their way out amid glowing paper lanterns and white twinkle lights.

He'd lost track of Francesca a little while earlier as he started talking politics with a few other men. Now, he picked up his champagne glass and went in search of his elusive fiancée. That sounded so odd to say, even just in his head.

He found her sitting alone at a table near one of the cherub fountains.

"Hey, there," he said as he approached. "Thought you'd run off on me."

Francesca smiled wearily and slipped off one of her heels. "I'm not running anywhere right now."

"Are you ready to go?"

"Yes. I think the party is over. And was successful, I might add. I got several people to agree to buying tickets to the Youth in Crisis gala next week."

"You're not supposed to recruit at our engagement party."

She shrugged. "Why not? It's what I do, just like you talk politics all the time with folks." She slipped her shoe back on and stood gingerly. *"Ahi, i miei piedi."*

Liam watched her hobble a few steps and decided the walk to the car would be too far for her. "Stop," he insisted, coming alongside her and sweeping her up into his arms.

"Oh!" she hollered in surprise, causing a few people left at the party to turn and look their way. They immediately smiled at his romantic gesture and waved good-night to them.

Francesca clung to his neck, but not with a death grip. "You didn't have to do this," she said as he walked the path to the front of the house.

"I don't have to do a lot of things, but I do them because I want to. Gray Lexus convertible," he said to the valet, who immediately disappeared to the car lot.

"I think I can manage from here."

"What if I'm doing this for selfish reasons? What if I just like holding you this way?" he asked. And he did. He liked the way she clung to him. The way her rose perfume tickled his nose and reminded him of their time together in the elevator. His body tightened in response to the press of her breasts against his chest and the silk of her bare legs in his arms. He didn't want to put her down until he could lay her on a plush mattress and make love to her the way he'd wanted to for days.

Francesca's only response was a sharp intake of breath as she turned to look into his eyes. She watched his face with intensity, reading his body's reactions through his expression. He saw an acknowledgment in her eyes—something that told him she was feeling the same way. She opened her mouth to say something when the car pulled up beside them.

Liam wanted to know what she was about to say, but instead, she turned away and struggled in his arms. He reluctantly set her down in the grass and went around to his side of the car and got in. The moment had passed and whatever she had to say was left unspoken.

It wasn't until the car pulled up outside her town house that they spoke again. And when they did, it was all at once in a jumble of words.

"Would you like to come in?"

"I had a great time today."

"So did I."

"Yes."

Francesca smiled at the way they'd talked over each

other. "Now that we have that all cleared up, come in
and I'll make us some coffee."

Liam was thrilled to get an invitation inside tonight.
He got out and opened her door, following her up the
brick stairs to her entranceway. He laid a gentle hand at
the small of her back as she unlocked the dead bolt and
he felt her shiver beneath it, despite the warm evening.
She couldn't help responding to his touch, he noted. If
he had anything to say about it, they wouldn't worry too
much about coffee until the morning.

They went inside and he followed her to the kitchen,
where she dropped her purse on the counter and slipped
out of her heels. "So much better," she said with a smile.
"Now, coffee." Francesca turned to the cabinets and
started pulling out what she needed to brew a pot.

While she scooped beans into the machine, Liam
slipped off his coat, draped it on one of the bar stools
and came up behind her. He wrapped his arms around
her waist and pressed the full length of his body against
her. He swept her hair over one shoulder and placed a
warm kiss on the bare skin of her neck.

The metallic coffee scoop dropped to the counter
with a clank as Francesca reached out to brace herself
with both hands. "You don't want coffee?" she asked,
her voice breathy as his mouth continued to move across
her skin. She pressed into him, molding her body against
his.

Liam slipped her sweater down her shoulders. "Coffee would keep me awake. I think I'd like to go to bed."
He pushed the firm heat of his arousal against her back
and let his hands roam over the soft fabric of her dress.
"What about you?" he asked. He knew Francesca had
been in a war between her body and her mind since they

met. She'd practically run from him the other night, yet when he kissed her, he could tell she wanted more.

But tonight, this step had to be her decision. Playing the happy couple would be much easier the next few weeks if he wasn't battling an erection whenever they were together. Sex wasn't required in their arrangement, but damn, being engaged was a really great excuse to indulge.

"No," she said.

Her words caused Liam's hands to freeze in place. *Had she just said no?* Damn. He must've been reading her wrong. Did she really only invite him in for coffee? Maybe she was a better actress than he thought.

Before he could pull away, Francesca turned in his arms to face him and wrapped her arms around his neck. She looked up at him with her large dark eyes, a sly smirk curling her pink lips. "I don't want to go to bed," she explained. "I want you right here."

Liam was all too happy to grant her wish. With a slide of his arm, he knocked her bag to the floor and cleared the countertop bar. He encircled her waist with his hands and lifted her up to sit at the rounded edge of the granite slab. His hands slid up the smooth length of her legs, pushing the hem of her turquoise dress high enough to spread her thighs and allow him to settle between them.

"How's this?" he asked, gripping her rear end and tugging her tight to him.

Francesca smiled and wrapped her legs around his waist. *"Perfetto."*

She leaned in to kiss him, and the floodgates opened. The moment their lips met, everything they'd held back for the past week came rushing forward. Their hands moved frantically over each other, pulling at zippers and buttons until they uncovered skin. Their tongues glided along one another, tasting, tempting and drinking it all in.

Liam couldn't get enough of her. The feel of her skin, the soft groans against his mouth as he touched her. He tried to be gentle as he unzipped her dress and pushed the hem up to her waist, but his patience was coming to its end. Especially when Francesca pulled the dress up over her head and he caught a glimpse of the hot pink lace panties and strapless bra she was wearing.

He took a step back to appreciate the view of her body and give himself a moment to recover. As badly as he wanted her, he wasn't going to rush this. Francesca delicately arched her back, reaching behind her to unfasten the bra and toss it aside. The sight of her full, round breasts was his undoing. His palms ached to cover them.

"Touch me," Francesca whispered, noting his hesitation. "I want you to."

"Are you sure? The other night…"

"That was then. Now I'm ready and I don't want to wait any longer."

He was ready too, but first things first. With his eyes focused on hers, he slipped off his unknotted tie and shrugged out of his shirt. The belt, pants and everything else followed until the only stitch of clothing on the two of them were those pink panties. Stepping back between her thighs, he put a condom on the counter and let his hands glide up her outer thighs to her lace-covered hip. "Are these your favorite pair?" he asked.

Francesca shook her head. He was glad. He was at the point of not caring if they were. He'd order ten pair to replace them tomorrow. His fingers grasped the fabric and gave it a hard tug. There was a loud rip, and the panties gave way as scraps in his hands.

At last. Her beautiful nude body was on full display in front of him. This time there was no power restoration to interrupt them, no reason for them to hold back.

Liam placed one forearm across the small of her back and used the other to press down on her chest until she was lying across the breakfast bar. He leaned over her and his lips joined both hands as they made their way over her breasts and down her stomach. His mouth left a searing trail down her belly, pausing at her hip bone as one hand sought out the moist heat between her thighs.

Francesca gasped and squirmed against him. Her back arched off the counter, her hands clawing futilely at the cold stone beneath her. She was ready for him, and as much as he wanted to take his time, he had to have her now. They had all night to savor one another.

Slipping on the condom, Liam gripped her hips and entered her in one, quick movement. Sinking into her hot, welcoming body was a pleasure he'd rarely experienced before. A bolt of sensation, like lightning, shot down his spine and exploded down his arms and legs, making his fingertips tingle where he touched her. He gritted his teeth, balancing on the edge of control as he eased out, then buried deep inside her again.

Francesca pushed herself up, wrapping her legs around his waist and her arms around his neck. Pressing her bare breasts against his chest, she whispered, "Take me," into his ear, flicking the lobe with her tongue.

Gripping at her back and pulling her so close to the edge she might fall without his hold, he did as he was told. He filled her again and again, losing himself in her until she cried out with pleasure and his legs began to shake. It was only then that he let go. Moving quickly, he gave in to the sensation of her body wrapped around his own and flowed into her with a deep growl of long-awaited satisfaction.

Seven

Francesca rolled over and snuggled into her blanket, opening her eyes only when a weight kept the covers from moving the way she wanted. The sunlight was streaming in through her bedroom window, illuminating the wide, bare back of Liam beside her.

What had she done?

She'd had a night of fantastic, passionate sex with her fake fiancé—that's what she'd done. Giving up on the blanket, she moved slowly onto her back, hoping not to wake him. She wasn't quite ready to face the morning after with the man she wasn't going to marry.

She glanced under the sheet at her nude body and cursed that she didn't think to slip into *something* once it was over. Bringing her hand up to her head, she swallowed a groan. This situation was complicated enough. Feigning an engagement wasn't for the faint of heart. Had she really added sex to the mix? On her kitchen counter, of all places? It was a good thing she didn't cook.

Now things were going to go from complicated to downright tricky. Liam was her boss. Her pretend fiancé. She had no business sleeping with either, much less both. And yet she was undeniably attracted to him. She couldn't help it.

He was handsome, wealthy, powerful.... He had a wicked sense of humor and a boyish smile that made her heart melt a little when he looked at her. And most important, he cared about his employees. They'd gotten off on the wrong foot over the budget, but that issue aside, she respected him for what he was doing. She respected him even more for the lengths he was willing to go to protect the network.

Liam was just the kind of man she could fall for— and hard. The only problem was that he wasn't the kind of man that would feel the same about her.

Francesca took relationships seriously. She wasn't one for flings, despite losing her sense in the elevator, and she certainly didn't make a habit of sleeping with men when she didn't see any relationship potential.

She wanted a marriage like her parents had. Victor and Donatella Orr had been married thirty years. When she was growing up, they'd set a good example of what a relationship should be. They argued, but they compromised and never held grudges. They were affectionate and understanding. They allowed each other their space, yet were always certain to spend quality time together as a family and as a couple.

At twenty-seven, Francesca had yet to run across a man she could have that kind of relationship with. Some were too clingy; others were too self-absorbed. Some were quick-tempered or arrogant. Then there were the kind like Liam—work-focused dreamers who looked at marriage as something they'd do later. They indulged in a variety of women, never taking anything but their jobs seriously. They were the kind of men who would wake up at fifty and realize they had missed out on their chance for a family unless they could find a willing younger woman with a fondness for expensive gifts.

Despite being engaged to Liam, he was the last man on Earth she would marry. And that's why she knew sleeping with him was a mistake. As a passionate woman, she put her heart in everything she did. But she couldn't put her heart into this. She couldn't look at her engagement ring and their portrait together and imagine it was anything more than a well-crafted fantasy.

Francesca turned to look at Liam as he grumbled in his sleep and rolled onto his back. The blankets fell across his torso, his hard, muscular chest exposed to the early-morning sunlight. She wanted to run her fingertip along the ridges of his muscles and bury her hands in the patch of dark hair across his chest. She wanted to reach under the covers and wake him up in the most pleasant way possible.

This sure didn't feel like a business arrangement.

Turning away, she spied her robe hanging on the knob of her closet door. Easing silently out of bed, she snatched the silk wrap off the handle and slid into it. She gave another glance to Liam, still sleeping, and slipped out of the room.

Downstairs, she found she could breathe a little easier. At least until she saw the scraps of her pink underwear on the kitchen floor. She snatched them off the tile and dumped them in the trash, and then went around gathering other bits of their clothing. She tossed the pile onto her sofa and went to the front door to pick up the paper. Laying it onto the kitchen table, she decided to make coffee. The caffeine would help her think so she could sort all this out.

The last few drops were falling into the pot when she heard Liam's shuffling footsteps across her hardwood floors. A moment later, he appeared in the kitchen wearing nothing but the suit pants she'd just gathered up.

"Morning," she said, pouring a cup for both of them.

"You snuck out on me," Liam complained, his voice still a touch low and rough with sleep. He ran his fingers through his messy hair and frowned at her with displeasure.

"I promised you coffee last night," she explained. "I had to come down here and make it so it was ready when you woke up." That sounded much better than saying she'd gotten weirded out and had to leave. "How do you take it?"

"One cream, one sugar," he said, sitting at the small round table in her breakfast nook. He unfolded the paper and started scanning the articles, oblivious to the nerves that had driven her to the kitchen.

Francesca busied herself making their coffee and grabbed a box of pastries from the counter. She set the two mugs and the carton on the table and plucked two napkins from the container in the center of the table. "Breakfast is served."

"Thank you," he said, looking up from the paper. "Our party made the society pages in the Sunday edition." Liam slid the section with their photo across the table to her. "I should clip it out and send it to the Queen Bee."

"I'm sure she hated missing it. My friends throw parties even she couldn't find fault with. Oh—" Francesca said, pausing to take a sip of her hot drink. That had reminded her of the important information she hadn't shared with Liam yet. "I forgot to tell you that Ariella said yes."

Liam looked up from the paper. "Ariella said yes to what?"

"I got a chance to talk to her at the party about the televised reunion show. I can't fathom why, but she's agreed to do it if the president is willing."

Liam's eyes grew wide, and he folded the paper back up as he grinned. "That's excellent. Wow. How could you forget to tell me something like that? We've been together since the party."

Francesca looked at him over her cup with an arched eyebrow. "Yes. We were together *all* night. And highly occupied, if you recall."

Liam grinned. "Indeed, we were. It's just as well because there was nothing I could do about it last night." He picked a pastry out of the box and set it on his napkin, sucking some icing from his thumb. "Well, now you'll need to contact the White House press secretary to see if President Morrow will participate."

"Me?"

"Yes. I told you that you would be in charge of the event. That means the ball is in your court."

"The Youth in Crisis gala is Saturday night. I've got my hands full with that."

"I have every confidence," he said with a meaningful gaze, "that you can handle everything I'm giving you and more. It's likely the ball won't really get rolling on the show until after the gala, and you just need to get White House buy-in. By the time everything is in place, the show will probably air in June."

Francesca could handle June. "I'll call over there Monday morning," she agreed. Part of her hoped the president and his staff would see what a bad idea this was. She knew it would mean good ratings, and maybe a boost in public opinion for ANS, but it felt wrong. If she had been adopted, she didn't think she'd want those first reunion moments captured for the world to see.

"Sounds great." Liam set aside the folded paper and reached his hand across the table to rest on hers. "Thank you for asking her. I know you felt uncomfortable about it."

"It's Ariella's decision to make, not mine. If she thinks it's the right choice, far be it for me to tell her no. It's her life."

"I think you'll do a great job running the show. I know it isn't something you've handled at the network before, but you'll do a bang-up job. Everything has been so crazy since I started at ANS, but I really believe that we can bring this network back. If all goes well, I'll get absolute control of the stock and we can end the fake engagement. The exclusive with the president and his daughter will earn us Brownie points and market share for our time slot. I know I can rebuild this network— with your help. So thank you for everything you've done so far."

"Don't thank me yet," she said, fidgeting with her coffee mug. A lot of pieces had to click together for these miracle scenarios to work out. And deep in her heart, Francesca worried that eventually, things would start to go awry.

* * *

Monday morning, Francesca breezed into Liam's office without Jessica's usual announcement. He looked up from his computer as she entered and a wide grin broke out across his face. He *should* be smiling after the weekend they'd spent together. "I see you're enjoying the new privileges of being the owner's bride-to-be."

"Exclusive access, anytime," she said with a grin.

Liam was glad to see her relaxed and happy. At first, he wasn't sure they could pull this off. Liam would never admit to that out loud; this had to work or he'd lose the network. And he knew Francesca had her own worries. She wore every emotion on her face. But after their time together this weekend, he was certain they both had sunnier outlooks on the arrangement. The lines of doubt were no longer wrinkling her brow, replaced with a contented smile that suited her much better.

Francesca set a to-go cup of coffee and a bag of Italian breakfast cookies in front of him. She was going to get him addicted to those things and he'd never be able to find them without her help.

"Grande drip with one cream, one sugar," she announced.

"Just how I like it," he said, turning in his chair to give her a hello kiss.

Francesca leaned into him but pulled away before his hands roamed too far. As much as it annoyed him to not be able to touch her when and where he wanted, he understood. Their relationship might be for the sake of the company, but public displays of affection at the office were a little much. She sat down in the guest chair with her own cup.

"Have you called the White House yet?" he asked.

"It's nine in the morning and I just handed you a hot, fresh coffee from the bakery. No. I haven't been to my office yet."

"Okay, sorry," he said, taking a sip. "You know I'm excited to move this plan forward."

"I know. I'll call once I get to my desk. Hopefully it won't take very long. I have a million things to wrap up this week before the gala on Saturday."

Liam nodded, but the details of the event didn't really interest him. The gala was really just a blip on his radar. And they were only doing it because she had agreed to be his fiancée. He couldn't have justified the expense given the state of the network. As it was, every mention of centerpieces and orchestras made dollar signs run through his mind.

"Now about the gala," she continued. "I've got most everything in place. Ticket sales have gone well and our sponsorship will see to it that it's the best year we've had yet. You'll need to make sure your tuxedo goes to the cleaners."

Liam made a note on his blotter so he wouldn't forget to ask Jessica about that later. "Check."

"And write a speech."

"What's that?" Liam looked up, his brow furrowed. He didn't like public speaking. As a matter of fact, he hated it. Avoided it at all costs and had since prep school debate class. Not even his aunt's declaration of mandatory matrimony made his stomach turn the way approaching a crowd of people with a microphone could do. There was a reason he preferred to be behind the camera instead of in front of it.

"As the major event sponsor, it's your job to give the

evening's welcome speech and encourage everyone to donate well and often."

"I don't remember Graham ever doing that." He tried to remember the times he'd gone. Maybe Graham did speak, but Liam was far too interested in his date for the evening to pay much attention. "Shouldn't that be the responsibility of the Youth in Crisis people?"

Francesca's red lips turned up with a touch of amusement. He must look like a damn deer in the headlights. "They do speak but not for long. Graham did it every year. And without bellyaching, I might add."

Liam grumbled under his breath and made another note to write a speech. This wasn't in their original agreement, but he could make concessions. Sleeping with him wasn't in their agreement either, but that had worked out splendidly. He would get something out of this. "Fine. I'll write a speech. But you'll have to go out to dinner with me tonight then."

"Why?"

Liam leaned across the desk, his most seductive gaze focused on her. "Because I'm going to ply you with sushi and expensive sake, and once you're drunk, I'm going to…talk you into letting me off the hook or writing the speech for me."

Francesca laughed. "I'm no speechwriter. But you do have several in your employ. I suggest you bribe them instead."

That wasn't a bad idea. Being a media mogul had its perks. If only he could get one of his news anchors to deliver the speech, too. He made another note on his blotter. "Does that mean you don't want to have sushi with me tonight?"

"I do. And I will. But first I have a president to cajole

and a charity ball to throw." She got up from her chair and leaned down to give him a goodbye kiss.

This time, because they were alone, Liam wasn't about to let her get away with just a peck. When she leaned down to him, he quickly reached for her and tugged her waist to him. She stumbled in her heels and fell into his lap. He clamped his arms around her so she couldn't get away.

Before she could complain, his lips found hers. He really enjoyed kissing her. He enjoyed kissing women in general, but there was something about Francesca's lips that beckoned him to return to them as soon as he could. Maybe it was the way she clung to him. Or the soft sighs and moans against his mouth. Maybe it was the taste of her—like a sweet, creamy sip of coffee. But he couldn't get enough of her.

Francesca indulged him for as long as she could, then pulled away. "I've got to get to work," she insisted, untangling herself from his arms. She straightened her skirt and rubbed her fingers along the edge of her lips to check for smeared lipstick.

"You look beautiful," he assured her. And she did. Dressed up, not dressed at all, perfectly styled or fresh from bed. He liked it all.

Liam wanted to tug her into his lap again and maybe make better use of his desk than he had since he'd moved into this office. But Francesca wouldn't hear of it—he could tell. As it was, that kiss guaranteed she would be on his mind all day. He probably wouldn't be able to focus on anything until after dinner, when he could get his hands on her again. But it had been worth it.

"You can flatter me all you want, but you're not getting out of this speech, Liam." She pulled away and sauntered out of his office, closing his door behind her.

Liam sat in his chair for a moment after she left. If he breathed deeply, the scent of her rose perfume still lingered in his office. Was there anything about this woman he didn't like?

He thought for a moment, then shook his head. Not yet. He'd been physically attracted to her the moment he laid eyes on her, but getting to know her had made the attraction that much stronger. She was beautiful. And smart. And thoughtful.

He picked up the coffee she'd brought him and took another sip. Her flaring temper could be a handful to deal with, but there were two sides to that passionate coin and he was certainly enjoying the other half at the moment.

The situation Aunt Beatrice had forced him into was unfortunate. But he couldn't regret asking Francesca to be his fiancée. Drawing her into this circus wasn't fair, but she was the right woman for the job. He couldn't imagine it going nearly as well with any of the women in his address book.

He liked being around Francesca. Working with her last week had been nice. Liam had gotten very comfortable having Francesca around, and that was saying a lot. He'd dated his share of women, never for more than a few months at a time. But he had boundaries. He very rarely had them over to his house and if he did, it wasn't overnight. They didn't meet any of his family or at least hadn't gotten to a point in the relationship where he thought it would be appropriate.

And he absolutely never brought them into his workplace. His romantic life and his work were two wires that never crossed. He usually didn't date at work, Francesca being a notable exception. He even tried to date outside the business. It took a bit of effort when you lived in D.C. not to date someone in media or politics—his usual circles—but he liked it that way. Usually.

Francesca was changing everything. This fake engagement was growing into something else with every passing moment. He didn't just want Francesca to come to his house; he also wanted her to help him decorate it. He liked starting his mornings chatting with her over coffee in his office or at her kitchen table. She may not have met his family yet, but if Aunt Beatrice had anything to say about it, she would—and soon. If the engagement went on for long, maybe he could convince his mother and sister to come to D.C. for a visit. He actually liked the idea of introducing them. He was certain his sister would really like Francesca.

All his rules were being broken. Stomped on with a red stiletto was more like it.

Normally, that would make Liam cringe. This woman he'd lassoed and pulled into his life was blurring all his boundaries. And he liked it.

A gentle rap at the door made him look up from their engagement photo. "Yes?"

Jessica came in, a couple of files stacked in her arms. "Good morning, sir."

"Good morning, Jessica."

She smiled as she approached his desk. "You're looking quite chipper this morning. Love looks good on you, sir. As does Ms. Orr's lipstick."

Liam grinned sheepishly and got up to look in the mirror over the minibar. He spotted a touch of reddish-pink lipstick, which he quickly wiped off. "Thanks, Jessica. She would've let me walk around like this all day, I bet."

"Of course. I've got those things you asked for this morning." Jessica set the stack of paperwork on his desk. "Last month's ratings numbers for the 5:00 to 7:00 p.m. weekday time slots, the budget breakout for the gala this weekend and the copy of *Italian for Idiots* you asked me to order came in from Amazon."

"Excellent. Thank you, Jessica. I've got a meeting with the CFO today, right?"

"At four."

Liam nodded. "Would you call and make reservations for Francesca and me at that nice sushi place in Dupont Circle? At six? I should be done with my meeting by then."

"I'll take care of it. Anything else?"

"That should do it for now."

When Jessica turned to leave, Liam thought of something. "Wait, one more thing. I'd like to send something to Francesca. An unexpected gift. Any suggestions?"

His secretary thought for a moment. "Well, for most men, I would suggest flowers or candy."

"Am I not most men?"

"Not at all, sir."

At least she was honest. "Then what would you recommend for the smaller minority of men?"

"Perhaps something for the gala this weekend? Do you know what dress she's wearing? Maybe something sparkly to go with it?"

Liam seemed to remember her saying something about that yesterday. That she had to go find a dress, but she didn't know when she would have the time. Perhaps he could help with that. Aunt Beatrice had the personal shoppers from Saks Fifth Avenue and Neiman Marcus come to her when she was choosing an outfit for an event. His aunt rarely left her mansion anymore.

"Check Ms. Orr's calendar for tomorrow afternoon and move anything she has to another time. Then call Neiman Marcus and have them send over a personal shopper."

"They'll need her size, colors and any other preferences."

Liam wrote down a few things on a Post-it note and handed it to her. "This is a fairly solid guess on her size, although tell them to bring a few things larger and smaller in case I'm wrong. I want the whole outfit, so shoes too. She wears an eight." He'd seen the label on her shoe as he'd carried her from the engagement party.

"Anything else, sir?"

"Yes. I want her to be the most stunning woman there. She is gorgeous on her own, but I'd like her to have a dress almost as beautiful as she is. And as such, let them know there's no price limit."

Eight

Liam had wanted to escort Francesca to the gala, but she'd insisted she had to go early and that she would just meet him there. He anticipated that she would be running around for most of the evening. That meant loitering on his own. Normally that wouldn't bother him, but lately being separated from Francesca brought on an awkward tightness in his chest. The only thing that would cure it was holding her in his arms.

As he walked through the front doors of the hotel's grand ballroom, he was greeted by the sound of a ten-piece orchestra accompanied by the dull roar of several hundred people mingling. The light was dim, but his eyes quickly became accustomed to it. He searched around the room for Francesca, but he began to think it was a lost cause. She was a needle in a haystack.

Despite the fact that he'd paid for the outfit she had chosen for tonight, he had no idea what she would be wearing. She had been exceedingly pleased with the gift and had thanked him in several ways over the past week, but the only details she would share was that it was a Marchesa and "*molto bellisima.*"

Then the crowds parted near the bar and he saw her. There was no mistaking this needle in any size haystack. The personal shopper from the department store had certainly taken Liam's requests into consideration. Francesca was the most stunning woman in the room tonight. He didn't even have to look around to check. He knew it in his gut.

The gown was black and gray with a swirling design. It was off the shoulder and clung to each curve all the way to the knee, where it fanned out into a delicate cascade of black marabou feathers. Her breasts were tastefully showcased by the neckline of the gown, which was trimmed with more feathers—there wasn't so much showing as to make him jealous of other men looking at her, but it was enough to make *him* notice. Her hair was swept up, making her neck look impossibly long and ready for his kisses. Her only jewelry was a pair of sparkling diamond dangles at her ears and a bracelet on one wrist.

When she turned to speak to someone, he noticed the feathers continued into a short train that draped behind her. It was grand, elegant and extremely sexy. And the best part was that *his* fiancée was wearing it.

He'd tried not to think too much of her that way. It implied more than there was between them, but he felt a surge of territoriality rush through him when she started talking to another man. He had the urge to rush to her, kiss her senseless and stake his claim before anyone got any ideas.

Then she held up her hand to show off her engagement ring. Even across the room, he could see the massive gem sparkle as her hand turned and she smiled. At long last, she radiated joy like a future bride should. The man said a few things, then they parted ways and she started walking in his direction.

The second her eyes met his, she stopped in her tracks. With a seductive grin curling her ruby lips, she held out her arms to showcase the gown and did a little turn for him. Lord, he thought, curling his hands into fists at his side. It was even more incredible from the back, where it dipped low to showcase her flawless, tanned skin.

Liam closed the gap between them as fast as he could without running across the ballroom. Up close, the dress sparkled as the lights hit little crystals sprinkled across the fabric, but it didn't shine as radiantly as she did.

"What do you think? Did I spend your money wisely?"

Not caring if he ruined the look she'd so carefully crafted, he leaned down and kissed her. He couldn't help it.

When he pulled away, Francesca smiled. "I guess so."

"Incredible," he said.

"Thank you for buying it for me. Having the woman from the department store just show up with gowns was perfect. I felt like I was an Oscar nominee with designers fighting for me to wear their looks on the red carpet."

"Hollywood is all the poorer for you not being on the big screen."

"Oh, stop," she said, smacking him lightly on the arm. "There's no one around to hear us, so you don't have to lay it on so thick."

Liam shook his head. "I mean every word. It wouldn't matter if we were all alone. I'd say the same thing. Of course, I'd be saying it as I unzipped you from the gown."

Francesca smiled and slipped her arm through his. "Let me show you where we're sitting. People are still milling around the silent auction tables, but the event should be starting shortly. You'll give your speech after the video plays about the youth facilities."

The speech. He'd almost forgotten about that weight dragging him down when he saw her looking so stunning. "Hooray," he said flatly.

"Did you bring it?"

He patted his lapel. "Got it right here. And I wrote it myself, I might add. No bribery was involved."

"I'm looking forward to hearing it."

They approached a round banquet table front and center, just beside the steps that led up to the stage. He helped her into her seat and took his own just as the orchestra music increased in intensity and the lights on the stage shifted to indicate the program was about to start.

Salads were brought to every place setting as the director of Youth in Crisis welcomed everyone and introduced the short video about their program.

Liam could only pick at his salad. With every minute of the video that went by, he felt more and more nauseated by the idea of speaking to three hundred people.

When the credits started rolling, Francesca sought out his hand and squeezed it gently. "It's time," she said, looking over to him. "You'll do great."

Liam took a large sip of wine and got up from the table. He made his way to the stairs and up onto the stage, where he was bathed in blinding white lights. He reached in his pocket for his speech, adjusted the microphone and tried to keep the frantic beating of his heart from being audible to the crowd. It was now or never.

"Thank you and welcome, everyone, to the eighth annual Youth in Crisis charity gala. As some of you may know, I recently bought the ANS network, which has a longstanding commitment to this organization. It's a partnership I'm proud of, and there are many people who work hard to make it possible."

He looked down in front of the podium, where he could see Francesca's dim silhouette. Her excited expression fueled his courage to continue. His heart seemed to slow and the subtle shaking of his hands subsided. He just might make it through the speech with her sitting there, silently cheering him on.

"First, I would like to thank ANS's Executive Vice President of Community Outreach and organizer of tonight's grand event, my beautiful fiancée, Francesca Orr. For those of you that don't know Francesca, she cares so deeply about this cause. With everything that has happened with our network in the past few months, there was some uncertainty about whether or not we could sponsor this event like we have for the past seven years.

"Well," he corrected, "I should say everyone *but* Francesca had some uncertainty. Come hell or high water, this gala would go on as far as she was concerned. The woman would give back her own salary to fund this event if she had to. I hope everyone rewards her determination by writing a big, fat check. I have agreed to match the largest private donation tonight as an engagement present for my bride, so feel free to stick it to me for a good cause."

The crowd laughed and Liam felt his confidence

boost. He shuffled to the next index card, gave Francesca a wink and continued in his bid to get the attendees to part with their money.

Francesca loved her dress. She really did. But after a long night, she was just as happy to change into a breezy slip dress and zip the gown into the garment bag she'd brought with her to the hotel. She couldn't stuff all those feathers into her little BMW and drive around. With that done, she stepped into the comfortable black flats she'd stashed away with her change of clothes and sighed in relief. Not only did her feet feel better, but the gala was a roaring success and—more important—it was over.

The ballroom was nearly empty by the time Liam found her gathering up the last of her things. "That was a very painful check to write," he said. "Remind me to kick Scarlet's fiancé for donating that much the next time I see him."

She smiled, standing and turning to look at him. His bow tie was undone, his collar unbuttoned. He managed to look casually sexy yet elegantly refined at the same time. "Daniel knows that it's for a good cause, as should you. And an excellent tax deduction," she added.

"It was worth it to see the look on your face when they announced how much money we raised."

"I can't believe it, really. We blew last year's donations out of the water. Everyone was buzzing about ANS tonight—and for a good reason." Francesca slipped her bag over her shoulder and took Liam's arm.

"It's about time," he said, leading them back to the front of the hotel where the party had been held. He approached the valet and handed him his ticket.

"I parked over there," she said, pointing to an area she didn't really want to walk to.

"We'll get your car in the morning," he said. "I want you to come home with me tonight."

That was an interesting development. Liam had yet to have her over to his place. She figured that it was a personal retreat for him. They'd always gone to her town house instead. And tonight, she really wished they were sticking with that arrangement. She had no change of clothes. She had what she had worn to the hotel and her dress. The designer gown, while fabulous, would look ridiculous in the morning.

"I don't have any clothes for tomorrow," she said.

"You won't need any," he replied with a wicked grin as the valet brought the car out.

Francesca gave up the fight. She was too exhausted after a long day to argue. They loaded her things into his convertible and she sat back in her seat, going with the flow. It wasn't until they reached his place that she perked up.

Liam had described where he lived as a town house, just a little bigger than hers, but he'd lied. As they pulled up the circular brick driveway, she found herself outside what looked like a two-story home. It was detached with a courtyard out front. Two stories of red brick with an elegantly arched front doorway and dormer windows on the roof.

"I thought you said you lived in a town house."

Liam shrugged and pulled the car into the attached garage. "It's close."

He came around the car and opened the door for her, escorting her toward a few steps leading up into the house. They entered through the kitchen. The cabinets were a stark white with glass fronts, set against stainless appliances and gray granite countertops. There wasn't a single dish in the sink and not a piece of mail sitting on the counter.

Liam took her garment bag and led her through to the front entryway, where he hung it in the closet. She set her bag containing the other items she'd needed tonight on the floor beside the door and wandered into the living room.

"It's a beautiful place," she said, walking over to the staircase and running her hand along the wood railing. The space had so much potential. It was a stunning home, but as he'd said before, it was probably just as it was when he'd moved in. White walls, hardwood floors, minimal furniture. There wasn't a single piece of art on the walls or personal item on a shelf. It looked like a model home or one stripped to sell. "But it does need a woman's touch," Francesca admitted.

"I told you I needed you to help me decorate."

"I didn't realize it would be such a large task."

Liam shrugged out of his tuxedo jacket and laid it across the arm of the couch. "Not what you were picturing?"

"I guess I was anticipating this place as more of a reflection of you. You seemed to guard it so fiercely that I thought coming into your home would give me some insight into who you are as a person."

"You don't see me in this place?"

Francesca glanced around one last time. "Not really. But I see what I should've expected to see. A house owned by someone too wrapped up in his work to make it a home. That speaks volumes about you, I think."

Liam's eyes narrowed at her. "My work is more important to me than the color of the walls."

"My work is important to me. But I make time for other things, too. I want to get married and have a family someday soon. When I do, I want not only a successful man, but also one that can take a step back from his job to enjoy family life. You'll burn out without that."

As Francesca said the words aloud, she realized she may have made a grave tactical error with Liam. He might not read much into what she'd just said, but it struck a painful chord with her. When she'd said the words, when she'd mentally envisioned getting married and having a family, she'd seen Liam in her mind. She had pictured this place filled with color and life and toddlers who looked like him.

She had let her heart slip away, piece by piece. It had happened so slowly over the past few weeks that she'd barely noticed the change until it was too late. Liam didn't know it, but Francesca had given her heart to him.

The man she could never really have.

It was unexpected, really. She was passionate about everything she did, but she knew from the beginning that this was business. There was no future for her with a man like Liam.

And yet she could see more now. Their future together was as crystal clear as the illuminated swimming pool she caught sight of from his living-room window.

"There's plenty of time for all that," he insisted.

This man, this workaholic, had so many layers to him she was anxious to explore. She knew there was more to him than he showed the world. The way he cared about his employees. The way he was handling the interview with Ariella. He had an attention to detail that went beyond just doing quality work. He was just as passionate about what he did as she was.

How could she not love that about him?

Love. Francesca swallowed hard and turned away from him to look out the window at his darkened yard and glowing turquoise pool. She couldn't look him in the eye with these kinds of thoughts in her mind. He'd know. And he could never know. Because it would never work between them.

Despite the future she could envision, there was a critical piece missing between them. He didn't love her. He wouldn't even be with her right now if it wasn't for his aunt and her demands. That was a bitter dose of reality to swallow, but the sooner she reminded herself of that, the better off she'd be when this "arrangement" came to an end.

"Would you like to see the upstairs?"

Pulling herself together, Francesca turned and nodded with a smile. Liam led the way up the stairs, showing her his home office, the guest room and finally, his bedroom.

Knowing they'd reached their final destination, she slipped out of her shoes and stepped onto the plush carpeting. She ran her hand over the soft, blue fabric of his duvet as she made her way to the window. She watched the glow of the city lighting the black night above the tree line, hiding any stars from her view of the sky. On a night like this, she really needed a sign to help her. Something to tell her she was making the right choices with Liam.

She reached for the *corno portafortuna* necklace she always wore and realized she'd taken it off tonight. It was in a pouch in her purse. She suddenly felt exposed without it, as though something could get through her protective armor without it. Looking down, she saw a rabbit sitting on Liam's front lawn. Before she could move, something startled it and the bunny shot across the yard, crossing her path.

A sign of disappointment to come.

Francesca took a deep breath and accepted the inevitable. She was in love with a man she couldn't have. She didn't need a rabbit to tell her disappointment was on the horizon.

The heat of Liam's body against her back was a bittersweet sensation. Just as her mind began to fight against it, her body leaned back into him. His bare chest met her back, his fingertips sliding beneath the thin straps of her dress to slide them off her shoulders.

The flimsy sundress slid down her body, leaving her completely naked with it gone. Liam's hands roamed across her exposed skin, hesitating at her hip.

"No panties?" he asked.

She hadn't worn any undergarments tonight. The dress was almost sheer and wouldn't allow for them. Besides, she knew how the night would end. "I can't have you ripping up all my nice lingerie," she said.

"That's very practical of you. I find that sexy. Everything about you just lures me in. I don't know that I'll ever be able to get away."

Francesca closed her eyes, glad her back was still to him. She wished he wouldn't talk that way sometimes. It was nice to hear, but it hurt to know it wasn't really true. The minute his aunt let him off the hook, this whole charade would end. At least now she wouldn't have to worry about faking the heartbreak when their engagement was called off. The tears she would shed on Ariella's shoulder would be authentic.

"Look at me," Liam whispered into her ear.

She turned in his arms, wishing away the start of tears in her eyes that had come too early. They weren't done just yet. She needed to make the most of her time with him.

When her gaze met his dark blue eyes, she felt herself fall into them. She wrapped her arms around his neck and stood on her toes to get closer. His lips found hers and she gave in completely. The feel of his hands on her body, his skin against hers, was an undeniable pleasure. She had to give in to it, even if it put her heart even more at risk.

They moved together, still clinging to one another as they slow-danced across the room to the bed. Her bare back hit the silky softness of the duvet a moment later. Liam wasted no time covering her body with his own.

As his lips and hands caressed her, Francesca noted a difference in his touch. The frenzied fire of their first encounters was gone, replaced with a leisurely, slow-burning passion. He seemed to be savoring every inch of her. At first, she wondered if maybe she'd had too much champagne tonight. That perhaps she was reading more into his pensive movements.

But when he filled her, every inch of his body was in contact with hers. He moved slowly over her, burying his face in her neck. She could feel his hot breath on her skin, the tension of each muscle in his body as it flexed against hers. When he groaned her name into her ear, it sent a shiver through her whole body.

Francesca wrapped her arms around his back and pulled him closer. She liked having him so near to her like this. It was a far cry from their wild, passionate encounter in her kitchen. Nothing like the times they'd come together over the past week. Something had changed, but she didn't know what it was. It felt like...

It felt like they were making love for the first time.

The thought made Francesca's heart stop for a hundredth of a second, but she couldn't dwell on it. Liam's lips found the sensitive flesh of her neck just as the movement of his hips against hers started building a delicious heat through her whole body. She clung to him, cradling his hips between her thighs as they rocked closer and closer to the edge.

When she reached her breaking point, she didn't cry out. There was only a gasp and a desperate, panting whisper of his name as her cheek pressed against his. His release was a growl against her throat, the intense thrashing of his body held to almost stillness by their tight grip on one another.

Instead of rolling away, he stayed just as he was. His body relaxed and his head came to rest at her breast. She brushed a damp strand of hair away from his forehead and pressed a kiss to his flushed skin.

As they drifted to sleep together, one of Francesca's last thoughts was that she was totally and completely lost in this man.

Nine

"Aunt Beatrice," Liam said, trying to sound upbeat.

After the maître d' had led Francesca and him to the table where the older woman was seated, she looked up at him and frowned. "Liam, do you ever wear a tie?"

He smiled, pleased he'd finally pushed her far enough to mention it. And now he got the joy of ignoring her question. He turned to his left and smiled. "This is my fiancée, Francesca Orr. Francesca, this is my great aunt, Beatrice Crowe."

Francesca let go of his hand long enough to reach out and gently shake hands with the Queen Bee. "It's lovely to meet you," she said.

Aunt Beatrice just nodded, looking over his fiancée with her critical eye. Liam was about to interrupt the inspection when she turned to him with as close to a smile on her face as she could manage. "She's more lovely in person than she is in her pictures, Liam."

He breathed a sigh of relief and pulled out Francesca's chair for her to sit. He hadn't been looking forward to this dinner. In fact, he'd deliberately not told Francesca about it until after the gala was wrapped up. She would just worry, and there wasn't any sense in it. His aunt would think and do as she pleased.

"I can't agree more," he said.

The first few courses of the meal were filled with polite, stiff pleasantries. His aunt delicately grilled Francesca about her family and where she came from. She was subtle, but Liam knew she was on a fishing expedition.

Francesca must've realized it also. "So what brings you to D.C.?" she asked, deflecting the conversation away from herself.

Liam swallowed his answer—that she was here to check up on him and their agreement.

"I'm speaking before a congressional committee tomorrow," Aunt Beatrice said, allowing the waiter to take away her plate.

She had mentioned that before, but Liam thought it had just been an excuse she'd made up. "What for?" he asked.

His aunt's lips twisted for a minute as she seemed to consider her words. "I'm speaking to a panel on federal funding for cancer treatment research."

Liam couldn't hide his frown. He also wasn't quite sure how to respond.

"Have you lost someone to cancer?" Francesca asked. Better that she ask the question because she had no real knowledge of her family history, as Liam should.

"Not yet," Beatrice said. "But the doctors give me

about three to six months. Just enough time to get my affairs in order before I take to my bed permanently."

Liam's glass of wine was suspended midair for a few moments before he set it back down. "What?" He couldn't have heard her correctly.

"I'm dying, Liam. I have stage four brain cancer and there's nothing they can do. Some of the treatments have shrunk the tumor and bought me a little more time, but a little more is all I'm going to get."

Unable to meet her eyes, his gaze strayed to her perfectly curled gray hair and he realized, for the first time, that it was a wig. How long had this been going on? "When did this happen? Why haven't you told anyone?"

At that, his aunt laughed. "Please, Liam. The sharks have been circling me for years. Do you really think I'm going to let them know it's close to feeding time?"

That was a true enough statement. The vultures had been lurking outside her mansion his whole life. This must be why she was so insistent on Liam marrying and taking over as head of the family. She knew the shoes needed to be filled quickly. She'd given him a year knowing she'd never live to see it come to fruition.

She'd been silently dealing with this for who knew how long. Worrying about her estate planning and altering her will even as she went for treatments and reeled from the aftereffects. "How can you go through this on your own? You need someone with you."

"I have someone with me. Henry has been by my side for more than forty years. He's held my hand through every treatment. Sat by me as I cried."

Henry. He'd never understood why her butler stayed around, even at his advanced age. Now perhaps he comprehended the truth. Neither of them had ever married.

They'd grown up in a time where they could never be together due to the wide social chasm between them, yet they were in love. Secretly, quietly making their lives together without anyone ever knowing it.

And now Henry was going to lose her. It made Liam's chest ache for the silent, patient man he'd known all his life.

"I don't know what to say, Aunt Beatrice. I'm so sorry."

"Is there anything we can do?" Francesca asked. Her hand sought out his under the table and squeezed gently for reassurance. He appreciated the support. Like her mere presence at his speech, knowing she was there made him feel stronger. As if he could handle anything.

"Actually, yes. I'd like the two of you to get married this weekend while I'm in town."

Anything but that.

"What?" Liam said, his tone sharper than he would've liked after everything they'd just discussed.

"I know our original agreement gave you a year, but I've taken a turn for the worse and I'm forced to move up the deadline. I want to ensure that you go through with it so I have enough time to have all the appropriate paperwork drawn up. I also want to see you married before I'm too much of an invalid to enjoy myself at the reception."

Francesca's hand tightened on his. It was never meant to go this far. He never expected something like this. "This weekend? It's Monday night. That's impossible."

"Nothing is impossible when you have enough money to make things happen. I'm staying at the Four Seasons while I'm here. I spoke to the manager this morning and he said they could accommodate a wedding and reception there this Friday evening. They have a lovely terrace for the ceremony and the Corcoran Ballroom is available for the reception."

Liam felt a lump in his throat form that no amount of water or swallowing would budge. He turned to look at Francesca. Her gaze was focused on her plate, her expression unreadable. She looked a little paler than usual, despite her olive complexion. Obviously, she was as pleased with this development as he was.

"I see no reason for you to wait any longer than necessary," his aunt continued, filling the silence at the table. "After all, you've found a lovely woman. By all accounts you two seem to be very much in love."

Her pointed tone left no doubt. His aunt had nailed them. He thought they had put on a good show. That it would be enough to pacify her until he could find the funding to buy her out. But he'd already heard from his accountant. The amount of money he needed was nearly impossible to secure, especially with the network in such a vulnerable place. They were looking at some other alternatives, but it would take time. Certainly longer that the few days they'd been given with her new deadline. That would take a miracle.

The Queen Bee was calling their bluff and he had too much riding on this hand to fold.

The waiter arrived then, setting their dessert selections in front of them. His aunt had never been much for sweets, but he noted a glimmer of pleasure in her eye as she looked down at the confection before her. He supposed that once you know you're going to die, there was no sense holding back on the things doctors told you were bad for you. What was the point?

Aunt Beatrice lifted a spoon of creamy chocolate

mousse and cheesecake to her mouth and closed her eyes from pleasure. Liam couldn't find the desire to touch his dessert. He'd lost his appetite.

"Don't make my mistakes, Liam. Life is too short to wait when you've found the person you want to spend your life with, I assure you."

At that, Francesca pulled her hand from his. He suddenly felt very alone in the moment without her touch to steady him. "We'll have to discuss it, Aunt Beatrice. Francesca's family is from California. There's a lot more to pull together than just booking a reception hall. But we'll be in touch."

Liam pushed away from the table to stand and Francesca followed suit.

"Aren't you going to finish your dessert?" his aunt asked, watching them get up.

"We've got a lot to sort out. I'm sorry, but we have to go."

His aunt took another bite, not terribly concerned by their hasty exit. "That's fine. I'll take it back to the hotel with me. Henry will enjoy it."

Liam's car pulled up outside Francesca's town house, but neither of them got out. It had been a silent drive from the restaurant. They must've both been in some kind of shock, although Francesca was certain they had different reasons for being struck mute.

When his aunt first started this, Liam had asked Francesca to be his fake fiancée. There was never even a mention that they would actually get married. He assured her it would never go that far. It seemed safe enough, even as she could feel herself slowly falling for him. Nothing would come of it, no matter how she felt. She wanted the kind of marriage Liam couldn't offer, but they only had an engagement.

Marrying Liam was a completely different matter.

Not just because it would never work out between them. But because a part of her wanted to marry him. She loved him. She wanted to be his bride. But not like this. She wanted to marry a man who loved her. Not because he had a metaphorical shotgun pointed at him.

When Liam killed the engine, she finally found the courage to speak. "What are we going to do?"

When he turned to her, Francesca could see the pain etched into his face. He was facing the loss of every-thing he'd worked for, and he wasn't the only one. She might not agree with Aunt Beatrice's methods, but she understood where the woman was coming from. Des-peration made people do crazy things. This was an ugly situation for everyone involved.

"She called my bluff. I'm just going to have to call hers. Tomorrow I'm going to tell her that the engagement was a setup and that we're not getting married. I don't think she'll sell her stock to Wheeler. It's not what she wants. She's a woman accustomed to getting her way, but she's not vindictive." He ran his hand through his hair. "At least I don't think she is."

Francesca frowned. She didn't like the sound of that plan. She didn't exactly get a warm maternal feeling from the Crowe family matriarch. His aunt had nothing to lose. If she was willing to go so far as to force him into marriage, she had no doubt she'd follow through with her threat. "You can't risk it, Liam."

"What choice do I have? I can't ask you to really marry me. That wasn't a part of the deal. I never in-tended for it to go this far."

Neither did she, but life didn't always turn out the way you planned. "When would you get the balance of the stock?"

Liam sighed. "It doesn't matter. I'm not doing it. She's taken this way too far."

"Come on, Liam. Tell me."

"I have to be married for a year. The ANS stock would be an anniversary gift, she said."

A year. In the scheme of things it wasn't that long. But she'd managed to fall in love with Liam in only a few weeks. A year from now, how bad off would she be? That said, the damage was done. Maybe a year of matrimony would cure her of her romantic affliction. It might give her time to uncover all his flaws. It was possible she wouldn't be able to stand the sight of him by May of next year.

And even if she loved him even more…what choice did they have? Their network would be destroyed. They were both too invested in the company and the employees to let that happen. Her heart would heal eventually. It was a high price to pay but for a great reward.

"We have to get married," she said.

Liam's eyes widened. "No. Absolutely not."

She couldn't help the pout of her lower lip when he spoke so forcefully. She knew what he meant, but a part of her was instantly offended by his adamancy. "Is being married to me so terrible that you'd rather risk losing the network?"

Liam leaned in and took her face in both his hands. He tenderly kissed her before he spoke. "Not at all. I would be a very lucky man to marry you. For a year or twenty. But I'm not going to do that to you."

"*To* me?"

"Yes. I know you're a true believer. You want a marriage like your parents. I've seen your face light up when you talk about them and their relationship. I know that's not what I'm offering, so I won't ask you to compromise what you want, even for a year."

She couldn't tell him that *he* was what she wanted. If he thought for a moment that their arrangement had turned into anything more than a business deal, he would never agree to the marriage. He'd chosen her because he thought she could keep all of this in perspective. Knowing the truth would cost ANS everything.

Francesca clasped Liam's hands and drew them down into her lap. "I'm a big girl, Liam. I know what I'm doing."

"I can't ask you to." His brow furrowed with stress as he visibly fought to find another answer. They both knew there wasn't one.

"You are the right person to run ANS. No one else can get the network back on top the way you can. Ron Wheeler might as well carve up the company if you're not running it because the doors will be closed in a few months' time." She looked into his weary blue eyes so he would know how sincere she was. "It's just a year. Once you get your stock, we can go our separate ways."

"But what about your friends and family? It's one thing to lie about an engagement that gets broken off. But to actually get married? Can you look your father in the eye and tell him you love me before he walks you down the aisle?"

Francesca swallowed the lump in her throat. She was very close to both her parents. They could read her like a book, and even as a teenager she couldn't lie to them without getting caught. This would be hard, but she could do it because it was true. Just as long as they didn't ask if *he* loved *her*...

"Yes, I can."

"What about your town house? You'll have to move in with me."

That would sting. Francesca loved her town house. She could hardly imagine living anywhere else. But she saw the potential in Liam's place. She could make that place her own for a while. "I'll rent out my town house."

"You don't have to do that. It's only fair I cover your expenses to keep it up even while you're not living there."

"Don't you think your aunt would find it odd if the place was left vacant?"

"This is going to sound a little harsh, but if what she says is true, she won't be around long enough to know what we're doing. She will probably write the marriage stipulation into the stock agreement, but she can't dictate what you do with your real estate holdings."

Francesca wouldn't put it past her. She didn't seem like the kind of woman who missed anything. "I suppose we can worry about the details later." She waited a moment as she tried to process everything they'd talked about. "So...is it decided then? We're getting married this weekend?"

Liam sat back in his seat. He was silent for several long, awkward minutes. Francesca could only sit there and wait to see what he said. "I guess so."

"You're going to have to work on your enthusiasm pretty quickly," she noted. "We'll have to tell our families tonight so they have enough time to make travel arrangements."

He nodded, his hands gripping the steering wheel as

though someone might rip it away from him. "I'll have Jessica call Neiman's again and get you a bridal appointment. Can you call Ariella and Scarlet tomorrow? They did a good job on the engagement party. Maybe they can pull off a miracle of a wedding in three days."

"I can. They'll think we've lost our minds."

Liam chuckled bitterly. "We have. Let's go inside," he said.

They went into her town house, and Francesca went straight into the kitchen. She needed something to take the edge off and she had a nice merlot that would do the trick. "Wine?" she asked.

"Yes, thank you."

Liam followed her into the kitchen as she poured two large goblets of wine. When she handed him his glass, he looked curiously at her hand for a moment before he accepted it. "Can I see your ring for a minute?"

Francesca frowned, looking at it before slipping it off. "Is something wrong with it?" She hadn't noticed any missing stones or scratches. She'd tried really hard to take good care of the ring so she could return it to him in good shape when it was over.

"Not exactly." Liam looked at it for a moment before getting down on one knee on the tile floor.

Francesca's eyes widened as she watched him drop down. "What are you doing?"

"I asked you to be my fake fiancée. I never asked you to marry me. I thought I should."

"Liam, that isn't neces—"

"Francesca," he interrupted, reaching out to take her hand in his own. "You are a beautiful, caring and passionate woman. I know this isn't how either of us expected things to turn out. I also know this isn't what you've dreamed about since you were a little girl. But if you will be my bride for the next year, I promise to be the best husband I know how to be. Francesca Orr, will you marry me?"

She underestimated the impact that Liam's proposal would have on her. It wasn't real. It lacked all those critical promises of love and devotion for her whole life, but she couldn't help the rush of tears that came to her eyes. It felt real. She wanted it to be real.

All the emotions that had been building up inside her bubbled out at that moment. Embarrassed, she brought her hand up to cover her mouth and shook her head dismissively. "I'm sorry," she said. "Just ignore me. It's been a rough couple of weeks and I think it's catching up with me."

"That wasn't the reaction I was hoping for," he said with a reassuring smile.

Francesca took a deep breath and fanned her eyes. "I'm sorry. Yes, I will marry you."

Liam took the ring and slipped it back onto her finger. He rose to his feet, still holding her hand in his. His thumb gently brushed over her fingers as he brought her hand up to his lips and kissed it. "Thank you."

Francesca was surprised to see the faint shimmer of tears in his eyes as he thanked her. It wasn't love, but it was emotion. There was so much riding on this marriage. She had no doubt that he meant what he said. He would be as good a husband as he could be. At least, as good as he could be without actually being in love with his wife.

Liam pulled Francesca into his arms and hugged her fiercely against him. She tucked her head under his chin and gave in to the embrace. It felt good to just be held by the man she loved. As she'd said before, this had been an emotionally exhausting couple of weeks. The next year might prove to be just as big a challenge. But somehow, having Liam hold her made her feel like it just might work out okay.

It felt like he held her forever. When he finally pulled away, they both had their emotions in check and were ready to face whatever the next week might hold for them.

"It's official then," he said with a confident smile. "Let's call your parents."

Ten

Francesca's precious retreat was a mess. Her beautiful townhome was in a state of disarray with moving boxes and bubble wrap all over the place.

Liam was maintaining the payments on her town house, so the bigger pieces of furniture she didn't need could stay, but everything else was going to his place. She'd probably need these things over the next year. This wasn't some overnight trip or long weekend she was packing for. She was getting ready to move in with the man who would be her husband in a few days' time.

Her parents had taken it well. At least they'd seemed to. Who knew how long her father had ranted after they hung up the phone. Either way, they were making arrangements to fly to Washington on Thursday afternoon. Liam's mother was thrilled. She didn't hesitate to say how excited she was to come and meet Francesca. Liam's mother and sister were coming Friday morning.

Their story was that they were so in love they didn't want to wait another minute to be husband and wife. Incredibly romantic or unbelievably stupid, depending on how you looked at it. But no parent wanted their child to elope and miss their big day, no matter what they might think about the situation.

Things were coming together, although it didn't look like it from where she was sitting.

The doorbell rang and Francesca disentangled herself from a pile of her things to answer the door. She'd asked Ariella to come over for lunch, hoping she and Scarlet could pull off the wedding hat trick of the year.

When she pulled open the door, she found her friend on the doorstep, but Ariella didn't have the bright smile Francesca was expecting. Her brow was furrowed with concern, her teeth wearing at her bottom lip. She had faint gray circles under her eyes as though she hadn't slept. And, most uncharacteristic of all, her hair was pulled back into a sloppy ponytail. That wasn't the Ariella she knew at all.

"Are you okay?"

Ariella's weary green gaze met hers as she shook her head almost imperceptibly.

Alarmed, Francesca reached for her friend's hand and pulled her inside. She sat Ariella down on one of the overstuffed living-room chairs that wasn't buried in packing tape and cardboard. "I'll make tea," she said, turning to the kitchen.

"Is it too early for wine?" Ariella called out.

Probably, but if her friend needed wine, she'd serve it with breakfast. "Not at all. Red or white?"

"Yes," she responded with a chuckle.

At least she was able to laugh. That was a step in the

right direction. Francesca quickly poured two glasses of chardonnay, which seemed more of a brunch-appropriate wine, and carried them into the living room with a package of cookies under her arm.

It took several minutes and several sips before Ariella finally opened up. She set the glass on the coffee table and reached into her purse. Pulling out an ivory envelope, she handed it over to Francesca to read the contents.

Francesca quickly scanned over the letter, not quite sure if what she was reading could possibly be true.

"It's from my birth mother, Eleanor Albert," Ariella said after a moment, confirming the unbelievable thoughts Francesca was already having.

The letter didn't give many details. It was short and sweet, basically asking if Ariella would be willing to write her back and possibly meet when she was ready. There was nothing about the circumstances of the adoption, the president or where Eleanor had been the past twenty-five years. Nothing about the letter screamed authenticity aside from a curious address in Ireland where she was to write back.

"When did you get this?"

"It came yesterday afternoon. To my home address, which is private and almost no one knows. Most of my mail goes to the office. I must've read it a million times last night. I couldn't sleep." Despite her weary expression, there was a touch of excitement in Ariella's voice. She'd waited so long to find out about her birth mother. Yet she seemed hesitant about uncovering the truth.

Francesca understood. The truth wasn't always pretty. People didn't always live up to the fantasy you built up in your mind. Right now, Ariella's mother was like

Schrödinger's cat. Until she opened that box, Eleanor would remain both the fantasy mother Ariella had always imagined and the selfish, uncaring woman she'd feared. Was it better to fantasize or to know for certain?

Francesca looked at the envelope and shook her head. After everything that had happened in the past few months, she'd grown very suspicious and protective where Ariella was concerned. It wouldn't surprise her at all if a journalist was posing as her mother to get details for a story. But she hesitated to say it out loud. She didn't want to be the one to burst the small, tentative bubble building inside her friend.

"Go ahead and say it," Ariella urged.

Francesca frowned and handed the letter back over to her. "I'm excited for you. I know that not knowing about your birth parents has been like a missing puzzle piece in your life, even before the news about the president hit. This could be a step in the right direction for you. I hope it is. Just be careful about what you say until you're certain she's really your mother. And even then, you can't be sure she won't go to the press with her story if someone offers her money."

Ariella nodded, tucking the letter back in her purse. "I thought the same thing. I'm going to respond, but I'm definitely going to proceed with caution. I don't want to be the victim of a ruthless journalist."

"I'm sure the letter is real, but it can't hurt to be careful."

Ariella reached for her wineglass and then paused to look around the living room. "What's going on here?"

"I'm packing."

Ariella's nose wrinkled as she eyed the boxes stacked around. Her mind must've been too wrapped up in the letter to notice the mess before. "You're moving in with Liam? So soon?" she added.

"Yes."

"Wow," she said with a shake of her head. "You two certainly don't move slowly. Next thing you'll be telling me you're getting married next weekend."

Francesca bit her lip, not quite sure what to say to that.

Ariella's head snapped toward Francesca, her green eyes wide. "Tell me you're not getting married in a week and a half. Francesca?"

"We're not," she assured her. "We're getting married Friday."

Ariella swallowed a large sip of wine before she could spit it out. "It's Tuesday."

"I know."

"What is the rush with you two? Does one of you have an incurable disease?"

"Liam and I are both perfectly healthy." Francesca wasn't about to mention his aunt's incurable disease. That would lead to more questions than she wanted to answer. "We've just decided there is no sense in waiting. We're in love and we want to get married as soon as possible."

With a sigh, Ariella flopped back into her chair. "Scarlet is going to have a fit. Putting together a wedding in three days will be a nightmare."

"We have a venue," Francesca offered. She loved how she didn't even need to ask her friend if she would do the wedding. It was a foregone conclusion. Francesca wouldn't dare ask someone else. "The Four Seasons. We've reserved the terrace for the ceremony and the ballroom for the reception."

Ariella nodded, but Francesca knew she was deep in planning mode. "Good. That's the hardest part with a quick turnaround. We'll have to use the hotel caterer, so I'll need to get with them soon about the menu for the reception. Did you guys have anything in mind?"

Francesca was ashamed to admit she didn't. As a child, she'd always fantasized more about her marriage than her actual wedding. And even if she had dreamed of a princess dress and ten thousand pink roses for the ceremony, none of that seemed appropriate for this. She wanted to save those ideas for her real marriage. One that would last longer than a year.

"We will be happy with whatever you two can pull together on short notice. We don't have room to be picky."

Ariella reached into her purse and pulled out her planner. She used her phone for most things, but she'd told Francesca that weddings required paper and pen so she could see all the plans laid out. "Color or flower preferences?"

"Not really. Whatever is in season and readily available. I'm not a big fan of orange, but I could live with it."

Her friend looked up from her notebook and frowned. "Live with it? Honey, your wedding isn't supposed to be something you *live with* no matter how short the notice. Tell me what you want and I'll make it happen for you."

She could tell Ariella wasn't going to let her off the hook. She would give her friend her dream wedding no matter how much Francesca resisted. She put aside her reservations and closed her eyes. Fake or no, what did she envision for her wedding day with Liam? "Soft and romantic," she said. "Maybe white or pale-pink roses. Candlelight. Lace. A touch of sparkle."

Ariella wrote frantically in her book. "Do you like

gardenias? They're in season and smell wonderful. They'd go nicely with the roses. And maybe some hydrangeas and peonies."

"Okay," she said, quickly correcting herself when Ariella looked at her with another sharp gaze. "That all sounds beautiful. Thank you."

"What does your dress look like? It helps sometimes with the cake design."

Francesca swallowed hard. "My appointment is tomorrow morning."

"You don't have a dress," she said, her tone flat.

She'd been engaged less than two weeks. Why would she have a dress already? "I don't have anything but a groom and a ballroom, Ariella. That's why I need you. I will make sure that Liam and I show up appropriately attired. The rest of the details are up to you."

"Please give me something to work with here. I know you trust me, but I want you to get what you want, too."

"I've got to buy off the rack with no alterations, so I'm not going in with a certain thing in mind because it might not be possible. I'm hoping to find a strapless white gown with lace details. Maybe a little silver or crystal shimmer. I don't know how that would help with the cake. It doesn't have to be very complicated in design. I prefer white butter cream to fondant. Maybe a couple flowers. I just want it to taste good."

"Any preference in flavor?"

"Maybe a white or chocolate chip cake with pastry cream filling, like a cannoli. My mom would love that."

"I can do that," Ariella said, a smile finally lighting her face.

"And speaking of food, I did invite you over here for lunch. Are you hungry?"

Ariella shoved her notebook into her purse and stood up. "No time to eat, darling. I've got a wedding to put together."

Francesca followed her to the door and gave Ariella a huge hug. "Thank you for all your help with this. I know I haven't made anything easy on you two."

"Do you know how many bridezillas we usually have to work with? You're easy. Anyway, that's what friends do—pull off the impossible when necessary. It's only fair considering you just talked me off the proverbial ledge over this stuff with my birth mother. And taking on a huge job like this will take my mind off everything, especially that upcoming reunion show."

The president had agreed to Liam's show proposal right before the gala. Francesca had jumped from one event to the next, getting everything in place for the televised reunion. "You don't have to do it, you know. You can change your mind."

"No, I can't." Ariella smiled and stepped through the doorway. "I'll email you our preliminary plans and menus to look over tomorrow afternoon."

Francesca nodded and watched her friend walk to her car. It all seemed so surreal. She would be married in three days. Married. To a man she'd known less than a month. To a man she'd grown to love, but who she knew didn't feel the same way about her.

A deep ache of unease settled in her stomach. She'd first felt the sensation when the shock wore off and she realized they were getting married on a Friday. That was considered to be very bad luck. Italians never married on a Friday. Unfortunately, the hotel wasn't available any other day.

Francesca hadn't seen a single good omen since that

ladybug landed on Liam's shoulder. Marrying Liam was looking more and more like a bad idea. But there was nothing she could do about it now.

Liam clutched a thick envelope of paperwork and a sack of Thai takeout as he went up the stairs to Francesca's town house. He'd met with his lawyer today to go over some details for the marriage. Now he planned to help Francesca with some packing.

"Hello," he yelled as he came through the door.

"I'm upstairs," Francesca answered.

He shut the door behind him and surveyed the neat stacks of labeled and sealed boxes in the foyer. "I have dinner."

"I'll be right there."

Francesca came down the stairs a few minutes later. Her hair was in a ponytail. She was wearing a nicely fitted tank top and capris with sneakers. It was a very casual look for her and he liked it. He especially liked the flush that her hard work brought to her cheeks and the faint glisten of sweat across her chest. It reminded him of the day they met.

God, that felt like ages ago. Could it really have been only a few weeks? Now here he was, helping her pack and clutching a draft of their prenuptial agreement in his hands.

"I see you've been hard at work today."

She nodded and self-consciously ran her hands over her hair to smooth it. "I probably look horrible."

"Impossible," he said, leaning in to give her a quick kiss. "I picked up some Thai food on the way from the lawyer's office."

"Lawyer's office?" Francesca started for the kitchen and he followed behind her.

"Yes. I got a draft of the prenup ready for you to look over."

Francesca stopped dead in her tracks, plates from the cabinet in each hand. Her skin paled beneath her olive complexion. There was a sudden and unexpected hurt in her eyes, as though he'd slapped her without warning. She set down the plates and quickly turned to the refrigerator.

"Are you okay?" Liam frowned. Certainly she knew that with the size of both their estates they needed to put in some protective measures now that they were making their relationship legally binding.

"Yes, I'm fine," she said, but she didn't look at him. Instead, she opened the refrigerator door and searched for something. "What do you want to drink?"

"I don't care," he said. Liam put the food and paperwork on the counter and walked over to her. "You're upset about this. Why?"

"I'm not," she insisted with a dismissive shake of her head, but he could tell she was lying. "It just surprised me. We hadn't talked about it. But, of course, it makes sense. This is a business arrangement, not a love match."

The sharpness in her tone when she said "love match" sent up a red flag in Liam's mind. He wished he could have seen her expression when she said it, but she was digging through the refrigerator. Then again, maybe he didn't want to see it. He might find more than he planned for.

He'd chosen Francesca for this partly because he thought she could detach emotionally from things. After she walked away from the elevator, he thought she could handle this like a champ. Maybe he was wrong. They'd spent a lot of time together recently. They'd had dinner, talked for hours, made love.... It had felt very much like a real relationship. Perhaps she was having real feelings.

Francesca thrust a soda can at him and he took it from her. She spun on her heel and started digging in the take-out bag. "So what are the high points?" she asked, popping open a carton of noodles.

She would barely look at him. She was avoiding something. Maybe the truth of the situation was in her eyes, so she was shielding him from it. If she was feeling something for him, she didn't want him to know about it. So he decided not to press her on the subject right now and opted just to answer her question. "Everything that is yours stays yours. Everything that is mine stays mine."

She nodded, dumping some chicken onto her plate. "That sounds fairly sensible. Anything else?"

"My lawyer insisted on an elevator clause for you. I couldn't tell him it wasn't necessary since we only plan to be married for a year. He said he likes to put them in all his prenups, so I figured it was better for it to be more authentic anyway."

"What is an elevator clause?"

"In our case, it entitles you to a lump sum of money on our first anniversary and an additional sum every year of our marriage after that. The money goes in trust to you in lieu of an alimony agreement. The longer we stay married, the more you're given."

Francesca turned to him, her brow furrowed. "I don't want your money, Liam. That wasn't part of our agreement."

"I know, but I want you to have it. You've gone far

beyond what we originally discussed and you deserve it. I'm totally uprooting your life."

"How much?"

"Five million for the first year. Another million every year after that. Milestone anniversaries—tenth, twentieth, etc., earn another five million."

"Five million dollars for one year of marriage? That's ridiculous. I don't want anything to do with that."

"If we pull this off, I'm inheriting my aunt's entire estate and all her ANS stock. That's somewhere in the ballpark of two billion dollars. I'd gladly give you ten million if you wanted it. Why not take it?"

"Because it makes me look like a gold digger, Liam. It's bad enough that we're getting married knowing it's just for show to make your aunt happy. If people find out I walked away after a year with five million bucks in my pocket...I just..." She picked up her plate and dumped rice onto it with an angry thump of the spoon. "It makes me feel like some kind of a call girl."

"Whoa," Liam said, putting his hands up defensively. "Now back up here. If we were getting married because we were in love, we'd probably have the same prenuptial agreement. Why would that be any different?"

Francesca shook her head. "I don't know. It just feels wrong."

Liam took the plate from her hand and set it on the counter. He wrapped his arms around Francesca's waist and tugged her against him. When she continued to avoid his gaze, he hooked her chin with his finger and forced her face to turn up to him. He wanted her to hear every word he had to say. "No one is going to think you're a gold digger. You will have earned every penny of that money over the next year. And not," he clarified, "on your back. As my wife, you're like an on-call employee twenty-four hours a day for a year."

He could tell his explanation both helped and hurt his cause. It justified the money but reduced her to staff as opposed to a wife. And that wasn't true. She was more than that to him. But if she was having confusing feelings about their relationship, would telling her make it worse?

"This isn't just some business arrangement anymore, Francesca. We're getting married. It may not be for the reasons that other people get married, but the end result is the same. You didn't have to agree to do this for me or for the network, but you chose to anyway. You're... *important* to me. So I'm choosing to share some of the benefits with you. Not just because you've earned them or because you deserve them. And you do. But because I want to give the money to you. You can donate every dime to charity, if you'd like. But I want you to have it regardless."

That got through. Francesca's expression softened and she nodded in acceptance before burying her face in his chest. Liam clutched her tightly and pressed a kiss into the dark strands of her hair.

It wasn't until that moment that he realized what a large price they were both paying to save the network and protect his dream. The reward would be huge, but the emotional toll would be high.

Five million didn't seem like nearly enough to cover it.

Eleven

Liam stood at the entrance to the terrace where the ceremony would take place. As instructed, he was wearing a black tuxedo with a white dress shirt and white silk tie and vest. A few minutes earlier, Ariella had pinned a white gardenia to his lapel. He looked every bit the proper groom, even if he didn't feel quite like one.

Beyond the doors was possibly the greatest wedding ever assembled on such short notice. Rows of white chairs lined an aisle strewn with swirls of white and pink rose petals. Clusters of flowers and light pink tulle draping connected the rows. A small platform was constructed at the front to allow everyone a better view of the ceremony. A large archway of white roses and hydrangeas served as a backdrop and were the only thing blocking the view of the city and the sunset that would be lighting the sky precisely as they said their vows.

About an hour ago, Ariella had given him a sneak

peek of the ballroom where the reception would be. It seemed as if an army of people was working in there, getting everything set up. The walls were draped in white fabric with up-lighting that changed the colors of the room from white, to pink, to gray. Tables were covered with white and delicate pink linens with embroidered overlays. Centerpieces alternated between tall, silver candelabras dripping with flowers and strings of crystals and low, tightly packed clusters of flowers and thick, white candles in hurricane vases. In the corner was a six-tiered wedding cake. Each round tier was wrapped at the base with a band of Swarovski crystals. The cake was topped with a white and pink crystal-studded *C*.

It was beautiful. Elegant. And completely wasted on their wedding, he thought with a pang of guilt.

Nervous, and without a herd of groomsmen to buy him shots in the hotel bar, he'd opted to greet guests as they came through the door. The wedding party itself was small with no attendants, but there were nearly a hundred guests. It had been a lightning-quick turnaround with electronic RSVPs, but nearly everyone invited had said yes, even if just out of morbid curiosity. So far, no one had asked any tacky questions at the door, like when the baby was due, but he was certain talk was swirling around the crowd inside.

"Ten minutes," Scarlet reminded him as she brushed by him in her headset, a clipboard clutched to her chest.

Ten minutes. Liam swallowed hard and pasted the wedding-day smile back on his face. In less than a half hour, he would be legally bonded to Francesca with all his friends and family as witnesses. A month ago, he'd been celebrating his purchase of ANS and looking forward to the excitement of fulfilling his dream of running a major network. Now he was about to marry a virtual stranger to keep the dream from crumbling into a nightmare.

"Liam," a proper female voice called to him.

He looked up to see Aunt Beatrice rolling toward him in a wheelchair pushed by Henry. He knew she was sick, but seeing her in a wheelchair was startling. Surely she could still walk? He thought back to every time he'd seen her in the past month. She had already been seated whenever he arrived. On their last few visits, she hadn't so much as stood up or walked over to get something from her bag. Now he realized it was because she couldn't. She'd done well hiding it until now.

"Aunt Beatrice," he said with a smile, leaning down to plant a kiss on her cheek. "And Henry," he added, shaking the butler's hand. He had a new appreciation for the quiet, older man who had served and loved his aunt all these years. "Seats have been reserved for you both in the first row on the right."

Aunt Beatrice nodded, and Henry rolled them into the room. There wasn't a "congratulations" or a "last chance to back out" from her. She hadn't even bothered to question him about his and Francesca's relationship any longer. He supposed that even if they were faking it, as long as it was legally binding, she was getting her way. She probably figured that within a year, they'd fall for each other for real. Or she'd be dead and wouldn't care any longer.

"Liam," Ariella said, approaching him quietly from the side. "We have a problem."

He wasn't surprised. As quickly as this had come together, things were bound to go awry. "What is it?"

"Security has spotted an uninvited guest in the lobby heading this way."

Liam frowned. "Who? A reporter?"

"Sort of. Angelica Pierce. How would you like us to handle this?"

Oh. That was certainly cause for a bit of excitement, especially where Ariella was concerned because Angelica had been suspended for her possible involvement in the hacking scandal that had revealed Ariella as the president's secret daughter. "Don't do anything. She's liable to make a scene if we have her escorted out. Better just to let her come and act like it's not a big deal."

Ariella nodded. "Agreed." She turned away and muttered into her headset. "Five minutes," she added, before disappearing toward the room serving as a bridal suite.

Liam busied himself greeting other guests and tried not to worry about Angelica. He'd only met the woman in person once, and he got the distinct impression that she was a suck-up who would do anything to keep her job. Right now, she was suspended pending the results of Hayden Black's investigation, so he wasn't surprised she'd shown up today. She was here to make an appearance and kiss up to her boss and his new bride.

He hoped that was all she was up to. He knew for a fact that Hayden and his fiancée, Lucy Royall, were already inside. Lucy was Graham Boyle's stepdaughter and there was some bad blood between her and Angelica. With any luck, they would sit far apart and not cross paths the whole evening. But he wasn't feeling very lucky today.

That's when he saw her. "Angelica," he said with a smile, accepting the hug she offered. "So good to see you." He wanted to keep this evening together, so he wasn't about to let on that she was an unwelcome party crasher.

Angelica seemed very pleased by the warm welcome. She'd certainly dressed up for the occasion, looking radiant even, if not a touch heavier than she had been a few weeks ago. Her face was rounder and her purple dress was a bit snug. The stress of Hayden's investigation must have been catching up with her.

"I wouldn't miss this for the world. I just love weddings. And my boss's wedding is an especially important event. I wish you both great happiness together."

Liam smiled and thanked her, turning to the next guests approaching. It was his rival network's former star, Max Gray and his new bride, Cara. They'd been married in March and had just come back from their extended honeymoon in Australia. The two of them were practically beaming with love for each other, and Cara's dress showed the gentle swell of her pregnancy. She had started doing public relations for D.C. Affairs since leaving the White House, but he could tell that motherhood was her true calling. She was just glowing.

As they approached the door, they both stopped to watch Angelica go inside. Max's jaw dropped, his eyes widening. His field research had helped uncover the hacking scandal back in January. "What is she doing here?" he asked.

Liam shrugged. "Trying to make friends, I suppose. Did you two have a nice trip?"

"Amazing," Cara said. "We slept in late, ate great food, did some sightseeing. It was wonderful. Where are you and Francesca going on your honeymoon?"

That was a good question. "We don't have anything planned yet. Things moved so fast and work has been so busy, we haven't had a chance. We're hoping things will slow down soon and we'll have the opportunity to get away. Sounds like a trip to Australia is a great choice. I'll have to talk to you two about it more later."

Max and Cara went to their seats and the last few arriving guests followed them. Liam straightened his tie and took a deep breath as he saw Scarlet and another man in a suit heading toward him with determination and purpose.

"Okay, showtime. This is your officiant, Reverend Templeton. He will go down the aisle first, then you. We'll seat the parents, and then the bride will come down the aisle with her father. Are you ready, Liam?"

That was another good question. He was ready as he was ever going to be for a corporate, shotgun marriage of convenience. The only thing that made him feel better was that he'd get to spend the next year with a sexy spitfire who made his blood boil with passion and excitement.

"I am."

Francesca sat still as stone at her dressing table, letting her mother pin the large, white gardenia in her hair. Looking at herself in the mirror, she was the perfect image of a beautiful bride on her big day. Her shiny, black hair was twisted up into an intricate updo, the gardenia pinned just to the side. Her makeup was airbrushed and flawless. She'd found the perfect gown in her size without much trouble. Even with such a time crunch, everything had worked out just as it should. It was as though this wedding was meant to be.

Only it wasn't.

Her persistent stomachache had kept her from eating

too much at breakfast or lunch. She had a plate of fruit and crackers beside her that she would pick at from time to time, but it just made the feeling worse.

Not even a saltine cracker could cure the ache of impending doom. This wedding was a mistake. She knew it. But the part of her that loved Liam and cared for ANS and its employees was overpowering her common sense.

She took one last look at herself in the mirror and inhaled a deep breath to pull herself together. Now was not the time to fall apart. Not while her parents' concerned eyes were watching her.

Since her father had come in, he'd been sitting in the corner, scowling in his tuxedo. Honestly, he'd had the same look on his face since she had met them at the hotel the day before. There had been a moment when he first saw her in her gown that his expression had softened and tears came to his eyes, but it hadn't lasted long.

Francesca was pretty sure her own wary appearance hadn't helped. But there was nothing she could do about it. She had to save her smiles and energy for the wedding and reception.

"Are you okay, *bella?*" her mother asked. She was a tinier version of Francesca, with the same dark eyes and warm brown skin. Her thick, brown hair was pulled back into a bun, with elegant streaks of gray running through it like professionally added highlights. She was wearing a shimmering gray dress with a jacket. Ariella had pinned a pink and white rose corsage to her lapel earlier. Her father had one very similar on his tuxedo.

Francesca nodded and stood, straightening her gown. She'd hoped for and found a white, strapless gown; there had been many to choose from because that style was in fashion. This one had a lace overlay that went to the floor and was delicately embroidered in a pattern with silver beads, crystals and pearls down to the chapel train. What she liked best about it was the silver sash around her waist with a crystal embellishment in the center. It accented her hourglass figure and gave the dress a little something special.

"Why do you ask?" Francesca asked innocently.

"You just don't look as happy as I was expecting. Where is my beautiful, blushing bride?" Her mother reached up to gently caress her face.

She stopped fidgeting with the dress and smiled, gripping her mother's hand reassuringly. "Yes, Mama, I am fine. I'm just a little nervous."

"You should be, marrying a man you hardly know," her father snarled from the corner.

"Victor!" her mother scolded over her shoulder. "We discussed this. We did the same thing, didn't we? And aren't you happy thirty years later?"

He shrugged and slumped into his chair. This was one argument he would lose, and he knew it. But he didn't have to like it. Francesca could easily see where she got her own stubborn streak and fiery temper.

"Mama, could you give me that small hand mirror so I can see the back?"

Donatella handed her the silver mirror and Francesca held it so she could make sure everything looked okay. Satisfied, she laid it on the edge of the dresser, but it tipped with the heavy weight of the handle and fell to the floor with a crash.

"Oh, no," Francesca lamented, crouching down to pick up the shattered hand mirror. There were only a few slivers of the reflective surface left, the rest scattered on the floor. Slumping into her chair, she looked at the broken glass and shook her head. "Seven years bad luck," she said. "As though I needed another sign."

"Nonsense," her mother chided. "Your *nonna* filled your head with silliness when you were a child. This means nothing aside from having to sweep up and buy a new mirror. Your marriage will be whatever you make it. And if you believe in your heart that it is doomed before it starts, you'll be right. You must fill your heart and soul with joy, not fear, as you walk down that aisle, *bella*."

Francesca hoped her mother was right. She should ignore the signs and try to make the most of her year with Liam. It was all she was going to get so she shouldn't spend the precious time she had moping about losing him.

A gentle rap sounded at the door and Ariella stuck her head in. "Mrs. Orr, it's time for you to be seated. I'll be back for the bride and her father in just a moment." She gave Francesca a quick wink of encouragement as they slipped out of the room.

Now was the moment Francesca was dreading the most. Five minutes alone with her father without her mother to be the buffer. Hopefully she could distract him with idle conversation until Ariella returned.

"How do I look, Daddy?"

The large Irishman crossed his arms over his chest and admired her for a moment before he spoke. "Like the saddest, most beautiful bride I have ever seen."

Francesca frowned at him. How could he see into her so well? "I'm smiling. Why do you think I'm sad?"

"There's something in your eyes. Something isn't quite right about all this—I can tell."

"Don't be silly, Daddy."

Victor stood up and walked over to her. He helped

Francesca up from her seat and held her hand tightly. "Look me in the eye and tell me that you love him."

Francesca fixed her gaze on her father. If she really wanted to back out of this wedding, this was her chance. All she had to do was say the word and he would have her on a plane to California before Aunt Beatrice knew what hit her. But she couldn't do that. Wouldn't.

She had to answer him honestly, or he would know. He sensed a problem, but he was barking up the wrong tree. If he wanted the truth of the matter, he should be asking Liam these questions. Without blinking, she spoke sincere words to him. "Yes, I love Liam. Very much."

"And you want to marry him?"

She did. It was fast, but she had fallen hard for her fiancé. Her trepidation was in knowing that no matter how she felt about him, their marriage would be over this time next year. How could she walk down the aisle knowing their wedding was a pointless exercise? Yes, it would save ANS and make a dying woman happy, but Francesca herself would be crushed in the process.

"Yes, Daddy. I want to marry Liam."

His gaze moved over her face, looking for a thread to pull at to unravel the truth, but there was nothing to find.

Another knock at the door came and Ariella stepped in holding Francesca's bouquet.

"It's beautiful," Francesca said as she took the flowers and admired them. There were pink and white roses, white hydrangeas and tiny white stephanotis. She'd given Ariella very little direction on this wedding, but with the bouquet, at least, she'd hit the nail on the head. Everything else would likely be just as perfect.

"Did you expect anything less?" she said with a smile. "It's time."

Francesca's father took her by the arm and led them down the hallway to the terrace. When she got the cue, Ariella opened the doors. They stepped onto the balcony to the sound of music from a string quartet. A hundred people stood up from their seats and turned to look Francesca's way as they kicked through rose petals down the aisle.

She was almost halfway down the aisle when she finally got the nerve to look at Liam.

Francesca had avoided it because she didn't want to see the truth in his eyes. He would likely look nervous. Maybe even fearful for what he'd gotten himself into. There would be no tears of love and joy. He would not be beaming with pride after seeing the woman he adored looking more beautiful than ever before. She knew she would be disappointed. But she looked anyway.

When her gaze met his, she felt her stomach do a flip. He looked so incredibly handsome. She'd seen him in a tuxedo before, but there was something different about the way he looked tonight. It was the expression on his face. There wasn't love there, but she did see admiration. Unmasked attraction. Deep respect. He knew how big a sacrifice she was making for him and he appreciated it. He just didn't love her for it. Not the way she loved him.

Francesca had to remind herself to smile and not get lost in her thoughts as they took the last few steps to the ceremony platform.

The minister began the ceremony, and her father leaned in to kiss her before handing her over to Liam for good. She couldn't meet his eyes then. If he saw the panic and fear there, he'd drag her down the aisle while everyone watched in horror. Instead, she closed her eyes and leaned in to his kiss.

"I love you, Daddy."

"I love you, too."

At that, he put her hand in Liam's and they stepped up together to be married.

Francesca thought she would be okay until she had to take that first step and her knees turned soft. It was only Liam's firm, reassuring grasp that kept her upright. He guided her to the minister, her hand clasped tightly in his.

"I won't let you fall. We can do this," he whispered with a smile and a wink.

She nodded and squeezed his hand.

The ceremony began, but it was a blur to her. The minister spoke, she repeated her vows, they exchanged rings and the next thing she knew, she was kissing her husband in front of a hundred people.

The roar of applause and the cheers were like a slap in the face, snapping her back into reality. The minister presented them as Mr. and Mrs. Liam Crowe as they turned to the audience. She clung to Liam's arm as they walked back down the aisle together as husband and wife.

When they rounded the corner to exit the terrace, Ariella was waiting for them. She escorted them back to the bridal room to wait for pictures while the guests made their way to the ballroom for cocktails.

Francesca rested her bouquet on the dressing table beside the broken mirror and slumped into her chair.

It was done. They were married.

They still had to sign the official paperwork for the license, but that would arrive any second now.

She almost couldn't believe it. She felt numb, like she was walking through a dream wedding instead of one in real life. It had been a beautiful ceremony, but it wasn't how she imagined her wedding day would be. No matter how many different ways she had pictured her big day, there was always a common element.

She looked over at Liam. He eyed the champagne glasses for a moment before crossing the room to pick them up. He handed one to her and held out his own for a toast.

"One day of marriage done. Three hundred and sixty-four to go."

With a sigh, she took a deep draw from her champagne flute and closed her eyes before the tears threatened to spill over.

One critical thing was missing from her fantasy wedding: a man who loved and adored her more than anything else on earth. And that was the one thing Scarlet and Ariella hadn't been able to provide.

Twelve

Liam was worried about Francesca. As she'd walked down the aisle toward him, she was literally the most beautiful bride he'd ever seen. The white gown was quite flattering against the warm color of her skin and it fit her curves like a glove.

For a moment, it had all become a little too real. His breath had caught in his throat. His mouth had gone bone-dry. His heart had raced a thousand miles an hour in his chest. Francesca was about to be his wife. And in that instant, he'd wanted her to be in every sense of the word.

It was a strange feeling. One he hadn't experienced before. He'd been fond of a lot of women over the years. He genuinely liked and respected Francesca. That was probably as close to "love" as he'd ever gotten. Marriage hadn't crossed his mind yet. He assumed he would get to that point in his life eventually. The Queen Bee had just accelerated his schedule.

Liam wasn't sure if it was the flowers or the music. The way she looked in that dress or the happy tears of his mother. But he was committed to the moment. He was excited to marry Francesca. Maybe this year wouldn't be so bad. Maybe...maybe there could be more than just a business arrangement between them. A real relationship.

He was snapped back to reality by the stony expression on Francesca's face. There was no happy, bridal glow. No tears of joy. No smile of excitement. She didn't look outright unhappy; she was covering it well, but Liam knew she was on the edge. The reality of lying to all their friends and family must be weighing heavily on her. He understood. That was why he'd given her the option not to go through with the marriage. But she'd insisted. She wasn't the type of woman to go back on her word. She would choke it down and do what had to be done.

Since they'd left the bridal suite, she'd become like a robot. She smiled, she went through the motions, but her dark eyes were dead. He wasn't sure what would happen when she couldn't hold in her emotions any longer. But he knew it wouldn't be pretty.

Fortunately, they were able to lose themselves in the smiles, handshakes and hugs of the receiving line. After that, the reception should be fairly short. With little notice, Scarlet and Ariella had only been able to arrange a catered hors d'oeuvres and cocktail reception. No band or dancing, no five-course sit-down dinner. Just an hour or so of mingling and cake, and then everyone would be on their way. It should be fairly simple to get through it without drama.

The last few guests came through the line and Liam and Francesca were able to leave their stations. He put his arm around her waist and leaned into her. "Are you okay?" he whispered.

Her wary eyes looked to him and she nodded. "I'm just a little overwhelmed."

"Do you want me to get you a drink?"

"Yes," she said with emphasis. "Please."

Liam left her side to get them both something from the bar. He was returning with a glass in both hands when he caught an unwelcome sight out of the corner of his eye. Hayden Black and Angelica Pierce were chatting. No, that wasn't the right word. They were having a discussion that verged on heated, if Angelica's stiff posture and tight mouth were any indication. What was she thinking, having a conversation with the investigator out to prove she was guilty? This couldn't be good.

As far as Liam knew, Angelica hadn't been called to testify before the congressional committee about the hacking scandal. He assumed it was because Hayden hadn't been able to piece together the details of her involvement. Or at least, to prove it. The suspicion of her guilt was nothing Liam could act on. He needed hard evidence to fire her, and if Angelica was involved, she had been very, very careful. She wasn't stupid. She was a ruthless, cunning reporter willing to do nearly anything to get the big story. He appreciated her ambition. But not her moral code.

Secretly, he hoped Hayden would find what he needed. Liam was nervous running ANS with Angelica still in his employ. He needed a reason to cut her loose permanently.

Their discussion was getting a little more animated. Liam searched the room for Ariella and Scarlet, but he didn't see them or the security they'd hired. He might have to intervene on this situation himself. Francesca's drink would have to wait.

As Liam got closer to them, he could hear what they were saying a little better. They were trying to speak quietly, but their passions were getting the best of them. At least, Angelica's were. Hayden was always very calm and collected.

"I find it laughable that people seem to think you were behind this whole thing," Hayden said. "As though the peroxide-bleached brain cells you have left could plan something more intricate than what kind of shoes to wear with what outfit."

A flush of anger rose to Angelica's cheeks. Her eyes narrowed at Hayden. She didn't notice Liam approaching them because she was so focused on their argument. "You think you're so smart, Hayden, but I'm not going to fall for your tricks. Is calling me a dumb blonde the best you've got? I expected better of you. All men see is what women want them to see. The hair and the makeup and the clothes blind you to the truth. But don't let appearances fool you. We may have the same hair color, but I'm not sweet and pliable like your precious Lucy. I earned my place at the company. It wasn't because my stepfather owned the network."

Liam expected Hayden to take offense at the insults Angelica was levying at his fiancée, but it didn't seem to faze him. "Yes," he agreed, "but Lucy has something you'll never have no matter how hard you work or how many people you trample."

Angelica nearly snorted with contempt. "And what's that? The love of a man like you?"

"Nope. Her daddy's undying affection. She's the beautiful little girl he always wanted. The one he raised as his own. He bought her ponies and went to her ballet recitals. He got her a convertible on her sixteenth birthday. I bet it breaks his heart that he'll be in jail and can't walk Lucy down the aisle when we get married."

Angelica stiffened beside him, but she brushed off his words with a shrug of indifference. "So what? Her stepfather spoiled her. Am I supposed to be jealous of her for that?"

"No. But you might be jealous because he didn't have to bribe people to keep *Lucy* a secret. He wasn't embarrassed of her."

"I don't know what you're insinuating," she said slowly, although the tone of her voice said otherwise. It was cold and flat, issuing a silent warning to Hayden.

It made Liam wonder what they were really talking about. He'd heard that Lucy and Angelica hadn't gotten along, but Lucy had left ANS to work with Hayden before he took over. He certainly didn't know anything about Angelica's past or her family. Why did Lucy's relationship with Graham make Angelica so angry?

Hayden really seemed to know how to push her buttons. Was he rattling her cage for amusement or was he trying to get her to make a mistake? Liam turned to his left and spied the wedding videographer, a field cameraman from ANS. Perfect. He waived the man over.

"I want you to very quietly, subtly, record their conversation. She can't know you're taping them."

The camera man worked on ANS investigations and undercover stings, so he was likely more comfortable doing this than taping greetings for the bride and groom. He eased into the crowd, coming up from behind Angelica, partially hidden by the towering wedding cake beside them.

Liam watched Hayden's gaze fall on the video camera for an instant, then back to Angelica. They both knew this was their chance to catch her at something when she didn't expect it.

"Admit it, Angelica. All this hacking business had nothing to do with presidential scandals or career-launching headlines. It was just a high-profile distraction to get what you were really after. The truth is that you were trying to ruin him. Getting your revenge, at last."

Liam held his breath, waiting to see where this conversation might go when she thought no one else was watching.

"That's a ridiculous, unfounded accusation. Graham was a lousy boss with questionable ethics, but he was hardly a blip on my radar. I've got better things to do with my time than try to ruin someone like him. In time, they always ruin themselves."

"It's interesting you would say that. But I've got a stack of pictures that say otherwise. Pictures of you modified to remove your fancy hairdo and contact lenses. It made me think of something Rowena Tate told me. She mentioned that you reminded her of a troubled, unstable girl at her private school. The girl had always gloated about her rich father, but he never showed up for parent weekends. He just mailed a check."

"I didn't go to private school," Angelica said, her jaw clenched tighter with every word he said.

"I did a little research and found old school records showing her tuition was paid for by Graham Boyle. Isn't that odd? He's always told people he didn't have any children of his own. It must've been hard growing up knowing your father didn't want anything to do with you. That you were just a mistake that could be fixed with enough money. If it were me, I'd want revenge, too."

"Shut up, Hayden."

"He didn't even recognize you when you came to work at ANS, did he? Sure, you looked different, but a father should be able to recognize his own daughter, right? Then you had to sit back and watch him fawn over Lucy, a child that wasn't even his."

"I don't have to listen to your wild stories. You're obviously grasping at straws." She shook her head, turning to walk away from their discussion.

"The sad thing is that you went to all this trouble, ruined so many lives, and in the end, you failed."

Angelica stopped dead in her tracks. She swung back to him, her eyes wide and furious. "Oh, really? What makes you think this isn't exactly the way I planned it? Those fools they arrested, Brandon and Troy, will take the fall for the wiretaps. All the evidence shows that Marnie Salloway orchestrated it. Graham Boyle is going to rot in prison and his precious network will be destroyed before too long. It sounds pretty perfect to me. My only regret is that in the end, I couldn't find a way to get Lucy's hands dirty enough to send her to jail with dear old dad."

"But he didn't go to jail because he loved you and wanted to protect you. It was pure guilt."

"I don't need his love," she snapped. "I've gotten this far in life without it. What I did need was to see that bastard brought to his knees. And I got that."

Hayden smiled wide and turned toward the cameraman. "You get that, Tom?"

The videographer pulled away from his lens and nodded. "Every single word."

Angelica's jaw dropped open, her skin flushing crimson in anger. "You bastard!" she shrieked. "You deliberately set me up. If you think I'm going to let you ruin my career with no physical proof of my involvement with the hacking, you've got another think coming. Even with that tape, no one will believe you."

Hayden just shook his head. "I didn't have to ruin your career. Like you said, in time, people always ruin themselves. I just happened to get that moment on film. I'm pretty sure ANS will terminate you when I show them that tape. And the FBI and congressional committee will find it very interesting. Soon, people will start rolling on you to cut a better deal for themselves. There's no loyalty among criminals. You'll be wearing matching orange jumpsuits with your daddy in no time."

Graham Boyle was Angelica's father? Liam frowned in confusion but was jerked away from his thoughts when Angelica reared back and slapped Hayden. He barely reacted to the assault, simply shaking his head and looking at her with pity in his eyes. "It's a shame you wasted your whole life on this. I feel sorry for you."

By now, a large crowd of the wedding guests had gathered around the argument. More witnesses. The more people that gathered, the higher Angelica's blood pressure seemed to climb. "I don't want your pity," she spat.

Liam watched her fingertips curl and uncurl as she tried to keep control, but she was unraveling quickly. At last, she reached out, and before anyone could stop her, she grabbed a large fistful of wedding cake. Less than a second later, she flung it at Hayden, silencing him with a wet slap.

"What are you looking at?" she screamed at the crowd. She grabbed more cake in each hand and started launching it at the crowd. Buttercream icing flew through the air, pelting the wedding guests. They screamed and scattered. Liam checked to ensure Francesca, Aunt Beatrice and his mother were out of the line of fire, but Henry wasn't so lucky. He took a large piece of cake to the front of his suit. But he only laughed, scraping it off his shirt and taking it in stride. After forty years with Beatrice, flying cake was probably nothing.

Before Liam could turn to get help, two burly security officers rushed past him. Angelica's eyes went wild when she saw them. She started kicking and screaming when they tried to restrain her.

"Don't you touch me!" she howled. "Let me go!"

Liam could only watch in amazement as she wrenched herself from the men's grasp, only to stumble backward into the cake table. It turned over, taking Angelica and the cake with it. Angelica landed smack-dab in the middle of the towering confection, coating her from hair to rear in buttercream. She roared in anger, flailing as she tried to get up and couldn't. When she did stand again, it was only with the help of the guards gripping her upper arms.

On her feet, she was a dripping mess. Her perfectly curled blond hair was flat and greasy with white clumps of frosting. Icing was smeared across her face and all over her purple dress. She huffed and struggled in her captors' arms, but there was no use. They had her this time. At last, Angelica had gotten herself into a situation she couldn't weasel out of.

"You know," Hayden said, "looking like that, I'm surprised people didn't see the resemblance before."

Angelica immediately stilled and her face went as pale as the frosting. "I don't look anything like *her*."

"Oh, come on, *Madeline*. There's no sense lying anymore about who you really are."

The calm in her immediately vanished. "Never call me that name. Do you hear me? Never! Madeline Burch is dead. *Dead*. I am Angelica Pierce, you understand? Angelica Pierce!" she repeated, as though that might make it true.

Several people gasped in the crowd. Cara stood stock-still a few feet away with Max protectively at her side. "Rowena and I went to Woodlawn Academy with Madeline," she said before turning to Angelica. "We were right. It *is* you."

"You shut up," Angelica spat. "You don't know anything about me."

"You're right. I don't," Cara answered.

The guards then escorted a wildly thrashing Angelica—or *Madeline*—out of the ballroom. By now, the local police were likely on their way to take her into custody. First, for disorderly conduct and assault. Then, maybe, for her involvement in the hacking scandal. Either way, a scene like that was enough cause for Liam to terminate her from ANS for good.

"I'm sorry about the mess," Hayden said, wiping some cake from his face. "I never expected her to come talk to me. She was so confident that she had me beaten. I couldn't pass up the chance to put a crack in her facade, but I didn't realize she'd go nuclear. It ruined your reception. Just look at the cake."

Liam shrugged. Somehow knowing it wasn't his real

wedding made it easier to stomach. "Nailing Angelica is important. You have to take every opportunity you can get."

He walked with Hayden out of the ballroom to where a few police officers were waiting outside. They answered their questions and gave out their contact information. Hayden opted to go with them to the station, but Liam knew he needed to get back inside and salvage what was left of his wedding reception.

When Liam returned, people seemed to be milling around, at a loss for what to do with themselves. "Sorry about that, folks," he said, raising his hands to get everyone's attention. "Please stick around and enjoy the reception. I'm sad to say there won't be any cake, though." A few people chuckled and most awkwardly returned to nibbling and drinking as they had before the fight broke out.

Liam noticed the drinks he'd fetched from the bar still untouched on the table. He'd gotten wrapped up in the scene and had forgotten to take Francesca her champagne. He picked them back up and turned, looking for her. After all that, they'd need another round pretty quickly.

But she was nowhere to be found.

Frowning, he searched the ballroom, finally turning to a frazzled Ariella for help. "Have you seen the bride?" he asked.

"Not since I put her in a cab."

"A cab?" Liam frowned. "You mean she's left her own reception? Without me?"

Ariella bit her lip and nodded. "About ten minutes ago. Right about the time Angelica started bathing in wedding cake. She needed to get out of here."

Liam glanced around the mess of a ballroom. Scarlet was frantically informing staff of their cleanup duties. The guests were still standing around, but despite his assurances, they seemed unsure of whether they should stay. It was a wedding disaster.

He didn't blame Francesca one bit for leaving.

Francesca couldn't get out of her wedding dress fast enough. The corset-tight bodice made her feel like she couldn't breathe. It was all just too much.

Initially, she'd been relieved when Hayden and Angelica started making a scene. For the first time that day, every eye in the room wasn't on her. It was a blessed break. It was the first moment since she started down the aisle that she thought she might be able to let the facade of bridal bliss drop and regather herself.

And then the cake started flying.

Her *nonna* had never specifically mentioned that having her wedding cake flung across the room was bad luck, but Francesca was ready to make her own deduction about that. Their reception was a disaster. Their sham of a marriage would no doubt be a mess, too. It was just one more thing, one more blazing neon sign trying to point her in the right direction. She'd ignored all the other portents of bad luck. The fates had ensured this last one would be undeniable.

When she'd asked Ariella to get her a cab, her friend probably thought she was upset about having her reception ruined. The truth was that she just couldn't pretend anymore. If she'd had to be in that ballroom one more minute, she would have blown everything for Liam and ANS.

Now that she was back at Liam's place, in a pair of

jeans and a light sweater, she felt better and worse all at once. Boxes of her things still sat around the ground floor of his town house ready to be incorporated into her new life with him. But they might as well go back onto the moving truck.

She poured herself a glass of wine to calm her nerves and went upstairs to the master bedroom to repack. The only things of hers that had been put away were her clothes and personal effects for the bed and bath. Those could easily be rounded back up, and she intended to do it right now.

If she hurried, she would be sleeping in her own bed tonight. Not quite the wedding night everyone was expecting her to have.

She had one suitcase filled and zipped closed when she heard the front door open.

"Francesca?" Liam called.

"I'm upstairs," she answered and pulled another bag onto the bed. She was stuffing it with lingerie and pajamas when he came through the doorway of his bedroom.

Francesca tried not to think about how handsome he looked in his rumpled tuxedo. His tie was undone, his collar unbuttoned. She liked him tousled. Despite everything, she felt her body react to his presence. Her pulse started racing, and her skin tightened in anticipation of his touch. But thinking about how much she wanted Liam wouldn't help. It would make her want to stay. And she needed to go.

"What are you doing?" he asked. His voice wasn't raised. It was quiet and tired. They'd both had a long day and didn't need any more drama. But this had to happen tonight.

"I'm packing my things and moving back into my

place." Francesca shoved another few items into her bag and looked up. "Don't worry, I'll lie low until Aunt Beatrice leaves town on Monday, but then I'm calling the moving company to come get my stuff."

Liam took a few steps toward her. She could feel the magnetic pull of him grow stronger as he came closer. She wanted to bury her face in his lapel and forget about everything that was going wrong. But she couldn't.

"Why?"

Francesca put the last of her clothes into the bag and zipped it closed. She looked at the bag as she spoke to ensure she could get all the words out. "I'm sorry, Liam. I thought I could do this. But I just can't."

There was a pause before he answered, his voice a touch strained. "Do you want an annulment?"

She looked up at him and shook her head. "No. I'll remain legally married to you for the sake of the network. Hopefully that will be enough because I can't play house with you. It's too hard on…" Her voice started to falter as tears rushed to her eyes. She immediately turned from him before she gave away how she really felt. "It's too hard on my heart, Liam."

He took another step forward, but stopped short of reaching out to her. "What do you mean?"

Francesca took a deep breath. "I want more."

"More than the five million?"

At that, Francesca jerked her head up to meet his gaze. "You just don't get it, do you? I don't want your money. I never did. I have plenty of my own. I want the things that you can't give me. I want love. A real family. A marriage like my parents have. I want a man who cares for me more than anyone or anything."

She shook her head and hoisted the strap of the bag

over her shoulder. "This isn't your fault. You were right when you said I was a true believer. I am. But I've been lying to myself. First, I told myself that I could be with you and it would be fine. That I could spend the next year pretending. But I can't because I was stupid enough to fall for you. Then I kept hoping that maybe, just maybe, you would fall for me and this could become more than just a business arrangement. Silly, right?"

Liam reached out to her, but Francesca sidestepped him. "Don't," she said. "Just don't. I know you don't have feelings for me. Anything you say right now will make it worse."

She extended the handle of her suitcase and rolled it to the bedroom door.

"Francesca, wait."

She stopped and turned to him. This was the moment everything hinged on. If she was wrong and he did care for her, this was the time for him to say it. She looked into his dark blue eyes, hoping to see there the love she wanted so desperately. Etched into his pained expression was desperation and confusion. He didn't want her to go, but he didn't know how to ask her to stay.

"Liam, would you have ever considered marrying me if your aunt hadn't forced us into this situation? I mean, would you even have asked me on a date after what happened between us in the elevator? Honestly."

Liam frowned and shoved his hands into his pockets. "No, I probably wouldn't have."

At least they were both telling the truth now. Nodding, she turned away and hauled her luggage down the stairs. It was time for her to go home and pick up the pieces of her life.

Thirteen

Liam signed Angelica's termination paperwork and pushed the pages across his desk. He thought he would be happy to see this issue put to bed, but he wasn't. He was the most miserable newlywed in history.

For one thing, he hadn't seen the bride since their wedding night. It had been a long, lonely weekend without her there. He'd quickly grown accustomed to having her around. Now his town house felt cold and empty.

The office wasn't much better. Francesca didn't greet him first thing with coffee and a kiss. He wasn't even sure if she was at work today. He wanted to call her. Email her. But he knew he shouldn't. It would make it easier on her if he took a step back and let her have the space she needed. She deserved that much.

But he missed his wife.

How quickly she had become that in his mind. She was no longer his employee. She was his wife. There was no differentiation in his mind about the terms of their marriage. Their engagement may have been a ruse, but the wedding and the marriage felt real to him. Frighteningly real.

Liam had never given much thought to a wife and family, but the minute Francesca walked out the door, a hole formed in his chest. It was as though she'd ripped out his heart and taken it with her. All he was left with was the dull ache of longing for her.

That didn't feel fake to him.

Yes, he'd been pushed into the marriage to please his aunt. He had to admit that much to Francesca because it was true. But now that he was married to her, it felt right. It felt natural. He no longer cared about Aunt Beatrice's opinion on the matter. He…was in love with Francesca.

"I love my wife," he said out loud to his empty office. There was no one to hear him, but saying it had lifted a huge weight from his shoulders. Unfortunately, admitting the truth was just the first step.

How could he prove to Francesca that he really did love her? That this wasn't about the network or stock deals? There was no way for her to know for sure that he wasn't just playing nice for appearances.

The only way to convince her, the only sure path, would be to take the stock deal and the network woes off the table. If his aunt had no negotiating power over him, then he stayed married to Francesca because he wanted to, not just because he had to.

But to do that without risking the company would mean that he needed enough stock to control ANS without his aunt's shares. That seemed virtually impossible. Unless…

Liam grabbed his phone and leaped out from behind

his desk. He had to find Victor Orr before they returned to California. Francesca had mentioned they were staying on a few days to tour the Smithsonian, so if he had any luck, they were still in D.C.

It took two phone calls and a drive to their hotel in bumper-to-bumper traffic, but Liam was finally able to track down Francesca's parents. He was standing at the door, waiting for them to answer the buzzer, when he realized he didn't know exactly what he was going to say to them. He would have to admit the truth. And that would mean that a very large, angry Irishman might be beating him senseless within minutes for hurting his daughter.

Victor answered the door with a frown. Without speaking a word, he seemed to realize something was wrong. Why else would his new son-in-law show up alone just days after the wedding? He led Liam into their suite and gestured for him to sit down in one of the chairs in the living room.

He watched Liam through narrowed eyes for a few minutes before Liam gathered the nerve to speak.

"There are some things I need to tell you," Liam said.

"I'm sure there are." Victor leaned back in his chair, ready to listen.

Without knowing the best way to tell the story, Liam chose to start at the beginning. He began with the stock arrangement with his aunt, delicately skipping over the elevator debacle, and followed with Beatrice's later demand that he marry to keep control of the network.

"And my daughter agreed to go along with this phony engagement?"

"Yes, sir. She seemed hesitant at first, but apparently she saw a sign that she should do it. A ladybug."

Victor shook his head. "Her and those damned signs. She gets into more trouble that way. Married to a man she hardly knows because of a ladybug!"

"We never intended to go through with the marriage, but my aunt was adamant we do it now. She's ill and wanted to make sure we followed through. I told Francesca she didn't have to do it, but she insisted."

"She's stubborn like I am."

Liam chose not to touch that statement. "What neither of us realized was that we might actually fall for one another. On our wedding night, Francesca told me she had feelings for me that she knew weren't mutual and she couldn't go on that way."

"You just let her walk out like that?"

Liam frowned and looked down at his hands. "I didn't know what to tell her. I wasn't sure how I felt about everything. What was real between us and what was a fantasy? I didn't know."

"And now?"

"Now I know. I love your daughter, and I want to ask your permission to marry her."

"Son, you're already married."

"I know, but things are different now. I want to be married to her for real. I want to go to her and tell her how I feel, but I need your help. Francesca will never believe our marriage is anything more than a business deal as long as my aunt is holding the stock over my head. I can't afford to buy her out. But if I could get enough minority stockholder support, I might be able to get majority control without her shares."

Victor nodded. "I don't think I have enough, but I've got a good bit. So does my friend Jimmy Lang. Together, that might tip the scales. Let me make a call."

As Victor got up and headed into the bedroom, a simmer of hope started bubbling in Liam's gut. He really hoped that he could pull this off. He didn't want to go to Francesca and tell her he loved her if there were any suspicions about his motives. This was the only way.

"Good news," Victor said as he returned a few minutes later. "I spoke with Jimmy and did the math. Combined with yours, we have fifty-two percent of the company stock. Close, but we made it. Jimmy and I are both really excited about the direction you're taking the network, so we have no qualms about delegating our voting authority to you. So," he said, extending his hand to Liam, "congratulations. You're still running this network."

Liam leaped from his seat and excitedly shook his father-in-law's hand. "Thank you so much, sir."

Victor shrugged. "I didn't do it for you. I did it for my little girl. You have my consent to marry her, so get out of here and make it right between you two."

Liam's eyes widened as he nodded. There was no arguing with Victor Orr, even if he wanted to. "Thank you again," he said as he turned and bolted from their hotel suite.

As badly as he wanted to rush to find Francesca, he had one other stop to make. Fortunately, that stop was located in the same hotel.

Liam rang the doorbell at the penthouse suite and waited for Henry to answer the door. The older man arrived a few minutes later, welcoming Liam with the same smile and nod he'd always received.

"Come in, Liam. I don't believe she's expecting you this morning. We're packing to return to New York."

"I'm sorry to pop in unannounced, Henry, but I need to talk to my aunt. It's important."

Henry held out his hand to gesture toward the bedroom. Liam didn't wait for him, moving quickly across the carpet and around the corner.

Aunt Beatrice looked up as he charged in. She was sitting in her wheelchair folding her clothes. "Liam," she said. "I expected you to be off somewhere basking in wedded bliss."

"No, you didn't," he said, sitting on the edge of the bed beside her. "You and I have been playing a dangerous game that could end up doing nothing but hurting people."

She didn't bother acting offended by his insinuation. "I did what I thought was best for the family. And for you, despite what you might think."

"I know," Liam agreed. "And I came here to thank you."

That, at last, got a rise out of the Queen Bee. She sat up straight in her chair, her eyes narrowing at him in confusion. "Thank me?"

"Yes. If you hadn't forced me to get married, I might've let Francesca walk right out of my life. I love her. And I hope she stays married to me for forty years—not for the network, or because of your demands, but because I want us to grow old together. That said, I'm not going to let you control me any longer. I don't need your ANS stock or you holding it over my head. I now have enough backing to maintain control of ANS without your shares or your billions. I don't care about any inheritance."

Aunt Beatrice sat silently for a few minutes, absorbing his words. After a while, he began to wonder if she was mentally going over the new changes to her will. He didn't care. Cut him out. Cut him *loose*.

"Those," she said at last, "are the words of a man who can take charge of this family." Beatrice smiled softly to herself and placed a blouse in her suitcase. "It's what I've been waiting for. I never intended to sell my stock to Ron Wheeler. I just wanted to see you settled down, in control and happy with your place in life. Francesca is the right woman for you. I knew that just as certainly as I knew you two were pretending. In time, I figured things would work out between you. Once you both stopped fighting it. It's a shame I'll be dead before I can see you two genuinely happy together."

"You knew we were faking the relationship?"

"It takes a smart, observant person to head this family. Very little gets past me, even now. But it's okay. I'm sorry for meddling in your private life. Blackmail really isn't my forte, but I did what I thought I needed to for the good of you and the family. I'll call my stockbroker this afternoon and have the shares of ANS transferred to you."

"What? Now?" He had years and millions to pay off before he owned those shares outright.

"It's your wedding present. Most people don't give networks as gifts, but you're not the typical bride and groom."

Liam reached out and took his aunt's hand. It was something he rarely did; she wasn't very affectionate, but he was seeing the dents in her armor. Her illness was revealing the person inside that she kept hidden. "Thank you, Aunt Beatrice."

She turned her head, dismissing his sentiment with a wave of her hand, but he could see a moist shimmer in her eyes. "It will be thanks enough when you save that company and take over handling our motley crew of relatives when I'm gone."

"Do I really have to be executor of the estate?"

"Absolutely. And don't worry. Eventually, you will grow accustomed to the constant ass-kissing."

Francesca left ANS early. She'd been a self-imposed prisoner in her office all morning, afraid she'd run into Liam in the hallway. She had had a few days to sit at home alone, licking her wounds, but she wasn't ready to see him again. Especially knowing that everyone still expected them to be a happy, newly married couple.

After overhearing Jessica tell someone on the phone that Liam was out of the office, she figured this was her opportunity to escape.

She made it back to her town house without incident. Relieved, she dropped her purse on the coffee table, kicked off her shoes and went into the kitchen for a drink.

When Francesca rounded the corner and found Liam sitting at her kitchen table, she nearly leaped out of her skin. *"Oh, dio mio!"* She jumped, pressing her back against the counter and clutching her rapidly beating heart. "What the hell are you doing here, Liam? You scared me to death."

He looked a little sheepish as he stood up and came over to her. "I'm sorry. I didn't mean to scare you. I thought you'd notice my car out front. You gave me a key, so I figured I would wait around until you got home. When I called Jessica she told me you'd left."

"I gave you that key when we were going to be a happily married couple. Using it after everything that happened is a little creepy. Why are you here, anyway? We don't have anything to talk about."

Liam shook his head and came closer. She was able to catch of whiff of his cologne and her body immediately began responding to him. Apparently, it hadn't gotten the message about the breakup of their nonrelationship.

"We have a lot to talk about. Starting with how much I love you and how miserable I've been since you left."

Francesca started to argue with him and then stopped. *Did he just...* She couldn't have heard him right. "What did you say?"

Liam smiled, sending her heart fluttering at the sight. He was wearing a navy collared shirt that brought out the dark blue of his eyes as he closed in on her. She noticed a few weary lines around them. He looked a little tired and tense, but she had attributed that to the stress of running the network and the fiasco of their wedding.

Could it be that he was losing sleep over her?

He stopped just short of touching her, forcing her to look up at him. His hands closed over her upper arms, their warmth sinking deep into her bones. "I love you, Francesca. I'm in love with you."

As much as she wanted to melt into him, she couldn't let herself fall prey to him. She ignored the excited flutter of butterflies in her stomach and pulled back out of his grasp, watching him with wary eyes. "You didn't love me Friday night. You could've told me then and you didn't. You let me leave. And now you show up singing a different tune. What happened? Did your aunt find out? Trying a different tactic to keep the network?"

Liam swallowed hard, a flash of resignation in his eyes. "I thought you would say something like that.

Which is why it took me so long to come see you today. I had some important business to take care of."

Francesca crossed her arms defensively over her chest, but she didn't think it would do much good. Her armor where Liam was concerned had been permanently breached. "It's always business first with you."

"You're right. First, I had to go confess to your father."

Francesca's eyes grew wide with unexpected panic. "You told my father? Why? He's going to kill me. How could you do that without asking me?"

"Because I needed his help. And his blessing to marry you."

"It's a little late for that."

"It's never too late where an overprotective father is concerned. Not only did he give his permission, but he and his associate have pledged their stock to support me at ANS, giving me a majority share without my aunt."

Francesca tried to process what he was saying, but she kept getting hung up on what kind of conversation he'd had with her father when she wasn't there. "You don't need your aunt's stock anymore?"

"No."

That meant they didn't have to be married. "But you don't want an annulment?"

"Absolutely not." Liam crowded back into her space, closing the gap she'd put between them. "I have no intention of letting you out of my sight, or my bed, for the next forty years."

The butterflies in her gut went berserk. She brought her hand to her belly to calm them. "Wait. You love me. You want to stay married to me. And it has nothing to do with the network?"

Liam nodded. "Not a thing. I told my aunt this morning that I wasn't going to play along anymore. I didn't want you to think for a moment that I wasn't one hundred percent sincere in my love for you. This isn't about my aunt or the network or appearances. It's about you and me and the rest of our lives."

His arms snaked around her waist and this time, she didn't pull away. She molded herself against him and let out a small sigh of contentment at the feel of being in his arms again.

"I am in love with you, Francesca Crowe. I want to stay married to you until the day I die."

Her heart skipped a beat at the use of her married name. She hadn't heard anyone use it since the wedding. "I love you, too."

Liam dipped his head down to capture her lips with his own. This kiss—their first as two people in love— blew away all the others they'd shared before. Every nerve in her body lit up at his touch. She wrapped her arms around his neck to try and get closer to him, but it could never be close enough. She lost herself in the embrace, letting his strong arms keep her upright when her knees threatened to give way beneath her.

Pulling away after what felt like an eternity, he said breathlessly, "I want us to get married."

Francesca wrinkled her nose and put her palm gently against the stubble of his jaw. "*Mio caro,* we're already married."

"I know," he said with a devious smile. "But I want a do-over. With a tropical honeymoon. And this time, it will just be the two of us. No family, no pressure and especially no cake throwing."

Epilogue

Francesca had no idea a vacation could be so perfect. With Ariella's televised reunion show coming up, they didn't have the luxury of taking a long honeymoon, but they did manage to sneak away for a long weekend in the Caribbean.

So far, they had sunbathed, swum in the ocean, dined on the best seafood she'd ever tasted and renewed their vows in a private white gazebo hovering over the water.

Their previous ceremony had been legally binding but tainted by his aunt's machinations and Angelica's tantrum. Their vow renewal had been just for them. A chance to say the words again and wholeheartedly mean it. Afterward, they drank champagne in their private bungalow and shared a tiny cake for two that no one could ruin.

Today they had planned a snorkeling trip in the morning, followed by marathon lovemaking and lots of luxurious naps. The snorkeling trip had been excellent. The water was crystal clear and a rainbow of fish was in abundance. They were on their way back to the bungalow when Francesca stopped and tugged at Liam's arm.

"Liam, stop. Look," Francesca said, pointing out the television mounted above the cantina bar.

It was the live coverage of Madeline Burch's arraignment. Before they left, the video of her confession had played repeatedly at every news outlet, with ANS breaking the story. The media had jumped on the tale about her involvement in the hacking scandal after both Brandon Ames and Troy Hall agreed to testify against her. The news of her double life was just the icing on the ratings cake.

For a moment, Francesca almost felt badly for Madeline. She looked awful. Orange was not her color. Going without her expensive hair coloring and extensions, she had mousy brown roots at the crown of her stringy, thin hair. Her last dose of Botox had faded away, as had her spray tan. Her colored contacts had been replaced with thick, prison-issued glasses. Several more pounds also had been added to her frame since their reception. There was no doubt that Angelica was Madeline Burch now.

"The news is out," Liam said as the news banner at the bottom changed. They couldn't hear what was being said on the television, but the words scrolling at the bottom announced the breaking news that investigator Hayden Black had testified that Madeline was Graham Boyle's secret, illegitimate daughter. Liam had told Francesca what he'd overheard during the argument at the reception, but her motivation for taking down Graham had been withheld from the press so far.

"Wow," Francesca said, shaking her head. "It's just so sad. And senseless. How many lives were ruined just so she could get back at Graham for the way he treated her?"

When she turned, Liam was pulling his phone out of his pocket. He had done well to unplug from the news world while they were on their honeymoon, but now that the news was out, all his journalistic buttons were being pushed.

He unlocked his screen and started typing something, and then he stopped. He pressed the power button and slipped the phone back into his pocket.

Francesca arched an eyebrow at him in surprise. "Really?" she asked.

"I am sure the network and my employees have this story well in hand. And even if they didn't, I am on my honeymoon. I couldn't care less about Graham Boyle's secret daughter."

He turned to face Francesca, snaked his arms around her waist and pulled her tightly against him. She melted into him, surprised to feel the firm heat of his desire pressed into her belly.

"Right now," he said with a wicked grin, "I'm more interested in making love to my wife."

* * * * *

A sneaky peek at next month...

Desire™

PASSIONATE AND DRAMATIC LOVE STORIES

My wish list for next month's titles...

In stores from 19th July 2013:

☐ Deep in a Texan's Heart – Sara Orwig

& Affairs of State – Jennifer Lewis

☐ His for the Taking – Ann Major

& His Instant Heir – Katherine Garbera

☐ Canyon – Brenda Jackson

& The Baby Deal – Kat Cantrell

2 stories in each book - only £5.49!

Just can't wait?

Visit us Online

You can buy our books online a month before they hit the shops! **www.millsandboon.co.uk**

0713/51

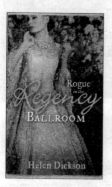
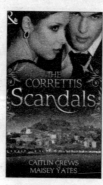

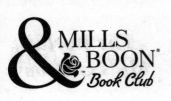 

The World of Mills & Boon®

There's a Mills & Boon® series that's perfect for you. We publish ten series and, with new titles every month, you never have to wait long for your favourite to come along.

Blaze.

Scorching hot, sexy reads
4 new stories every month

By Request

Relive the romance with the best of the best
9 new stories every month

Cherish™

Romance to melt the heart every time
12 new stories every month

Desire™

Passionate and dramatic love stories
8 new stories every month

What will you treat yourself to next?

Ignite your imagination,
step into the past…
6 new stories every month

INTRIGUE…

Breathtaking romantic suspense
Up to 8 new stories every month

Medical Romance

Captivating medical drama –
with heart
6 new stories every month

MODERN™

International affairs,
seduction & passion guaranteed
9 new stories every month

n o c t u r n e™

Deliciously wicked
paranormal romance
Up to 4 new stories every month

RIVA™

Live life to the full –
give in to temptation
3 new stories every month available
exclusively via our Book Club

LΠ 07/13